P9-DCH-394

NEW
JERUSALEM
NEWS

NEW JERUSALEM NEWS

A Novel

JOHN ENRIGHT

YUCCA

Copyright © 2015 by John Enright

All rights reserved. No part of this book may be reproduced in any manner without the express written consent of the publisher, except in the case of brief excerpts in critical reviews or articles. All inquiries should be addressed to Yucca Publishing, 307 West 36th Street, 11th Floor, New York, NY 10018.

Yucca Publishing books may be purchased in bulk at special discounts for sales promotion, corporate gifts, fund-raising, or educational purposes. Special editions can also be created to specifications. For details, contact the Special Sales Department, Yucca Publishing, 307 West 36th Street, 11th Floor, New York, NY 10018 or yucca@skyhorsepublishing.com.

Yucca Publishing® is an imprint of Skyhorse Publishing, Inc.®, a Delaware corporation.

Visit our website at www.yuccapub.com.

10 9 8 7 6 5 4 3 2 1

Library of Congress Cataloging-in-Publication Data is available on file.

Cover design by Yucca Publishing

Print ISBN: 978-1-63158-044-4
Ebook ISBN: 978-1-63158-054-3

Printed in the United States of America

NEW
JERUSALEM
NEWS

Chapter 1

It was Brenda's idea. That was the summer of Brenda's bright ideas—mango margaritas, golden carp in the swimming pool, hanging the guys' sweaty T-shirts and shorts about the yard to keep the deer from eating her garden plants. Charlie had long since learned just to let his wife have her way with such things, and Dominick felt that as their houseguest he really had no say in the matter. Brenda was his hostess; she could do what she would with his dirty laundry. This idea, however, involved more than just the three of them and random wild animals.

It all started on a visit to one of those quaint little villages up the coast. They all ran together in Dominick's mind—marinas filled with otiose unpeopled pleasure boats, heavy square buildings with plaques attached attesting to their longevity, fish and chips shops and pubs with cute names that sold clothing declaiming them, and tan flotillas of teenage girls showing the maximum amount of skin allowed by law. Brenda was off trolling the curio shoppes and boutiques. Charlie had found a stool and a drink in the dark cave of a bar lit solely by plasma TV screens playing the afternoon Red Sox game. Dominick plopped his considerable self down on a shaded bench in front of one of the ubiquitous realtor's offices and lit a cigar.

Firing up a Romeo y Julieta Churchill had always been a distinctly personal pleasure for Dominick, a curtain (of smoke) going up on a fine half hour of solitary sedentary drugged meditation. But now, in this strange new smokeless land, the public employment of his private enjoyment had become the occasion of civic drama. What he was doing there on a bench on the sidewalk was not against any law, but he might as well have been fondling some ewe's genitalia. Children stared, men scowled, and women mimed mustard gas poisoning. In a minor way Dominick enjoyed the performances, but they could sometimes become a distraction. One should not be distracted from a good cigar.

But then this was New England after all, home of Hawthorne and the Reverends Mather, where the evil inventions of teenage girls had once sent scores of their betters to horrible deaths for far lesser offenses. To be a sinner was to break some god's rule. It did not necessarily have to be your god, if you happened to have one, who made rules and cared about them enough to go about punishing people. The fine fumes of the Churchill in his head led Dominick off into a consideration of the etiology and evolution of the concept of punishment—the same root and basic meaning all the way back to the Greek—and of punishments in different civilizations, varieties of castigation. Was punishment or just its specialization a human invention? There were outcasts throughout the animal kingdom. Could a culture's refinement be measured by the sophistication of its criminal code? Dominick's meditation was interrupted by a henna-haired woman from the realtor's office behind him, who threatened to call the police if he did not move on.

There was a certain type of woman to whom Dominick had always been attracted. They were invariably foreign and full-bodied, medium to tall in height, and wore high heels. They would be slightly over-dressed for whatever occasion in garments that looked as if they were meant to be shed and that showed off the fullness of their ample breasts and constrained décolletage. They had a look in their eyes that said they expected to be treated with the respect due to them as women. His henna-haired verbal attacker was such a woman. He could not place her almost hidden accent. Russian? Dominick rose to his feet to receive her, bowing slightly. "Madame?"

Brenda arrived on the scene simultaneously with the police cruiser. Dominick had, of course, refused to move on as he hoped to make the acquaintance of this feisty foreigner, and he had no intention of ruining his now perfectly tuned Churchill by stubbing it out to placate her. He expected the respect due to him as a man. She would not give him her name. A small crowd had stopped to watch and listen, blocking the sidewalk pedestrian flow. Dominick heard a small child say, "Look, I think his thumb is on fire."

Brenda took Dominick by the arm. "Lord Witherspoon, I am so sorry to have stranded you here like this. What on earth could be the problem?"

"This charming lady," Dominick began.

"I will not have this foul tobacco smell invade my office and affect my clientele," his temptress said, stamping her foot like a Parisian. A bejeweled hand swept her bangs away from her face.

The policeman got out of his car the way they always do, as if burdened once more with the obligation to interfere.

"But, ma'am, we are your clientele, or rather would have been," Brenda said. "I am assisting His Lordship in the search for the proper property here at the shore. We were about to inquire into your top listings, but if this"—Brenda gestured to the policeman now standing beside them—"is your idea of customer service, we will take our inquiries elsewhere. Come along, Lord Witherspoon." And Brenda led Dominick through the crowd and down the sidewalk.

"Good god, Brenda, Lord Witherspoon? Could you not come up with something better than that? I feel like a fugitive from a Brontë novel," Dominick said, giving his Churchill a few puffs to keep it burning. "Didn't you find her a bit alluring?"

"I can't stand that perfume. Where's Charlie?"

"In the saloon at the corner. Look, I will wait here." Dominick had found another sidewalk bench and sat down there to enjoy what was left of his cigar. "Take your time."

Thus was the character of Lord Witherspoon created. Henceforward restaurant reservations and takeout pizza orders were placed in his name. "Lord Witherspoon, party of three," always turned heads, and they got better tables. It did not seem to make any difference with the pizzas. Dominick wondered out loud once why more parents did not name their children Lord and Lady. Charlie just went along with it, calling Dominick "ya lawdship." Brenda bought Dominick several silk ascots. They were uncomfortably warm, but he looked good in them. He started to trim his moustache differently, a more colonial look.

The nationwide real estate crisis had hit the second-home market, and suddenly there were lots of seaside mansions for sale. In local parlance these lavish eight- and ten-bedroom century-old monstrosities were called "cottages," though they each sat on many manicured acres and carried multimillion-dollar price tags. A drive down the coast road now was a for-sale-sign tour of descendants of old families turning their backs on their Gilded Age past. Even the named estates were up for grabs—Westwind, Cliff Retreat, Surfhead, Rockledge, The Pines.

It was Brenda's idea. It was a hot, still afternoon. The summer had been especially warm, and they all were getting tired of it. Charlie proposed going for a drive, perhaps out to the lighthouse at the end of the island where there might be a sea breeze. But Brenda suggested that they go for a tour instead. "A tour of what?" Charlie asked. "Someplace air-conditioned, I hope."

"Oh, yes, all very cool. Dominick dear, go change your clothes and come back as Lord Witherspoon. I'll dress up, too. Charlie, you'll be fine as you are as our driver."

They took Dominick's car, because it was the newest and closest to being upscale. They drove into the village, to the block with most of the realtors' offices. Charlie waited in the car while Brenda and Dominick went into the office that had in its windows the most photographs of seaside mansions. Within ten minutes Brenda and Dominick were back in the car and Charlie was following the real estate agent's Lexus out of the village and down the oceanside drive.

"What a strange creature," Dominick said. "Do you think she is ill?"

"She is a real estate agent, Dominick, a salesperson. Her life is hell. She would like to smile, but she has forgotten how."

"Do you think she believed us?"

"She really has no choice. Did you see any other customers in there?"

"Where are we going?" Charlie asked.

"That's her call, really," Brenda said. "We told her that at this point price was not a consideration, that His Lordship was looking not so much for another home as for a family investment property now that the market seemed so favorable. She'd be a fool not to start at the top of her list."

4

"This is fun," Dominick said. "Perhaps tomorrow we could do it with that lady who took such umbrage with my cigar. Do you remember what village that was?"

They were on a stretch of wooded road where occasional gated driveways led off toward the coast. The Lexus signaled long in advance of turning into one of these drives. Charlie followed. There was a chain across the drive, suspended from two vine-covered stone pillars. The agent got out of her car to unlock the chain. In her high heels she stumbled in the uneven gravel and almost fell. There was a dark sweat stain down the back of her green silk blouse. She didn't appeal to Dominick at all. If this was their new game, it needed some refinement. They ought to have a better choice of the players, for one thing.

The driveway curved scenically, unnecessarily for maybe an eighth of a mile through a young evergreen forest before opening onto a broad expanse of undulating lawn surrounding a multistoried, turreted, cream-colored copy of a French villa set against the two pale blues of the sea and the sky. A fairy-tale castle.

"Must be fun to heat in the winter," Charlie said. "Do you think they'll have the air-con on?"

Inside, the house was grand and empty and stiflingly hot. It felt as if no one had ever lived there. "A tragic story," the agent began. "A husband built it for his wife, who died before it was completed." She opened some French doors leading out to the seaside patio, and a cool breeze swept in as if the house, awakened, was gasping for air. The agent went on with her fairy-tale story for the fairy-tale house, but Dominick and Charlie walked out through the French doors to the lawn sloping down to an empty dock. Brenda and the agent went off on a tour of the many rooms.

"Could you live here, Charlie?" Dominick asked, loosening his ascot.

"I'd like to hunt deer here, my own private game reserve. There's got to be a dozen acres at least."

They looked at four other houses before calling it a day, none quite as grand as the first but some nicer and two still occupied. It was a diverting afternoon. Brenda especially had a marvelous time, lying to and dueling with the real estate agent, whose name was Alice or Alisha or Alison or something similar. "Poor thing," Brenda said. "It's her job to know everything and never be wrong. She has to be two steps ahead of every conversation. What a suck job."

Lord Witherspoon house tours quickly became one of their main summer pastimes. Charlie even got all of the golden carp out of the swimming pool. God knows what he did with them. They honed their visitation routine. Charlie now took digital photos wherever they went. Brenda carried a fancy notebook in which she made secret notes. Dominick found it most comfortable to say nothing at all, just make small grunts and throat-clearing sounds now and then, and look bored and vaguely disappointed. Soon they were getting calls back from agents with a new—"perfect," always "perfect"—estate to show them. It certainly was a buyer's market. They became jaded clients, hypercritical, always finding the cons to counter the agents' pros, never satisfied. And it never had anything to do with the price.

The Jamesons were the most charming couple Dominick had yet met on the island. Lydia and Atticus. Lydia would have always been petite, but her seven decades had refined it. She was an ad for the well-kept woman, and she had also somehow preserved, for her own amusement, a young girl's outlook on life. It showed in the lights in her eyes, her amused lips, and the tilt of her head as she watched you as if you were unique. Atticus was not much bigger than his wife, a yachtsman shrunken with age and years in the sun. Dominick came to think of them as fine bottled spirits—brandy and port—that aging had brightened and mellowed and deepened. Atticus liked a good cigar, and Lydia claimed to love its aroma in her house. "All the men who smoked here," she sighed. "What fond memories that aroma brings back." Atticus also fixed a fine mint julep.

They called their house Mt. Sinai, although it was not listed as such. The village had only recently learned to act ambivalent toward Jews and things Jewish. Not that the Jamesons were Jewish. Their house had been built atop a large rock outcrop, and from the seaside its flat, double-arched façade resembled the outline of certain famed tablets. "Calling the house Mt. Sinai was my grandfather's idea of a joke,"

Lydia said. The house had come from that side of the family. Mt. Sinai was for sale, which was how they made the Jamesons' acquaintance.

It had started out as a normal visit. The real estate agent—a new one, a mysteriously obsequious Persian woman—had made the appointment for them and then had not shown up. So the opening was awkward. Without the mediating salesperson present, what exactly were their roles? Brenda, Charlie, and Dominick were well aware of their duplicity and felt exposed without the agent's shield of authenticity. The Jamesons had never been retailers but were practiced hosts. Iced tea was offered, seats on the veranda, small talk—the record-breaking hot weather, gardening, the story of the house's name—but no one knew quite how to broach the purpose of their meeting. The topic just seemed impolite.

There was a squall approaching—dark sky and lightning off in the distance. Charlie asked if he could take some photos of the grounds and the view before the rain arrived. Lydia offered to take them on a quick tour of the grounds. She was proud of her flowers and wanted to show off her potting shed and small artist's studio on the edge of their rock outcrop. She led Brenda and Charlie off down a garden path. Dominick and Atticus stayed behind. Dominick was too comfortable in his cushioned settee and had no interest in seeing flowers.

"How about something stronger than that?" Atticus asked once they were alone.

Dominick gave one of his Lord Witherspoon grunts that were meant to sound agreeable and handed his host his half-empty glass. Atticus vanished into the house. The air was thick with that stillness that arrives before the storm. Dominick's view was out over treetops to the still-sunlit sea. There was something about this house that he had not felt in any of their other visitations, a déjà vu feeling of being at home. Without really thinking about it, he pulled a Churchill out of his sport coat's breast pocket and lit it up. He could tobacco meditate here. When Atticus returned with their two tall and icy mint juleps, he accepted with a little bow the fresh Churchill that Dominick wordlessly offered him in return for his drink. They sat, silently sipping and puffing, looking out at the same view.

"You don't really want to buy this place, Mr. Witherspoon," Atticus said, studying his thick cigar.

Dominick cleared his throat, trying to make it sound like a question.

"It's way overpriced for one thing, and the market for this sort of property has nowhere near bottomed out yet."

Dominick managed an agreeable sounding noise in his throat.

"None of these ridiculous 'cottages' were built to be lived in before June or after September, unheated, uninsulated."

"But you and the missus live here all year long?"

"This will be our first winter here. We will close down most of the place and just live in the kitchen and a couple of rooms. All exposed like this, the place takes a beating in winter nor'easters."

As if summoned by stage directions, the squall hit. The wind and the rain came from the back of the house, so the veranda remained dry, but all the foliage in front of them bent to the fury of the first onslaught.

"Figures," Atticus said. "Lydia likes to be out in her little place when it rains." The squall brought the end to their conversation. By the time the shower had ended and Brenda and Charlie and Lydia had come back into the house, Dominick and Atticus were in an upstairs billiards room shooting pool, still tending their Churchills and sipping the last of their bottom-sweet mint juleps. That was where Lydia delivered her praise of the past in the smell of cigar smoke. Just the simple sharing of a squall had brought them all into a closer circle of acquaintanceship. The sun broke through the clouds and the wavy old lead glass windows of the billiards room. Lydia and Brenda settled themselves into a window seat and continued their conversation. Charlie took photographs. The reason for their visit was never mentioned again.

A few days later Dominick gave Atticus a call. The Jamesons' number was in the phone book. Brenda and Charlie were off somewhere. An hour later Atticus and Dominick were back at the pool table, this time drinking Dominick's dark 'n' stormies. Lydia brought them a plate of deviled eggs and went off to her garden.

A couple of racks into the afternoon Atticus asked, "What exactly is the point of your game?"

"Which game is that?" Dominick said, lining up a shot.

"The one about you being an English peer looking for investment properties, the one that realtor woman tried to sell us."

"Are you calling Lord Witherspoon's bluff?" Dominick missed the shot.

"Do you think I'd have you back if I thought you were a real English lord? Is it just theater to make the seller feel like the realtor is doing her job? Or is it staged to make other potential buyers think they have competitors? Or was the purpose of your visit simply to get Lydia and I used to the fact that strangers, foreigners, might come bursting into our home at any time? Why else would that realtor woman not show up?"

Dominick waited while Atticus took and made his shot. "If you don't want to sell the place, why did you put it on the market?" Atticus made his next shot, too, leaving just the eight ball up against a cushion.

"You haven't answered my question. End pocket," Atticus said, pointing with his cue stick, an impossible shot.

"It was just an idea for a way to spend summer afternoons, really, visiting rich peoples' houses, an off-the-beaten-track mansions tour. No hidden motives, no harm intended. Maybe we have sparked a little false hope here and there."

"No one is paying you to do it?" Atticus missed his eight ball shot, scratching.

"That would make it a bit like work, would it not? No time off to play pool." Dominick leaned his pool cue against the wall and took his and Atticus's glasses to the sideboard to freshen. "Now you answer my question."

"Lydia and I are not selling the house. Mt. Sinai isn't ours to sell. We just live here now, temporarily."

"I thought your wife grew up here, summers anyway."

"Oh, yes. The house has been in her family since it was built a hundred and twenty years ago, still is actually. Last year we did what everyone said was the smart thing to do to avoid estate and inheritance taxes. We set up a trust fund for the kids, sold the house in Westchester, and moved in here full-time. Mt. Sinai was part of the deal. It belongs to our daughters now."

"And they put it up for sale? Cold."

"To get us out of the cold, supposedly, and into some safe, warm Florida condo."

"Not ready for that yet?"

"You ever been to Florida?"

"Know what you mean. Dantesque, deadly."

"Best avoided."

"Sorry about your daughters."

"Oh, they're good girls. They think they mean well, but both of them are married to zero-sum accountant types for whom Lydia and I are just impediments to sound fiscal management."

"That was pleasantly bitter." Dominick handed Atticus his fresh drink. "No way to stop them?"

"You don't have any children, do you?" Atticus said. "Or you wouldn't have asked that. They are our daughters. The whole point has always been what's best for them."

"Like a big cash influx by the end of this fiscal year?"

"Sometimes it's like that."

"Life is what happens while interest rates change."

"So rack and break. I scratched." Atticus ended the conversation, turning away, a small gnarled man, standing as tall as he could against the light. Real life is filled with equalizers.

It took Dominick a week to decide. Brenda and Charlie were off to a wedding on the Cape, so he had the place to himself, which meant the air-con was off and all the windows were open and the floors got wet when it rained. The Persian woman realtor was clearly losing it, but after a couple of days she returned his calls and—surprised—accepted Lord Witherspoon's verbal bid on Mt. Sinai. The bid was ridiculously low—two-thirds of the asking price—but not so low as to be dismissed, negotiable.

Dominick was fond of Brenda and Charlie. They were easygoing hosts, but there was always a point when it was best to move on and save that place for a future visit. Dominick had pretty much always lived as a guest in other people's homes. He knew better than anyone the protocols, the fine art of being a houseguest. When the host couple started whispering in the house it was time to find a new nest to borrow. Mt. Sinai felt like the next new place to be, and it was large enough so that he could be almost alone even with Atticus and Lydia still living there. What would the winter be like? The three of them in the old manse?

Of course, Atticus and Lydia would have to agree to give up a guest room in exchange for his services. Dominick would present the deal to Atticus, guaranteeing that he could delay and complicate the negotiations on Lord Witherspoon's bid for Mt. Sinai virtually forever or at the very least until one of them had a stroke or they got tired of having Dominick around. His only bad habit was his cigars. Of course, Dominick had neither the money nor the intention to buy the place, but, playing Lord Witherspoon, he knew that he could keep the house in limbo and off the market. Screw the daughters. They could wait their proper inheritable turn. This was New England not King Learland.

The next time Dominick invited himself over to the Jamesons' he brought a gift, a hand carved and painted wooden duck decoy of old but unknown provenience that he had picked up somewhere. He introduced it as the Witherspoon duck as he presented his scheme to both Atticus and Lydia over tea at the kitchen table. Lydia asked Dominick if he had a preference as to which way his room faced.

Chapter 2

After Labor Day the boats began to disappear from the marinas and their embayment anchorages along the shoreline. One by one they were hoisted up onto the hard, demasted, and shrink-wrapped in white plastic. The process fascinated Dominick. Like many expenses he never incurred—property taxes, mortgages, insurance, alimony, rent—this bizarre expenditure mystified him. Atticus tried to explain that a winter in these waters could be very hard on a pleasure boat and that the cost of maintenance and year-round insurance actually made a haul-out cheaper, but Dominick could not get it. "It's like putting a forty-foot toy in your attic every year," he said. "Surely your father and grandfather never did this."

"Some boats, the big boats, still winter in the water here or head south to Bermuda or the Caribbean like in the old days," Atticus told him. "Around this time every year when I was a boy, I used to crew my dad's yacht down to a Florida marina. That was always a good time. Take the train back. I was always late starting school." Atticus's dad's sloop had been called Covenant II. There was a portrait of it, under full sail on a starboard tack in heavy seas, in the dining room at Mt. Sinai. But there was no longer a boat in the family. The last one—something considerably smaller than Covenant II, Dominick was told—had been liquidated along with the rest of the estate. Liquidation seemed a proper fate for a boat, Dominick thought. The topic was a sore spot with Atticus.

The end of summer also meant the end of the summer people. The streets of the village were returned to the care of the locals. The SUVs with out-of-state plates and the nifty convertible sports cars went wherever it is they go when the days get shorter and the nights get colder. At first Dominick felt a bit deserted, left behind. He was, after all, one of them, a fair-weather visitor. His limited wardrobe was all summer clothes, plus a couple of ascots. It had been many years since he had stayed north for the winter.

It was Lydia who took him to the thrift shop in the basement of St. Edgar's Episcopal Church, open only on Wednesday and Saturday mornings. Dominick's XXL-Tall pear shape was not a common one, especially here in New England, where the beer bellies and fat asses so popular now among most American males had not yet become fashionable. Dominick knew from his research that his height, size, weight, and shape—none of which had changed in decades—matched almost exactly what was known of General Washington's founding father endomorphism—perhaps the most physically fit of all the presidents and definitely the finest horseman. Dominick's great-aunt Dorothea had always claimed a sort of Washington-slept-here family descendance from the first president, though they would never let her into the D.A.R.

Dominick flicked through the rack of "pre-owned" men's jackets, looking only for ones with the longest sleeves. Elsewhere in the shop Lydia was searching for the largest men's sweaters and woolen shirts. The relative wealth of the island was reflected in the fancy brand names of its castoff clothing, only the best and barely if ever worn. Dominick pulled out a North Face down jacket that looked like it might fit. As he was trying it on, a woman spoke from behind him: "Lord Witherspoon, what a happy surprise to have you back among us." It was one of the realtors he and Brenda and Charlie had dealt with, maybe that first one, with the dark sweat stain down the back of her green silk blouse.

"Ah, yes, back again. Hello," Dominick said, putting the down jacket back on its hanger and sticking it back on the rack. "Flying over, I thought I would stop by and visit your charming village in a different season. Not much to do here off-season, is there?" He moved away from the men's clothes rack to examine a shelf of books. "I mean, here I am reduced to church flea markets for entertainment. Have you read this?" He pulled a John Grisham novel from the shelf.

"No. I don't read pulp airport novels, probably because I don't get to fly away very often. I hear you made a bid on the Jameson place. Here to rethink that? Prices are still in play, you know."

"Just passing through," Dominick said. He put the book back on the shelf. Lydia walked up behind him and held a bulky Aran Islands cable-knit sweater up against his shoulders, shook her head, and walked away.

"Bargain hunting?" the lady realtor asked, sardonic, ironic, dangerous.

"Always," Dominick said. "Especially for investment properties. Ta-ta now." And he walked to the exit and up the steps and went and sat in his car until he saw the realtor lady leave. Then he went back to fetch Lydia. He bought a used copy of a coffee-table book entitled *Great Bordellos of the World*, which he felt obliged to remove from the Episcopal Church basement. Between St. Edgar's thrift shop and the Salvation Army—"Salvation Armani" Lydia called it—over in New Jerusalem, Dominick built a basic winter defense wardrobe. Nothing matched, but that seemed to echo the local fashion sense.

Dominick's sole quandary about his new attire was it provenience. Somewhere in his heritage a hex had been placed on dead men's clothes, and a few of his new plaid shirts and woolen sweaters and especially a pair of rubber winter boots never seemed like his but borrowed. He knew that these were widows' thrift-shop gifts, the passed-on harvest of closets cleaned out after himself had passed on. There was one well-worn denim jacket with leather elbow patches hand sewn on that he especially took a liking to. He often wondered during the course of the winter as he wore the jacket to town, to the gas station and the grocery store, if there were not locals—maybe even the widow herself—who saw it and recognized it and thought immediately of its original occupant—a man his height and size and wingspan—then had to swallow that memory when a stranger was standing there.

Dominick also noted that while he had heard women brag about pieces of fine clothing picked up as flea-market steals, men—of his acquaintance at least—never bragged about their secondhand clothes. When he shared this observation with Atticus, his host had no idea what Dominick was talking about. Secondhand clothes?

New Jerusalem was the closest mainland town, the place where their island ferry dropped them. It was an old fishing and shipping port down on its luck for a hundred years but rebounding a bit with the new visitor industry age. Derelict dockside districts that no one had gone to the expense of demolishing had become slowly gentrified for the summer trade. But a block or two back from any Harbor View boutique the old houses on their narrow streets still pushed up against one another as if for warmth, crowding the cobblestone right-of-ways. There was still an old-world smell there of dampness and mold, old wood and things left alone too long. Up one of these alleys was a tobacconist's shop that sold Dominick's cigars. At the next corner was a Portuguese fishermen's saloon.

Dominick would not take his car on the New Jerusalem ferry. He would find a side street parking spot near the village ferry dock and walk on and off. It was much cheaper, and everything he needed in New Jerusalem was within easy walking distance of the wharf where the ferry docked. In his new-used local mufti, including a blue knit watch cap, he passed for a local and nobody noticed him. He was not Dominick or Lord Witherspoon here; he was nameless, which was nice. Even in the Portuguese saloon no one ever asked his name or offered theirs. Dominick prized the anonymity.

At some point in October the ferry changed from its on-season to its off-season schedule. That possibility had never occurred to Dominick, so one brisk dusk as he returned to the New Jerusalem wharf to catch his ferry home he was surprised to find the wharf deserted and the gate to the ferry dock closed and locked. Only then did he see the posted notice of the new shortened hours. He had missed the last boat. Perplexed, he returned to the Portuguese saloon and resumed his seat at the bar. "Missed your last ferry, did you?" the bartender said as he placed a fresh glass of ale in front of Dominick. Dominick wondered where he would spend the night.

Dominick had never fallen for that cell phone entrapment scam nor bought one, but when he looked around he could see no public telephone in the bar. The bartender confirmed that they hadn't had one of those in years. "Not since everyone started carrying their own." A man down the bar, a regular, leaned over and handed Dominick his black compact gadget. "Here, mate, use mine."

Without looking at it Dominick handed it back. "No, no. I would only break it." Dominick had never used a cell phone. "But if you would dial a number for me." He gave the man Atticus and Lydia's number to dial, then took the phone back and walked away from the bar. The phone rang many times. Dominick could see it on its assigned end table at the end of the hall. It was an old black office-style phone with a polite ring. If the kitchen door was closed you could barely hear it in there. He waited. No message machine or voice-mail service kicked in. It just kept ringing. Finally Lydia answered with a surprised "Hello?" as if she had just found a kitten abandoned inside her front door.

Dominick only wanted to let the Jamesons know he had missed the last ferry and would not be home that night. He knew they would worry; they had little else to do. There would be plenty of empty tourist rooms in New Jerusalem in October. He would find a place to stay. But Lydia would hear none of it. She gave him the name and address of a friend. She would call ahead and let her friend, a Ms. Arnold, know to expect a guest for the night. "And do bring her a bottle of port, dear. Spend what you'd spend on a room for a bottle of something vintage, ruby. Martha is much more entertaining on good port."

It was three days before Dominick finally caught a ferry back home. He had had no idea how interesting New Jerusalem could be in the off-season. Of course, Lydia had told Martha that the houseguest she was accidentally sharing with her for the night was Lord Witherspoon. Whether Mrs. Arnold believed this or not was of little matter, as she really did not care. "It gets so boring here," she told Dominick early on their first evening, "with just the same old farts." She would not let him drink the port—"a woman's drink"—and put out a bottle of aged single malt for him. They sipped their separate drinks neat. "No iced drinks after Labor Day," she announced.

Martha kept him busy—joint errands around town and manly things to do around the house, like changing lightbulbs, tightening doorknobs, exchanging screens for storm windows. From the start she called him Lord Witherspoon and would not give it up even after he asked her to call him Dominick. She rather liked calling him Lord Witherspoon. In return he called her Mrs. Arnold until she corrected him with the information that Arnold was her maiden name; she had never married. "But I do miss having a man around the house. It was so nice of Lydia to loan you to me." Dominick could not guess her age, although she had fond memories of World War II, which had ended well before Dominick was born.

For a day, Dominick's lack of a change of clothes didn't seem to matter, but the second night Ms. Arnold wanted to go out for dinner, and Dominick's patched denim jacket, green woolen turtleneck, and dark watch cap just would not do. The night before, Ms. Arnold had shown him his guest bedroom and said good-night. They were both a bit tipsy by then, and Dominick hadn't really seen the room, just the bed. Now Ms. Arnold took him back to the room and opened the closet, which was hung with men's clothes—jackets and slacks and suits and sweaters. "My brother Ben's. I never could bring myself to get rid of them. He had such wonderful taste in clothes. There are shirts and things in the dresser. See what you can do, Lord Witherspoon, and perhaps a bath? I'll make reservations for eight o'clock. You will need to wear a tie, I'm afraid."

Brother Ben had been a big man, bigger even than Dominick. The first suit he tried on—after his bath—fit him swimmingly, tailored for a mogul with yards of fine fabric. Its double-breasted cut was so forties retro it was almost back in style. He found socks and suspenders and, still folded in crinkly paper from a Chinese laundry, a starched white dress shirt that was actually a size too large for him around the neck. There was even a selection of silk cravats. There were no shoes. Dominick did what he could to buff up his scuffed brogans. Downstairs in the parlor at a quarter to eight when he met Ms. Arnold—dressed all in black like a widow except for the pearls at her throat—she said, "Ah, the real Lord Witherspoon emerges from behind his proletarian camouflage."

In the dim indirect and candle light of the ristorante, Martha Arnold was really quite striking. In the purposeful gloom, her pale face was striking above her high black lace collar and her string of pearls. Her thick white hair pulled back and up in a casual chignon held by a silver comb completed the regal look. She liked being dressed up, and out in public. Dominick had to admit that he was enjoying it too, disguised by his period costume and his nom de plume. "Lord

17

Witherspoon party of two" still turned heads even in this fanciest of
New Jerusalem eateries. They got a good table, removed but where no
one could miss catching sight of them. They ordered only the best from
the menu. Ms. Arnold vouched for the freshness of the oysters. They
would share a lobster and the prime rib.

It was a delightful meal. The wine was fine. Ms. Arnold continued
her monologue from the night before about the famous historic rogues
and idiots, scoundrels and scandals of New Jerusalem. Chronology
meant nothing to her. The story of an eighteenth century minister
caught in bestiality would be followed by an account of a recent city
councilman arrested for shooting his mistress's pimp. History was just
a dateless porridge of human frailty and fuckups. Dominick found it
charming. He seldom had to say a word, just laugh, and she would go
on, a Baedeker of broken commandments.

The waiter had cleared and they were awaiting their coffee and
cognacs when a wiry, gray-haired man approached their table and
Ms. Arnold introduced Lord Witherspoon to her cousin Carlos.
Dominick cleared his throat and grunted a hello. He was craving a
cigar with his coffee and cognac—an impossibility that especially irked
him after so fine a meal. But no, that would, of course, be committing
a crime. Carlos had an irritating voice—nasal and whiny. He was complaining about something to his cousin. "Do you believe that? Claimed
he never heard of it!"

"That man and the truth are sworn enemies, Carlos. I don't know
why you deal with him. By the way, I don't know what your plans are,
but Lord Witherspoon here has expressed an interest in purchasing my
portion of the general's letters. Perhaps he may be interested in your
portion as well."

Carlos looked at Dominick and Dominick looked at Ms. Arnold,
like passing a question mark.

"Don't you think that might be best? Their ending up quietly back
in England?" Ms. Arnold asked. "Without any messy auction and pub-
licity here?"

Carlos was now looking back and forth from Ms. Arnold to Lord
Witherspoon like one of those bobblehead dolls only much larger.
The waiter returned with their after-dinner drinks, and Carlos had to
step aside.

"But now is not the time to discuss such things, is it? Ta-ta, Carlos. We'll talk tomorrow."

They had both sampled their coffee and cognacs before Dominick asked, "Your portion of the general's letters?"

"Oh, Carlos has been pestering me for months now to sell him the letters that I have, so that he could have them all. But I don't want to. We've kept them a secret thus far. I want you to have them and take them back to England and do whatever you want with them. They will only become more valuable with time."

"But we had not discussed it."

"Hadn't we? I thought we had. I've gone over our conversation several times in my mind. But the offer still stands. I will sell the letters to you rather than Carlos, and I think you should purchase his as well, put an end to this whole unfortunate mess, take it all away with you and make a nice profit on it later." Ms. Arnold reached across the table to put her hand on top of Dominick's. "When you arrived last night, Lord Witherspoon, you were like a prayer answered, my humble knight in hiding come to save me."

Dominick paid the fat check with a credit card.

Ms. Arnold allowed Lord Witherspoon his occasional cigar only if he stood by an open window. It didn't seem to matter if the breeze wafted the smoke back into the house, just that he be by an open window. It was a cold October night when they got back from dinner. Rather than chill out her parlor, Dominick smoked his Romeo y Juliet Churchill outside the closed front door. He took a snifter of single malt with him. The cold did not bother him, but there was nowhere to sit down on the stone stoop, and he disliked standing when he smoked. He made the best of it. Inside, Ms. Arnold was fetching the letters she wanted him to buy so that he could examine them. As if he knew anything about old letters. He only half-finished his cigar before going back in. He was not enjoying it properly, not giving it his undivided attention.

Ms. Arnold had the letters displayed on her dining room table. The lace tablecloth beneath them was a nice touch. The letters were old. The once-folded pages were yellow and dry, the ink turned sepia. There were maybe twenty of them, each of multiple pages, written in an open cursive with what must have been a quill pen, judging from the occasional blots and uneven ink density. Most were accompanied by their original postal envelopes. The first page of each letter bore a date in its upper right-hand corner, all from the 1790s. The last page of each letter bore the bold, backward-slanting signature of Benedict Arnold.

"They were only discovered four years ago," Ms. Arnold said. "I can give you all the details, their provenience and authentication. It was my aunt, Carlos's mother, who came across them. She was dying, going through her attic. She secretly gave them to me—there were twice as many then—because she didn't trust Carlos to do the right thing by them."

Dominick was carefully picking up pages, examining them, and setting them aside. It occurred to him that he ought to be wearing gloves of some archival sort. He stopped.

"They have all been copied and transcribed. The transcriptions are here," Ms. Arnold said, picking up a ring binder, " along with the experts' authentication certificates.

They are letters the general sent secretly to his family back here in New England after he moved on to London."

"And you want to sell them?" was all Dominick could think to say.

"After the old lady died, Carlos raised a stink about my having the letters. It was holding up the probate, so I agreed to give him half of them. I'm afraid my half-wit cousin Carlos and his white-trash wife are going to auction off his letters a piece and a parcel at a time, destroying their integrity and just feeding the anti-Arnold forces."

"And you want to . . . ?" Dominick retreated from the table and its letters to a sideboard where he had left his snifter.

"Why, keep them altogether and protected and properly cared for."

"And hidden somewhere in England."

"General Arnold's story is much, much more complex and intriguing and sympathetic to him than American historic demonology has allowed. Don't you see, Lord Witherspoon? If you agree to purchase my set of letters, Carlos would readily settle to sell you his as well, not for any altruistic or family loyalty reasons but because he needs—he always needs—the ready cash."

Dominick took a sip of scotch and made a several-syllable affirmative sound in his throat.

"And I will sell you my half of the letters for a fraction of their appraised value—I don't need the money—thereby setting the price for Carlos's parcel."

"A win-win situation, as they say. Except for Carlos."

"Carlos and those profiteers at the auction houses and those so-called scholars eager to misconstrue anything in order to further demean the general's character. There are people out there, Lord Witherspoon, who deserve to lose."

Dominick took the ring binder of transcriptions and papers to bed. He found the letters quite boring, which, he surmised, was testimony to their authenticity. Parts of the letters were in a yet unbroken cipher code, which a footnote explained was common practice for international business correspondence at the time, when transoceanic correspondence was almost as likely to end up in a competitor's or enemy's hands as its intended recipient's. More proof of their authenticity. There were references to payments for the education of a minor child in St. Johns, New Brunswick, whom historians had reason to believe and this would prove—another footnote—was Arnold's illegitimate child. A handwriting expert had matched the letter signatures to those on other official documents. But nowhere was there the hint of a human being behind the letters. No one emerged, not even a mask. And if the documents had been appraised, there was no figure mentioned anywhere. Not that it mattered, as Dominick had no intention of Lord Witherspoon even pretending to have an interest in purchasing them.

Dominick slept late as usual. He preferred rising during those quiet hours of late morning after everyone else in the house had already rushed off on their daily business and neighborhood children were safely caged in school. The housewife's soap opera hours, every homestayer's secret sweet spot in the day. He was determined to head home that day, but Ms. Arnold was not about when he came downstairs, and he really could not leave without a proper farewell and a response to her offer. Dominick was wearing his own clothes again. He had hung the gangster suit back in the closet. He had decided that he would thank Ms. Arnold for her offer to sell him the letters, but inform her that a family injunction precluded him from expending any estate money on antique art or documents—the family had been burned too many times before—and really all he had to spend was estate money.

Dominick finally lost patience waiting and was writing a note at the dining room table when he heard the front door open. It was Ms. Arnold with her cousin Carlos in tow. Or was he pursuing her? They were in mid-conversation. " . . . has nothing to do with it," Carlos was saying, "and neither does she. It's you."

"Oh, it's me, is it?" Ms. Arnold answered him, then she called out, "Yoo-hoo, Lord Witherspoon, are you up and about?"

They met in the hallway. Dominick was crumpling up his note.

"Witherspoon, I can't let you take those letters out of the family and out of the country." Cousin Carlos was wasting no time on pleasantries. "I have offered Martha what I think is a decent and fair sum for them, and I would appreciate it if you could respect our family peace and patriotism enough to let that be the end of the matter." He paused as if waiting to find out what else he might have to say, thought of nothing. "Thank-you."

"Lord Witherspoon, I am so sorry. I told Carlos that you hadn't even named a sum yet."

"I'll match it," Carlos said with a nod of his head and a firm lip.

"I had no idea of the . . . eh . . . deep family concerns here," Dominick said.

"Do you have any idea, sir, can you imagine, sir, if your surname was the national synonym for traitor?" Cousin Carlos took a step closer. "These letters can only refresh those ugly elements again. They must be suppressed, and I am willing to make any sacrifice to see that they do not leave New Jerusalem."

"Well, I . . ." Dominick felt compelled to say something, but what?

"Carlos." Ms. Arnold turned on her cousin. "How dare you impugn Lord Witherspoon's intentions with the suggestion that this is anything more than a simple business exchange."

"There you go again, Martha. I'm not impugning anything." And they went off on an argument about their relative purity of motive, or something. Their voices grew quickly louder and overlaid one another. It was an ancient argument in which Dominick had no part. He walked off toward the kitchen, unmissed. He was putting some water on to boil for tea when he heard Carlos leave with a final loud "You know where I stand."

When Ms. Arnold came into the kitchen, Dominick asked, "Where do you keep your tea?"

"You mustn't pay too much attention to Carlos," Ms. Arnold said as she pulled a can of Earl Grey down from a cupboard. "He gets excited easily." She spooned loose tea into a Chinese teapot. "Are you interested in the letters, Lord Witherspoon? Carlos's remonstrations mean nothing."

Dominick explained to her his familial restrictions against his buying anything besides real estate. "I had an uncle who managed to lose a large portion of the family fortune through foolish purchases and scams. Hence the estate prohibits any investments save property. And I myself make a point of not collecting anything. Thanks for the offer, though. Sorry."

"No harm done, my lord. It was just an offer. Even without a real bidding war between you and Carlos, his offer is quite acceptable. I'll take it."

Dominick was watching the tea kettle not boil. "You will take it? But I thought . . ."

"Oh, your interest put quite the scare into Carlos, along with my willingness to sell an Englishman some of our dirty family linen. He won't do anything with them. He'll hide them. Maybe he will even burn them." The kettle was now whistling, and Ms. Arnold poured the steaming water into the Chinese teapot. "It doesn't matter."

"So, you're not afraid of . . . ?" What was it she had been afraid of? "What do you mean, it does not matter?"

"Oh, the letters and the authentication papers are all fakes, forgeries. Good enough to fool Carlos but not any reputable auction house expert. They're worthless, really, all of them, including the half, the bait, I'd already given Carlos."

"But you were willing to sell them to me as real?"

"Oh, yes. You're an outsider. And if you had bought Carlos's letters as well, then we both would have made out fine. But no matter, I'll take Carlos's money and be done with it. He'll probably never find out the truth." Ms. Arnold was setting out teacups and saucers for them. "Cream and sugar, Lord Witherspoon?"

Chapter 3

It was just fucking cold and there was nowhere to go to get warm. Their eighteen-foot aluminum dory rose and fell and bounced on the dirty-dishwater-colored waves. Every ninety seconds a foghorn sounded off to their right. Sometimes the fog cleared enough so that they could see the next oncoming wave and prepare, sometimes not. Atticus was crouched in the stern over the currently dysfunctional outboard motor—something about the carburetion. Dominick sat on the center seat, his back to the prow, just able with his six-foot-plus wingspan to grasp simultaneously both the port and starboard gunwales. Although all of him was cold, his sneakered feet were coldest, awash in the frigid seawater that sloshed back and forth in the bottom of the boat.

The soiled and worn yellow foul-weather gear that Atticus had found for Dominick to wear was several sizes too small for him. The sleeves ended on his forearms. The pants were a laugh. But Dominick was not laughing. "Where are all the other boats?" he yelled as calmly as he could, trying to sound as if all this were just foreplay for a larger adventure.

Atticus did not answer. He did not have his hearing aid in, so even if he did hear he would not have to answer. The motor came briefly to life then died. The foghorn moaned again, sounding even closer. Atticus was whistling now, something that sounded frighteningly like a sea chantey, and a wave hit them broadside, spilling more sea into the boat. "You might bail," Atticus said. Crouched down in the stern, he was up to his asshole in water. Dominick went back to bailing with one hand, never letting go of the boat with the other.

Occasionally, being a houseguest entailed making huge mistakes. It was essential not to have or express any political ideas at all. They were the proper property of those who owned real property and paid real taxes, like your hosts. Transients did not deserve the vote, or even an opinion. Local and party politics—like religion—were topics to be avoided. They only led sooner or later to dysfunction and departure. Dominick knew the rules—do not take a position, do not get involved. So, how had he gotten himself here, adrift in an open boat on a wintery sea as part of a demonstration in protest against something he did not understand? A huge mistake, and he had his host Atticus to thank for it. He stopped bailing to try and blow some warmth into his fingers. The motor started up again, belched out a cloud of blue smoke, then stayed alive, running rough but steady.

"We'll head back," Atticus said; although how he could tell which way was back escaped Dominick.

Dominick had once joked that the reason New Englanders liked boating so much was that then they could enjoy being wet, cold, and uncomfortable all year long. That was not funny now. Atticus was in his element here. His face was lit up as if there were a fire burning inside him. His eyes sparked with life. He was whistling again, just softly, badly, but contentedly to himself. Dominick couldn't stand watching and turned around to face forward. As the boat got up speed the prow rose up and all the bilge washed backward around Atticus's happy, snuggly sea-booted feet. Damn the ancient mariner and all his causes, Dominick thought. He still could see nothing beyond twenty feet in front of them.

Supposedly out there with them on the bay was a flotilla of similarly protesting private vessels. But who knew? Who could tell in the fog? It had not been long after leaving the marina that the other small boats that left with them vanished from sight and then sound. "We have to spread out," Atticus told him, "form a curtain they can't get through." Atticus set off on his own course, without compass or chart, toward the mouth of the bay. Dominick said something about never liking the alternative connotations of the term "dead reckoning." But Atticus assured him, "Don't worry. This bay has been my backyard since I was just a kid in a skiff."

Dominick was not quite sure what it was they all were forming an impermeable—albeit invisible—curtain against. This lack of a seemingly important fact arose from his professional practice of ignoring all news of the day. That morning Atticus had asked him if he would mind giving him a hand moving a boat. The boat was already up on a trailer. All they had to do was get it to the water and put it in. "But I thought everyone was taking their boats out of the water," Dominick said. "Oh, she's just going in for the day. Then we'll take her back out," Atticus answered.

This made so little sense to Dominick that he refused to pursue it. How bad could it be, putting a boat in the water then taking it out? It was a balmy late autumn day with a hazy egg-yolk sun in the sky. He went off to put on some outdoor clothes, never asking what the point was of putting a boat in the water and then immediately taking it out. New England seasonal customs. He wondered if they still planted corn with a dead fish for fertilizer the way the original natives taught them.

The boat was borrowed. The last of Atticus's vessels had gone with the estate. He was, after all, supposed to be in a Florida retirement condo by now. The boat was up on its trailer parked in someone's backyard. The owner—in an incongruous Red Sox sweatshirt and Yankees cap—was loaning them his pickup truck as well to haul the trailer. "I'm with you on this one, Mr. Jameson," he said to Atticus. "A hundred percent behind you. I wish I could go with you, but you can have her for the day." The boat was a battered but sturdy-looking aluminum-hulled working dory, mounted with a large if also well-used-looking outboard engine. The pickup truck was newer, an F-150. Atticus drove, looking like a little kid behind the wheel.

Dominick hadn't thought through the rest of his day. Now he figured they would back the boat into the water on a ramp at one marina or another, and he would wait out Atticus's return there, hopefully in a nearby pub. But where they stopped to put in was at a remote public park beach ramp. "Don't belong to a marina anymore," Atticus said. It wasn't that hard launching the boat. Atticus did most of the work. They loaded the boat with the coolers and gas containers Atticus had brought along and parked the truck and trailer in an almost empty parking lot. Dominick had no choice but to get on board. He was already wet when Atticus handed him his foul-weather gear. He had been shanghaied. They motored back to a marina where they met up with the other small crafts and fishing boats before setting out. Atticus pulled a bottle of scotch out of a cooler, and they passed it back and forth. Dominick had to admit his adrenalin was up. "What exactly is it we are going out to catch?" he asked.

"Them," Atticus said, "the despoilers."

They never did catch them that day. In fact, in the fog and the failing light Atticus could not even find the park beach ramp where they had put in, and they ended up tied to the end of a marina dock. A fellow protestor gave them a ride home. Only the next day did Dominick ask about the backstory to what he now saw—in dry, warm, and well-rested retrospect—as a mini-adventure memory. By the time Dominick came down to the kitchen that morning, Atticus had already retrieved and returned the boat and trailer and truck, with the help of their owner, and was sitting at the kitchen table drinking tea. Atticus tried to explain it to him.

"So, it was the Coast Guard we were looking for out there?" Dominick asked. "Isn't that sort of backwards?"

"No, no," Atticus said. "They were supposed to find us, but I guess they never went out."

"Why were they supposed to find us? Were we in danger?"

"No—Jesus, Dominick—they were supposed to find us because we weren't supposed to be there."

"Where were we supposed to be?"

"Not there."

"Why?"

"Because the Coast Guard was running an exercise, a practice run for an LNG tanker entering the bay."

"Oh," Dominick said. He had set about fixing himself a small pot of French-press coffee. He could not stand tea in the morning, and he was really no good before that first cup of joe. "What's an elengied anchor?"

"You really aren't from here, are you, Dominick? I never did learn where you do hail from."

"My mother now lives in the Washington area," Dominick said.

"So, you haven't heard about the natural gas terminal they want to put in up the bay? It's only been the biggest political news around here for the past two years."

"I'm afraid I do not know what that is, a natural gas terminal." Dominick brought his coffee to the table.

"It's a big shoreside facility where they unload liquid natural gas from supertankers, process and deliver it."

"And the problem is?"

"The problem is nobody hereabouts wants it, and we mean to stop it."

Dominick knew he did not want to hear the reasons why this terminal was a bad idea, just like he did not want to hear why it was a great idea. "Which leads somehow to the Coast Guard running—or not running—some sort of anchor test?"

"I swear sometimes you are worse than Lydia, Dominick. What are you talking about?"

"Okay, let's start at the beginning again. Why exactly were you and I and the others out there in our little boats yesterday?"

"So that the Coast Guard would see that bringing one of those supertankers filled with liquid natural gas into the bay to go up to that proposed terminal was not possible."

"Ah, good tactic, preventative defense." Dominick smiled at Atticus, who had begun to act a tad hyper. "And how were we going to show the Coast Guard this? Was someone going to blow something up and the rest of us were just out there as decoys?"

"What? Are you crazy? No one's going to blow anything up!" Atticus was getting excited again.

"Calm down, Atticus. I was just joking—hoping—about blowing things up. Don't we all sort of envy terrorists for their freedom to do outlandish things for a cause?"

Atticus stared at Dominick for a full thirty seconds before answering, "No, I don't envy terrorists. I despise them. Cowards hiding behind threats and the murder of innocents. And part of the problem. Because of your enviable terrorists, these liquid natural gas supertankers have become potential targets of mass destruction, ready-made floating bombs. We don't want anything blowing up. We want them out of here."

"I can understand that," Dominick said, "but how does what we did yesterday . . . ?"

"Because these LNG supertankers are so dangerous, special security measures have been invoked. Their arrivals and departures—at least three times a week—are unscheduled and kept secret, just announced at the last minute. In American waters—like our bay—the Coast Guard must enforce a security zone around the tankers three miles long and a half mile wide. No vessel is allowed inside that security zone, no vessel whatsoever, be it a freighter, a yacht, a lobsterman, or a kid in a Sunfish."

"That seems a bit extreme. Ferries and things too?"

"The works. Nothing. Even bridges farther up the bay would be closed to all traffic."

"While these surprise tankers moved through."

"You're getting the picture."

"So we were out on the bay . . ."

"Because we got the Coast Guard to agree to make a dry run to see what it would take to clear the bay like that."

"And your tactic was to flood the zone."

"Right."

"And they never showed up? That was unsportsmanlike."

"Well, they won't say, I gather. But if they did try to come through pretending they were a supertanker, no one saw them, and there had to be boats inside their sacred four-and-a-half-square-mile security zone. We had the outer bay covered."

The next day there was an article in the *New Jerusalem News* about the protest, under the headline "Anti-Gas Armada Stymies Coast Guard." Atticus made a point of showing it to Dominick.

"Stymies is not a good headline verb," Dominick observed, putting the paper down.

"No, read the article," Atticus said. Dominick did.

The article reported that the Coast Guard had gone ahead with its planned supertanker rehearsal run in spite of foggy conditions on the bay. A cutter out of Boston would escort a fictional LNG tanker through the bay, maintaining the proscribed security zone, including bridge closures. However, due to weather conditions and the cutter's radar detection of "abnormally high vessel activity in shipping lanes," the exercise was postponed.

The protestors were calling it a victory for their cause. Atticus's local group, Bay Savers, had been joined by national organizations Greenpeace, Nature Conservancy, the Wildlife Foundation, and others in mounting a Blockade to Save the Bay Day. International support was also mounting. "The British Green movement was represented by Lord Witherspoon, who spent the day on the bay with the other boating protestors."

Atticus had wandered off to another part of the house while Dominick read. Now Dominick went off to find him. He found him in his study, where he was watching the local news on TV. "What is this? What is this!"

"I know, I know," Atticus said, not even turning around. "That's Lydia's work. She knows the reporter. I guess she thought your presence would add a little punch to the coverage. We need all the traction we can get right now. Both the state and the feds have come out in favor of the terminal."

"But . . . but Lord Witherspoon . . . Lord Witherspoon isn't green."

"Why not? Don't chameleons change color?"

"Lord Witherspoon is colorless."

"Was. Lord Witherspoon was colorless. Now he's green, for the time being at least. What's the difference?"

"I look awful in green. It doesn't match my complexion, makes me look like a corpse."

"Talk to Lydia."

Lydia claimed to know nothing at all about how Lord Witherspoon came to be named in the article. "But most people," she said, "would take some pride in having their name associated with such a worthwhile cause."

It was four days before the men in suits arrived. Dominick was home alone at Mt. Sinai when the front door bell rang. He ignored it at first, but whoever was pushing the button would not give up. Some variety of door-to-door Christian was Dominick's guess. Well, he would give them a piece of atheistic dismissal. But the two men in dark suits and ties on the doorstep did not look like missionaries. They were empty-handed for one thing, no Bibles.

"Mr. Jameson?" The taller one spoke. Why was it always the taller one who spoke first?

"Mr. Jameson is out," Dominick said, and instinctively he went to close the door. The taller one's foot and shoulder stopped him. "And you are?" the man asked.

"A houseguest," Dominick said. "Who are you?"

Both men produced little wallets with gold badges inside. "Federal agents, ICE, conducting an investigation. May we come in?"

Dominick was still examining their badges and photo IDs. "Why, of course not," he said without looking up, "not without a warrant. This is private property, and not even my private property to give you permission to enter. What is it you want?"

"Okay, play it that way," the shorter one said, and they both took a step back from the threshold. "As a federal law enforcement officer I do have the right to ask you to produce some identification."

"Certainly. Wait here," Dominick said, and he walked off into the house. His wallet with his driver's licenses was in his back pocket, but he wanted a little time to think. He briefly imagined the two agents as lovers, then as a vaudeville duo. What an awful job that must be, being a cop—the chain of command and the bureaucracy and all that driving around in cars. He wondered if they were armed. Then he wondered what in the world they could want. Had Atticus and/or Lydia broken some federal law? Had their daughters called in the feds to evict them? And what was *ice*? "Federal agents, ice," hadn't one of them said? Dominick chuckled to himself, imaging the phrase as an ungrammatical autobiographical index entry—"Federal agent, I is."

Dominick stopped in the kitchen for a minute and pulled his wallet from his pocket. The simple truth was that Dominick had nothing to fear from the police state, even federal agents, as he had done nothing wrong, or at least chargeable. He walked back to the front door and handed over his Florida driver's license. He chose that one because it was from the farthest-away state.

The shorter man took the ID and examined it, then took a photo of it with his cell phone. He said thank you when he handed it back. "Is Lord Witherspoon at home?" he asked.

"Who?"

"Lord Witherspoon. We'd like to speak with him."

"I don't know anyone of that name."

"An acquaintance of Mr. Jameson. We have reason to believe he is a houseguest here."

"The only people staying here are Mr. and Mrs. Jameson and myself."

The shorter one pulled a business card out of his coat breast pocket and handed it to Dominick. "Have Mr. Jameson give us a call. This is a Homeland Security matter." As they walked back to their car parked on the road Dominick saw from the business card that ICE stood for Immigration and Customs Enforcement. Perhaps it was time for Lord Witherspoon to disappear.

Chapter 4

Dominick was reading about New England privateers during the War for Independence, a book he had found in Atticus's library. He was pleased to discover what an unruly lot of mostly freebooting anarchists they had been, many of them barely teenagers. In many of New England's small fishing ports the entire employable male population would have been at sea as privateers, some in proper brigs and schooners but others in everything from coastal sloops to whale boats converted into temporary ships of war. High-seas piracy had become suddenly legal, or sort of legal anyway, with the proper piece of paper and a promise to share any prizes with the folks who issued the piece of paper.

Israel Rutman was typical. He began a family shipping empire by running a fleet of small privateers out of several ports in Maine, harvesting seemingly at will the coastal British supply ships running down from Halifax to New York, then black-marketing the captured war supplies to the Continental Army. General Washington had his own set of high-seas supply captains, some of whom he had to fire for being too blatantly just pirates. It was a free-market war on this seaboard, with the merchants winning many more engagements than the military. Breaking the law for profit's sake was what the revolution was all about, anyway—the birth of American industry, the eternal profits of a nation at war.

It was Israel Rutman's profits that several generations after his death had built Mt. Sinai for his great-whatever descendants. His portrait was in the library. When Dominick made the connection—Israel's name was not only on the portrait but also first on the brass plaque inside the grandfather clock in the sitting room—Lydia filled in the details. The deep past was very clear to her.

"Oh, yes, the commodore made the family fortune. After the war—which was very good for him—he got in at the end of the triangle trade and imported slaves. He had many. There are more Negro than white Rutmans in New Jerusalem County these days, you know. He once owned most of the docks there, controlled everything in and out. He knew General Washington, you know. They were friends. There are letters somewhere."

"He was a powerful man, then," Dominick said.

"Oh, all men want to be remembered that way, don't they?" Lydia was dismissive. "He had only daughters, no sons. So the white side of the family name vanished. There is a Rutman's Swamp up near Potters Falls, but that had nothing to do with him really, strictly coincidental and after the fact."

Dominick had found Lydia out in her combination gardening shed/artist's studio. She had an easel set up in front of a pair of glass French doors that looked out and down over now almost barren tree-tops to the ocean and a distant horizon. It was a painterly view if the sky and the light were right, but the painting that she was working at on the easel was of a completely different scene, pastoral with cows and a distant windmill. It was chilly in the studio. Lydia was wearing many layers—all of which clashed—and a pair of gray yarn gloves with the fingers cut off. The backs of the gloves were many colors where she had unloaded or cleaned a brush.

"Oh, men just love having things named after them," Lydia said as she stepped back from her canvas and stared out at the view. "Macy's, Neiman Marcus, Jacksonville, McDonald's."

"Women don't?"

"Fahrenheit, Ohm, Watt, Doppler, Sandwich," Lydia continued. "They even make a wife change her name to her husband's, as if that would make a difference about how she feels."

"Well, there is the downside, too—Quisling, Ponzi, Edsel, Benedict Arnold."

"None of the elements are named after women, but there is Einsteinium and Fermium and Copernicium." Lydia went back at her canvas with a brush.

"Don't forget Neptunium and Promethium."

"I never heard of those."

"They're newer. Some guys just invented them. How about Curies? Stuff is measured in curies."

"Yes, but after Marie or Pierre? They wouldn't even give the poor woman her own Nobel Prize. She had to drag her husband along to share the honors."

There was silence for a while as Lydia dabbed at her canvas. "Beef Stroganoff, Eggs Benedict," she said.

"Bloody Mary," Dominick answered as in some church litany, "Margarita."

The silence returned. It was a nice silence, not pregnant with anything at all.

After a while Lydia asked why Dominick had become interested in Commodore Rutman.

"Oh, Atticus and my little voyage last week you might say wetted my interest in sailing hereabouts. Just reading up on past bad guys on the bay."

"You know, I was very glad you did that with Atticus. He used to be much busier with things like that, water things I mean. But none of his old salt friends are still around. Why don't you two do more things like that? Atticus doesn't have much time left, you know. You'd be doing a good service to get him out more often."

Dominick had no idea about the state of Atticus's health, nor especially did he want any. He said nothing.

"Prostate, cancer, spread," Lydia said, three separate words, each delivered with a stab at the canvas with her brush. "I'm not supposed to know. He hasn't told me. As if you can keep something like that from your wife. But the prognosis is now measured in months. I don't know, maybe he is in denial."

"Oh," Dominick felt compelled to say.

"But if he is, you can help him out. Get him out of the house more, you know, doing guy things. Keep his mind off it. Get out on the water, go golfing. I don't know."

"It's a bit late in the season for both boating and golf, I'm afraid," Dominick said, glad to have something to say.

"Well, whatever. He wants to do this alone, without me. That's his choice, but at least he should be having some fun these last months while he still can. He's not a bad guy, you know."

This was a new one for Dominick. He had become comfortable at Mt. Sinai. His days there were spent as he liked to spend them—unplanned. The essence of his existence was the absence of obligation. Did Atticus truly need a playmate? For the next few days Dominick avoided his host. The autumnal weather broke and gave way to one last glorious good-bye to sunlight and warmth, and each of them took advantage of those valedictory Indian summer days to be out of the house on their separate errands. But in course the skies lowered and closed and darkened again, and one early dusk Dominick and Atticus found themselves together in the den. Atticus was cleaning an old flint-lock rifle. Dominick came in to fix himself a drink.

Perhaps there was a slight tremor in Atticus's hands Dominick had not noticed before, a caution in movement that tried to mask pain. Atticus never did mention how he was feeling, as if it was not a topic open for discussion. Dominick wondered, if he were dying and could hide it, would he want others to know? Probably not.

"That'll be it for the summer wardrobe," Atticus said, looking up.

"Good-bye seersucker," Dominick said. "Fix you a drink?"

"Thanks, just a scotch, straight."

"Heard any more from our friends at ICE?" Dominick asked.

"Ice? No ice, thanks. Oh, those guys? No, nothing more."

Dominick had passed on the message and calling card from the short federal agent, and Atticus had called him. Lord Witherspoon? He didn't know anything about a Lord Anybody. It had just been Dominick and him out on the bay that day. The agents must have been misinformed. Who was this Lord Witherspoon, anyway, Atticus had asked. That's what the feds were trying to find out.

"Excuse me for asking, Atticus, but how old are you?"

"Seventy-five this year. Born the same day Will Rogers died."

"But your parents didn't name you Will or Roger."

"No, Atticus was my dad's idea. He was a classics professor, Swarthmore. I was named after Cicero's best friend."

"A rare honor."

"My mother disliked the name. She always called me Teddy for some reason that I never discovered. Grew up that way, never sure if I was a Roman aristocrat or a Rough Rider."

"Tough."

"Not really. Easy, actually. I never had to worry about money, just make more of it. Married my distant cousin."

"Lydia?"

"Oh, yes. My roots go back to that Rutman tree too."

"That sounds a bit like royalty."

"Does it? Never thought of it that way. More like a cage that I couldn't escape."

"But it has kept you healthy."

"Can't take much credit for that. Longevity runs in the family."

Was that a sideways suspicious glance Atticus shot at him from his armchair?

"But I did get shot once, when I was just a boy," Atticus went on. "Buckshot in the back while out hunting quail with my uncle. Still got the scars from where they had to dig them out. Only time I've been under the knife."

"Still hunt?"

"Haven't in years."

He has family, kids and grandkids, Dominick thought. Why don't they come and play with him? When I get to that stage I won't have anyone. "How about a game of pool?" he asked.

Charlie called. Brenda had already headed south to their place in the Keys, but Charlie wasn't ready to migrate yet. He was wondering if Dominick wanted to go hunting. "Season's on for most varmints," Charlie said, "and we don't have to worry about licenses over here. The Fish and Wildlife folks can't spare a warden for the island. It's always worked pretty much on the old honor system here. Especially if you're on private land, no one questions."

"And which private land would that be?" Dominick asked. "Your backyard?"

"Remember that first place we looked at out on the coast road? That empty French villa-like place? Well, it's still vacant, and the folks to the north and the south of there are gone for the season. I checked it out. It's a private Sherwood Forest, man. Let's play Robin Hood and do a little poaching."

"It's safe?" Dominick said. "I mean, from the authorities and all."

"Look, those billionaires should be happy if we go in there and do a little varmint culling for them for free. No one will even hear the gunshots."

Dominick was not a stranger to hunting. He had opened his home-less career in Virginia horse country, where shooting parties were de rigueur. "The weather has to be good," he said. "I want to shoot dry, happy beasts."

And so it was that three days later when the rain let off that Dominick, Charlie, and Atticus found themselves in Charlie's Bronco stopped at the locked chain across the French villa's driveway. They had with them a collection of shotguns and rifles—Charlie's and Atticus's. Charlie had not been clear on exactly what they might be hunting. "Well, deer, of course, but then maybe turkey and pheasant or quail, depending on what's there. Maybe an opossum or bobcat. I'd love to get myself a coyote. They're in there." So they had brought with them a varied-purpose arsenal, including Atticus's ancient flintlock muzzle-loader from Commodore Rutman's time.

Charlie got out of the driver's seat. The chain was fastened by a big Yale lock in the middle, but Charlie easily unhooked it through a broken link at one end of the chain, rehooking the chain after they drove through. "I told you I had scoped it all out," Charlie said as they headed up the pointlessly curving drive through the pine forest. All the trees were the same height and were planted almost too perfectly equidistant from one another, so that it looked more like a German park than a French one.

"Of course, they had to tear a real forest out to plant this one," Charlie said.

"This is the Hitchenses' place." Atticus said from the back seat. "He got caught in a defense contract scam during the Reagan years and was sent up just as he finished the place, so the trees are that old."

They parked on the gravel drive in front of the house, which looked even more forlorn and lost in the non-summer light. Charlie had brought an old two-wheeled golf cart and empty golf bag, which he got out of the back of the Bronco first. Then he loaded their collection of weapons into the bag and filled its side pockets with the various ammo they required. "Our gun boy," he said, swinging the cart around by its handle and heading off. "This way, I suggest. Canada geese for a warm up."

It was not a bad afternoon of shooting. They did get some geese right away on the seaside lawn. Then they each took their weapon of choice and headed off on their own. State law required every hunter to wear so many square feet of bright orange vest and hat, but they were dressed just in their normal warm hiking clothes. There would be no other illegal hunters out there. They just had to take care not to shoot one another. Dominick was slightly troubled by this. Not that he thought they were in any danger of repeating Atticus's uncle's mistake, but because years before he had adopted a rule of only breaking one law at a time. If you were driving drunk, you did not speed. If the girl you were with was underage, you did not cross state lines. Breaking the hunter's dress code was more of a superstitious worry.

Atticus had luck with his Minuteman special and brought in two rabbits. Dominick had missed most of what he had shot at, but late in the day he had bagged an opossum, which kindly fell out of its tree when it died. What he was most proud of, however, was what he had not shot. Deep in the woods he had gotten an eight-point whitetail buck dead in his sights but had not pulled the trigger. It wasn't a Bambi moment. He did like venison. It was just the thought of dressing the deer and dragging it out alone that put him off. Atticus and Dominick were back at the car with their trophies as dusk thickened. Atticus seemed happy and relaxed, no worse for wear from his ramble in the woods.

It was almost dark when Charlie came hiking up the driveway, dragging something large behind him by the tail. It looked like Charlie had gotten himself his coyote.

"You know there are good coyotes and bad coyotes," Charlie said as he walked up to them. "The good ones you never see. They're afraid of humans. The bad ones, the ones that cause trouble, are the ones you do see because they've lost all respect for us. This varmint was so ballsy it tried to stare me down. So I shot him." Charlie pulled the dead animal up to the back of the Bronco where they could get a good look at it.

"There's only one problem," Atticus said.

"Right," Charlie said. "It ain't a coyote."

Dominick could see how Charlie in the wild could have mistaken the canine laying there bled out for a coyote. The size was right, and coyotes come in different shades of brown, especially this time of year when their winter coats were coming in. But this animal was plainly some sort of Alsatian mix. Its long nose gave it an almost wolfish look.

"Wild dog," Atticus said.

"But someone's pet once. Look." Charlie reached down and pushed aside the matted fur on the animal's neck to show the tattered remnants of a collar.

"What are you going to do with him?" Dominick asked.

"Take him home and bury him, I guess. Same as I would have done with a coyote."

The ride home was pretty quiet. At one point Charlie asked, out of nowhere, "Which one was it liked to eat dog? I forget. Lewis or Clark?"

"Meriwether Lewis, I believe. He preferred it to venison," Atticus answered.

"Are you sure? Clark was the more, you know, rugged type."

"No, Lewis preferred dog over elk or horse even."

"I wonder how they fixed it?" Charlie said, ending the conversation. But Charlie did offer to skin, dress out, and freeze the meat of Atticus's and Dominick's kills for them. "I like the pelts. I cure them."

When Charlie dropped Dominick and Atticus off at Mt. Sinai it was well after dark. All they had to take from the back of the Bronco was their ammo and weapons—two shotguns, a .22 rifle, and Atticus's musket. In the dark they had not noticed the black car parked across the street, but as they headed toward the house they heard two car doors open and shut and steps approach behind them.

"Mr. Jameson, a word with you, please." It was the duo from ICE, only this time they were in uniform—blue jeans and midnight-blue windbreakers with their badges plainly showing. The uniforms amplified their Mutt and Jeff vaudevillian possibilities. They met on the front steps in the light of the porch lamp.

"Put down your weapons, please, gentlemen," the short one said. The tall one already had his windbreaker pulled back and his hand on his holstered sidearm.

"Who the heck are you?" Atticus asked. Dominick remembered that they had met only over the phone.

The short one turned around to show them the bright white capital letters spelling out ICE POLICE on the back of his jacket.

Dominick was already leaning his two guns up against the front of the house. "Here, I'll take those, Atticus," he said, gesturing for him to pass his guns over, which he reluctantly did.

"Assembling an arsenal, gentlemen?"

"No, just back from hunting," Atticus answered.

"No, you're not. You're not dressed for hunting, and you've brought back no game, and how many guns do you need to go hunting?"

"What business is it of yours?" Atticus was getting some heat up.

"We'd like to speak with Lord Witherspoon."

"I've already told you I don't know any lords."

"We have reason to believe he is in the country illegally. Harboring an illegal alien is a federal offense."

"What's so important about this Witherspoon guy?"

"He is a person of interest in an ongoing investigation."

"An investigation into what?"

"Seeing as the investigation is ongoing, I'm not at freedom to say, but it does come under the auspices of the Homeland Security laws."

"We don't like terrorists," the taller agent said.

"Or even outside agitators," the shorter one added. "Your cooperation now could preclude you from subsequent charges of conspiracy and obstruction."

"Are you threatening me?" Now Atticus was cooking.

"We do not threaten, sir. We are only here looking for Lord Witherspoon. Is he in the house, sir?"

"No, there is no Lord Witherspoon in the house."

"Have you seen or been in touch with Lord Witherspoon recently?"

"I don't even know if this Lord Witherspoon exists. Do you? Now get off my steps, get off my property. This is all about that goddamn LNG plant, isn't it? Just hassling people with the common sense to oppose it. Hand me back my long gun, Dominick." Dominick did no such thing.

"Alright, Mr. Jameson, we're leaving. But you should be aware that recent events, especially this morning's occurrence, have raised this investigation to a level red. I would advise you to get a lawyer."

"Another goddamn threat," Atticus said, and he turned and pushed Dominick aside to grab his Revolutionary War weapon from against the wall. By the time he returned to the top of the steps the two agents were almost to the street; the white sans serif capital letters on the backs of their dark windbreakers ICE POLICE seemed to glow in the dark.

"That's not loaded, is it?" Dominick asked.

"I wouldn't waste a rabbit slug on them."

For the first time, Dominick noticed that the gun was longer than Atticus was tall.

The next morning's *New Jerusalem News* informed them what the previous day's "occurrence" had been. It was front-page, above-the-fold headline news: "Terrorist Attack in Old Grofton!" In the early morning hours a bomb had blown up the trailer offices of a construction company at a waterfront site up the bay. The site had been deserted at the time; there were no injuries. The Old Grofton Fire Department had extinguished the fire before it spread to any other structures. A sweep of the site by bomb-sniffing dogs discovered another, undetonated incendiary device attached to the gas tank of a large piece of earth-moving equipment nearby. The State Police bomb squad had safely inactivated and removed that device, described as quite sophisticated. A government official, speaking on the condition of anonymity because of the ongoing nature of the investigation, speculated that the second explosive was meant to go off after the first had attracted emergency response and law enforcement officers to the area. He called it "a common terrorist tactic to maximize casualties."

The site on Darby Point was in the process of being cleared for the construction of a proposed new Hercules Corp liquid natural gas terminal and processing plant there. Sources close to the investigation said that while there were as yet no suspects in the case and no one had claimed responsibility for the act, authorities would be questioning leaders of the local groups opposed to the multibillion dollar project.

"Someone is not playing well with others," Dominick said as he put down the paper. Atticus and he were sitting at the kitchen table. There was a damp chill in the house, and Dominick was wearing a bathrobe over his clothes.

"No one I know, no one from Bay Savers," Atticus said. "You don't peacefully demonstrate one week then go blow something up the next. Who knows how to make a bomb?" The phone in the hallway rang. They could just hear it through the closed doors. Atticus went to answer it.

When Atticus came back he was shaking his head. "They're making a federal case of it now. That was one of the ladies from our group. It was just on the local TV Eyewitness News. The FBI held a news conference to announce that the bomb they recovered and probably the one that blew up were both of a type never used in the States before, a type only used before by the IRA and other terrorist outfits in Great Britain."

There was silence for a while. Dominick raised the collar of his bathrobe against the chill. Would the house be like this all winter, he wondered.

"They're calling it an international terroristic attack on American soil against American industry."

"Atticus," Dominick said, "do you think you could turn on the stove?"

Chapter 5

"**B**ullshit, Dominick. Burgoo is Kentucky. Ain't nothing more Kentucky than burgoo."

"I'm not saying it's not, Charlie. I only meant to suggest that the word for it is much older."

To say that Charlie grew up in Kentucky would be to drastically understate his Kentuckiness. There are some places that imprint upon their native sons a template so indelible that they are not just *from* there but are *of* there, never to be changed.

"So do not sit there, eating my good Kentucky burgoo, and tell me it is some variety of rag-head dish."

"I did not say that. All I said was that your native name for this wonderful hunter's stew you have fixed us—burgoo—originally comes from the Persian term for a bruised-grain gruel that they fixed long before there was a Kentucky."

"How do you know that?"

"Why don't you? It's your dish. Look it up."

"What's to look up? I grew up with it."

The burgoo was a thick and aromatic mixture of many tastes—mutton, pork, opossum, rabbit, potatoes, corn, lima beans, tomatoes, and okra at least, along with many spices. Charlie claimed it had been brewing over the fire for more than a day. It was the opossum gave him the idea, he said. He hadn't had possum since he was home on the Ohio. He had called Atticus and Dominick and asked their permission to use their game in his old Kentucky home concoction; he'd share it. The next day, Atticus, Lydia, and Dominick got an invitation over to dinner. When Dominick asked what they could bring, Charlie said, "I find bourbon goes well with it."

On the drive over to Charlie's, Atticus wondered if Charlie might not have come up with a recipe for serving them dog à la Meriwether.

From the back seat Lydia asked, "Who's that?" Since before they had left the house, she had been ignoring them, her earphones in, listening to something on her iPod. They had pretty much forgotten she was there. "Who is Allah Meriwether?"

"A joke," Atticus said.

"You shouldn't make religious jokes, Atticus. No one thinks they're funny. Remember they wanted to kill that cartoonist." Lydia put her earphones back in and looked out her backseat window.

"She always has been fun to be around," Atticus said.

Charlie served up the burgoo in bowls with slices of French bread. He apologized for the bread. "Back home you'd get a side of potato salad and some barbeque mutton on a hamburger bun, but I don't make those, so you got to settle. Of course, also back home, growing up, the burgoo wouldn't have been quite so fancy, nothing store-bought, just what veggies you had and probably roadkill. Who had time to go hunting? You'd keep it going for days, adding stuff as you went along, cooking it till it all broke down. Brown dinner. I came to dislike squirrel and corn burgoo."

"Any coyote in here?" Atticus asked.

"We don't eat dog in Kentucky."

"It's like New England chowder," Lydia said, "only without fish and cream."

"Dominick," Atticus said, "what is your strongest childhood food memory, good or bad?"

"Can't say I have any. I have always found it curious how people claim to have these vivid memories of their youth when so much has come in between."

"You never ate squirrel and corn burgoo for days on end," Charlie said.

"No. Maybe that is it—being untraumatized by my youngest years, I have no memory of them."

"Or maybe your childhood was just so upsetting that you have suppressed all those memories," Lydia said. "I had a friend like that once. The men in her family did terrible to things her as a child, but when she grew up she remembered them all as saints, wouldn't hear a word spoken against them."

"No," Dominick said, "I'm pretty sure my youth was uneventful. It's the future I'm suppressing."

"The past is just what we make of it anyway," Atticus said, using a piece of French bread to clean the bottom of his bowl. "In this case, a memorable stew."

"What do you mean by that?" Charlie asked.

"That I'd like another helping," Atticus said.

Charlie got up to refill Atticus's bowl. "No, I meant what you said about the past being just what you make it? The past is the past. You can't change what happened."

"At the very least he can choose what he wants to remember," Dominick said.

"But that doesn't change what did happen." Charlie put Atticus's bowl back in front of him and cut some more French bread. "Other people could set him straight on that."

"So, we rely on others to confirm or deny our version of the past?" Atticus said.

"Some sort of consensus, yeah, I guess, but it is what it was."

"So, the truth about the past relies upon some sort of consensus. You know, the past can get pretty complicated."

"Doesn't change the facts."

"But what if the consensus changes? Doesn't that then change the past?"

"I think people forget the complications," Lydia said. "And some people lie."

Charlie was shaking his head. "I know what you're saying," he said, "but that's not history. That's propaganda. It's like the liberal media always twisting the news to make America look bad."

Now that the conversation had become pointedly political, Dominick totally withdrew from it. He knew that Charlie didn't mind his smoking a cigar in the house, but he went to the back door anyway and opened it to smoke, just to get away from the table.

"So, there you are, Charlie," Atticus said. "The same set of events, two different ways of seeing it."

"But only one way is correct. It's like them terrorists blowing things up. I suppose they think they're right, but they're dead wrong. You can't twist that around and justify it."

"Is everything so black-and-white, Charlie?" Lydia asked. She was stacking their empty bowls to take to the sink. "God knows, I've been wrong about plenty of things I didn't fully understand."

"Well, I suppose you could be initially misinformed about things and have to refine your opinion later, but if you have the right set of beliefs to guide you, you'll get it right. You can't keep changing history to suit yourself is all I'm saying."

"I'm afraid, Charlie, that is all history is—arranging the past to suit ourselves," Dominick said from the doorway.

"Or to fool others," Atticus added.

"Then your history is bunk," Charlie said. "Give me Fox News and the Bible."

"*De gustibus non est disputandum,*" Dominick said.

"To each his own fantasy," Atticus agreed.

"I'll drink to that," Charlie said, and he poured them each more Maker's Mark from the bottle Dominick had brought. The doorbell rang, and Charlie went to answer it.

In Atticus's library Dominick had found a history of lighthouses on the bay and their keepers. At one point in history there had been a good dozen lighthouses marking the entry into and the twists and hazards of the bay, and, since they burned whale or coal oil, they needed constant tending. They could never go dark, and the horns or bells that were their fogbound voices must always be ready to speak. It was what Lydia said about black-and-white that had set Dominick off on this train of thought. He had seen her black-and-white as a lighthouse light flashing its signal against the night, that simple binary missive—I am here; this is who I am—because each light had its own identifiable interval, and each lighthouse's foghorn or bell had its own constant pitch and tone and timing. Their constancy was essential. They could not go dark or silent, could not change, could not move, or they would not only lose all meaning but become themselves the enemy, part of the hazards they were meant to defend against, luring the unwary to destruction.

Wasn't that Charlie's point, in a way? That safe passage through life required constancy, certainty, assuredness? To insure that the harbor you return to is the same familiar harbor that you left? Good guys and bad guys, the safe channels of our forefathers versus the shoals of shipwreck? As political analogy, how romantic.

But what Dominick had been most curious about were the keepers of the lights. For obvious geological reasons few of the lighthouses were located in easily accessible places. Most were reachable only by the sea, on remote rocks or islands, doomed by purpose and design to occupy the most inhospitable locations. A lighthouse cannot cower from the sea. David-like it must confront its Goliath nemesis, rock face to wave face—in this case the North Atlantic and its famed nor'easters. These were places where no normal human being ever chose to live. But lighthouse keepers did live there, sometimes with a wife and family. One had to wonder at the choice, as none were exiled there nor sentenced there, and there was competition for positions. The pay was paltry, even by the standards of the day, and the living quarters often mean and always cold and damp. Retired seamen were preferred, sailors home from the sea, because their hard lives had left them unpampered and they knew the value to a man at sea of that light ashore. But the solitariness—every watch your own and every watch alone—must have been daunting for men who had lived their lives as members of a close-knit crew. Of course, there was no captain; that might have been a plus for some of them after years of rigid hierarchy. At a lighthouse you were captain and crew.

They had to be men of the sea, because even on land now the sea was their closest and constant companion, and a small craft that they could manage and maintain alone was their sole connection to the world behind them. In their small boats they saved the lives of many shipwrecked sailors. Some lost their own lives in storms. To a man they liked to fish. An uncommon number of lighthouse keepers were the sons of lighthouse keepers. Dominick wondered if the sense of duty was an inheritable trait, because the life of a lighthouse keeper was all about duty, not personal gain. Beyond the danger and the solitude and the discomfort there was a further basic subjugation—that he was a servant of the light, a vassal to a beacon and its sole server.

Whereas the privateers Dominick had read about had been in their game wholly for themselves, changing history as they went along and as it suited them, the lighthouse keepers—their fellow New England seamen—had taken the opposite tack. Their game was not about themselves and profit and change but about service and solitude and constancy. Very black-and-white.

Well, not always about solitude. If you were young enough and in lust enough, a rustic cottage for two on a cliff above a scenic panorama could be an ideal romantic setting. The passion of the pounding sea, the freedom of being alone together, free to make love at any time of day and anywhere you wanted. Dominick always wondered about all the clothes they wore back then—heavy clothes, wool and muslin, with petticoats, buttons, long johns and leggings—and infrequent baths. How would you rewrite passion into that historicity?

In the lighthouse history book only one such occasion had been included. A lone keeper at a remote island station had requested permission to bring his mother to live with him and to hire a housekeeper to help her. Permission granted; only the mother never arrived, just the housekeeper. Her name was Catherine, a very proper name. Three years of—one would like to think—bliss and a child ensued before poison rumors infected the chain of command and a pair of Lighthouse Service inspectors (was one tall and one short?) arrived unannounced at dawn one day. The keeper answered the door in his pajamas. It was all written up by hand in a five-page report. He was asked "why he kept his clothes in her [the housekeeper's] room. He said he always did as that room was drier. When informed that no other room in house showed signs of having been occupied and asked where he slept, he said he slept in a chair in dining room." His resignation was asked for and received on the spot. That keeper's record for keeping the light had always been ranked as excellent. He had received a commendation the year before for saving the lives of a boat owner and his wife. After his dismissal he vanished from the Service and from local history. Dominick liked that. At least when he vanished he left behind a slew of unpaid bills.

The lighthouses—those that were left—were all automated now. All the lighthouse keepers were gone. Electronic-light buoys marked the channel now, and, of course, all the bigger boats and ships had radar and global positioning gizmos, revolving antennae and satellite hook-ups. Instead of sailing ships tacking in and out of the bay, huge container ships and tankers now screwed their arrow-straight courses and precisely angled turns down the shipping lanes without even having to look out the bridge window. Modern meteorology had stripped storms of their advantage of surprise. An occupation had disappeared. The privateers were all gone too, Dominick thought, all moved ashore.

When Charlie returned to the kitchen he was speaking over his shoulder. "Sure, come on in. These folks will verify who I am. Guys, meet the front line in our fight against those terrorists we were talking about—two gentlemen from Homeland Security."

Sure enough, following behind him, in their jeans and windbreaker uniforms again but this time with ICE baseball caps, were agents Mutt and Jeff. "They just need to confirm with you who I am and that I do live here. They're investigating that attack up in Old Grofton."

Dominick was still standing by the back door, smoking his cigar and meditating on the life of a lighthouse keeper. Lydia was at the sink, rinsing and stacking dinner dishes. Atticus was still seated at the kitchen table. No one said anything. Charlie didn't seem to notice. "I guess the Florida plates on my Bronco in the driveway raised an eyebrow."

"Actually, sir, we had some difficulty tracing you and your car to this address. The house is not in your name."

"No, the wife's. She's got the deep pockets in this household. But glad to help. Let me get that driver's license for you. That's from Florida, too, you know." Charlie went cheerfully on out another door. Silence in the kitchen.

"A little cell meeting, gentleman?" the short agent finally spoke, a slight knowing smile on his lips.

"Burgoo," Atticus said.

"Say what?" the tall agent said. His hand flicked to and away from the grip of his sidearm beneath the windbreaker.

"Burgoo," Dominick said, blowing cigar smoke out the door. "We are here for a burgoo feast. That's an Arab word, you know."

"Atticus, who are these men?" Lydia asked.

"These men are from the federal government, dear. They are our public servants."

"But those hats."

"Yes, the icemen cometh."

"Why don't they take them off, indoors and all?"

"Can't you see it's a uniform, dear? Ignore them like you do all men in uniform."

"We'll deal with you in a moment, ma'am," the tall one said.

"You'll take your hat off in the kitchen," Lydia said.

"We'll deal with you in a moment, ma'am."

Charlie came back into the kitchen with his wallet, pulling out his driver's license. "Here you go. Charles Owens. That's my Florida address, but these good folks here can tell you that me and the missus spend close to half the year here in this house. Now, how can we help you catch your terrorists? You think they might be hiding out here on our island? What sort of suspicious stuff should we be on the lookout for? You guys like a cup of coffee or something?"

"Is that your weapon, Mr. Owens?" the short one asked, handing Charlie's license back to him after barely looking at it.

"Which weapon is that?" Charlie answered, still smiling, eager to help.

"That firearm there, sir," shortie said, pointing to an over-under shotgun leaning in the corner by the outside door. "Would you step away from the weapon," he said to Dominick, who had not even noticed the shotgun before. Dominick took a few steps into the room.

"Well, yeah. I just been cleaning it," Charlie said. "Why?"

"Turn around, Mr. Owens." The tall one this time, stepping forward, his windbreaker pulled back clearing his sidearm. "You." He motioned to Atticus still at the table. "Up, over next to him. You, too." He pointed to Dominick to join them. "Turn around, hands on the wall. You too, ma'am."

They were all four thoroughly frisked by the tall man. Lydia's face turned scarlet. Atticus's turned white with rage. Charlie could not understand what was happening. "Wait, wait. What's going on here?

This is my house. That's my shotgun. I got rights here—second amendment, fourth amendment. Take your hands off the lady!"

The tall agent pushed Charlie hard against the kitchen wall. "You don't want to assault a federal officer or interfere with the performance of his lawful duties," he said. "That's a felony." When he got to frisking Dominick he had to lean close because of Dominick's size, and Dominick could smell the sweet scent of fruity chewing gum on his breath. It had been so long since Dominick had been touched by human hands that the brisk pat-down first registered almost as an electric shock then lingered as a pleasurable tingling.

When the tall one had finished his frisking, the short one asked, "Is there anyone else in the house?"

Atticus went to Lydia's side to put his arm around her, but she shrugged him off. She was staring intently, quizzically at the short agent, her eyes slightly squinting, her head tilted to one side, as if trying to remember or recognize something familiar.

"You'll pay for this," Atticus said.

"I asked if there was anyone else in the house."

"No," Charlie said. "There's no one else here."

"Are you expecting any more members tonight?"

"Any more members of what?" Charlie asked.

"I'll ask the questions. Who is this woman?" The short one had his little notebook out.

"This is my wife," Atticus said. He was looking at her now with some concern. Lydia hadn't moved, but her face had taken on a perplexed look, her lips pursed.

The agent flipped back a few notebook pages. "That would be Lydia Jameson?"

"You're Allah Meriwether, aren't you?" Lydia said. "You're an evil man."

"Are you Lydia Jameson?"

"Allah Meriwether. A disgrace to his family."

"Yes or no."

"Yes, you are. The Bristol Meriwethers, I bet. There was always that side of them, the ones they tried to hide, the runts of the litter."

"What's wrong with her?" the tall one asked. "What is she talking about?"

At the word runt the short agent had stopped making notes and closed his notebook. "Look, your game is up. Cooperate and deliver any illegal aliens or foreign agents associated with your little group or face the consequences. You all should be aware that you and others with whom you are associated are subjects of an active and ongoing investigation. My name is not Meriwether, ma'am." And they left.

"What the fuck?" Charlie said. "Are they smoking it or taking it in the arm? What other members? What aliens? What foreign agents?"

"Looks like you are an enemy of the state now, Charlie. See how easy it was for that consensus to change." Dominick said. His cigar had gone out and he was relighting it. "All you had to do was invite them into your house."

"Dominick, I think we'd better be going," Atticus had gotten Lydia's coat and was trying to get her to put it on, but she wasn't helping. She was playing with her iPod. She hadn't moved from the spot where she had been frisked.

"Atticus, how come you broke this? It won't work." Her color was normal now, her voice even.

"Time to go, dear," he said, draping the coat over her shoulders.

"I went before I left the house. You broke my thing. It won't play."

Atticus gently put the earphones into her ears. "How's that?"

Lydia smiled. "But I fixed it," she said.

"Atticus, you two go ahead. I'm sure Charlie will give me a ride home later." It was time for Dominick to play the distance card he always held in his hand like a Get Out of Jail Free card, the one that said I am not family, even an old friend, just a temporary houseguest; I hold indemnity against all moments tragic, intimate, dramatic, and/or interpersonal. Wherever Lydia had gone only Atticus need follow. Besides, in the car he couldn't finish his cigar.

They drank more Maker's Mark as Dominick made a stab at explaining to Charlie the agents' interest in aliens, explosives, and Lord Witherspoon.

"But why bust into my house? I don't know any aliens. I despise all bombers. And Lord Witherspoon doesn't even exist."

"But Lord Witherspoon, the terrorist alien, has become central to their understanding of events. That's their history of the case and they are sticking to it."

"So, what if we just told them Witherspoon doesn't exist?" Charlie asked.

"We could, I suppose, but I doubt it would work. They'd just think we were lying, deepening the conspiracy, hiding our outsider coconspirator. No, now they have uncovered their cell of local terrorists and—in their minds—the Englishman's fingerprints are almost on the bomb. Lord Witherspoon has become a creation of necessity."

"But he does not fucking exist."

"Ah, there's the rub."

"Why us?"

"Charlie, that is the single most popular question of all time."

Chapter 6

There was nothing very remarkable about their little village. There was just the one business street stretching several blocks up from where the New Jerusalem ferry docked, with one each of the requisite shops and churches, the post office, and the volunteer fire department house, plus the cluster of realtor offices on Water Street facing the marina. You could exhaust the sites in a ten-minute walk. The British had gone to the trouble of burning the whole place down during the War, so there were no colonial era buildings. There was a handful of restaurants that catered mainly to the summer crowd, a pizza place, and one saloon for the locals. Dominick avoided the village, especially now that the summer crowd had left and it had been returned to control of the natives. He did not belong there. It was just as well that he not be seen there. But there was the matter of his mail.

The village post office was the obverse of quaint—a one-story, four-corner, flat-roofed, unadorned, cement-block blob from the fifties, ugly in its extreme utility, that could have just as well been (and not belonged) in any one-silo corn-state town or some exurban mall. But there was no avoiding it, and it was normally devoid of other customers. At the beginning of the summer, when he arrived at Brenda and Charlie's, Dominick had taken a P.O. Box there. Not that he got much mail, but for occasional business and legal purposes he needed to have an address other than general delivery wherever he was. This entailed his checking his mail every so often and recently mailing off things in return.

Although Dominick's expenses were few, he had not yet discovered how to live totally for free. From time to time he had to restock his

checking account and pay off his credit cards. This entailed correspondence with agents and lawyers in Richmond and Washington.
His assets were real and so not difficult to liquidate, but there were
always the middlemen and -women who had to be involved and who
justified their skimming by prolonging and complicating the sale.
Middlewomen. And how are you today, madam? Good to middling,
good to middling, she would say, not knowing that in the original old
dirty English, middling referred to a man and a woman putting their
middles together. There was that French auction house woman from
Alexandria whom he would not mind middling with again, but too
many years had passed. She had probably retired.

Everything that Dominick had to sell had been given to him, left to
him. He liquidated the pieces one at a time because he knew that their
value increased as they aged, as he aged. In a sense, their mutual sur-
vival was like cumulative interest accruing. This was truer for the old
maps and prints than it was for the antique cars and motorcycles. Also,
the old paper did not leave puddles of oil and command storage fees.
So, the ranks of his father's collection of motorized memorabilia had
been depleted first. There were just a few prize pieces left, and a man
in Las Vegas had been interested in buying the lot. Not needing the
cash, Dominick had been putting him off. But now his agent informed
him that there was another interested buyer, an Emirates oil sheik who
wanted to start a museum in honor of the invention that had made
him rich. With two eager bidders in play, it was time to sell. The sale
would set Dominick up, cushion him from the need for further transactions or interactions for years to come, maybe even until forever.
Forever was Dominick's term for death.

Dominick did not share his father's passion for collectibles.
Dominick did not share much of anything with his father. All they
really had in common was a woman—Dominick's mother, his father's
one-time mistress. He had grown up knowing father only as an abstract
term indicating something masculine, removed, symbolic—Father
Time, Father Christmas, Father of the Country, Holy Father, God the
Father. His mother would never speak of him. Dominick remembered
only vaguely the few times they had met when he was just a small
boy—rides in the big car, ice cream cones on a pier, a nightmarish
trip to a zoo, getting sick on a sailboat ride. He could recall the events

but not the man. He was a teenager before he figured out that his unmarried mother did not have to work because his unknown, absent, abstract father paid for everything. By the time Dominick got to graduate school at Oxford he knew that he too would never have to find and hold a job. Then his father had died and left him not property or cash or an endowment—all that stayed in his real family—but a few of his eccentric collections—minor things, given all his millions—that his widow and legitimate sons could not quibble about in probate.

Was it guilt money he had lived on all his life? Did it matter? Was the ease of his existence just a simple way to ease another man's conscience? Dominick doubted it. He had read about his father, how he had taken over the family business and expanded it many times over into a financial empire. The man had no conscience. The yearly stipend for his mother and him had been a fraction of the maintenance cost of one of his yachts. The money meant nothing to him. It was a gratuity, the tip a man of his stature left for a whore. For Dominick's college graduation his father had sent him a vintage Mercedes, but he had not come. When Dominick inherited the car collection, he noted that his father owned three other Mercedes of the same vintage; his had been just an extra. His mother had been a kept woman, he a kept bastard son. What was it they were being paid to keep? Why, their silence, of course, their complicity. And now his father was gone—forever—and it all meant nothing.

This Monday afternoon Dominick had to stop at a lawyer's office before going to the P.O. There were papers to be notarized before mailing, and Dominick used Atticus's lawyer's office for that. The secretary was a notary. She did it for free. When Dominick mentioned to Atticus that he would be stopping there, he decided to come along. Atticus had not been out of the house since the dinner at Charlie's several nights before. He had been sort of hovering around in the wings watching Lydia. A dynamic had changed in the house, an arrow of attention had changed direction. Now, rather than Lydia fussing over Atticus, Atticus had become the caretaker. Dominick had distanced himself as much as possible, but he could not help noticing. Nothing much else had changed.

Lydia did not seem different, perhaps just a bit more removed, but her new iPod addiction could account for that. She hummed to herself and sometimes sang along to what was in her earphones in that strange off-key way people sing when they cannot hear themselves.

The first nor'easter of the season had been predicted, and the clouds were already lowering and rushing, gray militias gathering for battle. Rust-colored gusts of leaves whisked down the road in front of them. The streets were deserted in a premature dusk. Dominick was struck by how many houses stood bravely dark and deserted, as if left behind to go it alone against the storm. He stopped the car at a rise where they could look out over the nickel-colored bay with its pinstripes of whitecaps.

"Nasty tonight," Atticus said.

"Ever been out there on a day like this?"

"Only once, as a boy, with my dad and the crew of Covenant II, trying to beat a storm into port. We had left to take her south, about this time of year, but we broke a spar and had to turn back."

"Your dad was a good sailor?"

"He was good, but he took too many chances. He almost bought it that time, racing a crippled ship into a storm. There's nowhere to hide on this side when she blows like this."

"Do you miss it?" Dominick asked. "The sailing, I mean."

"Oh, you can miss things but not want them back. You got to be realistic. The wife and I once had a great sex life, but I can't imagine doing that again. Know what I mean?" The first spray of rain raked the car. "I miss my daughters, and they're still around, but the daughters I miss grew up and left a long time ago. What do you miss, Dominick?"

"I don't know. I have never really needed anything I didn't have, so I guess I have never wanted anything enough to miss it when it's gone." Dominick turned the windshield wipers on.

"Ever go sailing with your dad?" Atticus asked.

"Once, just once that I recall."

"Was he a good sailor?"

Dominick put the car in gear and headed on down the gradual slope into the village. "I wouldn't know," he said. "I was too young to notice."

Dominick parked in the handicapped space next to the door of the lawyer's office so that they wouldn't have far to duck through the rain. No actual handicapped person should be out on a day like this, which gave everyone a handicap anyway. Atticus had brought a large envelope with him that Dominick figured he was taking to the P.O., but now he brought it into the office with him. While Dominick was signing and getting his documents notarized, Atticus went in to see his lawyer, but he was quickly back out again, followed by the lawyer, a large man in shirtsleeves and a wide tie.

"No, Jameson, I don't think so, not in this current climate, and I never put any kind of sticker on my car. You never know what potential client you might offend. You know, they did a study, and the people with the most bumper stickers on their vehicles are the people most likely to engage in road rage."

Atticus was still holding out a green-and-white bumper sticker. "How about you, Agnes?" he said, turning to the secretary. "I know you're with us, and no one would dare take offense from you." In bold white type on a Kelly-green background the bumper sticker read SAVE OUR BAY and there was a circle with a diagonal line over the initials LNG.

"Why, no, thank you, Atticus," she said, handing Dominick his finished papers. "My husband happens to think that new facility is just what's needed hereabouts to perk up business now that the fishing industry's collapsed. It wouldn't stay on my car long."

"You know, there are a lot of people who feel the same way, Jameson," the lawyer said, "that what we need is more shipping on the bay, not less, that we need the jobs."

"This isn't shipping. These are giant liquid natural gas tankers, potential Roman candles three football fields long. Their comings and goings will totally shut down all other activity on the bay at least a hundred and seventy times a year. Don't they care that the tankers, the terminal, and their miles of pipelines under the bay are potential terrorist targets that could take us all out?"

"It's anti-progress, Jameson, anti-business. The government's got no problem with their going ahead. And talk about terrorists, who was behind that bombing a week ago? That didn't win your cause any supporters."

"No one from Bay Savers was involved in that, I can assure you."

"Well, it didn't look good, and now outsiders are involved. No one likes that." Trying to terminate the conversation, the lawyer turned to Dominick and stuck out his hand. "I don't believe we've met."

"No, we have not," Dominick said, shaking the offered hand. "Well, come along, Atticus, before it gets worse outside." And he hurried Atticus out the door. Back in the car he said, "Atticus, please do not get involved in such conversations when I am with you. This is your cause, not mine. And do not even think of putting one of those stickers on my car." He glanced over at Atticus, who looked suddenly pale and shrunken and old, and Dominick remembered his terminal condition. "You okay?"

Atticus was looking straight ahead into the rain. "Fucking assholes," was all he said.

The nor'easter blew throughout the night, rattling the windows and shaking the old house, whose flat sail-like façade took the brunt of the gale full on. Dominick could not sleep. It was too much like being inside a creepy amusement park ride. The wind moaned through deserted rooms. Something on the floor above him came loose and knocked constantly like someone left outside in the storm pleading to be let in. Beneath it all was the sound of the sea—the waves booming against the cliffs, the growl of the surf, an almost human howl of elements meeting on the worst of terms. It all grew closer as the night worn on. Wrapped in a quilt, Dominick sat in the dark in an armchair close to the window of his room and lit a cigar. He thought he could hear voices in the cacophony, deep choral voices arguing in a foreign tongue. He could not imagine being at sea on a night like this, the monstrous seas. How insignificant it must make you feel, how crushable. Drowning would be an unpleasant forever. In a cold sea like this it would be a dry drowning. No water would be found in your lungs. You would have just stopped breathing, suffocating yourself. Forever.

Why had Atticus asked about his father? What business was it of his that Dominick even had a father, much less if they had ever gone sailing together? The things people thought important. Things long gone and best forgotten. The fear of memories, afraid of the past. How can you fear something that has already happened? You are free of it; it has passed. That last huge crashing wave didn't get you, did it? As the past grew deeper, darker, longer, more removed, the future foreshortened and flew in your face. Dominick flicked his long cigar ash onto the floor. There was just the distance between here and approaching forever that mattered. The past was just a good-bye. Why did people choose to live there, asking ancestor questions? So that by searching for beginnings they could avoid turning around and facing the end?

Storm thoughts. In his pajamas, robe, and slippers, but still wrapped in his quilt and smoking his cigar, Dominick went down to the kitchen to fix himself something. He wasn't sure what—a pot of tea, a sandwich, a stiff drink? It was hours after midnight. Lydia was already there, standing at the stove, wearing a green down vest over her nightgown and a pair of men's slippers. She was watching a pot that was not yet boiling. "Oh, I hope I didn't disturb you, Dominick."

"In this racket, hardly. Like minds."

"Were you having bad dreams too?"

"No, I meant coming to the kitchen in search of something comforting."

"Tea?" she asked

"Tea? Yes, that too," Dominick said, going to the sideboard where the scotch was kept and pouring himself a stiff one.

Lydia was singing to herself now, "Tea for two and two for tea, me for you and you for me." Without her earphones in she sang on tune, a young girl's voice. She forgot the words and hummed instead. Then she lost the tune and stopped altogether. Dominick walked through the house with his glass and cigar to the front door and switched on the porch light to watch the storm. There was not much to see—just bright curtains of rain slicing in from the surrounding darkness then back out again—but you could feel it here, just inches away, bouncing off the door and pushing at the foyer windows. Unlike some beast it will never tire, Dominick thought. Storms are perceived like sunsets over water—always focused just on you. This storm could be a hundred miles wide, but it would always seem that you were its central point of attack. He could feel the frigid ocean air seeping through the cracks around the door and windows, not giving up, undaunted by walls. You had to like storms. If there was any one entity Dominick felt worthy of deification it would be storm, the storm god—pointless to worship or supplicate, too deaf with its own howling to hear prayers, mindless and terrifying, wholly impersonal but also able to make you feel as real as you will ever feel.

Back in the kitchen Lydia had a pot of tea brewing under a cozy and was setting out cups and saucers, cream and sugar. Dominick went to the sink, extinguished the stub of his cigar, and dropped it into the trash. Lydia poured and passed.

"You know, Dominick, there are two questions that women everywhere always ask, and I've never asked you."

"No, I am not married, and no, I have no children."

"You're so lucky. Children are an unmitigated curse. We have two, you know, twins, so I know. I never wanted any, but Atticus tricked me, got me pregnant, then insisted I go through with it. I never let him trick me again, I'll tell you that."

"Twins," Dominick said.

"Two more useless and bothersome creatures I've never known. They're Atticus's girls, not mine. He spoiled them rotten."

"But they are out of your life now. That must give you some relief." Dominick got up to pour himself another scotch.

"Oh sure, out of my life just as I have next to no life left. Ungrateful little witches. You'd rather drink whiskey than tea? I never could stand the taste of it myself, no matter what they mixed with it."

"I noticed there are no pictures of your daughters in the house."

"I wouldn't stand for it. And they know enough not to try and set foot here."

Ah, the present tense, the future tense lurking. Dominick felt more comfortable here. "And do they know of . . . of their father's condition?"

"You mean that death stalks their parents? It couldn't happen soon enough for them. Then they can take everything their father hasn't already given them."

Privateers, Dominick thought. "Where do they live?"

"One is in London, the other over in Boston."

"Both married?"

"Why? You looking for a wife? I wouldn't wish either of them on you."

"No, no. I have no need for a wife. Just curious."

"They both have husbands, last I heard. The one in London married an Arab. The one in Boston married some nothing doctor. They don't eat meat."

"Strange for twins to live so far apart."

Lydia laughed. It was much too close to a cackle for such a dark and stormy night. "They can't stand each other. They have that much sense anyway. They were always in competition, first for their daddy's attention and then for everything else. God, they were awful. The lies, the deceptions, the just plain meanness. There's not another creature in god's creation—except maybe cats—that can act as evil and mean as little girls to one another. And I know, because I was one once. But those two just never grew out of it."

Lydia fumbled in the pocket of her down vest and pulled out her iPod. "Talking about them depresses me. The doctor says I shouldn't get depressed because I can't take those pills at the same time as the other ones he gave me. Do you have a doctor, Dominick?"

"No, ma'am. Again no need. No wife, no kids, no doctor, no pills."

"Lucky you. Keep it that way. Don't even go in for a checkup. It's their job to find something wrong with you to treat." Lydia pushed back her hair and slipped the little bud earphones into her ears and played with the iPod settings. Dominick noticed that she was wearing fancy earrings, only they didn't match. Lydia looked away, and just like that it was as if he wasn't there. She began bobbing her head to the tune she was hearing, tapping her fingers in time on the table beside her teacup. Dominick knew the past, the present, and the future; but what time was this that Lydia had escaped to? He watched for a while, then she closed her eyes and was totally gone, to a land with no tenses whatsoever, a neverland just this side of forever. When Dominick rewrapped himself in his quilt and went off to his room, Lydia never noticed.

It was well after noon by the time Dominick came back to the deserted kitchen. The storm had passed. The day was too bright, unnaturally bright. The windows were painful to look at. He poured what was left of the morning pot of coffee down the sink and fixed a fresh pot. He had taken Lydia's bad dreams back to bed with him and had slept poorly. It was one of those dreams that you couldn't escape from, waiting for him every time he got back to sleep. He was trying to get somewhere, a train station, to meet up with friends for a departure. The cityscapes were all familiar but all wrong. He kept getting lost. He kept losing his luggage. There were catwalks and cliffs to negotiate. He was dressed in one of Ben Arnold's antique suits, which got soiled and ripped. He was late, and getting to where he was supposed to be seemed to take forever. Forever, and he would wake up again, his pillow wet with sweat. Even the trick that his mother had taught him to deal with his earliest nightmares—to change pillows and roll over on to his other side—had not worked. He was glad there was no one about, because he was not in the mood to be nice.

He must have been broadcasting that, because when Atticus came into the kitchen he at first said nothing to Dominick. He poured himself a cup of coffee and took a seat at the other end of the kitchen table. Dominick didn't look up. Atticus stirred his coffee as if he were winding something up. Commodore Rutman's grandfather clock in the front sitting room chimed the half of some hour.

"The realtor called this morning," Atticus finally said.

"What realtor would that be?" Dominick asked, looking up, bothered.

"The one with whom Lord Witherspoon placed his bid for the house."

"Oh. What did she want?"

"She wanted to let me know that they had another bidder on the place and that, seeing as they had heard no more from Lord Witherspoon about negotiating his bid, she had been instructed to open dealings with the second bidder."

"Instructed by whom?" Dominick got up to pour himself another mug of coffee.

"By my daughter Angie, who is handling the sale. She's over in Boston. The realtor said that if Lord Witherspoon still wishes to pursue the purchase he has to deal directly with the seller on the price. I'm sure those are Angie's instructions. It sounds like her."

"And Angie is in Boston."

"Right."

"Angie has a twin?"

"Yes, her sister Rey, but she's in England and not involved in this."

"Maybe Lord Witherspoon should go to Boston."

"You think so? Angie's no fool."

"No, of course not. She just invented another buyer to force our hand."

"You think she is bluffing?"

"One way to find out," Dominick said. Was it just his bad mood or was he getting bored? But he felt like he needed a little engagement. A disguise, an evil twin, a nice quiet drive to Boston, maybe he would visit a few museums. He would be financially flush again soon. A small splurge in a first-class hotel and some fine restaurants? Why not? "Yes, a trip to Beantown seems quite in order," he said. "Nothing to lose. By the way, Atticus, Angie and Rey? What sort of names are those for twin daughters? They could almost be prizefighters."

"Oh, those are just their nicknames. I don't think even they use their given names anymore."

"Which are what?"

"Angelica and Desiré."

Dominick wondered which of those names would end up engraved on the brass owner's plaque inside the door of Commodore Rutman's grandfather clock, which now chimed three quarters into some hour.

Chapter 7

The comfort of pretense. How appropriate that it was almost Halloween. As Lord Witherspoon, Dominick called the realtor pretending he was somewhere far away, maybe in England, maybe someplace in the opposite direction. He asked what time it was there and apologized if his call was inconvenient. He was just checking in. Of course, he knew nothing of the realtor's call to Atticus or of Angelica's ultimatum. When informed of the situation, Lord Witherspoon insisted that he was still interested in the property. He had just been waiting for a counteroffer. Yes, he would be happy to contact the seller directly, if that was necessary. The realtor had both a phone number and an e-mail address for the seller. Dominick copied them both down and thanked her. He gave her to understand that if she could hold off a week or two on the other offer to give him a chance to respond, there would be something extra in it for her at closing.

Costumes, masks, Mardi Gras freedoms, the relief of not having to be yourself. Who can deny the pleasure of it? Mythomania is built into the species. "And who do you want to be when you grow up?" How do you want to be remembered after you're gone? Fool others, fool yourself. Do card tricks with your days and make things vanish in the night. Pretending was different from lying because your fabrication is for everyone, even yourself. The Internet, for instance, made it dirt simple for someone to be anyone he or she wanted to be out there in the cyber world, where every other self-invented, self-invested character knew better than to question if what was represented on the screen was real or not. So, it was a simple choice for Dominick to e-mail Angelica rather than to call her.

Dominick was not an active Internetter. At some point business necessity had caused him to acquire an e-mail address, but he refused to be its slave. He had never owned a computer. Atticus and Lydia still had a black bakelite dial phone. Charlie had a computer with Internet connection. Dominick went over there. Charlie was packing the back of his Bronco. "Headed south," he said. "Things are getting a little weird around here for me."

"Ah, the agents of change," Dominick said, holding the door open for Charlie to pass through with an armload of stuff. "It's all Brenda's fault, you know, for inventing Lord Witherspoon in the first place."

"Don't go there, Dominick. Whatever you and Atticus have going down with the feds, I'm not part of it, and neither is Brenda. We are good, mostly law-abiding American citizens. I got no beef with the authorities."

"Neither do I, Charlie, neither do I. By the time you guys get back here in the spring this will all be so blown over it won't be worth mentioning. But you can do me one favor before you go."

Charlie set Dominick up with a new e-mail account and address— lordwitherspoon—and Dominick got an initial e-mail off to Angelica, suggesting a meeting. He had planned a flight to Los Angeles in a few days and could make a stopover in Boston if she wanted to meet and discuss the Mt. Sinai sale, Cheerio.

"I'm taking this with me, you know," Charlie said as Dominick finished and he closed up his laptop, "but you can get online at the library for free." Charlie showed Dominick where a key to the house was hidden in the garden shed and where the thermostat was to turn the heat up above the forty degrees it was set at. "Feel free," he said, "just don't have any of your secret terrorist cell meetings here."

The next day, at the library, Dominick received Angelica's e-mail reply. She suggested a place and a time for a meeting three days hence in Boston. Dominick confirmed he could be there. He asked if there was anything he could bring her from London, but he left the library before she had a chance to reply.

The drive to Boston should have taken only a couple of hours, but it was longer because Dominick took back roads and got lost several times at traffic circles. He found himself at one point in a perfectly deserted beach community, the one street through sand dunes empty and windblown, the ramshackle cottages shuttered, seagulls the sole animate presence. He stopped to smoke a cigar. Such a location was a rare gift, the setting of a thousand post-cataclysmic sci-fi stories and movies. At any minute now some pseudohominoid figure covered with scales or fur or feathers would come walking down the middle of the empty road, or perhaps someone dressed in rough colonial woolen garb and a flat-brimmed Puritan hat carrying a blunderbuss. A bird three times the size of a herring gull, with the long pointed wings of a spy plane drifted low above the dunes, coming toward him in an effortless glide. Dominick had never seen an albatross before—how many people had?—but he needed no introduction. It zeroed in on him, sitting there alone in his long black car. It almost seemed to pause, studying him, its head turned to one side as it passed above him.

Dominick's pleasure with it all emerged as a chuckle. Oh, what could be read into it all? The pretense of portents. To read the future in the accident of a meeting—he gets lost and an omen bird finds him. Thank you, Samuel Taylor Albatross. Even more bogus than reading the past as a personal message was subjecting the future to such an analysis. "It is an ancient mariner and he stoppeth one of three." Of such superstitions are religions made and died for, to read forever in a happenstance. Then the bird circled back as if to take another look, and Dominick started up the car and drove away. Those birds spend all their lives alone in flight far out at sea, he thought. What do they know? Omens and amens—people trying desperately to pretend that their lives had some overarching meaning, were part of some grander scheme than just another ordinary organism eating, shitting, sleeping, reproducing, dying.

When Dominick checked in to the Mandarin Oriental in the Back Bay—as Lord Witherspoon comma his own name—he asked for a room on the highest floor available. He needed to look down on the city. It didn't matter how far away he was from the in-house spa. He enjoyed a lavish solitary Indian dinner and then a cigar on a chilly bench in a little pocket park not far from the hotel. His meeting with Angelica was scheduled for the following afternoon, and before going out to dinner he had asked at the front desk for directions to the address she had given him for a club in Braintree, south of the city. They had the directions ready for him when he returned—a computer printout with a map. He slept well in the huge bed, the drapes open to the bright lights of the city below. Now that he was in a city, he had no dreams of being lost there.

The directions said it would take Dominick twenty-five minutes to drive to his destination, so he doubled the time and left his room an hour early. His car had been valeted away somewhere when he arrived and now had to be redeemed, and he needed extra time in case he got lost. He had shopped in New Jerusalem for an appropriate outfit. Now, as he dressed as Lord Witherspoon, he made a mental effort to enter the character as well, and he discovered that Lord Witherspoon was a tad put out by being asked to travel an hour round-trip for the meeting. Surely Angelica could have made the effort to meet him here at his hotel or at one of the many fine establishments in the neighborhood. It was Dominick's fault, actually. He was too obsequious. He should not have just acquiesced to that woman's request for a meeting out of town but e-mailed her back insisting on a more convenient rendezvous. Dominick needed to firm up his act a bit. Now this bother of finding his way through a foreign city, where they drove on the wrong side of both the auto and the road. He practiced his repertoire of British noises and throat sounds.

But it wasn't that bad—though the traffic was heavy—just on and off an interstate headed south. He wondered what sort of club he was headed for. The F1 Boston Club. Some sort of country club or private spa? An elite retreat in the suburban woods? He wondered what Angelica looked like. How would he know her? Ask the maître d', of course; announce himself. She would have to find him. It was her club. The directions deposited him on an industrial road beside the freeway. He was a half hour early. He found the address about a half mile on—a large parking lot in front of a long, low, red metal-sided building. A flashy expensive sign above a glass entrance said F1 Boston. This was all so wrong that Lord Witherspoon almost drove by and left, but Dominick's curiosity was tweaked and he parked. It was as

Dominick that he walked down the landscaped stairs to the glass entryway and went in.

The maitre d' was just a teenager in a black-and-white checkered shirt, who asked if he had reservations. Dominick said no, he was just meeting someone in the lounge. The boy smiled and waved him on. Down some more polished steps there was a sort of entry hall adorned with racing car paraphernalia. In the middle of the floor was a sleek red racing car. There were shops and displays, all about auto racing. At the end of the hall was a neon sign for the Ascari Café. Dominick headed there, dawdling along the way at NASCAR displays, trying to absorb what he had walked into.

The café was really a bar that served food, what once was called a bar and grill not a café. No one was drinking coffee. An all-glass and burnished-aluminum affair, it was semicrowded, with most of the crowd at the long bar that extended the length of one wall. This crowd was almost exclusively male and of an age, midtwenties through thirty, with a few women on bar stools the centers of their attention. It was a loud crowd, beer drinkers. The far wall of the room was all windows looking out into another much larger enclosed space. There was a high counter with tall stools that ran the length of the windows. No one was sitting there, so that was where Dominick went, as far away from the crowd at the bar as possible. None of the women there would be Angelica; they were all too young.

The windows looked out onto a large low-roofed arena that held a twisting gray track maybe eight yards wide that dipped and turned and rose and disappeared into the further reaches of the building, and around this miniature roadway raced a fleet of identical go-karts, each with a number on its side, each with a helmeted, orange-jumpsuited driver behind the wheel. Dominick could hear them now, though being electric they were not that loud and the windows muffled them. There were maybe a dozen vehicles in all. They went round and round, each lap taking maybe two to three minutes. Dominick seemed to be the sole spectator. A waitress came over from behind the bar to take his order. She was young, like everyone else there at least half his age. He felt out of place in his gray slacks, navy blue sports coat, and Argyle sweater. He ordered an ale and asked for a menu. She smiled. He was afraid she was about to call him Pops.

Lord Witherspoon was ready to leave, but Dominick was hungry. He had not had lunch. When the waitress returned with his draft and a menu, he ordered a cheeseburger without opening the menu. Her name tag said Christy. He called her Christy as if she were an old friend's daughter. She liked that. "You looking for someone?" she asked.

"If she comes in she'll find me," he said.

"No, I was wondering if you were a cop. My dad was a cop, and you remind me of him. We're cop friendly here. We don't want any trouble."

"No, I'm not police or any type of authority figure." Who did she remind him of? Someone from so long ago. Long hair like hers, a similar chin that drew attention to itself, perfect skin. "My condolences on the loss of your father."

"Thanks. He could be a jerk but he had a big heart. How do you want that burger?"

"Well," he said, "well."

"Done?" she said, laughing.

"That too."

She laughed again. Why did that happen? That thirty years can just fold into nothing like that and someone so forgotten can just reappear? You can't trust your brain. It is so densely wired that it is bound to go haywire now and then. When she laughed he could see her charmingly familiar uneven teeth.

"That comes with fries," she said.

"Doesn't everything?" he said. She took back the unopened menu and shook her head.

As they were talking, the race down on the track was coming to an end. A young man was waving a checkered flag on a stick over the heads of the kart drivers as they drove past him at the finish line. All along, Dominick had been thinking of the drivers as kids, thinking that must be fun for them, pretending to be adults in their little go-karts, but now he saw that the drivers were all grown-ups—adults pretending to be kids.

His cheeseburger and fries arrived at about the same time as the next heat began, and they were finished almost simultaneously. As usual, half of the French fries went uneaten. When Christy took his plate away he ordered another ale and looked around the large room, which was filling up. Fit young men, no longer in orange racing jump-suits but in jeans and polo shirts and carrying their colorful personalized helmets, were coming up steps from the level below. They piled all their helmets on one table and headed for the bar. Dominick turned back to watching the track, where a new string of karts was entering and taking a warm-up lap.

He saw her reflection in the window first, so her "Lord Witherspoon" did not surprise him, but it was Dominick who responded, not Lord Witherspoon. "How did you do?" he asked as he turned to face her.

"Isn't the normal question how do you do?" Angelica, too, was dressed in jeans and a polo shirt with a team logo above the breast pocket. She was carrying a helmet. She was medium height and blonde and broad shouldered. Only her eyes—Lydia's eyes—bore any resemblance to either of her parents.

Dominick stood and offered his hand, and then Lord Witherspoon took over. "I was referring to how you placed in your race."

"I came in sixth, but that doesn't matter. It's team racing. Our team placed second, so we get to go on to the next round. So nice of you to come all this way. I thought you might enjoy it."

"A change, yes."

"I didn't know if you would come or not. I was beginning to wonder if you actually existed or were just the nameplate on some real estate scavenger outfit."

Lord Witherspoon made an I-am-amused noise in his throat and took a sip of ale. "No, I am real, and I have a real interest in your family property. Would you like a drink?" Here he was offering her hospitality in her own club.

"You don't sound very British, Lord Witherspoon."

"We don't all sound like Prince Charles. I went to school here in the States, in Virginia. I come here often, I don't mind passing for an American. Are we to discuss our business here?"

"I suppose all I really need to hear from you is that you are real, that you are serious in your bid, and that you would consider increasing it, because your past offer is clearly unacceptable."

"I came all this way for that? Interrupted my trip? All that was needed was for you, through your agent, to make a counteroffer for us to consider and respond to." Lord Witherspoon was put out.

"Well, we could have a proper meeting, I guess, and see if we can come closer to an agreement. That real estate agent is really quite useless. You are kind of cute when you get angry like that. I like a man who can strike right back." Angelica's tone had softened and her face had relaxed into something approaching a bemused smile. "Shall we do dinner tonight, Lord Witherspoon? I have another race coming up right now, but this evening? If you're not busy, that is."

"I am free. But at a proper place in the city, not out here. I am staying at the Mandarin, Boylston Street. You know the neighborhood?"

"Of course. There are some fine restaurants around there. Shall we have a date, at eight, say? I'll meet you at your hotel, and we can start out with drinks at that excellent bistro there?" Now Angelica was being charming. With a toss of her head she flicked an errant strand of blonde hair away from her face and smiled, showing perfect teeth.

High maintenance, Dominick thought, but Lord Witherspoon said, "Well, yes, that would be fine. At eight then."

Angelica stretched out her perfectly manicured hand for him to shake, elbow locked, palm down the way women do sometimes, as if giving you the option of bowing and air-kissing the back of their hand. "And let's decide to be friends no matter how our little business deal works out."

Driving back, Dominick did get lost, missed his exit and ended up somewhere in Cambridge. He hadn't been paying attention. It had been some time since his last date. He couldn't even remember whom it was with. Dating was just something that when you reached a certain age you didn't do, and in any event the women he met to whom he might have felt attracted were invariably married or burdened with children or too worldly and sardonic to take any overture seriously. He could not remember the last time a woman had asked him out. And an attractive woman at that. He found a bridge back across the river to Boston and then found Boylston Street and finally his hotel, where he delivered his car to the valet, glad to be free of it.

Why was it, the more expensive the hotel the more embarrassing the bathroom mirrors? Drying himself off after a shower, Dominick had a many-sided, morgue-lit view of his physical self. The corpus revealed was not the same as the one he held in his mind's eye. It was wider, paler, lumpier—a collapsing pile of flesh, his private parts dwarfed by the roll of flesh above them. There were good aesthetic reasons why no one else had recently viewed this travesty. When he shaved he could see every facial blemish and scar and exploded pore. He tried to clip his protruding nasal hairs with a fingernail clipper, but succeeded only in painfully yanking out the most obvious ones. He opened both tiny bottles of Glenfiddich from the minibar and poured them over ice. Dominick told himself this was not a date, just a business dinner, a flimflam exercise that had nothing to do with him personally. It was Lord Witherspoon's gig. Only His Lordship was not around, just Dominick wondering what he was doing there.

When the call came it was half an hour late and Dominick had opened and finished the other two mini-bottles of lesser scotch in the bar. Angelica was down in the lobby bistro, waiting for Lord Witherspoon. By now Lord Witherspoon was ready. He brushed and gargled to take the taste of whiskey out of his mouth and dabbed on some extra cologne. In the lounge Angelica was seated at the bar. The place was full, a younger crowd, not hotel guests but young cosmopolitan types cruising. It was a place to be seen. Floor-to-ceiling windows looked out onto busy Boylston Street. There were no empty seats at the bar, so Lord Witherspoon stood beside Angelica's stool and ordered a rusty nail.

Angelica was in a short black basic evening dress, over which she was wearing an open, long-sleeved, pumpkin-colored, embroidered and hand-beaded, textured cotton jacket with Mandarin buttons— something a woman in the foothills of the Himalayas had spent many days creating. Her long blonde hair was swept back from her face and held with a silver butterfly clip. She was wearing no jewelry whatsoever, not even earrings or a wedding ring. Her tanned athletic legs were crossed. She did not look like a go-kart racer. She was drinking a martini. Though older than the crowd around her, she was still closer to their age than Dominick's.

When his drink arrived, they clinked glasses and she toasted him, "To your health, Lord Witherspoon." They sipped their drinks. "I can't keep calling you that. It's four syllables long. What do your friends and lovers call you?"

"My friends call me Dominick. That's only three syllables. My lovers call me less often. And what shall I call you?"

"I'm pretty much Angie to everyone, but I wouldn't mind it if you came up with your own private name for me, as long as it is polite and endearing. I'm tired of being just Angie. What say for just this evening we pretend I'm Lady Witherspoon? That would be fun. I've never been a ladyship before. Or is there already a Lady Witherspoon?"

"No, no Lady Witherspoon since my mother passed on."

"That wouldn't be too painful then? I mean, I don't want to be your mother or anything, just not Angie for an evening."

"No, m'lady, that would be fine. We shall pretend thus. Might I then presume to say that your ladyship is looking very fine tonight?"

"Why, thank you, my lord." She smiled. "I like this already. Where shall we eat? This place is so . . ."

"Loud," he suggested.

"No, beneath us."

There was a four-star steakhouse nearby, Morton's, that Angelica suggested. They walked there. There was a chill wind off the harbor, and she took Dominick's arm and pressed against him away from the wind. She came up to his shoulder. She had already made reservations there for them, for Lord and Lady Witherspoon. The meal was superb. They drank champagne and lingered over cognacs and coffee. She laughed at his monologues and his imitations of American speech. Angelica asked about England and his family there. Lord Witherspoon invented something thin and dismissive. When he in turn asked about her family, she demurred, reminding him that tonight she was Lady Witherspoon. "So, you tell me my family tree and who I've been."

"Your great-grandfather was a British admiral best remembered for getting lost in the fog on his way to the Battle of Dogger Bank," Dominick began. It was a fun fictional evening.

On their stroll back to the hotel, Angelica told him how refreshing it was to be in the company of a non-American male. "They are so raised to be crude. Only the crude seem to survive. The meek are eaten, and the polite ones are trampled underfoot. I've enjoyed your company tonight, Dominick, your Old World charm and chivalry."

"But I don't believe we once talked business, did we?" Dominick said. He wondered if this was going to be so simple and easy.

"No, we haven't," Angelica agreed. "Let's do that over a nightcap back in your room."

Chapter 8

Dominick's cock was not particularly long, but it was thick and uncircumcised. This seemed to delight Angelica. She made cooing, approving noises—"Oh my, oh yes, yes"—as she wrapped one slender feminine hand around it and her tongue flicked at his foreskin. In her other hand she held the heft of his testicles as if they were some fragile Tiffany gift. She licked the length of his shaft. "Oh, Lord Witherspoon, you are so gorgeous." She wrapped her mouth around him, sighing.

She cannot possibly be pretending that, could she? Dominick wondered, watching Angelica as if from a very great distance as she made herself comfortable along the long white bolster-sized pillow that was his extended leg and her head moved slowly up and down and in little circles in his crotch. For the first time he noticed the dark, deep roots of her hair. She was still wearing her short black dress, though she had shed her shoes and jacket. She was squirming with pleasure, crushing her breasts against his leg, grinding her pelvis along his foot.

Dominick had long suspected that the pleasures of fellatio were mainly pretentious. The idea of a male member in his mouth repulsed him, so he had trouble imagining how anyone else might enjoy it. It was demeaning, subservient to be the fellator. Popular culture concurred on that. She was servicing him. What fun was that? Yeats's line, "But Love has pitched his mansion in / The place of excrement." Angelica moaned deep in her throat. Her eyes were closed, but it still looked like work.

There was a philosophical basis for his suspicions as well. As the cheap simulacrum of an essential actual action, fellatio committed the fallacy of equivocation. For Dominick to ejaculate into Angelica's mouth could only be syntactically and falsely substituted for a coital and perhaps mutual ejaculation. The act's unnaturalness encompassed a lack of engagement and commitment on the part of the actors. There was, of course, the question of altruism. But lust and altruism had nothing in common beyond the four shared letters in their names. Angelica stroked him harder, sucking now like a calf at its mother's teat.

She knew that with an older man like Dominick if she could make him come once her work in that department would be done for the night. That would be fine with him. He reached down to squeeze her breast inside her dress and bra. She liked that and moaned and turned more onto her side so that his hand could reach farther down onto her belly. He pulled up Angelica's dress, and she shifted and turned, moving between his legs and pulling her knees up so that he could now reach his hand down between her legs and up her smooth thigh to her—what was that word from the porno classics?—quim, her warm, moist quim beneath her sheer panties. His thick fingers found the swollen crease beneath the hair and with one slip opened her outer lips. Angelica shuddered and groaned and her legs opened wider.

But Dominick was going soft in Angelica's mouth. The truth was he disliked blow jobs and had never come while getting one. Was it the thought of the teeth? Wasn't a woman's mouth the true and original *vagina dentata*? Or was it just that the distance left too much room for thought altogether. In any event, an erection was nothing to be toyed with, and now it was going away. Just the ghost of erections past, Dominick thought, a miasma.

As Dominick's erection vanished, first in her mouth and then her hand, Angelica seemed mystified. She yanked at his flaccid member and squeezed it as if she were working an exhausted tube of toothpaste. This hurt, which only made him shrink faster. It was as if his penis was an entity entirely to itself, no longer part of him, a misbehaving pet. He pulled his hand out of her panties and touched the side of her head, pushed the hair away from her beautiful ear. "Angelica," he said.

"No, I'm not Angelica," she said. "And you are not my father, who is the only person alive who still calls me that. What? Are you gay? You don't find me desirable?"

"No, I find you very desirable." Dominick spoke softly. Absentmindedly he raised his fingers to his face to sniff them, smell her there. "Only . . ."

"Only what?"

"Only I enjoy getting oral sex only up to a certain point."

"And then?" Angelica had abandoned her attempts to rearouse him and sat up, pulling her dress back over her lap.

"And then I would like to move onto something more mutual."

"Oh, bullshit, Your Lordship. I've never met a man who didn't enjoy a good blow job, at least American men, and I give a good blow job. And if you expect me to let you stick your thing into me on our first date, you are sadly mistaken. What kind of girl do you take me for?"

"Is this our first date?" Dominick suddenly felt very vulnerable and unattractive lying there in just his socks and shirt. She had strewn his pants, shorts, and shoes on the floor beside the couch as she had stripped them off of him.

"Well, I was looking forward to our getting to know each other better." Now she was rearranging her hair. Grooming, always grooming. "I've never been to England, you know."

"Look, I'm sorry. Perhaps you are used to younger men."

"I've never had that happen to me before. Are you alright? Physically, I mean?"

"It has been a long time," Dominick said as he sat up and reached for his clothes on the floor, becoming Lord Witherspoon as he did so. "So, you were hoping to fellate your way to a transatlantic invitation?"

"Look, just because your prick isn't working is no reason to get insulting."

"Enjoyed playing Lady Witherspoon, did we?" He got back into his shorts and pulled up his trousers.

"Wait, Dominick, don't get all huffy on me. As a matter of fact, I did enjoy being Lady Witherspoon. I enjoyed your company. I . . . don't know what to say right now."

The bar had been restocked with scotch. Lord Witherspoon poured himself one. "We have yet to discuss our business," he said, his back to her, as he went to the drapes and opened them on the lights of Boston.

"Your shirt's not tucked in in the back," she said. "May I have a drink, too?"

"Help yourself," he said, putting down his drink to unbuckle his trousers and tuck his shirt in properly. He was still in his stocking feet. "By the way, Angie, you have very comely ears."

"So, there is hope for us."

"Why do you not wear any jewelry?"

"I suppose because my mother never did. I never learned how, never felt safe with my choices, so never got in the habit."

Dominick thought of Lydia's mismatched earrings. "Not even a wedding ring?"

"That really is nobody else's business, is it? Some ancient now meaningless custom, one of the easiest public lies to tell without saying a word." Angelica had poured herself a glass of white wine and was now standing beside Lord Witherspoon, looking down on the lights of the city. "Scary, isn't it?'

"The expanse of it? All that wasted energy?"

"No, the height, I mean, looking down on it. I don't like heights. You meant that? About my ears?"

"Exceptional."

"Where do you go from here?"

"On to Los Angeles, estate business. A lawsuit in progress, a deposition, American attorneys." The Lord Witherspoon fictions were coming quicker and thicker. Dominick suddenly felt very tired of it all. "Listen, Angie, about Mt. Sinai, your bargaining position is poor—prices are still dropping—but I have been authorized to sweeten our initial bid by fifty thousand on the condition that you or your agent present a bona fide authorized competitive bid from another potential buyer. We are prepared to negotiate a higher price if necessary, but not against some phantom player."

"You're dismissing me, aren't you?"

"I'm tired. I have an early departure tomorrow."

"Will you be stopping back in Boston on your way back home?"

"I was not planning on it. Why?"

"I thought we might try a second date. You know, even if you are gay, I would still like to be friends."

"Yes, well we have each other's e-mail address now. We can stay in touch." Lord Witherspoon was a bit put off by Angelica's assumption of his homosexuality. Dominick thought it was funny. "Please do get back to me about whether we still have a window of opportunity on the Mt. Sinai negotiation. Perhaps we could celebrate a closing some day."

"Let me sleep on it. I think I will be changing agents. You really do like my ears? No one has ever told me that before."

"I think you are altogether exquisite. I love the way you smell and the way you do your hair." Dominick wondered if Lord Witherspoon knew how faggoty he was sounding. "You've maintained yourself wonderfully. Yes, of course, do let us get together again."

Angelica went off to the bathroom. Now she seemed miffed, but when she returned she was composed. She had fixed her hair and reapplied lipstick. She put on her shoes and retrieved her wine glass from the coffee table and finished her drink in one swallow. "I will be in touch, Dominick. May I still call you Dominick? And the negotiations on the house are still open. And we will get back together again, I assure you. I am not so easy to get rid of." She slipped into her beaded coat of many colors. "You do have a beautiful cock, by the way." She came over to where Lord Witherspoon was still standing by the windows, pulled down his head with both of her hands, and gave him a lingering kiss on the lips. "Let's try it again sometime."

When she left she forgot her small handbag, and Dominick had to run down the hotel corridor with it, catching her just in time as the elevator doors opened. He was still in his stocking feet and shirtsleeves. He could taste her lipstick on his mouth.

"Oh," she said and laughed when he handed her the bag. "Thank you, sweetheart. You make me forget things." And she gave him another kiss on the cheek. A couple was coming out of the elevator and was stopped by the exchange. They gave each other a knowing look and smile—the conclusion of a hotel liaison, older man, younger woman. In their minds, at least, Lord Witherspoon had just gotten laid. The fact that it had not actually happened did not matter.

Lord Witherspoon felt like saying, "No. You don't understand. She is just the daughter of a friend. We were talking real estate." But instead he discovered that his fly was still unzipped and, as Dominick now, he lingered there at the elevator after the doors had closed in order to give the couple a head start down the corridor. He heard the man say something that made the woman laugh. He zipped up his fly. Ah, romance.

When Dominick got back to Mt. Sinai, no one was home and the house was cold. The Jamesons' car was gone. There was several days' mail in the mailbox and two *New Jerusalem News*es in their clear plastic sleeves near the front steps. There were two unwashed coffee cups in the sink. It was just another deserted house, but it was home. Funny how that worked. When you have a base—no matter how temporary or borrowed—and leave it, when you return there, it is home. It was that way with campsites and hotel rooms and even weekend house visits. If you leave and return, the place you return to is olly-olly-home-free "home." Your stuff is there. You can take off your shoes and empty your pockets, change your clothes. Safe haven. Home—its deep root was the Greek *kei*, meaning to lie down, to rest, then to lie down with others, and so on to *heim* and subsequent uses, all the way to what missiles do before they explode. Was there an older word than home?

Dominick went to bed. Lord Witherspoon's rich repast at Morton's the previous evening had brought on intestinal havoc and he had slept poorly. The drive home had exhausted him. He was feeling his age and would rather not think of it. Lie down was what you did when you got home—rest, hide behind the gates, beneath the covers.

Next morning he still had the place to himself, and he started to worry. He couldn't remember Atticus saying anything about a trip, and they had left the house in a bit of a mess, as if they had been searching for something before they left. Where would they have gone? Dominick knew none of their friends. He had no numbers to call—except for Angelica's, and he could hardly call her to inquire about her parents' whereabouts. What if Atticus's forever time had suddenly arrived and he was in a hospital somewhere or a funeral home? But then surely there would be friends or relatives coming to the house, phone calls. Dominick prized his solitude, but this silence was unnerving.

There was Ms. Arnold over in New Jerusalem, but Dominick had never had her number, only her address. When the next day arrived with still no Atticus or Lydia or word, Dominick caught the ferry to New Jerusalem. His supply of Churchills was running low, so a visit to his tobacconist was also in order. It felt good to be back in his local garb, his denim jacket and knit watch cap. The midmorning ferry was nearly deserted. The wind off the bay was like a frozen knife, and all the other passengers remained inside. Dominick had the open deck and the railings all to himself. He found a snug corner on the lee side out of the wind where his view was up the bay, which was also nearly deserted—no sailboats, no fishing boats, just an empty, rusted freighter resting high at anchor off to the left of the channel.

Dominick knew from old maps that both shores of the bay and its many islands had once been spotted with forts and coastal batteries from three centuries of waiting for war. Each new installation had been state of the art of defense for its time, and each had been eclipsed by the next advance of offensive ordinance. But not since the Revolution—how many American wars before?—had a shot been fired there against any enemy. War was such an excellent industry. The profits of endless paranoid preparation, with the added bonus that if hostilities actually did occur your product was either fired away or blown up and had to be immediately replaced, at your prices. Not one of those forts and batteries, camps and bases was still in service, useless defenses against ballistic missiles or terrorists. Most were abandoned, overgrown, and forgotten a few were now parks.

Dominick's favorite bay war story was from early in the Revolution when a farmer on their island had, on his own initiative, jammed the barrel of a small canon between two boulders on the shoreline of his farm to take potshots with rocks at passing Royal Navy vessels. When he finally hit one—took out a sail on a little sloop—the tars came ashore and spiked his gun. A Second Amendment kind of guy before there even was one, a local hero. Of course, they burned his house and barn and crops and took all his livestock and him. What war was really all about was things changing hands. Dominick wondered how the hero's wife felt about it. Somewhere up that bay was Old Grofton, where the LNG port was going in. There would not be any patriots taking rock potshots at those ships going by. The ferry turned into the wind so that there was no lee, and Dominick ducked inside with the rest of the passengers. A small boy shot at him with a toy gun, and with his finger Dominick shot him back.

He stopped at his tobacconist and the Portuguese fishermen's bar before heading on to Ms. Arnold's house. She seemed pleased to see him. "Lord Witherspoon, what a pleasant surprise. Come in, come in."

"I was just in the neighborhood, thought I would pop in to say hello."

Ms. Arnold led him into the front parlor. "Lydia, dear, look who is here," she called. Lydia was seated in a chair in the front window. She had her iPod ear pods in. She must have seen him walk up to the house, but when she turned to face him there wasn't a hint of recognition in her face. "Lydia, you remember Lord Witherspoon," Ms. Arnold said, as if introducing someone from her garden club.

"Where is Atticus?" Lydia asked. Then she turned back to look out the window.

Ms. Arnold took Lord Witherspoon to the kitchen. "Poor dear has had a bit of a shock, I'm afraid. Her house was raided earlier in the week, awful experience. I understand they went through the entire place basement to attic, tearing everything apart, looking for god knows what. I never did trust that little weasel of a husband of hers. I guess the authorities finally caught on to him. You do know how he made all his money, don't you? Building submarines. That's right. The company he worked for built those giant submarines, like Sean Connery's. She just sits there by the window with those things in her ears waiting for him to come back."

It was hot in the kitchen, which smelled like a roast was cooking. Dominick took off his cap and jacket and draped them on the back of a chair. "Ah . . . and where is Atticus?"

"God knows where he goes. They came here after the invasion. She couldn't stay in that house. I've got plenty of room. Poor Lydia, she comes and goes. She's better when he is around, but he's gone all day and a few evenings. Where are you staying now, Lord Witherspoon? Just visiting?"

"Oh, with friends on the island," he said, confused. Had he only been gone the two days? Again time had done one of its peculiar folds in the plain. Everything changed. A year could have passed since he last took a seat at Ms. Arnold's kitchen table. "Submarines, you say? I didn't know." The house had not been in such bad disarray.

"Yes, the ones that fire missiles. And he is from the other side of the commodore's family, the side that left and came back. He is part Indian, you know."

"Part Indian."

"That's what they say."

"That would have been a long time ago."

"Memories are long here. Will you stay for dinner, Lord Witherspoon? Just a simple family meal, but you are welcome."

"Lydia didn't recognize me."

"Like I said, she comes and goes. I think it's that music that she listens to. What do they call it? Those awful Negroid-sounding rhyming songs with no melody? Wrack? And then she'll go on about how terrible the Meriwether family is. Why, there haven't been any Meriwethers hereabout since she and I were girls. Poor dear."

"Are you expecting Atticus back this evening?"

"I don't expect anything from that man. Why, I wouldn't be surprised if he didn't just leave Lydia here with me indefinitely and never come back. He's been very angry, not at all nice to be around. But do stay. I'm afraid I can't offer you a drink. Atticus has drunk all the liquor in the house."

"You would have no idea how I could contact him?"

"Stay for dinner. He might show up."

Dominick left a sealed message for Atticus instead. If he stayed much longer he would miss the last ferry back, and he needed to get out of that house no matter how good the roast smelled. He had supper instead in the village, fish and chips at one of the restaurants that stayed open year-round in the block above the ferry. On the boat ride home he had decided he would grow a beard. It would come in white, like Sean Connery's in that movie. He would keep it trimmed. The fish and chips were good, but it was not the roast he craved.

The "raid" on Mt. Sinai meant a search warrant, surely federal, had been issued. The ICE guys were grasping at straws. When he got home, Dominick went through the piled up issues of the *New Jerusalem News*, looking for updates on the Old Grofton bombing. All he found was one story saying that although there were no suspects yet in custody or identified, the investigation was ongoing and deepening and that other law enforcement and intelligence agencies had become involved, including Interpol and British antiterrorist agents. The president had issued a statement condemning the attack and vowing federal vengeance against the "cowards and enemies of our God-given freedoms."

Dominick went to his room and looked through his things. He had not noticed anything amiss before, but now he saw that the books on his end table seemed out of order—the lighthouse book he had just finished was at the bottom of the pile— and that a notebook in which he wrote down memorable quotations was not where he normally kept it. Someone had gone through his drawers as well, because the white clothes and the colored clothes were no longer clearly segregated as he always kept them. But nothing seemed to be missing.

He went back down to the kitchen, where he could hear the phone if Atticus called, and poured himself a drink—bourbon tonight because he was feeling like an American, a wronged American, a volunteer for the whiskey rebellion. Maybe he would let his hair grow long as well. He wondered if the house was being watched, but he didn't bother going to see if there were any suspicious vehicles in the road. He wondered if the house was being bugged, if they had planted microphones like in the movies. Atticus didn't call.

That night Dominick awoke himself with his own snoring, in his dream mistaking it for a lighthouse foghorn. He had been following an albatross that led him to the edge of destruction on the rocks in the fog before the warning sound awakened him. He switched pillows and rolled over and went back to sleep.

Chapter 9

Crows. It was crow time. They owned the new dead season when the woods were just black branches against a brooding sky. All the sunshine birds were gone. The only calls were caws and the now-and-then lament of seagulls higher above. Black rulers of an empty roost, strutting across brown lawns, pecking at macadam road kills, unbeautiful birds with attitude. What sort of creatures thrived at margins, this border time at the edge of snow? They traveled in brazen gangs now. They distilled starkness.

Dominick watched them from the windows of the house. He was still there alone, although Atticus stopped by at times to check on things or fetch something, always hurrying back to Lydia in New Jerusalem. They had left Ms. Arnold's and moved to the seasonally vacated home of another friend, Lydia refusing to return to her violated Mt. Sinai. Wild birds were the perfect pets. Their freedom freed you. The pleasure they gave was gratis. Here he was in the cage of this house, looking out at them free on whatever wind. Free to be crows.

Dominick's camera bag was still in the trunk of his car. He had never brought it in when he moved from Brenda and Charlie's, but he thought of it now that the weather was turning colder. He had not taken a photograph in months. It went that way sometimes. It was as if for a stretch of time he could not see anything, and then suddenly everything would become very clear. Baseball batters talked like that, whether they were *seeing* the ball or not. For Dominick it was as if all of a sudden his eyes were a viewfinder and his mind worked through f-stops and apertures, focal lengths and shadows. Always in black-and-white—the posing crow's absolute absorption of light against that marbled sky.

He went out to the car and brought in his camera bag. It was like meeting an old friend in a pub for a drink—well, many drinks. He and his cameras and lenses went on a binge. He had left all his black-and-white film stock in Brenda and Charlie's freezer. After he shot all the film in his cameras he drove over there, found the key to the house where Charlie had shown him, and retrieved it all. He felt ten years younger. On the way home he stopped and reloaded and shot black-and-white cows in a field and a one-shade-of-gray horse against a line of another-shade-of-gray trees. He was a danger on the road.

Not since graduate school in England had Dominick spent a winter in the north. He was a migratory not a hibernating creature. He had forgotten the slanting distant light of a November afternoon, forgotten the thin transparency of frozen air, the vulnerable fragility of barren trees. The cold had never bothered him much. It was the inconveniences of northern winters that had always drawn him south to Florida or the islands. He was a camp follower of the highest tax bracket, and the idle well-off liked it warm. In recent years he had noticed, though, that the fewer people he had to be around the better, and in his memories winters were the cloistered season, a time of solitary walks and empty rooms, a black-and-white time. Now he had a place entirely to himself, with zero social obligations, the human world stripped back to basics. He didn't even have to speak. He could just shoot.

He did have to get his film developed, however, and purchase more. Neither of these once simple transactions was a given any longer. Black-and-white film photography had ceased to be commercial. Stores no longer sold black-and-white film. Getting film developed and having prints made had become a specialist's trade, or you did it yourself. Dominick checked the Yellow Pages and made a few phone calls, but no one locally had a clue. Try in Boston was the most common suggestion. He was left with the quandary and photos he couldn't see.

The New Jerusalem Historical Society Museum occupied one of those houses with a bronze plaque beside the front door. This one was a tall Victorian, returned part of the way to its original rococo splendor, but with too much of its once-buffeting grounds now an unfortunate parking lot. Dominick had trouble finding it in the warren of the old town streets. It was a nasty afternoon of cold spitting showers and shifting winds, but he was on a mission. He wanted to look at photographs, old photographs. He might not need a community, but his photographs did. How had this landscape appeared to earlier cameras? What thematic traditions might his photos be accidentally mimicking, mocking? How did this place come across arrested in black-and-white a hundred and more years before?

Dominick paused on the porch beside the plaque to stomp the rain from his shoes and remove his wet knit cap. It had been ten days at least since he had last shaved. In his dark turtleneck sweater and wet denim jacket with the patches on the sleeves and his bristling stubble face he would look like some bum coming in out of the cold and rain. Would some old maid curator just try to shoo him away? As he opened the door and stepped into the foyer, a voice did call out to him from somewhere, but it was a man's voice. "You can hang up your wet jacket there by the door." Dominick looked around, and sure enough beside the door was an empty, very antique-looking coat rack fashioned from deer antlers. He hung his jacket and his knit cap there. "How can I help you, sailor?" the voice asked. Dominick couldn't see the source of the voice until he walked further into the foyer and looked through an open doorway to his left into a well-lit room that looked to be the library. Standing behind a counter there was a tall man with a shock of white hair. The man laughed. "I could see you in the hall mirror there as you came in. A bit of a nasty day out there?"

Dominick just nodded. He was now standing at the juncture of a foyer, a hallway, and two large rooms with open sliding doors. In front of him an ornate carpeted staircase with a sweeping banister led up to a stained-glass-window landing. The house was warm, and everywhere he looked old furniture, framed prints and paintings, and glass display cases glowed in indirect amber lighting. There was the smell of paste wax. No one else was around, just the past cast in amber.

"No other visitors today," the man said as if reading Dominick's mind. "Off-season, the weather, the general lack of interest in finished things. What brings you?"

"Photographs," Dominick said, "old photographs of hereabouts."

"Anything specific? Is your family of here?"

"No and no."

"Well, feel free to peruse what we have hanging, and I'll pull out a few albums for you to look at as well. Would it be ships and fishing that interest you?"

"No, not really. Landscapes, houses, period shots. If it's not too much trouble."

"No trouble at all. It's what we're here for. Might I ask if there is a purpose for your search?"

"I take photographs," Dominick said. "I want to see what other photographers saw here."

The man came out from behind the counter where books and papers were spread. He was as tall as Dominick, but trimmer. He was impeccably dressed in a dark-brown wool suit and forest-green tie. He was very handsome in a self-preened way. He extended his hand to shake. "My name is John Starks," he said. "I'm curator here, and I would be quite happy to assist you on your search. You are?"

"Dominick," Dominick said, "just Dominick." He was definitely not Lord Witherspoon. They shook hands.

The next several hours passed quickly and pleasantly. Mr. Starks had a fine eye for photographs and knew his collection well. He avoided all studio portraits and posed family scenes. "I have few interior shots without people in them," he apologized, "and not real people anyway, more like mannequins posed in period costumes." In the outdoor landscape, panoramic, and real estate photos that they looked at, people were either totally absent or just small, indistinct, insignificant figures. The seascape views of the bay were among the most interesting. This was where the unnamed photographers with their boxy wooden cameras and fragile glass plates had felt most free to indulge their aesthetic expression. There were several truly majestic skies, studies in contrast and chiaroscuro. "Amazing what they could do," Starks said. Dominick could only imagine the labor involved—hauling all that heavy, breakable gear in a horse-drawn buggy over farm trails to a cliff edge to set up and hope for the light to be right and for the rain to hold off. No point and shoot, better pack a lunch.

The phone never rang. No one else came in. At one point Starks went off and came back with two demitasse cups of freshly brewed espresso and another old album. "Shipwrecks," he said. John Starks was openly, brazenly gay. The way he talked, the queenly way he walked and carried himself. This was no fag in hiding. He was himself and confident about it. If you had no use for it, then that was your problem, not his. Dominick found this lack of pretense relaxing. They talked about the photographs, Starks giving what details he knew, anecdotes and background. Dominick asked questions, studying details. The old ferryboats captured him. There was something so portly and maternal about them. Here was one washed up onshore in the hurricane of '38, an injustice somehow greater and more personal than the other shipwrecks.

Then it was time for Dominick to leave if he was to catch the last ferry back to the island. Starks said for him to come back, that he had more photos to show him. Dominick said he would. "You said you were a photographer. What are you shooting?" Starks asked. When Dominick told him black-and-white but that he couldn't find a local shop to develop them, Starks told him to bring him the film, that he would develop them. It was his hobby, too, only he had a darkroom. "Tomorrow then?"

The next day, Dominick brought his rolls of exposed but undeveloped film and gave them to Starks, and they went back to looking at photographs. Dominick had been struck by the barrenness of the country in the old photographs. A tree was like a special event. Every vista was of empty land, with isolated, stark four-corner buildings stuck here and there like enemies both of one another and the tundra landscape. These days, trees and forests filled all the empty spaces. The bay islands, which now were covered with seemingly primordial woods, had once been stripped so bare that they looked like naked flesh in sepia—a thigh, a hip, a knee of some drowned giant. The coastal plains behind New Jerusalem were similar—boundless fields that could have been Iowa after a corn harvest. John Starks explained that this place astride the protein bounty of the bay had always been prime real estate and that the original human inhabitants liked to burn off the understory to keep the forests clear and parklike for better hunting. "Even though they didn't graze, they pushed the forests back."

Then came the next wave of inhabitants, the ones who came on wooden ships and built wooden houses and kept sheep and cattle that needed pastureland. "They also burned a lot of wood. It was their only fuel." A typical New England farmstead would consume a dozen cords of firewood a year. A small hamlet would clear several acres of forest a year just to burn. "Combined with what they took from the bay and the outer banks, it was a real striptease," Starks said. "Our forefathers didn't fool around."

Generally, Dominick had little idea as to what day of the week it was. It made no difference to him. There was no event or anticipation that set one day off from another, so he often lost track. His was not a life of calendar events. "Three days from now" was about as complex as his scheduling ever got. But he knew that on Friday and Saturday nights there was an off-season late ferry from New Jerusalem. He had a suspicion it might be the weekend, so when he got on the ferry that morning he had asked, and was told, yes, there would be a late boat that evening, seeing as it was Friday. He would not have to hurry back to the dock at dusk.

John Starks knew the ferry schedule, too. As the afternoon darkened he asked, "Can you take the late boat back tonight, Dominick?"

"I was planning on it; maybe have supper over here somewhere."

"Good. Let me close up shop early and we'll go," Starks said, and he set about turning off lights and turning on alarms. He returned dressed for departure—tan leather gloves, a raw silk scarf, a camel hair overcoat.

It was only a three- or four-block walk—an old-town block up, a brick block over, another narrow block in, and then down a short Sherlock Holmes-style alley. On the way they continued their discussion of digital photography, their shared disdain for Photoshopped lies and deceptions, colors so enhanced they were a different color altogether, the dozens of framing and focus and contrast and brightness tricks that could be played with one lackluster shot until something better emerged, all the crispness and clarity and honesty of true photography murdered. Starks had a special hatred for those huge, pixel-blurred, printed-on-canvas works that pretended to be Impressionist paintings: "The neon-colored dories afloat on a never-to-be-seen blue sea, the cut-and-paste still lifes of flowers that grow in opposite seasons, blaze-doctored sunsets that even Turner would have been embarrassed by. If they want to be seen as painters, then why don't they learn how to paint, instead of pushing their computer mouse around and just clicking?"

They entered by a low side door. Now that no one could smoke in pubs anymore there was no tobacco aroma to mix with and mask the sour-sweet smell of spilt beer and drinkers. The noise was the same though—the din of many layers of simultaneous conversations, men's and women's voices mingling, snorts and peals of laughter. Occasional full phrases came through—"Cheap as shit," "So I called her again," "No lie," "He never did it again, I'll tell you that." Down a few steps to a low-ceilinged room with three dartboards all in use and through there to the busy barroom itself. John Starks led the way. He was a familiar there. They found an empty corner booth away from the bar. A waitress trailed them there with a tray and a rag to clear and wipe off the table. "Good evening, Sir John," she said. "You're a bit early. The usual?"

"Yes, thank you, Annie. Dominick?"

It was an Irish pub. Even their waitress had an old-country lilt to her voice. "A pint of Guinness," Dominick said. They removed their coats and sat down. "Sir John?"

"It's their joke name for me here in The Harp. I'm not one of them. I don't have to work with my hands and I don't have to work outdoors in all seasons like most of these gents do. So they pretend I am from a different class—different, not necessarily superior—and have mentally knighted me. I've been Sir John here for so long that some of the newer regulars think it's my actual name. I had one chap ask me what kind of a surgeon was I then."

"Probably had a bad back."

Starks chuckled. "Actually he did, wanted a referral."

"And a consultation."

"I don't do bar calls. Thank you, Annie. Anything special on the menu tonight?"

"No oysters, no chowder," she said, putting down their drinks. Starks was having an Irish coffee.

"It being Friday, I'll have the fish and chips. Dominick, I'd recommend the shepherd's pie. Not the usual pub fare, a specialty of the house." Dominick nodded in agreement. "And a shepherd's pie. Tell Malcolm it's for me."

Dominick waited for the head on his Guinness to thin. "So, are there other members of The Harp's royalty class, or are you the sole survivor of the revolution?"

"Oh, there are a few others. You can't have many, you know. It spoils the illusion. There's the Duke, who owns the place, and Queen Emma, who may actually be royalty somewhere outside The Harp. There's the dead Prince. It being Friday, they may stop in later. Not the dead Prince, of course."

"Cause of demise?"

"A fatal DUI or overdose. No one seems to remember for sure, but he was quite the favorite here before the gods took him."

"A different class of people."

"Absolute social necessity, even in a microcosmic culture like this pub." Starks took a long sip of his drink, leaving a thin line of cream on his upper lip that he licked away. "Without contradictions there can be no definition. There has to be an other before you can have a self. More basic to our nature than walking upright."

"So, why create classes? Why not just be yourself?"

"If everyone lived like a shaman in a hut on the edge of town, there would be no town to be around. Besides, creating classes gives one the comfort of solidarity. You know, the old us-against-them thing. There's a lot of power there."

"I've seen the documentaries."

"Also, you are spared the effort of trying to understand differences. You just lump the strange stuff together and call it theirs. You will have noticed that there is not a non-Caucasian person in this establishment. Those other racial classes are wholly excluded here. They have their own places to go. This is a working-class Irish bar, basically mono-class. Oh, some may be foremen by now and some retired, but it's all one when it comes to who they are. Good people, don't get me wrong." Starks had finished his Irish coffee and motioned for Annie to bring him another. "Being peons with no one below them, they created an aristocracy, a mythic class of not-them."

"Sir John," Annie said as she came to the table with their dishes.

The shepherd's pie was excellent—thin crusted, herbal, succulent, with tender lamb and sirloin chunks. "A royal peasant dish," Dominick said, pushing his empty plate aside.

"Don't confuse things," Starks said. He had eaten only half his fish and chips and ordered another Irish coffee. "But don't you agree that human societies invariably create an upper class? Why is that? In many cases they even worshipped them, deified them. From what Darwinian need did that impulse arise? Adoration of the wealthy is more prevalent in America today than it was in ancient Rome. No progressive movement will ever wipe that out." Annie had come to take their dishes away. "Thank you, sweet Ann, but aren't you getting a little bit broad in the hip there?"

"That would be because I'm pregnant, Sir John, and none of your fookin business."

"Of course, no longer having life or death powers does lessen the level of respect," Starks said as she walked away.

"You did call it an illusion."

"Yes, an essential one. In order to accept me they must create a category that is not them."

"Does your being gay have anything to do with it?"

Starks laughed. "Oh, I'd say so, yes. The sexual lives of the royal class have always been of special interest to the hoi polloi, the more outré and risqué the better. Every pantheon and royal family is filled with sex-obsessed superstars and deviants. What do tabloids feed the masses? Where would Zeus be without his sacred Priapus? Which brings us to you, Dominick of no last name." Starks turned and caught Annie's eye and waved her over. "Annie, bring us brandies that we might toast your new baby."

He turned back to Dominick. "First off, I don't believe your name is Dominick at all. It was just the first word that came to your mind when I asked you your name and you couldn't come up with a last name to match. No one is named Dominick anymore, at least not in this country. And you are from this country, though you have spent time abroad, England or Ireland. The way you said 'a pint of Guinness.' But that's alright. No matter what your given name may be, you are Dominick to me. I respect—nay, I admire—your chosen anonymity."

Annie came with two snifters of brandy, and they toasted her. "To your beautiful belly, may it bring forth a beautiful child," Starks said loud enough for others around them to hear. His toast was answered by a ragged chorus of "Here, here" and "I'll drink to that" and "To Annie's fair belly."

"You," Annie said, blushing. "If you weren't such a great tipper, Sir John, I'd throw you out."

Starks turned back into the booth. "Back to you, Dominick. In spite of your chosen appearance, your working class attire and your . . ." Starks waved his hand toward Dominick's face.

"Be kind and call it a beard."

"Whatever. In spite of your affected disguise, you are not a member of the general class at all. You are not the sailor I first mistook you for when you came into the museum. For one thing, you have done very little real labor in your life. A working man by your age has broken, sprained, and strained so many parts of his body that he moves with certain cautions and restraints, rather than your relaxed—dare I say?—floppiness. Your hands—though quite handsome—are soft and unmarred. I can tell by your teeth that you were raised with care, and you have yet to mispronounce a foreign word. No, Agent Dominick, you pass undercover poorly. Remember those Cold War spy movies where the American spy would get caught because he switched knife hands to cut and eat his meat?"

"Agent? Agent of what? Or should that be of whom?"

"Oh, that doesn't matter either. I have nothing to hide. I just find it fascinating, that's all. Someone who is not whom we pretend him to be. You, Dominick, are just a visitor to my museum, a man interested in old photographs, a photographer himself as it happens. You are not gay, so neither of us is sexual prey. A possible friend perhaps, but just as possibly someone who will vanish like any other tourist."

"Well, you do have my film, which you have kindly offered to develop."

"That's right. I have a temporary purchase on your return. Which reminds me." Starks reached over and fumbled around in the pocket of his camel hair coat. "Here," he said, handing over to Dominick four 35mm film canisters, "Kodak T-Max 400, twenty-four a roll. It's what

I've been shooting. I'm sure you must be out or close to it. The only place you can buy it these days is online, and you don't strike me as an online type of person."

"Why, thanks, John. As a matter of fact I am almost out of film. What do I . . . ?"

"I'll put it on your bill." Starks waved him off. "Ah, look, Queen Emma has arrived."

Dominick looked toward the bar, where a tall woman in a cape had made an entrance. Her back was to them. After receiving the greetings of those at the bar, she turned to survey the room and saw Starks and Dominick sitting in their corner booth. Starks blew her a kiss, and she smiled a queenly smile. If everyone else in the room was 100 percent Caucasian, Queen Emma was not—jet-black hair pulled back in a bun, a broad face with a permanent tan. Part something, not African, maybe Incan or American Indian or Pacific Islander. She was a large woman, but large the way a panther was large, not a bear. She was young. In her thirties maybe? Hard to tell. Her movements were graceful. She carried herself with an easy regality. Dominick could see why she had been granted royal standing. Someone handed her a glass of red wine. She headed in their direction.

"There you are, Sir John, my precious princess," she said as she came up to them. "Have you been hiding from me?"

Starks stood up to give her a hug and a kiss on the cheek. "Hiding? Who can find you? You are never where you say you will be."

"Well, I just got back and now you can avoid me no longer." She glanced at Dominick dismissively. "We really must talk."

Another round of drinks arrived at their table, unsummoned—another brandy for Starks, a brandy and a pint of Guinness for Dominick, and another glass of red wine for Queen Emma. Starks made no move to introduce Dominick to Queen Emma, and as she sat down Dominick got up and took his new drinks to another empty booth, back into the anonymous crowd as it were, leaving the nobles alone to their privileged conversation. He didn't mind. He had less need of Queen Emma than she had of him. He'd had his fill of those types. He sipped his drinks and watched the crowd as it changed from guys just off work to a younger contingent getting an early jump at

Friday night. Annie brought him another brandy, "From Sir John," she said.

By the time Dominick retrieved his coat from where it was hung near the corner booth both Starks and Queen Emma were gone. He hadn't seen them leave. In the pocket of his denim jacket were the four film canisters he had left on the table. He wondered what time it was.

Chapter 10

The front-page above-the-fold story in the next morning's *New Jerusalem News* was headlined "Terrorists Strike Again at Old Grofton: Submarine Bomb":

Federal, state and local authorities have again converged on the Old Grofton waterfront after a second suspicious explosion there. According to eyewitness reports a large underwater explosion off Darby Point at about noon yesterday sent a plume of water 30 feet into the air. The wave of water caused by the explosion, estimated at least 10 feet high, caused extensive damage to boats and docks at nearby Larsen's Marina. No deaths or injuries were reported.

The incident occurred in the same area as an explosion and fire on land last month that federal agencies have called an act of terrorism. The area is the site of the proposed Hercules Corp liquid natural gas terminal and processing plant.

Following the explosion the Old Grofton Police quickly cordoned off and evacuated all of Darby Point, and bomb-sniffing dogs were brought in. In the previous incident a second, undetonated device was found. There were no reports of other bombs being found this time.

By midafternoon several teams of divers from the State Police, Coast Guard and Navy were on the scene conducting underwater searches.

Special Agent Kerwood Rexroth of the FBI said that although the investigation was only in its preliminary stages, there was every reason to suspect that the explosion was connected to the earlier incident. "We have the same location, the same M.O., a similarly sophisticated and powerful explosive device. Only this time they struck in broad daylight, endangering lives and property."

No individual or group has claimed responsibility for either attack, and authorities have not released the identities of any possible suspects.

According to informed sources familiar with the construction plans for the Hercules Corp facility, the explosion took place in the approximate location where sea-floor pipelines would enter the terminal from an offshore tanker pump-out station. A project engineer, who spoke on condition of anonymity because he lacked authorization, speculated that the purpose of the attack was to expose vulnerabilities in the design of the facility.

By late afternoon there were reports of large numbers of dead fish washing ashore in Old Grofton and as far north along the bay as Destin Roads.

Dominick was reading the *News* as he ate breakfast in the Harbor House Hotel restaurant. He had had to plead for his breakfast. Breakfast was only served until eleven, and he had arrived at a quarter past. Luncheon menu only. The only other customers in the place were an old couple in a window booth. "So, the chef is too busy to fry some bacon and eggs?" he asked the waitress, who went off to get the older woman from behind the cash register. Just what Dominick needed to start his day—a little confrontation over arbitrary rules.

The older woman's name tag pegged her as an Elinor. "What's up?" she asked.

"I was hoping for breakfast." Dominick knew he should smile, but he couldn't manage it.

"You're late," she said. "You want coffee?"

"For starters. Checkout is not until twelve. One should be able to buy breakfast at least until then."

"Says who? You a guest here?"

"I just checked out. Elinor, I had a bad night and I am asking for your mercy, and a little breakfast."

"What do you want?"

"Pancakes, bacon, orange juice, coffee. Please."

"No problem. I don't know why they don't serve breakfast all day long. It's what a lot of people feel safest eating when they travel." She sent the young waitress off with the order. "That wouldn't be decaf, would it?" When she came back with his coffee she brought a refolded copy of the morning's newspaper as well. "You can hide behind this till you feel better."

Dominick's bad night had begun when he left The Harp. The brandies and Guinnesses had mellowed him out to the point where he got lost in the backstreets of New Jerusalem on his way to the ferry dock. He stopped in another pub to ask directions and saw on the clock behind the bar that he had already missed the boat. He stayed for another shot and draft beer and watched silent sports highlights on the wide-screen TV above all the back-bar bottles. He seldom got tipsy anymore. Those Superman days were behind him, the pot and red wine then the cocaine and Stolichnaya years. He had forgotten this pleasant confident glow. Not until you get older and have learned to live with all the small and various pains of a body past its prime does the phrase *feeling no pain* take on any real meaning.

So, Sir John Starks thought that Dominick was just a made-up name of the moment. Maybe he should rename himself then. A new name to go with his new beard and northern exposure. Vladimir. He had always liked that name, but you needed an accent. How about just Nick? Shit, he could try out whatever he wanted until one clicked. But with whom? He introduced himself as Nick to the man sitting on the next bar stool, who couldn't have cared less if his name was Barbara. "The Celtics are going to suck again this year," he said.

The Harbor House Hotel was close by the ferry dock, which he found by remembering to always turn downhill when faced with a choice. He checked in around midnight. No, no luggage. He was suddenly very tired, and the soft hotel bed felt good when he hit it. But he was denied sleep. On the other side of his thin bedroom wall was another bedroom, this one occupied by a pair of heterosexual humanoids in a state of persistent lust. She was a yelper; he was a bed-banging groaner. In the time-outs between coital trysts they partied and laughed. Dominick couldn't bring himself to knock on the wall or complain to the front desk. Their use of a hotel room seemed more legitimate than his. He had just missed his boat. They were the reason his species prevailed. But he had a bad night nonetheless.

Breakfast was good. The news was bad. In addition to the front-page article there was an editorial denouncing the terrorist bombings, which somehow turned the LNG terminal project into a sacred patriotic commitment. The editorial questioned the naiveté of opponents of the project, warning them about their "anarchist or worse bedfellows." Atticus's group, Bay Savers, was mentioned by name. The editorial ended with a call for the authorities to spare no effort or expense in searching out the perpetrators and saving the bay community from further such atrocities.

Dominick caught the early afternoon ferry back to the island and walked to where he had left his car the day before. When he got home, Atticus and Lydia were there. Or at least their car was there. They were nowhere around. Then he noticed that the door to their room was shut. None of his business. Now, with daylight savings time over, the sun set a little after four p.m. It was disorienting. Rising late, as Dominick normally did, that gave him only five or six hours of daylight. That day's light was fading already, and he had done nothing. He went to his room, changed into his night clothes, and got into bed. There were no winter sunset bird songs, only some distant crow calls. Darkness came quickly and so did sleep.

Lydia was painting again. Her doctor in New Jerusalem had gotten her onto a new pharmaceutical regimen, and she had decided she wanted to return home and paint. Atticus seemed pleased to be back home, but tired. They both had aged—a click or two more frail and uncertain. Another one of those little folds in time where a week or two might as well have been a year for its effect. Dominick kept to himself as best he could. The house was frigid now in the mornings. They no longer ate together. A sort of hibernation had set in. Then one afternoon several days into their new routine, Atticus caught Dominick coming in from a run to the store and asked a favor of him.

"Lydia's been out in her studio for some time now. Would you mind walking out there to check on her? She just yells at me if I go out there."

"Sure."

"Then would you take her this tea as well?" Atticus had a tray ready with a teapot under a cozy and a cup and saucer.

Lydia's studio at the far end of the garden was unheated. Being just one end of a potting shed, it wasn't meant for habitation—all that uninsulated glass. She had an electric space heater there, but it wasn't turned on. Lydia was dressed in many layers—a long cotton nightdress over jeans and boots, a cardigan sweater beneath her green down vest. On her hands were her painter's gloves with the fingers cut off. In her ears were her iPod earphones, their white cord disappearing into a down vest pocket. Her back was to him. She must have seen his reflection in the windows, She couldn't have heard him come in. He could hear the hum and thud of the music from her earphones. She half-turned to look at him, a bothered look on her face. "Oh, it's you, whoever you are," she said a bit too loud. "Put it down anywhere."

On the easel in front of Lydia was the large pastoral landscape that Dominick had last seen her working at—cows and a distant windmill, with lots of sky. She had divided the canvas up with randomly spaced parallel horizontal and vertical lines, making different sized rectangles, which she was randomly filling in, Mondrian style, with solid blocks of deep Rothko-like colors.

Lydia watched Dominick curiously as he placed the tea tray on a workbench. She took off her ear buds. "Now, which one are you?" she asked.

"I'm Dominick, ma'am."

"Yes, of course you are, but which bitch are you married to, and why are you here spying on me?"

"I'm not one of your sons-in-law, Lydia. I'm a boarder, a friend of Atticus."

"And where is useless Atticus?"

"Atticus is busy up at the house. Why are you doing that?" Dominick stepped sideways to get a better view of the painting on the easel.

"Why, I'm fixing it, putting in the holes that I left out."

"So, those holes go through the painting?"

"Yes, those are the colors behind the painting. I was always too lazy before to show them."

"All right corners?"

"That's not my fault. It's so that other people can see them."

"I like it."

"Then here, you can finish up. It's all pretty obvious." Lydia handed Dominick the long-handled paintbrush she was holding and went to pour herself some tea. "I was getting bored with it."

Dominick stood there with the paintbrush awkwardly in his hand. He could see his breath. "I'm afraid I don't do my colors well. I'd ruin it."

Lydia poured herself a cup of tea. There was no sugar or cream on the tray. She didn't seem to miss them. "Tell me . . . I'm sorry; I've forgotten your name already."

"Nick," Dominick said.

"Tell me, Nick, does madness run in your family?"

"Not that I know of, at least nothing dramatic." He looked around for a place to put down the brush. "Mostly they die fairly young, though. So they don't get a shot at that late-stage crazy stuff." He laid the brush along the lip of the easel.

"So, you haven't had the chance to be much around mad people."

"I don't think they're called mad people anymore. Addled, perhaps, or people with special needs or of diminished capacity. The terms you hear most now are Alzheimer's and dementia."

"I like addled, and dementia has a nice sound to it, but what's wrong with just mad?'

"It could mean just angry, and only temporary. As a term meaning whacko, mad has lost a lot of power."

"Things do change, don't they?"

"Why do you ask?"

"Ask about what? Oh, about mad people in your family. Because I think I may be going mad, and I was thinking . . . you know . . . I don't know . . . that you might offer an opinion."

"What do the doctors say?" Dominick hugged himself, sticking his hands into his armpits. The dampness of the room sucked the heat from your clothes.

"Oh, the doctors don't tell me anything. They'll talk with Atticus, but what good is that? What could they know anyway except what Atticus tells them?"

"What is mad anyway?" Dominick was struck by how much Lydia's eyes resembled Angelica's—their distance apart, how there seemed to be no sockets surrounding them.

"I don't remember yesterday," she said.

"Perhaps it's not worth remembering."

Lydia looked at Dominick and laughed. Her eyes laughed, too. "I like you. You're freezing, run along. But I do hope you come to visit again." Still carrying her teacup she pulled a fresh brush from a jar of them beside the easel. "What color is a cow inside, in the dark, where no one can see it?" She dipped the brush in black and then red pigment. "How streaked should dementia be?"

There was no reason for Dominick to answer. Lydia already knew the answers. He left as he had come in and went back to the house. Atticus was waiting for him in the kitchen. Dominick assured him that his wife was fine, happily working away. "You know how artists are. They get lost sometimes."

It was a week before Dominick got back to New Jerusalem and the historical society museum. Hibernation. It was a Saturday, and for some reason he rose early and was out of the house in time to catch the midmorning ferry. John Starks seemed neither surprised to see him nor curious about his absence. The museum closed at noon on Saturdays, and Starks was just closing up for the weekend when Dominick arrived.

"I've developed your film. It's at the house. If you're not busy we can go there to get it when I'm done here." Starks was putting things away. "I've had Mormons in here all week doing genealogical searches. Did you know that if you are a Mormon you can save your ancestors who are already dead? Now there's a twist. You're not Mormon by any chance are you?"

"No, and I have no progeny, so I guess I will never be saved. What exactly does that mean, anyway? Saved?"

"Not sure." Starks went around turning off the amber lights inside display cases. "The opposite of lost, I guess."

"Don't you save things for later?"

"Well, they do call themselves the Latter-day Saints."

"Later or latter?"

"What's the difference?" Starks came back with his coat on. "By the way, the beard is looking much better. It's almost time to start trimming it. You should think about shaving your neck, though. That is so geriatric. Have you ever done this before?"

"Done what?"

"Grown a beard."

"No, never."

"It's coming in all white, you know. Do you want that?"

"It's just a disguise."

"Are you pretending to be hiding from someone?"

They drove to Starks's house in his Jaguar, the only car left in the parking lot. It was an old Jag sedan, maybe thirty years old. Its fawn leather seats were worn, but it drove well. In no time they were on the tree-lined roads outside of town. This was new country for Dominick—two-lane country roads winding around the fields of large estates, big old houses set up on knolls way off the road. They had the roads to themselves. They pulled into a paved driveway and parked beside what once had been the gatehouse or carriage house of the big ramshackle mansion farther up the drive. The first floor was all garages, but the second story was a residence. Wordlessly Starks led the way up the stairs at the side.

From the living room windows you could just see the ocean on the horizon. The room was furnished sparsely but with antiques, except for a long, low red sofa facing a fireplace. The ceilings were high and peaked and beamed. The only artworks on the walls were framed and matted photographs, all black-and-white. The broad-planked wood floor was polished and bare. There was a Spartan feel to the place, which surprised Dominick. At the museum Starks was so immersed in collectibles on display that one assumed it was his natural habitat, but here in his home it was all open space and clean sight lines.

"Make yourself at home," Starks said and headed off down a hallway. When he returned he had shed his overcoat and suit jacket and tie and was wearing a crimson old-style letter sweater, one of those ones with buttons down the front—unbuttoned—and with a large gold capital E on the breast. He was carrying a manila envelope, which he dropped on a table beneath the seaside windows. "Can I get you something? An ale or something stronger?"

"An ale would be fine," Dominick said. Starks kept on walking toward the kitchen. "What does the E stand for?" Dominick asked.

Starks answered from the next room, "Enfield Academy, one of the places where I went to school. This old thing is still the most comfortable sweater I own." He returned carrying two brown bottles of ale.

"And your letter was in?"

"Track and field, hundred yard dash. I always came in second. I like your photographs, Dominick. You have been doing this a while." He handed Dominick his ale and went to the table beneath the window. "I made contact sheets of all your rolls and printed out some eight by tens of a few that especially jumped out at me. I hope you don't mind. Sit down."

They sat at the table—old straight-back dining room chairs—but Starks didn't open the envelope. Instead he reached out and pulled toward him an ornately carved wooden box, which he opened, and took out a film canister and a long-stemmed pipe. "Home is the sailor, home from the sea, and the hunter home from the hill," he said. "Do you smoke, Dominick?"

The pipe was a beauty—a delicately decorated blue-and-white porcelain bowl with a slender, intricately worked pewter stem—an object from a place and time that no longer existed. "An opium pipe?" Dominick asked.

"Yes, very old, but only hashish to smoke today. Will you join me? My afternoon off."

Starks packed the pipe, and they passed it back and forth in silence, sipping their ales in between tokes to soothe their throats. The sun was trying and failing to break through the clouds. If it ever won, it would be a fine sunset. When the pipe was done, Starks set it back in its box. "Now for your photographs," he said, opening the manila envelope. "I'll tell you what I like about them.

"First, there are no people in them. Not only are there no people, there is no evidence that people even exist, nothing human at all. In a way they could be historical photos, as there are no temporal markers. They are timeless in that sense. But at the same time they are ahistorical because they are also placeless. They could be from just about any temperate zone place." Starks laid out three eight-by-ten prints from the envelope. Then he opened the carved box again, repacked the pipe, lit it, smoked, and passed it to Dominick. "This could be a Sung Dynasty crow."

"Second is your incredibly narrow depth of field, the tight focus, foreground and background all indistinct shades of gray." Starks retrieved the pipe from Dominick and took another long toke. "There are features within the frame that the viewer is denied the possibility of identifying. The tight focus and use of light creates multiple secrets while showing one thing delicately clear. This one, for instance." A lone bare oak in a foggy pasture—what is called a wolf tree—stenciled against a troublesome sky.

"Third is their anonymity. The photos are so cold and impersonal that not even the photographer is present. They should never be signed. It's like the omniscient narrator in prose, never projecting himself into the story, no need to."

The hashish buzz was so peaceful and familiar that it was like slipping into an old comfy letter sweater. Dominick saw what Starks meant in the photos, but he was more interested in what he could see out the window. The photos seemed like dim memories now. They were, after all, shots he had already taken. There were no trees in the view of sepia pastures rolling toward the sea, just as in the old photos. The sun was shining now on the ocean's distant horizon, a bright stripe like a strip of chrome on a two-tone gray '50s muscle car. This was a full-depth-of-field shot, not a true color in it. Of course, he didn't have a camera with him.

Starks was still talking. "Dustin Hamlin, the photojournalist, once told me that all good photographs were merely accidents, and that all a good photographer could do was increase the incidence of happy accident. You have a high incidence of such happy accidents here." Starks put down the pipe. "Perhaps happy is an inappropriate adjective for these; entrapping would be more accurate. Are you stoned?"

"Delightfully so, thank you. It has been a long time since my last pipe of hashish. Thank you also for your words. I heard them. I am humbled. Do you have another ale?" Dominick's bottle was mysteriously empty. The strip of bright horizon chrome vanished like that. Starks was no longer sitting beside him but was off in the kitchen. Time messing around again, skipping ahead like a poorly spliced film. Starks returned with two more ales and some bread and cheese. They sat and talked at the table—Dominick didn't remember about what— until the light was almost gone. Then Starks excused himself. He had an evening engagement back in town and had to change. He would drop Dominick at the ferry in plenty of time to catch the last boat.

It was biting cold on the deck of the ferry, so Dominick had it all to himself. The manila envelope with his negatives, contact sheets, and prints was tucked safely inside his denim jacket buttoned up to his neck. He found a seat in the stern as out of the wind as he could and lit up a cigar. He had been craving one since he'd put down the hash pipe. He watched the lights of New Jerusalem shrink into a spangled line between the blackness of the bay and the lighter darkness of the sky. The cigar was good. It warmed him. The night was good. It was his alone. Being stoned was good. How personal it made the world, almost small enough to care for.

Chapter 11

The hammering awakened Dominick. Then it stopped, and he went back to sleep, vaguely wondering what Atticus was up to. When he came down to the kitchen later in the morning he found out, only it hadn't been Atticus hammering. It had to have been Lydia. Nailed to the kitchen wall were four pieces of burned toast. The hammer and more nails were still on the table. As Dominick fixed his short pot of coffee and then sat and drank it he studied the crucified toast as if it were a piece of installation art or the start of some coded message. They seemed randomly spaced on the white wall between the stove and the doorway to the hall, at about the height that Lydia would nail them but not aligned in any way—an angry sort of graph in black-and-white.

Dominick heard someone coming up the steps to the back door. It was Atticus. He walked through the kitchen headed for the doorway to the hall with his head down, ignoring Dominick, who couldn't resist—"New art work?"

Atticus stopped at the hall doorway and looked at the wall. "Lydia got angry at breakfast."

It was none of Dominick's business, but again he couldn't resist. "Angry about what?"

"Why, angry at herself, angry about burning the toast. She nailed it up there to remind herself not to burn the toast."

"That might work. Or you could buy her a new toaster that doesn't burn the toast."

"She'd find a way to burn it. I think she likes the smell of burnt toast, one of those smells that brings back the past. That sense of smell, you know it goes straight to our brain stem."

"Our earliest brain, our snake brain," Dominick said, agreeing. "Burnt toast."

Atticus went on out into the hallway, then he returned. "Dominick, I don't suppose you could miss noticing that Lydia has been, well, a little stressed out since the raid and all. She's better now, but . . . anyway, I don't mean to impose or anything, and there certainly is no obligation, but, well, would you mind sort of keeping an eye and an ear out for her when I'm not around? You can say no if you want to. I'd understand. It's really not your problem, and she is fine by herself. It's just that I'll feel less guilty about leaving the house if I can think I'm not leaving her totally alone. Know what I mean?"

"Yes, I can understand that, Atticus. Rest assured that when I am here, I am here for Lydia. Though she seems fine in her own little world. Doesn't she have other friends in the neighborhood that she could visit with or who could stop by, lady friends?"

"They're all either gone for the season or dead, and she won't have the girls here."

"No problem. Where are you going to be?"

"I volunteered to do some patrol shifts. If there are enough of us, it won't be that often, but I will be on call."

"Oh. What exactly will you be patrolling?"

"Darby Point. We've taken on that duty, a twenty-four-seven sea patrol."

"We being?"

"Bay Savers."

"And why would Bay Savers be patrolling Darby Point?"

"To stop the bombers, discourage them, maybe even help in catching them. We'll just be out there incognito as it were, pretending to be fishermen or civilian boaters going about our business, but keeping an eye on the place and any unfamiliar boats in the area."

"Ah, Atticus, you don't have a boat anymore."

"I know that. I'll be on one of the fishing boats out of Larsen's Marina."

"Isn't that the place that got busted up in the last explosion?"

"That's right, right there in Old Grofton."

"But I thought . . . wasn't Bay Savers sort of implicated in that explosion? Anarchist bedfellows and all?"

"Oh, that's just the feds and the *News* talking. The locals know we had nothing to do with it. All the water people up there are against the terminal. Hell, Bill Larsen, whose dad owns the marina, is the Bay Savers vice president. Nobody who works the bay is going to blow up a bunch of fish. That's an act of war to those folks." For all his wrinkles and thinning white hair and geriatric shrinkage, there was still a lot of Boy Scout—make that Sea Scout—inside Atticus.

"These bombings have been bad for us. No politician can oppose something that is under terrorist attack. Our fund-raising has bottomed out. As far as cable news and the radio talk shows are concerned, we might as well all be Muslims. We've got to stop the attacks, try to prove it wasn't us or anybody else who has any real interest in saving the bay."

"So now our modern day Minutemen are defending the Hercules Corp's LNG site at Darby Point? Not exactly any enemy of my enemy . . ."

"Don't be dense, Dominick. This isn't war; it's politics."

"Politics with a private armada. If patrolling the waters off Darby Point is so important, why aren't the authorities doing it?"

"Good question. The Coast Guard hasn't increased its patrols. The State Police Marine Patrol doesn't do surveillance. The FBI guys all went back to their office in Boston. And the Old Grofton police don't even have a boat much less a marine patrol unit. The place is wide open for another attack. The first one probably came from the bay side as well. So we have to do it."

"Well, it would seem you have it all figured out then," Dominick said, getting up and taking his coffee cup to the sink. "But what about the cops? Won't your people look suspicious just floating around outside ground zero all day and night?"

"Like I said, the feds aren't there. It's not the Coast Guard's job. The only cops that might get suspicious are the Old Grofton police, but they're our partners in this."

"Partners? Protesters and police? How refreshing."

"Nobody in Old Grofton except the mayor wants that terminal there. In the long run it will only mean a handful of local jobs. The cops are dead against it. They know we weren't responsible for the explosions. They think it was, and I quote, 'a rag-head attack,' and they would like to get credit for catching them. But they have no marine patrol capabilities."

"So."

"So we cut a deal with them. We coordinate our efforts. They cover the landside; we cover the waterside. We stay in constant cell phone contact. Any collar is obviously theirs."

"What if the bombers don't strike again?"

"Then at least we've stopped them. But we think they will. That magic number three. They have to prove that they mean business."

"What if they do strike again and they're successful, and Hercules just decides to go somewhere else after all, somewhere they are more welcome?"

"That's too many future ifs for me, none of which I have any control over," Atticus said.

"Well, at least you'll be back on the water."

"So, you'll keep an eye out for Lydia then when I'm not here?"

"I will be sure Lydia knows that if she wants or needs anything, all she has to do is ask. Don't you think we should put the hammer and nails away someplace?"

The first few times Atticus was out on patrol, Lydia didn't even seem to notice that he was gone. She had taken to ignoring Dominick almost entirely, and he stayed out of her way. He was working his way through the local history books in Atticus's library and had come across one that was giving him some pleasure—a 500-plus-page, 1955 edition of *A Cruising Guide to the New England Coast*. He was slowly reading his way north from Long Island Sound to the Bay of Fundy, through shoals and crosscurrents and dungeon fogs, into difficult or piece-of-cake anchorages, with numerous narrative trips ashore to visit old fishing villages and historic sites. His style of sailing—excellent writing. There was even an appendix on "Birding Under Sail" that whetted his interest in photographing seabirds. The book was inscribed in brown ink on the title page, "To Atticus, With every wish for many happy hours together on our dream boat far from the madding crowds, Lydia, Christmas 1956."

Then one afternoon when Atticus was gone—not on patrol but at some meeting—there was the sound of an ambulance under siren leaving a house up their road. Dominick was reading in bed, fully dressed under the covers, making the run into Newagen, Maine: "Approaching from the westward, make the lighted bell in the middle of Sheepscot River and head for the houses in Cape Harbor. As you close in, pick up num 2 and leave it well to starboard. Head for a white cottage on the northern side of the entrance until within 100 yards of the northern shore. Then follow the northern shore eastward into the harbor, leaving the red beacon to starboard." Dominick wondered if the white cottage was still there fifty-five years later, if it was still white.

"Atticus! Atticus! Where are you?" It was Lydia downstairs, sounding panicked.

By the time Dominick was headed downstairs Lydia was standing in the open front door, looking out at the road. She was wearing her layers of studio clothes and her paint-smeared gray gloves with the fingers cut off. When she heard Dominick on the stairs she turned on him. There were dabs of paint on her face—French blue and ochre.

"Atticus. Where is Atticus? What have you done with him? I heard the ambulance. They took him away, didn't they? He died, and you wouldn't come to tell me. Why? Why wouldn't you tell me? I have a right to know. I'm his wife. I'm his widow. I have rights."

"Lydia, Atticus isn't dead. He's fine. He's just away at a meeting right now, that's all." Dominick stopped on the stairs.

"You, you whatever your name is, lurking around here like some angel of death. Why not take me now, too? Go ahead, call another of your ambulances to take me away. Then you can have this place all to yourself."

"Lydia, stop being a fool. Atticus is not dead. Atticus was not in that ambulance, which did not come from here. Besides, they don't turn on their siren if the person inside is already dead."

Lydia looked back out the front door. "That's right, they don't, do they? The ambulance didn't stop here? Atticus wasn't in it? He's not dead?"

"Right on all counts, Lydia. Just a little unnecessary panic on your part. Why not go lie down for a bit? Panics can be pretty draining. Atticus will be home soon, I'm sure. Just a meeting."

"You would tell me, wouldn't you? The wait is awful, waiting for him to die. Nobody tells me anything." Lydia headed up the stairs toward Dominick. He pressed himself against the wall so that she could brush by. "Yes, I am going to go lie down. It's so cold in this house, isn't it, Dominick? Why does Atticus keep it so cold? The old skinflint."

It was probably inevitable that one day Atticus would come to Dominick with an urgent request for him to crew on one of his patrols. Dominick had not told him about Lydia's ambulance panic attack. She had remained near invisible since, a silent housemate. At the very last minute, just as he was leaving the house, Atticus had gotten a call informing him that the crew mate for his patrol shift would not be there. It took a minimum of two to man the fishing boat on duty. No one else was available. Without a crew mate Atticus could not take the boat out.

"There would be nobody else out there all afternoon. Our ranks are getting a little thin," Atticus said. "It won't be like last time. The Lucy Anne II is a regular little fishing boat, with a heated cabin and all. I'd only really need your help casting off and tying up at the marina dock. We won't be going far, just back and forth in the bay outside the point."

Dominick looked outside. It was a clear, crisp December day, no wind to speak of. "How long?" he asked.

"Just a four-hour watch, till dark. There are more volunteers after working hours, just not many of us retirees to cover the daytime shifts. What do you say? You can bring what you want to eat and drink. Everyone else does."

Except for a few brief trips to the village, Dominick had not been out of the house since his last trip to New Jerusalem. The light was good. What would it be like on the water? With the big lens and the extender, he could try his hand at shooting seabirds. "What about Lydia?" he said.

"She seems alright, don't you think? Nothing too bizarre in days."

Dominick didn't know. "Hold on," he told Atticus. "Let me check." He found Lydia in her studio, where the space heater was turned on and she was seated in an old stuffed armchair, staring at a blank canvas up on her easel. In her lap was a gray cat Dominick had never seen before. Her ear buds were not in. "Lydia."

She looked up from petting the cat. "Oh, hello, Dominick."

"Lydia, Atticus and I are going to go out, some business to attend to. Will you be alright or could we drop you somewhere?"

"Drop me somewhere?"

"You know, if you wanted to visit someone. We will be taking the ferry to New Jerusalem, if you wanted to go see Ms. Arnold or anyone."

"I'm hardly dressed for visiting, Dominick, and around here we don't just stop in on people. We make dates well in advance. But thank you for asking. No, you and Atticus go ahead. I'll be fine."

"We'll be back by supper time, I think."

"Then bring back a pizza. I feel like pizza. What do you think of this painting?" she said with a nod toward the blank canvas.

"I think there's nothing there."

"I mean do you think I should just leave it at that?"

"No. I think you have to fill in the hole."

"Dominick."

"Yes."

"You know all those times I ignore you as if you're not there?"

He said nothing.

"It's because I can't remember who you are or why you are here. It's embarrassing. I know I should know who you are."

"What's the cat's name?" he asked.

"It doesn't have one, doesn't need one. Cats never answer to names anyway, so why name them?"

"We'll bring back a pizza then. What do you want on it?"

"Oh, mushrooms and peppers and little girls' fingers, extra cheese."

"Be good, Lydia. Fill in the blank spaces."

They went in Atticus's car. Dominick packed a quick lunch and a six-pack of ale in a cooler and brought his camera bag. He also took time to change into the warmest clothes he had. Atticus was eager to leave, but he had no choice but to wait until Dominick was ready to go. Old Grofton was a ways up the bay, a good half-hour drive from New

Jerusalem. Larsen's Marina was a place it would be hard to find if you hadn't been there before, on the other side of the tracks and through a ghost-town neighborhood of deserted old brick warehouses with every window broken. The Old Grofton waterfront was not exactly a happening place. Dominick stayed in the car while Atticus checked in with someone in the marina office.

The Lucy Anne II was a small, old trawler with a rust-stained hull. She was still set up for fishing and smelled of fish and diesel fuel. There was a single small wheelhouse cabin forward that was still warm from the previous shift and reeked of smoked cigarettes, a smell Dominick always found particularly unpleasant. Atticus started up the engine and took the wheel, while Dominick struggled with the bow and stern lines. The boat was like an old quarter horse who knew its routines even better than its rider and it pulled slowly away from the dock and through the other moored boats toward open water. Dominick joined Atticus in the cabin only to be sent back out again to pull in the bumpers.

"Do we have to pretend to be fishing or anything?" Dominick asked.

"No. Nobody to playact for. We just get a ways off shore and watch. We have every right to be here. We're not breaking any laws. If the Coast Guard cruiser does appear, I just pick up some speed as if we're going somewhere, just to avoid answering any questions. Nice day, isn't it?"

It was a nice day out on the water, the bay as calm as a pond and sparkling in the cold sunlight. When they were out maybe a quarter of a mile in the cove south of Darby Point, Atticus clicked the throttle back to idle and went out on deck with a pair of large binoculars to scan the bay and the point. It was an activity that perfectly suited him. On the ride to Old Grofton they had somehow gotten into talking about sports, and Atticus had let it out that he had played baseball in college—Dartmouth, class of '57. Like probably every college ballplayer, he had toyed with the idea of going pro when he graduated, continuing his youth indefinitely, but he went on for his MBA instead, married his cousin Lydia, whom he had known as long as he could remember. He had played shortstop, back in the days when shortstops were still short. But Dominick couldn't picture Atticus at bat or in a baseball uniform.

He belonged like this—legs apart, balanced, on the deck of a bobbing boat, binoculars up and steady, admiral of all he surveyed.

A small gang of herring gulls came to check them out. Dominick went out to study them as they hung in the breeze beside and above the boat. Then he went back into the cabin to get one of the sandwiches he had packed. He ate it back out on the fantail, sharing it with the gulls, occasionally tearing off pieces of bread or bologna or cheese and holding it out at arm's length. One of the gulls would glide down to take it gently from his fingertips. The bread seemed to be their favorite. Dominick went back inside and came out with a bag of potato chips and his Nikon with the big lens. It took some trial and error, but after a while the gulls got used to the idea that if they stayed around and did a fancy turn or two in flight there would be more chips coming. A gull that wasn't a herring gull—smaller, whiter, sharper winged—tried to join the potato-chip party, but was viciously repulsed. Dominick got some good shots of the attack.

It must have been the way the wind was blowing, but the helicopter was upon them almost as soon as they heard it, coming in low. It made one pass and then came back, buzzing them. Dominick wasted some film, clicking off shots of it as it went by. It was black and bifurcated in his view finder, like an insect, a wasp or dragonfly or something Amazonian. He and Atticus met at the cabin door. "What was that?" Dominick asked.

"Not a friend," Atticus said, clicking the throttle out of idle and up to slow forward. "Our side doesn't have any of those."

"And wouldn't yours be painted green? Where to now?" Dominick opened two ales and passed one to Atticus.

"Back to port, but first a little diversionary tactic." Atticus clicked the speed up another notch and headed for shore in the opposite direction from Larsen's Marina. Sure enough, the helicopter made one more pass before turning and heading inland. When it was out of sight, Atticus turned the trawler around and headed back where they had come from, running in close to the shoreline. "What the hell were you taking photographs of out there?"

"Just the gulls," Dominick said. "I've never been so close to gulls before."

"Filthy, useless birds, the definition of pests."

"Yes, they do seem to rule hereabouts."

Somewhere in the cabin a cell phone started making one of those disagreeable sounds that passed for a ring.

"Find that, would you?" Atticus said.

The sound got gradually louder until Dominick found the little black device in a net bag hanging on the back of the steersman's chair. He handed it to Atticus, who flipped it open. "Lucy Anne II," he said and then listened. "Yes, we just got buzzed." Pause. "Negative, no idea, no markings." Another pause. "Roger, we're coming in. We've been made. Can you get another boat out here? Something may be coming down." Atticus flipped the phone shut and handed it back to Dominick.

"I thought you said we were within or rights out here," Dominick said.

"Absolutely. Unless they decide to accuse us of being spies, and I can't spare the time. You don't want to flaunt your rights too often, because what the state giveth the state can taketh away."

It was another ale each before they got back to Larsen's Marina, where they tied the Lucy Anne II up where they had found her, dropped her keys at the office, and drove away without incident. It was still light out. They easily caught the last ferry back to the island and stopped for a takeout pizza at the pizza place in the village. Mushrooms and peppers with extra cheese.

Chapter 12

On one wall of the short entryway between the back door and the kitchen at Mt. Sinai there was a board with a line of pegs for hanging up coats. In warmer weather it was almost empty, but now it was almost full with the various outer garments they each needed for the variety of weather days. There was no mistaking whose was whose. As various as the weather was from day to day so was Lydia, alternating back and forth between a mutual world and one she occupied all alone. One morning she showed up in full makeup, which, seeing as she never wore makeup, was applied badly, making her look like either a very cheap whore or a corpse. But the next morning she was just Lydia again and remembered Dominick's name and didn't nail the toast she burned to the wall. She just automatically threw it in the garbage as if that's what one does with things that come out of toasters. Another day she mistook Dominick for the plumber and told him to go away, that nothing needed fixing.

Both Atticus and Dominick now just went along with whatever scenario was playing. That was easiest—both for them and for Lydia—and what harm could it do to indulge her? Dominick thought of them as circus days, never knowing what to expect. Then one day around lunchtime they all found themselves in the kitchen simultaneously. It was now the only room in the house kept warm, with the oven. Lydia was still in her layers of paint-spattered studio clothes, no earphones. She seemed as herself as she ever had. She wanted to talk and asked them to stay and sit down.

It was a long speech for Lydia. She wanted them to know that she knew sometimes she acted strange and that they put up with her and that she appreciated that. "I know I'm going batty, but I'm harmless, I think. You don't have to watch me all the time. I don't need a babysitter.

"Dominick, I have come to think of you as family, almost like the son I never had, and I am so glad you are here to help out Atticus and keep him company. You know, it's quahog season. Why don't you two go quahogging? If you catch them, I'll clean and cook them up."

Up to that point Lydia had been making sense. Dominick wasn't aware that there was any particular season for quahogs, those thuggish local cousins of clams, but finding them involved getting wet while slogging around tidal mudflats in hip boots with a rake and a bucket, not something even the looniest and hungriest of natives would do on a near-freezing late November day. "I think I will pass on that," he said.

"What? You don't like quahogs?" Lydia asked.

"To tell you the truth, they have always tasted to me like the last thing from the sea you would want to eat no matter how they were fixed, just a nasty chewy vehicle for neurotoxins."

"It's one of those acquired-taste things, I guess," Atticus said.

"How can anyone not like my quahog stuffies?" Lydia asked, sounding miffed.

Any further discussion of the relative culinary merits of bivalves was cancelled by the sound of a helicopter closing on and then hovering above the house. "Them again," Lydia said and went to the window. "Yep, the same black one." She raised an imaginary can of aerosol spray and pointed it at the window, making a hissing sound. Atticus and Dominick joined her at the window. The helicopter was the same as the one that had buzzed their boat. It circled again and hovered and then sped off. Atticus and Dominick exchanged a mutually bewildered look.

"Again?" Atticus asked.

"Oh, it was here the other day when both of you were gone, though it stayed longer that time. It got so low I thought it was going to land."

The phone in the front hallway started ringing, and Atticus went to answer it.

"I thought maybe I had imagined that helicopter, too," Lydia said. "It was one of my off days. I thought it was coming to get me, so I took Atticus's old gun outside and pointed it at them. That's when they left.

That seemed too easy, and it left so fast I wasn't sure afterwards if it was real or not. But now you've seen it too, so it was real."

Atticus came back from the hallway. "That was Angie," he said. "She's on her way here."

"Angie?" Lydia said. "You mean your lovely daughter Angelica? Coming here? What the heck for?"

"She said she is worried about us."

"Strange timing," Dominick said.

"If she wants something to worry about, she can worry about her face if she steps foot in my house."

"Lydia, dear, try to remember that she is your daughter."

"That's no excuse."

"And that, legally at least, this is her house."

"If she wants us out, she is going to have to carry me out dead or alive."

Dominick hated to interrupt this little skirmish. "You said she was on the way here. Where did she call from?"

"On her cell phone from New Jerusalem. She said she was waiting for the ferry."

"So, she could be here anytime. I should make myself scarce then."

"Why is that?" Lydia asked.

"Because I met with your daughter in Boston as Lord Witherspoon. If she sees me here, that game is up."

"And your car?" Atticus asked.

"She never saw my car, but the Virginia plates might make her suspicious that something was going on here. I'd best leave." Whatever bad news Angelica was bringing really did not belong to him anyway. It was Atticus and Lydia's problem, not his.

"Then I'm not staying either. Dominick, you can take me with you. I'm not setting eyes on that woman. Atticus, you deal with her. I'm going to change. Dominick and I are going out on a date."

"Lydia, really . . ." Atticus addressed her departing back.

"Can you deal with it, Atticus?" Dominick asked when they were left alone.

"Of course I can. She's my daughter. This is all overreaction."

"I don't like the black helicopters, Atticus."

"We've done nothing wrong. We have nothing to fear."

"Atticus . . ." Dominick didn't know what to say. "I'm going up to change, too. I'll pack a few things to take with me as well. I'll drop your wife back when the coast is clear, but I'll be staying away a few days until things have settled down."

"Sure, of course." Atticus went to the sink and started washing the few breakfast dishes still there. "I'll just straighten up a bit. It's been almost two years since I've seen Angie."

As Dominick was changing and packing he heard the helicopter return and hover at a much higher altitude than before. He didn't like the fact that they would see him leave. There was no tree coverage. He wasn't sure why he didn't like it. What would they do? Follow him? He didn't even know where he was going. If Lydia went with him, he couldn't leave the island because there would be no late boat back to return her home, and he wasn't about to check into a New Jerusalem hotel with her. But if he didn't leave the island, where would he stay? There was always Brenda and Charlie's. He knew where the key was. But that wouldn't be much of a hiding place, not from the feds. Dominick dawdled a bit, waiting for the sound of the helicopter to go away. It finally did.

Lydia was waiting for Dominick at the bottom of the front stairs when he came down with his rucksack. She was wearing a full-length mink coat, cut in an old sort of Betty Davis style with squared-off shoulders and wide lapels. He couldn't see what she had on underneath. She was ready to go.

"Let me get my coat," Dominick said. He turned toward the hall to the kitchen, where his denim jacket was hanging on a peg beside the back door, when he heard car tires crunching the driveway gravel.

Lydia looked out the window beside the door. "It's her," she said, "Massachusetts plates."

Dominick kept going toward the kitchen door. Lydia was right behind him. Atticus was drying dishes.

"Atticus, your little girl is here, and so, still, are we," Dominick said as he glanced around the kitchen for an escape route. Lydia rushed by him like a bear on the run and out the back kitchen door. The doorbell rang. "Stall her," Dominick said. He was still carrying his rucksack. The only other door out of the kitchen was the one that opened on the stairs down to the cellar. He could hear Atticus and Angelica exchanging greetings at the front door. He had enough time to settle himself and his rucksack comfortably on the top steps of the cellar stairs before closing the door behind him. The darkness smelled ancient, an unforgotten smell. For some reason it made him think of buried treasure and pirates.

Dominick heard Angelica's voice first as they came into the kitchen. "Daddy, why do you keep it so cold in here? See, this is why I worry about you. You're not taking care of yourself. It's freezing in here."

"Ah, it's not that cold, honey, but keep your coat on and I'll turn up the oven."

"Daddy, it is the twenty-first century. People do not heat their houses with their kitchen stoves. Where is Mum?"

"Oh, she is . . . um . . . out."

"Out? How can she be out? You're here. The car is here."

"I can't lie to you, Angie. When she heard you were coming she went out to her studio. You know she doesn't like surprises."

"She doesn't like me, you mean."

"She knows you are here. If she wants to see you, she will come in. Let's leave it at that, okay? It's good to see you. You're looking fit. I'll fix some tea. Have you lost weight? How's the hubby?" From behind the closed cellar door Atticus sounded like some adolescent on his first date.

"Daddy, I do not understand why you and Mum are not already at the condo in Florida. This is so silly, you just camping out here off season while the condo is just sitting there waiting for you."

"Angie, I happen to know you have rented the condo out for the season."

"Well, what was I supposed to do when you refused to follow the plan? Just leave it sit there empty, sucking up maintenance costs? I could cancel those rentals."

"No, Angie, we're busy here, and besides, someone has to look after the house, keep it up, show it to potential buyers, if there are any."

"Busy? You're busy? Busy with what? Your terrorist friends and their plots?"

The teakettle started to whistle.

"My what?" Atticus sounded truly mystified. "My terrorist friends and their what?"

"Plots, Daddy, their plots to blow things up and stuff."

"Angie, I don't know what you've heard or who you have been talking to, but—"

"The FBI, Daddy, that's who I've been talking to, the frickin FBI, about my parents and my property!" Angelica had jettisoned her daddy's-little-girl disguise. The teakettle was still whistling. "That's why I am here. Why I dropped everything and drove all the way here today, because the frickin FBI came to my house and asked me what the heck was going on here."

"Why would they . . . ?"

"Because I am the registered owner of the property now. They looked it up and found that out. And do you know why they care about that? Because if there are activities taking place here that are against their frickin Homeland Security laws they will seize the property. That's right—seize the property."

"Angie, I can assure you that there are no such activities occurring here. That's ridiculous." Atticus must have turned off the kettle because it stopped whistling.

"This is the FBI, Daddy. They don't make this stuff up. They don't lie. They told me that they have an ongoing investigation into an underground terrorist operation, including foreign agents, which they suspect is using this house as a base of operations in the area. They called them armed and dangerous, suspected bombers. They said that people in this house have threatened federal agents with guns, for chrissakes."

"Did they tell you they already raided us and found absolutely nothing?"

"They said a federal judge issued a search warrant, but that the group must have been tipped off because when the officers arrived only the elderly couple was here. The elderly couple—you and Mum, my parents! And my house being raided!"

"They found nothing, Angie, nothing for all their trouble and upsetting your mother terribly."

"They said that the absence of evidence only meant that the evidence was absent. Daddy, there is a grand jury looking into those bombings your group was involved in."

"Now, hold it right there, young lady. Bay Savers had absolutely nothing to do with those bombings, nothing. We have never threatened anyone. I can't believe you believe that."

125

"They have photographers, Daddy. They showed them to me—Mum taking a shot at them, you on board a boat with binoculars spying on the target site with another, bearded sailor taking photos with a telescopic lens." There was the sound of a chair being pushed back. "I want you and Mum and your terrorist friends out of this house immediately. The agents wanted me to come here and spy on you. They said that if I, as property owner, cooperated with them, they wouldn't pursue the seizure. But I don't trust them, or you. I just want you and your coconspirators gone."

"What coconspirators? What terrorist group?"

"I don't care if the place is empty, if it doesn't sell."

"Angie, will you listen to me?"

"No coconspirators? How many other people are living here? Whose black sedan with Virginia plates is parked in the drive? Who do all these man-sized coats by the back door belong to? Come on, Dad. I don't have to listen to you. If everything is so innocent, why all the secrets? You can't explain it away. It's not like you assuring me when I was six that there wasn't a giant slug beneath my bed that was going to eat me when the lights went out. Maybe Mum is right. What's the point of talking?"

Dominick had the impulse to burst through the cellar door and say, "Wait. This has gotten way out of control." Federal grand juries and children throwing their parents out of their house. Trumped up charges and exaggerations—more than a little bit out of control. Why not just blow open this whole Lord Witherspoon hoax? So then Angelica will know, so what? He stood up. But wait. So what? Angelica would tell the feds—she would have to—and it wouldn't solve anything. Angelica would just feel doubly duped and even more suspicious, and she would still throw them out of the house for sure. She was just aching for an excuse. The feds would just feel confirmed in their suspicion of a conspiracy going on—people switching identities—and that we—"the terrorist group"—were hiding the actual "Lord Witherspoon," the agent provocateur passing as an English noble, whoever he was. Had it gotten that far along? So that it didn't even matter if Lord Witherspoon existed or not?

It struck Dominick that Angelica had not mentioned Lord Witherspoon's name. Had the FBI not mentioned him to her as one of their suspect foreign agents? Of course, they had no way of knowing that she had met with His Lordship, and surely by now their British counterparts would have informed them of His Lordship's nonexistence. And he, Dominick, whose car was in the drive and whose coats were on the wall and who had been sitting in the dark ten feet from them—and whose member Angelica had recently attempted to fellate—might not have existed at all. Even in the photograph of him and Atticus on the trawler, he went unidentified, just "another, bearded sailor." Call him Nick.

Maybe it would be best if instead of bursting onto the stage, both Dominick and Lord Witherspoon vanished as far into the wings as possible. Way too many questions to answer otherwise. Maybe, as soon as the coast was clear, he should pack up all his things, load the car, and head south. Savannah was nice this time of year. He could rent a small boat and take more seabird photos somewhere his hands didn't freeze on the camera.

As it happened, any entrance Dominick might have made was preempted by an entrance from the opposite direction. Dominick heard the back door fly open and then shut, then Lydia's voice, sounding just like an outraged mother, "Of all the nerve. Of all the nerve."

"Mother! Mother, put that down!"

"Lydia! Lydia, stop right there. Now give me that. Hand it over."

"You come in here, you . . . you witch, out of nowhere, and tell us we have to leave our own house? I should have drowned both of you when you were born. So, you're on the side of the black helicopters, are you? Accusing your own father of all sorts of things. I rue the day I gave birth to you. Now, you get out of my house and stay out, or I'll take that sickle to your made-up face. Go on get out!"

"I do not believe this, mother. You wandering around the grounds in your mink. You threatening me with a garden tool. And what is this? Burned bread nailed to the wall? I'll have you arrested. I'll have you committed. I'll have you out of this house. You'll see."

"No, you won't, Angie." It was Atticus talking, sounding calm and in charge. "You won't do any of those things, not in this town, not while I'm alive. I think you better leave."

"I am not going to be thrown out of my own house!"

"I'll give your mother her sickle back."

"Daddy! Alright, I'll go. Who wants to stay in this freezing house anyway? But you have not heard the last of this. You are both crazy."

"Good riddance," Lydia said.

Angelica had one more pronouncement to make from the front hall, yelled loud enough that Dominick could hear it on the cellar stairs. "Everyone is against you, you know. You haven't a chance." The front door slammed.

Dominick waited a minute before opening the cellar door, and it was as if he were still invisible. Neither Atticus, who was studying the rusty dull sickle he was holding, nor Lydia, still in her mink and tearing the burnt toast off the wall, noticed him. He took a step into the kitchen, feeling like he was intruding on a private family moment. Then he saw the handbag on the kitchen table, a large, expensive-looking handbag. It had to be Angelica's. She had done it again. He wondered if she did it on purpose. Dominick stepped quietly back through the door and shut it softly behind him.

In less than a minute Angelica was back in the house and coming through the kitchen door from the hallway. Without a word to or from her parents, she grabbed her handbag and left again. Again the front door slammed. She sprayed gravel on the underside of her car as she gunned it backwards out of the driveway. It was like her curtain call, coming back for her purse.

It was like barnacles on a docked boat. If he stayed in any one place for too long, things just accumulated—clothes, books, stuff. Dominick would have to do some triage and jettisoning of things if he was going to pack and depart. He started right in on it. He was headed south, so the winter wardrobe could stay behind. He would chose just a few of Atticus's books to take on permanent loan. Then he heard the helicopter again, hovering high above. What in the world were they doing? The afternoon light was fading. Were they waiting for someone to leave, so that they could follow them? Where would their quarry go? To another coconspirator's house? There was only the one way off the island. Or was it just psychological? Trying to get someone in the house to panic and leave?

Dominick stopped packing and sat on the bed. Why had the feds sicked Angelica on them? She said it was because the feds wanted her to spy on them. But the fact that she did not live there and was not welcomed there made her a poor choice for spy. No, they recruited her and sent her in there just to stir things up, to increase the pressure, to see if they could make something pop, like shooting the cue ball into a cluster of balls with no particular objective in mind other than just breaking things up to see what happens. The purpose of the helicopter was to see if there were any immediate results from Angelica's visit and to apply some paranoid pressure from above. They knew they could be heard in the house. They were there to be heard.

Dominick realized that if he did leave, he would then become an individual focus of interest. It wasn't just the helicopter. The helicopter was just sort of the sacrament, the outward sign of their surveillance. They knew who he was and by now they would have discovered his credit card and banking records, his rap sheet from the old Florida bust. Who knew what else? They would follow and track him even if he slipped away. For all he knew they already had a tracking device on his car with hopes he would lead them to other terrorist cells, make their boring jobs mean something.

He unpacked what he had packed. Better to hide in plain sight and act innocent, at least for now. After all, he had to remind himself, he was innocent. When he decided not to leave, the helicopter left.

Chapter 13

There was a fireplace in the rear parlor at Mt. Sinai. From the looks of it, it had been well used in its day but not recently. Dominick asked Atticus about it, who said the chimney hadn't been cleaned in years. Dominick had seen the stacks of rather ancient-looking firewood under an eave at the back of the house. He hauled some inside and started a fire with papers from the recycling bin. Atticus had gone out. Lydia was off in her somewhere else world. The flue was cold and wouldn't draw, and smoke started coming into the parlor. So he crumpled up and piled on more paper and kindling until flames were licking up into the flue opening. He was counting on there being no birds nest or blockage farther up. Smoke was still coming into the parlor, so he piled on more kindling, trying to get the fire hot as quickly as possible. This would either work or become a smoky disaster. With a whoosh and plop a large clump of twigs and leaves fell out of the flue onto the fire and burst into flames, and the chimney began to inhale. He still had to air out the room, however. He opened a window and the door to the front hall and then the front door. A chill breeze swept through the parlor—the opposite intent of the fire. He went and put on his denim jacket and knit cap and returned to tend the fire.

What had Angelica referred to their living here as—camping out? Perhaps he should search the kitchen for marshmallows. But the smoke cleared quickly, and he closed the room up again. It would still take some time and fire tending before the room heated up at all, but now there would be an option to his arctic room. The parlor had cozy potential. He pulled a stuffed settee and a reading lamp over in front of the fire, then an end table and a stuffed wingback chair. He went to his room for his book and then to the kitchen for a glass of scotch. The parlor was warm enough now for him to take off his jacket and cap. He lit a cigar and settled back into the settee to watch the fire and enter a nicotine meditation.

The fire was like a pet that he fed and that in turn kept him company. As always the life of its flames was hypnotic. How basic was that? How all the way back did that go? Fire, the first psychedelic entertainment—just your mind and the inanimate dance of the flames. Campfires made myths tellable. What was TV but a hearth light flickering at you? But TVs were cold. They gave off no heat, no comfort. How many cords of wood was it Starks had said a New England farmhouse would burn in a year? All that staring into fires on early unfriendly dusks like this, all the questions to ask yourself, searching for elusive self-justifying answers.

One history everyone got to write was their own for themselves. Such histories were especially unreal, beyond inaccurate. Too much was too easy to forget, like the damage one left in one's wake. You never got to see that; you'd be long gone. As long as there was forward time to look ahead to, the past was just random memorable mileposts with vast blank stretches between them. All mirror images were vain. But then no one had a better view of your life than you. Anyone else had only a snippet here or a snapshot there, and everyone lies in their letters. Who wrote letters anymore? Probably these days they lied online, creating persona that existed solely in digital space. A life lived as a lie was probably best ignored anyway, like a Photoshopped image of a scene that never existed.

Lydia stuck her head in the hall doorway. "I smelled smoke," she said. "Is that you, Lord Witherspoon?"

"No, just me, Nick."

"St. Nick. Is it Christmas already?"

Ah, a pair of made-up lives, Dominick thought—St. Nick and Christ—celebrated together. "No, not quite. There's still time to wait. Come on in, Lydia. Take this chair by the fire."

"I'll get myself some tea. The fire is nice."

When Lydia returned, Atticus came with her, and the three of them sat in front of the fire—Atticus in the wingback chair, Lydia and

Dominick on the settee. They sipped their drinks and watched the fire as darkness settled in outside. Nobody spoke. They listened to the fire.

There was a school bus in the parking lot of the New Jerusalem Historical Society Museum, and inside was a class of students, maybe eighth graders. John Starks was busy, surrounded by kids. Dominick caught his eye and pointed to the case where the historic photo albums were kept. With a nod and a wave Starks gave him the okay. Dominick was only there to see if Starks had developed the roll of film he had dropped off several days before, but as long as he was there and had to wait he might as well look at old photos.

Dominick had taken his time walking from the ferry dock to the museum—a stop at his tobacconist and a few other shops, a circuitous route. Maybe he was just feeling self-important, but he had the feeling he was being followed. When he had walked onto the ferry he had glanced back at the dock and saw a man standing there in the cold, not in line to get on the boat, with one hand on his ear and talking into his shoulder. He was wearing city clothes not island clothes.

When they got to the New Jerusalem dock maybe another forty walk-on passengers disembarked with him. He split quickly from the crowd and headed up a side street. No one seemed to follow him. But at the top of that block was a square where all the streets up from the dock met, and there was a woman there in a blue down ski jacket talking on her cell phone. During his wandering to the museum he saw her several more times, window shopping, walking away across a street, waiting for a light at an opposite corner. She was a good-looking young woman, hardly more than a girl. Maybe that was why he kept seeing her. Did the FBI employ people like that? On the last few blocks to the museum he did not see her or he would have kept walking. So this was intro to paranoia? Black helicopters and pretty girls? Men addressing their lapels?

"You know, maybe you should just let your beard grow, it's coming in so full and white. Christmas is coming up. You could get a job as Santa Claus." Starks had seen the last students out the door.

"Ho ho. Maybe next year. I'm not quite ready for that role yet."

"Looking for anything specific today?"

"Actually, I was looking for photos of Darby Point. If that's what it was called back then."

"It was also once called Strawberry Point and then Fort Darby for a while. Hold on, I think there may be two or three Fort Darby photos, gunnery crew posed with their cannon sort of things, not your cup of tea." Dominick returned with a black archival box with loose prints inside and started flipping through them. "Might I ask why our photographer of birds is suddenly interested in Darby Point?"

"I was there photographing birds. That seagull roll of film I gave you. Just curious, you know, the way it looks now and the way it looked then."

"The birds have changed," Starks said. He had brought back to their table a manila envelope along with the archival box. He pulled out several eight-by-ten prints and laid them out. "These predators weren't there back then." They were the photographs Dominick had taken of the black helicopter as it hovered above the trawler. "Nice shots. Look how they match up." And Starks spread out a similar number of seagull shots in which the white-and-gray birds hung and twisted and looked at the camera just as the opaque helicopter seemed to. They both laughed.

"I was feeding them potato chips," Dominick said. "Probably not good for them."

The old-fashioned store bell above the museum door that jangled when someone came in made its sound. They both looked up toward the mirror at the end of the hall where you could see who was there. It was the girl in the blue down ski jacket, looking innocently around. Then the bell jangled again and a man entered, also warmly dressed.

"Customers," Starks said, "out of towners," and he went out to greet them.

Dominick picked up the prints of his photographs and put them back in the manila envelope with the contact sheet and negatives. Then he placed the envelope with the other old photos in the black archival box, which he closed up and put on the floor beneath the table. He wasn't sure why, but he was becoming sufficiently paranoid to suspect that taking photos of black helicopters might somehow be a crime. He casually got up and put on his jacket and cap and headed for the door.

He had to walk past Starks and the girl in the main hall. "Thank you for your help," he said without stopping.

Starks seemed mildly surprised but said only, "Oh, you're going? Well, you're welcome. Come back again."

The man who had followed the girl in was still standing by the door, his hands clasped behind his back, pretending to examine an old chart on the wall. As Dominick brushed past him to open the door, he couldn't resist. "Agent," he said both as greeting and farewell. The man didn't respond.

By now Dominick didn't care if he was being followed or not. He had to remind himself that he had nothing to hide. He headed out for and found The Harp and went directly to the quiet corner booth where he and Starks had sat. A different waitress. He ordered an ale and pulled from his jacket pocket the book he had brought to read on the ferry, a paperback collection of essays by the New England historian Samuel Eliot Morison. He was on his second ale and reading about clipper ships when Starks showed up and joined him maybe forty minutes later.

"If you're not careful you may end up as a member of The Harp's royalty as well," Starks said as he sat down. "I doubt any of these other customers have the FBI following them around."

"Maybe you will now."

"I've already been knighted. What's up, Dominick? Your sudden interest in Darby Point, your photos of the black-op helicopter, the FBI asking questions about you?"

"So, that girl was FBI then? She showed you a badge?"

"ID, Penelope something. She had bad breath, by the way. I'll bet their medical insurance doesn't cover dental." Starks was drinking Irish coffee again. "She asked what you were doing there."

"And?"

"And I told her the truth, that you came in and asked to see old photographs, that I didn't know your name, which I don't."

"Darby Point?"

"Never mentioned it."

"Developing photos for me?"

"She didn't ask."

"The guy with her?"

"He wasn't. Ukrainian gentleman, barely spoke English, just a tourist coming in from the cold. I suspect he had been following her around for purely prurient reasons. He stayed around after she left. I had trouble getting rid of him."

"What is the world coming to when you can't tell the difference between a Ukrainian tourist and an FBI agent?"

"I just wish you answered questions as well as I do," Starks said, getting the waitress's attention for two more drinks. "For instance, did you know that you are just about to miss the last ferry back to your Gilligan's Island?"

"I thought I would give them something to ponder."

"And perhaps give a few of our worthy public servants the chance to earn some overtime? Where will you be staying tonight, then?"

"Probably down at the Harbor House."

"No, come out to my place. I'll fix us some dinner and ply you with drinks. I want to get some answers out of you, hear your story. You are a mystery to me, Dominick."

There were in Morison's essays certain historic figures whom he especially admired—shipbuilders or captains—the surface of whose lives was so perfected that the men themselves became obscured behind it. They were notorious for their attention to order and detail, as if they had lived only to be memorialized, stuck in some maritime museum, a portrait with a name plate, very public but unknowable men. During the course of the evening at Starks's house Dominick came to view his host in a similar way. There was something so practiced and perfected about John Starks's solitary style of life that it drew attention away from the man himself, the way his polished wood floors reflected the light. The man's house was like himself—pleasingly calm and confident, uncluttered and open, but unrevealing. Perhaps what rhymed about such lives was their seeming lack of need. These were men who asked no favors, who needed nothing you could give them. There was no valence there, only self-sufficiency.

Frank Sinatra sang while Starks fixed dinner after another shared pipe of hashish and some ales. Dinner was simple, just salmon and salad. Talk was easy because nothing was forced or needed to be edited. Starks's candor eased honest banter, and topics ran the range of free association. They discovered they were within a year of age, but neither of them talked about their families or their youth. Men play this chess game of personal display when learning one another—move forward the pawn of a funny embarrassing memory, then follow with a rook's assertion, always guarding the hidden queen. It was established where each of them had been when they learned of Jimi Hendrix's death. Dominick had been at Oxford. Starks had been sitting in a café in Piazza San Marco.

However, when Starks asked about Darby Point and the FBI, Dominick found himself being evasive. The whole anti-LNG thing was Atticus's trip not his, and it didn't feel right discussing his host's politics. That would also entail entirely too much explaining. And as for Lord Witherspoon and the feds' interest in him, there was no point in going there at all. "It's all a matter of mistaken identity," he said. "I'm sure they will sort it out themselves."

"But how did you know that blonde was an FBI agent?"

"She was following me, and I'm sure it wasn't for prurient reasons."

"Are you some sort of spy? I mean, the helicopter photos."

"No, I'm not any sort of spy. I was out there on a fishing trawler taking seagull shots when it flew over us and then went back to shore, that's all. I asked the guy driving the boat where we were, and he said off Darby Point."

"Okay, we'll leave it there. You have every right to be evasive, and I rather like the lingering mystery."

Dominick excused himself to go outside and smoke a cigar. Starks said he appreciated that courtesy. There was a built-in bench on the small porch at the top of the outside stairs, and Dominick settled in there in his jacket and watch cap to smoke. There was not a light in sight in the landscape. Even the big house at the top of the driveway was perfectly dark, just a blacker shape against the night. A lovely chilly emptiness to meditate in.

About halfway through the cigar, Starks came out, wearing a parka and bearing two glasses of port. "You know, I envy you smokers your always available excuse to slip away."

"You've found us out. It isn't the nicotine we are addicted to, but the freedom from being around nonsmokers." He took a sip of port. It went well with the Churchill. "Tell me, John, what's the story of the big house?"

"It's known as Broadmoor. No one has lived there since my parents died. I keep meaning to burn it down, but there is always something else that needs to be done first."

"Family?"

"Only child. I'm not sure which one of them decided to go celibate after I was born."

"Why not sell it?"

"Because it's not mine. It belongs to the bank. I bought this piece. It's all I need."

"So, the Starkses are landed gentry."

"I have an ancestor who is acclaimed for killing more Indians than any other original settler hereabouts. There's a street named after him in town. He didn't rate an avenue."

"Ever go up there?"

"Quite often, actually. I kept a key. I check on things. There are many memories lurking in those rooms."

"Then why burn it down?"

"I'm of two minds about memories."

"So, you will be the last of the Starkses."

"Not necessarily a bad thing. There's a certain nobility in extinction, don't you think? The Aztecs, saber-toothed tigers, Tyrannosaurus Rex?"

"No stars tonight."

"You are a master at changing topics, Dominick. No, no stars, no moon, no sky. No anything out there really. If this was the first minute of your awareness, that would be your world—nothing and you, a nice dichotomy."

"You forgot my cigar, and the cold."

"See how quickly life gets complicated? It's freezing out here. I'm going in. Your room is the one with the light on down the hall. Goodnight, Dominick or whoever you are."

The next morning they stopped for breakfast at a working-class diner on the non-touristy part of the waterfront, another spot where Starks was a regular, although no one called him Sir John here. When the waitress brought their coffees all she said was, "The usual?" and Starks just nodded. Dominick just had coffee. He never ate breakfast. Eggs repulsed him, and it was as if his digestive tract needed longer than the rest of him to wake up. As it was, he was up long before his usual hour. Starks had awakened him as he was getting ready to leave. "Last Jag to town," he said as he shook Dominick's shoulder.

If Dominick did not eat upon rising, Starks did not talk. He was uncharacteristically quiet on their ride into town—not hostile, just silent. He picked up a copy of the *New Jerusalem News* from the pile on the counter beside the cash register when they came into the diner. This was his daily routine. Dominick was just along for the ride. He looked out the window as Starks unfolded and read his paper, thankful that no conversation was expected from him. This was an alien time of day for Dominick. Outside, people were bustling off to their jobs, most of them with their heads down against the cold wind off the bay. A few—mostly women—were talking into cell phones.

Starks had awakened him in the middle of a vivid dream that lingered still, like a freeze-action shot on a stopped video. It had been in full color, which was special. Maybe the hashish had something to do with it. He had been in the great cabin of a clipper ship on a starboard tack, the cabin tilted that way, the ship beneath him straining and shivering for extra speed. It was a fine sunlit cabin, the glow of polished oak. There were other people in the cabin with him. They were sharing a moment of relaxed satisfaction, as if an agreement had just been reached or a goal accomplished. Atticus and Starks were there, dressed like naval officers, and his father was there as a very young man.

In fact, they were all young, of an age. Dominick struggled to recapture what it was they had been celebrating. Was it a race they had just won? It was the feel of the boat that made the dream so real.

"Your Darby Point is in the news again." Starks said.

"What was it you called it? Strawberry Point?"

"The authorities have picked up a, quote, 'person of interest' in their investigation of the bombings there. You do know there have been bombings there, don't you? I mean, you can admit to knowing that."

"Yes, of course, the LNG plant or whatever."

"Well, it seems they finally have a suspect, or at least a lead."

"That's good."

"Not surprisingly, the young man has an Arab name."

"Ah, the usual suspects."

"Are you Muslim, Dominick?"

"Not that I am aware of. Wait, John. Why ask such a ridiculous question? Of course I'm not Muslim. What is it? The beard? Do I look like an imam or something?"

"One never knows these days. Of course, you do drink alcohol, but that could be just a clever cover. Before I woke you up this morning, you were talking in your sleep. It sounded like Arabic, like some sort of prayer."

"I was sailing a clipper ship."

"Oh, that explains it."

"I don't know any Arabic."

Starks started to laugh. The waitress came with his plate—two eggs over easy, bacon, toast, and hash browns. He put his paper aside. "Dominick, what do you expect? You persist in your mysteries. I get to make guesses. You are a tabula rasa. I get to invent things about you."

"Why?"

"Why not? Life's a game."

"Here. I will prove it to you." Dominick reached across and took a piece of bacon from Starks's plate and ate it.

"Okay, so I guess you're not Jewish either."

"Allah be praised," Dominick said.

Chapter 14

One of his names was Mohammed. An Art Institute student, he was the only person on the Bay Savers membership list with an Arab name. Atticus had never met the man, had no idea who he was. In fact, no one seemed to know anything about him beyond the fact that he was in federal custody. Find someone named Mohammed and arrest him. Oh, yes, he was Canadian, which made him an even more likely suspect somehow. A foreigner, in any event, not an American, thank god. The *New Jerusalem News* editorialists were quite relieved on that point. The idea of a homegrown New England terrorist had obviously unnerved them. The editorial even dubbed him "the non-suicide bomber," implying that he was too much of a yellowbellied coward to blow himself up with his own bombs.

When they left the diner, Starks had handed the newspaper to Dominick, who read it in the ferry waiting room. According to the front-page news story, Mohammed had been picked up by Homeland Security officers for questioning. He had not yet been charged with anything. He was not only a "person of interest" but also a "possible prime suspect," whose apprehension was "precautionary" and meant to prevent any more immediate bombings. An ICE Agent named Kaczynski was quoted as telling the *News* that the suspect had come under scrutiny when irregularities were discovered in his Canadian papers. It did not say why he was being investigated in the first place, only that the search for other possible unnamed coconspirators was ongoing. It was the editorial that mentioned the leaked information about Mohammed's Bay Savers membership—the group's brochures and bumper stickers had been found in his room—by innuendo implicating the group as the unnamed coconspirators.

When Dominick got home to Mt. Sinai, Atticus had not yet heard the news, and Dominick had to break it to him. Bay Savers had now been painted permanently with a big black brush. That was when Atticus started making phone calls to discover that no one knew this Mohammed. He had signed up on campus but never seemed to have come to a meeting. Someone was assigned the task of drafting a suitably irate response. Then Atticus headed off for an emergency meeting.

For Dominick it was a long-overdue town errand day—the laundromat, grocery shopping, the post office, the library to check his e-mail, St. Edgar's Church basement thrift shop. He needed a warmer winter coat. Real life. It was a suitably shitty-weather day for such tasks. He made a list and found Lydia to ask her if she needed anything from town. All she wanted was a bag of chocolate-covered doughnuts. "The cheap ones," she said, "the ones that never go stale."

Finally hungry, Dominick had lunch at the deli down by the ferry dock. This was one of the rewards for going to town. They made a good roast beef sandwich, and the place was staffed entirely by lovely young women. The deli was owned and run by women, and somehow they managed to hire only the comeliest local postadolescents to work there, girls with perfect skin in that magic potent flash between high school and first marriages. The girl next door you wanted to ravage when you were that age. Something to watch as you munched your sandwich and chips. And they liked being watched—male attention like sunlight on a young plant's leaves—they dressed to attract it. Dominick tried to recall how long it had been since he had crossed over to the old-man's spectator part of the game, from which any fantasy of actually being a player had been wholly excised. There should be separate words for a sport you can still actually play and for one that you can only imagine having once played. The girls' almost cinematic distance did not matter. They were still lovely to look at. One poignantly reminded him of his first and only wife. What was the name of that slim geriatric Japanese novel? *The House of Sleeping Beauties?*

While his clothes were in the washing machine at the laundromat Dominick went to the church basement thrift shop. It being a fairly miserable day, there were few customers, so he didn't feel rushed as he went through the racks of men's coats and jackets. He couldn't believe his luck. There was both a tan London Fog raincoat with liner that looked like it had never been worn and a well-worn but still sturdy dark-blue peacoat, and they both were large enough to fit him. He debated which to buy, then bought them both for twenty-five dollars. He wore the peacoat out of the shop, the collar turned up.

When he got online at the library, there were a couple of business queries to answer—"Yes, the Bugatti is for sale as is, even if it's not running"—and an e-mail from Angelica. It was a long e-mail, long and disturbingly intimate. She missed him, his company. She thought of him daily, wondering where he was and what he was doing. She wanted to fly over to London to be with him, if only for a few days and if she could come up with a good excuse to tell her husband. She had never been to England. What was his life like there? Did he have any children? She gushed and rambled on like this for half a page with no paragraph breaks and ended: "My menstrual cramps were severe this last period. I know it's because I never took that gorgeous cock of yours inside me and my pussy was punishing me for that."

Dominick leaned back from the computer screen and looked around him. All the other Internet computers at the long library table were in use. No one seemed to be paying him any attention. He wondered how secure his messages were here. Funny how in this instance secure meant private. Surely the library had rules against or filters blocking pornography, and Angelica was getting pretty close. He wasn't sure he wanted to read on.

But the next block of prose was about her parents, how much she loved them, how dear they were to her, how she worried about them in that big old house. "Old people just get so stuck in their ways. I know they would just love the condo I got for them in Sarasota if they would only go there." It was all Daddy and Mum and how they deserved a golden retirement. But—it took Dominick another five lines to reach the *but*—they needed one more incentive to move, which was knowing that the old family house (she refused to call it Mt. Sinai) would be loved and well cared for. This was where the nongenital part of Lord Witherspoon came in. If she was going to do what was best for her parents, she would have to be able to tell them that the house had a new owner as devoted as they were to maintaining it—Lord Witherspoon. It was the right thing to do, even if it meant her selling the house at a loss in a buyer's market. Her lovely parents didn't have that many years left to bask in Gulf Coast sunlight. So, she would be open to another bid from Lord Witherspoon—not as low as his first, but closer to that range.

Darling, just type a number out and send it to me and we can negotiate from there, maybe even face-to-face again in another hotel room with a lovely view. I long to hear from you. I imagine you out hunting real estate deals in countries I'd have to find on a map or on a safari somewhere hundreds of miles from the nearest computer. But do get back to me. That house means a great deal to me. I spent every summer of my youth there. Just think, when you own it you and I can make love in the big master bedroom where I used to watch Mommy and Daddy do it, peeking through a keyhole.

Dominick had to go outdoors. He wanted to smoke a cigar and think, but it was much too cold and wet outside to enjoy one, and there was nowhere public indoors anymore in this so-called civilized world to do so either. In his new peacoat and watch cap he stood for a while out of the rain in the shelter of the entryway. After the Boston visit with Angelica, Lord Witherspoon had pretty much vanished. Perhaps he had had a small say in the purchase of that other coat today, the London Fog, but generally speaking Lord Witherspoon might just as well have been out of the country. Dominick seriously considered leaving him there. A nonresponse to Angelica at this point might well be just as effective as responding and continuing the charade. That would be the reasonable thing to do. Kill Lord Witherspoon. He could even reply to her e-mail as someone else, an executor or relative, informing her of Lord Witherspoon's unfortunate demise in a Bulgarian car crash.

But then, how many such adventures did Dominick have in his life anymore? He may well be lashed to the mast of his superannuation when it came to the deli sirens, but Lord Witherspoon was being invited as a player out onto the court—or in Angelica's case was it a racecourse? What would it hurt to play along further? A sudden death could always end Lord Witherspoon's career whenever Dominick pleased. Let him live a scene or two longer into this caper. Angelica's athletic body was still unexplored. He returned to the library as Lord Witherspoon. What the hell.

Dear Angelica: I was thrilled, of course, to get your e-mail. Sorry for the lag in response. I have been, in fact, off on another family acquisition mission in the north of Ireland, godforsaken Donegal, where the dearth of sunlight is exceeded only by the lack of Internet cafés. The bottom has fallen out of the Irish real estate bubble. (Do bottoms fall out of bubbles?) To the extent that newly foreclosed developments can be had for a fraction of what they cost to build. Busy. I have no immediate plans of returning to the States, though your personal enticements might bend a man's resolve in that respect.

As per Mt. Sinai. I am touched by your concern for your parents' well-being, and I must say the family foundation is still interested in diversifying its holdings in New England. (Like my buying spree here in Ireland, it is a bit like buying the escaped empire back one piece at a time.) However, that being said, I must be honest with you, dear, and say that I have not received any authorization to augment our initial bid. BUT, but your personal appeal has not fallen on deaf ears, and I will pursue seeking an offer more in your favor. I cannot give you a new figure today, but I will get back to you soon. If only the market there would take a tick upward to justify our reconsideration.

You ask if I have children. No, no children. No wife. I am still waiting for the right woman to come into my life.

It was dusk before Dominick finished all his town errands. Shopping was last, with a final stop at the liquor store. It was only four o'clock, but the solstice was approaching, days were shrinking to less than nine hours of daylight. On his drive through the village he was surprised by all the Christmas lights—on houses, stores, trees. They seemed early.

Or were they? Whatever schedule they were on had nothing to do with his. What a special mixture of hubris and generosity were Christmas decorations. People spent hundreds of dollars decorating a public space—the outsides of their houses—for the pleasure of others, while at the same time taking part in a competition that drew attention to themselves and the extent—or lack—of their esthetic sense. Just the electricity bills for some of the displays had to be meaningful. In any event, it was another one of those impulses that remained a mystery to him.

He was at the edge of the village headed home when he remembered the one thing that had not been on his list—Lydia's chocolate doughnuts. He turned around and headed back to the food mart. He found her box of desired treats and resisted reading what was in them. On a table by the checkout line was an array of small, tabletop synthetic Christmas trees with tiny colored lights—the sort of thing you saw in offices. On an impulse he bought one. It was all of eighteen inches tall.

Back at Mt. Sinai Atticus already had a fire going in the parlor. Dominick set up his Christmas tree on the end table there between the settee and the wingback chair and plugged it in to the extension cord for the reading lamp.

Neither Atticus nor Lydia mentioned the tree. It was as if it had always been there or was meant to be there. That evening as the three of them sat in front of the fire—Dominick reading, Lydia knitting, Atticus just watching and tending the fire—the tree was like a fourth in their party. It was hard to imagine it not being there, but it wasn't like it had anything to do with Christmas.

"Tell me, Dominick, do you think of your body as your enemy or your friend?" Lydia looked up from her knitting as she spoke.

"I try not to think of it at all. I've found that is best." Dominick didn't look up from his book.

"But when we are young we love our bodies, the source of such pleasure."

"I still feel that way when I fall asleep."

"Then at some point they become an embarrassment. They stop us from doing what we want to do. They hurt."

"Is it all about pleasure or pain then?"

After a long pause Lydia said, "Yes, I think it is. That's what it is all about. It's really quite simple, pleasure and pain."

The big Bay Savers meeting was to be held on the mainland up the bay, in the evening. In the evening was the problem part. Atticus had to admit that for years his night vision had been getting gradually worse, but recently it had gotten so bad that he had to give up driving at night altogether. His solution was for Dominick to take him to the meeting. Only that would mean a night off-island for both of them, and Atticus did not want to leave Lydia alone that long. So Atticus called Ms. Arnold in New Jerusalem and had her call Lydia back to invite her over for the evening. Atticus had it all arranged before he informed Dominick of his essential involvement. "What else would you be doing?" Atticus asked.

They dropped Lydia off at Ms. Arnold's after catching the early afternoon ferry. Dominick used the excuse of not being able to find a parking space to avoid going in. He cruised instead, circling the block, or blocks actually. New Jerusalem, with all its two-hundred-year-old narrow streets, held the record for Do Not Enter signs. It could take blocks before you found a street going the direction you wanted to go. Another age-induced dysfunction, Dominick thought. By his third pass Atticus was back out on Ms. Arnold's stoop, waiting. "All quiet on that front," he said, getting into the car.

Atticus gave Dominick directions on how to get out of town, headed north on a main route. The ride was like a trip forward in time. Ms. Arnold's eighteenth-century neighborhood gave way to blocks of more stately nineteenth-century houses on larger lots, which yielded to suburban split-levels and ranch-style houses with fairway lawns and proud garages. Then came the omni-present of strip malls and drivethroughs and ubiquitous cement. Funny how the past was place specific and the present could be anywhere.

"You know, Dominick, I never asked you about how your visit with Angie in Boston went. There was all that other stuff going on, the raid and Lydia's . . . ah . . . little crack up."

"Have you heard anything more from Angelica since her visit?"

"No, nothing. But how did it go in Boston? Did you guys have a good meeting?"

"She was much more charming with me there than she was with you here."

"Oh, the feds had gotten her all riled up, that's all. She always was one to fly off the handle."

What else flies off the handle besides weapons, Dominick wondered. How would Atticus like to hear that his favorite daughter prided herself on the professionalism of her blow-job technique? "Did you know that your daughter races go-karts?" he asked.

"No. What?" Atticus laughed. This was good news to him.

"We met at a go-kart race course, between heats. What's with her husband?"

"Slim? I call him Slim. Haven't seen him in years. You didn't meet him?"

"No, we did not meet. Angelica and I did have dinner though, later, and reached a sort of agreement to continue our negotiations. I think we're on hold through the winter at least."

"You know, in the old days fathers had some sort of say over who their daughters married."

"It was seen as more of a real estate deal back then, feelings came second. But I thought her husband was a doctor. That is usually not a bad business deal."

"Slim? Yeah, he's an MD, but not worthy of her in my estimation. And he's a homosexual."

"Why do you say that?"

"Well, for one thing they haven't given me any grandkids."

They had wandered into territory where Dominick did not want to be. "Say, that meeting isn't for hours yet. Let's find a place to get something to eat. We have plenty of time." He had in mind a proper inn or restaurant with a bar, some place with a history, but for the longest stretch all they passed were fast-food places, twenty-first-century purveyors of impersonal fodder.

The Bay Savers meeting was at the Quanticut Yacht Club. Dominick stood in the back, in his peacoat and watch cap. He had been careful not to go in with Atticus. He had used the excuse of smoking a cigar to hang behind outside in the parking lot and watch the others arrive. He had counted the other men who had beards—none. He was not yet used to appearing in public as the white-bearded gent. He noticed that his carriage and gait had adapted to his new appearance—he walked slower, with his shoulders back, like an old guy looking for a fight. He wondered what General Washington would have looked like with a beard, a white beard, as white as that funky wig he wore in Gilbert Stuart's portrait of him on the dollar bill. No one would recognize him. Funny how beards went in and out of fashion, not to mention powdered wigs. Would they ever make a comeback? Much less as a sign of highest authority?

It being a New England meeting, it started promptly on time at seven, even though people were still arriving and the yacht club parking lot was full and people were walking from blocks away where they had to park on the street. Dominick had found a secluded spot to park his car between the shrink-wrapped hulls of hibernating yachts on an adjacent chandler's dock. Dominick slipped in and stood at the back of the hall near the main door. The few seats still available were up near the front.

At the Boar's Head Inn where they had eventually stopped to eat, Dominick had downed enough drinks to put him over the state DUI level. He was on this trip under protest. Atticus was one of the six people seated at a table in the front of the hall. None of them were wearing white wigs. There was only one microphone, and one of the others was using it, welcoming people, directing them to the still-empty seats in the front. Behind them was a computer projection screen on which someone was trying to find the right PowerPoint file.

The hall was unheated but warming up with the assembled bodies. There had to be fifty or sixty people there. Dominick had no real interest in the meeting—especially now with the PowerPoint setup, which meant someone would be reading to them what was already up on the screen, as if they were beginners in an English as a Second Language class—but it was colder outside and he had nowhere else to go. A seventh person joined the group seated at the front table, and with a start Dominick realized he recognized her—tall and catlike, black hair pulled back, cape and all. It was Queen Emma from The Harp. The meeting took on a little more interest for him. He looked around the hall more carefully. Maybe there were other people there he knew. And sure enough, standing by a side door, confiding to her cell phone, was the pretty young woman in the blue down ski jacket, Miss FBI Agent of the Month. She snapped shut her little phone and took one of the empty chairs near the front. He wondered if she had made him.

He also wondered how many other agents, infiltrators, and plants the feds had in the crowd. There would be three factions present—the feds and their friends there to learn what they could, those true believers clever enough to know that there would be moles among them and so would speak guardedly, and those true believers innocently ignorant of the game being played around them. The purpose of the meeting seemed to be to rally the base in the face of the new allegations against them and to reconfirm publicly the group's opposition to all acts of violence.

The sound system wasn't good, and some of the first few speakers didn't know how to use a microphone, so that there were calls for "Louder" and "Speak up" from the back of the hall. Queen Emma was introduced by her chiefly Indian name and tribe, both of which Dominick missed in the shitty transmission. People continued to come and go by the side door, but all was quiet by the main entrance where Dominick was standing. About the time that the PowerPoint presentation began, the sounds of a scuffle and raised voices came from outside. Dominick took the opportunity to slip out.

A TV crew had arrived and was being stopped by a group of men dressed like anyone else at the meeting. Dominick ambled into the shadows around the side of the building to watch. This had to be more interesting than the PowerPoint show inside. The TV crew—a cameraman, a sound man, and a female reporter—were putting up a protest about being denied access to the meeting, but they were also being pushed slowly backwards toward their transmission truck parked in the street. Dominick saw someone hold up in the reporter's face an ID case. The cameraman tried to film this but was stopped. There was no one in a uniform there, but they won anyway, and the TV crew returned to their truck. One man stayed there by the truck, while the rest of the posse—maybe eight or nine men—huddled together, some of them talking into their shoulders.

Dominick found an open back door to the hall at about the same time that the posse came into the hall through the side and main doors. Some man with a very good voice and a New York accent was telling everyone to stay where they were and not move. People were getting to their feet. Folding chairs were being pushed back and collapsing. A scuffle broke out near the main door. Someone was yelling into the microphone about constitutional rights of assembly and free speech. Dominick came up behind Atticus and tapped him on the shoulder. "Let's go," he said, jerking his head toward the open back door. "Party's over."

Atticus nodded his agreement, got up, and followed Dominick out the door. Two other people from the table followed them out. One was Queen Emma.

Chapter 15

It was a very fast boat, fast and sleek and clean inside the cabin. After a stealthy lights-out crawl away from the Quanticut Yacht Club marina, they had opened up to full throttle, and the prow of the speedboat rose out of the water and raced for the deepest darkness toward the mouth of the bay. Inside the cabin were Atticus, Dominick, and Queen Emma, all sitting in silence, feeling the rhythm of the wave tops the hull kissed as it bounced over. They were joined by the other man who had left the hall with them through the back door, whose boat it was. Dominick recognized him as the man who had made the opening remarks at the meeting, a small robust hairless man in a black turtleneck and a windbreaker.

Queen Emma spoke first. "This is all very nice, Theo, but why and where are we going?"

"Well, there was no point in staying there and being treated like criminals, was there? Besides, they were looking for new people to suspect; they already know you, me, and Atticus. But I don't believe I know this gentleman here, who provided us with our escape route."

"Oh, this is Dominick," Atticus said. "He's with me. I can vouch for him."

"Dominick, Theo Neisner." They shook hands. "Welcome aboard."

"But where are we going, Theo?" Emma asked again.

"There was no getting out of there on the land side, as Dominick here told us, but as luck would have it, I came by boat," Theo gestured to their surroundings, "so we could leave that way. Hold on a second." Theo left the cabin.

When they had come aboard, unpursued, Dominick had noticed a crew of at least two waiting for them, who had immediately untied the boat and gotten underway. Theo must be giving them instructions, because the boat slowed down and changed course. Theo came back. "Emma, I thought we would go somewhere out of harm's way and see how this develops."

"And where might that be?"

"I have a place on Teapot Island no one knows about, a nice private spot, just the one house and the dock. But it has everything we might need."

"For the night?"

"For the night at least, I'd think. Until we learn what this was all about and what the fallout is and how we should respond."

"But I'm parked illegally on the street back there," Emma said.

"We will get your car back for you, Emma, but not tonight."

"I need a drink," Emma said.

"The cabinet there above the sink is stocked," Theo said. "Help yourself. It will be about another twenty minutes. Dominick, can I have a word with you?"

Dominick followed Theo out on deck and then through another door into a smaller cabin with bunks and a fold-out table. Theo wasted no time. "You're Lord Witherspoon, aren't you? I remember you, without the beard, from our flotilla action. You were with Atticus, and it was Lydia who called me up and gave me your name to use in the press release."

"Lydia's grip on reality is not the best. She calls me many things."

"Okay, whatever. Look, I am going to frisk you. I want you to take off your peacoat and to empty your pockets onto the table first. If you have nothing to hide, you'll have no trouble doing that."

Dominick did as he was asked, and Theo gave him a very thorough, professional pat down. Once again, being touched all over his body was a foreign, strangely exciting sensation. On the table were just his car key, a money clip of folded bills, a cigarette lighter, a handkerchief, and the small leather card case with his driver's licenses and credit cards. Theo examined his peacoat and pulled out the burnished aluminum four-cigar case. "No cell phone, no wristwatch?" Theo asked.

"No weapons or wires either."

Theo opened the cigar case and sniffed. "Nice," he said. He looked at Dominick's licenses and cards.

"And no Lord Witherspoon," Dominick said.

"What's your game, then?" Theo handed Dominick's coat back to him and gestured that he could pick up his pocket things. "Why pass yourself off as Lord Witherspoon if you're not?"

"That was Lydia, remember? Not me. I just look after Atticus sometimes. I only came tonight because he can't drive after dark."

"You know I'd be a fool to just accept that as the whole truth and nothing but the truth, but there's not much I can do about it now. You're here. You're with us. But I'll be keeping a close eye on you. You understand why I can't wholly trust you?"

Dominick put his peacoat back on and picked up his things from the table. "Of course. And for all I know you are a fed and this boat was a drug-bust prize."

Theo laughed. "See, you think like a cop. Let's go join Emma in a drink."

"Maybe she is the fed among us," Dominick said as they left the bunk room.

"Nah, she wouldn't have worried about being parked illegally. Emma and her tribe have been with us since the git-go. She has no dark shadows. She gets a little horny when she's drunk, but that's about as dangerous as she gets."

A switch near the throttle turned the dock lights on. Theo was taking the boat in, himself. Dominick was standing beside him in the cockpit. The two crew members were out on deck. The wind had picked up, and the channel around Teapot Island was choppy. The dock lights moved up and down in the blackness off to starboard. "Not to worry," Theo said. "It's calmer inside the cove." Theo deftly maneuvered the boat up to the dock and the crewmen had her quickly bumpered and secured. Emma needed help getting from the deck to the dock, but no one got wet.

When they were all ashore, the two crewmen got back on the boat, untied her, and took off into the night. "She takes too much of a beating tied up here in these easterlies," Theo explained when Dominick asked. He was experiencing a strange new sensation—that of being marooned.

"Besides, she needs to be refueled, and if she's safe in her slip ashore and not tied up here, no one would think to look for us here."

There was a long flight of wooden stairs from the dock up a rocky cliff face. With the flick of two switches Theo turned on the stair lights and turned off the dock lights, and they headed up. At the top of the steps Theo flicked another switch and lights went on at a house at the top of a sloping lawn maybe thirty yards away. A gravel walk led to it. Theo switched off the stair lights. Behind them now was only darkness, not a light to be seen. Dominick noticed how closely they all were clustered together, almost touching. In fact, Emma reached over to hold on to Dominick's forearm as they started up the walk. They fell behind the shorter and spryer Atticus and Theo.

"What's your name again?" Emma asked.

"Nick," Dominick said.

"In my language nick is the word for shit. I can't call you that. I'll call you Nickel instead. Tell me, Nickel, what do you think of all this?"

"I wasn't prepared to be on the lam tonight."

"Got a late date? You can always call her and tell her you are stranded on a deserted island."

"No, I did not bring enough cigars to be marooned."

"Just don't tell her you're with me." Emma laughed, almost a giggle.

The house was lit just by twin porch lamps beside the front door. It was not a big house nor at all ostentatious, two stories but humble, the traditional saltbox design. As they got closer Dominick could see why its style seemed so traditional—because it was an original. The house had to be at least 150 years old. From its stone front stoop to its shuttered second-floor windows the house was like a projection of the past emerging from the gloom, getting clearer and more real with every step. What had struck him first as humility now seemed better defined as forbearance.

Emma tightened her grip on Dominick's arm. "Whoa. Stay close to me, Nickel. This place gives me the creeps."

Theo unlocked the front door and turned on a hall light, then went to a keypad on the wall to punch in the code to disarm the burglar alarm. The house was cold, but warmer than outdoors. Theo switched on other lights and turned up the heat at a thermostat in the hall. The rest of them stood clumped together just inside the front door, like kids entering a Halloween haunted house.

"The place was supposedly haunted once," Theo said, interpreting their obvious thoughts, "the keeper who died here in the '38 storm that took out the lighthouse. But I had a priest out here to do the full de-spooking thing. No ghosts since." Theo turned and led the way back to the kitchen, turning on more lights. "Something hot to drink, I think."

"So, this was the lighthouse keeper's house?" Atticus said.

"Yep, built in 1837 and abandoned a hundred and one years later. After the hurricane took out the light, they decided they didn't need one here anymore. They just put a light buoy farther out. Coffee, tea, cocoa?"

"And how did you . . . ," Atticus started.

"Estate sale. The island always had been private property, an old local family, but nobody wanted it. Basically, it cost me back taxes."

"Theo, you have liquor here? Or was happy hour over on the boat?" Emma had let go of Dominick and was prowling around. The kitchen, like the rest of the house they had seen, was sparsely furnished, sort of like a barracks or a public place.

With a key from his crowded key chain Theo unlocked some cabinets. "We're roughing it out here, Emma, only vodka or Canadian whiskey, and the cuisine is pretty much canned, but make yourself to home. Let's find out if there was anything on the news. Dominick said there was a TV news team there."

They left Emma in the kitchen as she fixed herself a drink and started looking through cabinets. Atticus and Dominick followed Theo through a swinging door into another room, which, when Theo clicked on the overhead lights, appeared to be an office with a couple of desks with computers and a big flat-screen TV. Theo unlocked another cabinet and threw some more switches. Off in the distance Dominick heard the dull throb of an engine start up. "Generator," Theo said. "Solar batteries won't last long with the heat on and all." The house was slowly warming up.

Theo sat down at one of the computer keyboards, and within a minute the flat-screen on the wall came to life, a car chase scene with lots of shots being fired. "Satellite," Theo said. "What channel was that news, Dominick?"

"The truck said Channel 4 News."

Another channel jumped up on the screen, another cop show. "They have news at eleven," Theo said, "another hour or so."

"All they could report is that they have nothing to report," Dominick said.

"Maybe the feds will have a statement to make."

"Theo, what is this place?" Atticus asked.

"My summer place, a space I can escape to but not disappear, still stay in touch."

"I don't sense a . . . ah . . . woman's touch," Dominick said. Nowhere in the house so far had he seen anything hung on the wall, any carpets or curtains, any fabric at all really—all tile and plastic and dry wall.

"No reason there should be. Not too many women visit. The place is a lot easier to maintain and keep clean without all that extra stuff."

"The soft stuff," Dominick said, agreeing.

"The beds are soft enough," Theo said, not looking up from his computer keyboard and screen, "but just sleeping bags, no sheets or blankets this time of year. The upstairs isn't too well heated, I'm afraid. In fact, I'm going to turn the heat down in here as soon as the chill is off the house. It's a big drain on the system."

Emma stuck her head in from the kitchen. "I found canned beef stew and some cabin crackers. Anyone else hungry?"

Theo stayed behind while Emma, Atticus, and Dominick had their late night snack. There was nothing about the Bay Savers meeting or the raid on the late night news, after which Theo declared he would stay up late to see what he could learn on the Internet. Emma had made a big dent in the Canadian whiskey and now wanted to call home, but announced that she had "no bars" on her cell phone. Theo admitted he had a satellite cell phone there, but that it was only for emergencies as he did not want calls traced back to it. Emma conceded that her not getting home that night would not be deemed an emergency, and Atticus also passed, on the grounds that Lydia in the care of Ms. Arnold was better off not knowing, and besides he couldn't remember the number. Dominick had no one to call. Theo took them upstairs and assigned them each their own bedroom and turned on the light in the bathroom at the end of the hall.

The rooms were like cloister cells or a dorm room at Kafka U—a single bed, a wooden chair, a two-foot-square table with a reading lamp on it, and in one corner a metal locker-room-style gym locker. There was a window, but the outside shutters were closed. The walls, the ceilings, and the locker were all painted an institutional off-white. There was nothing on the walls, although Dominick could easily imagine a crucifix above the bed or the portrait of some other fearless leader. Inside the locker was a rolled-up down sleeping bag, a hard pillow, and a towel. On the top shelf were some candles in a medal dish and a box of matches. Ah, minimalism, Dominick thought. He tested the door lock to make sure he would not or could not be locked in if he shut the door.

Dominick took inordinate comfort from the fact that the window and shutters opened. It might be a fifteen-foot drop to the ground below, but it was a second way out. One must always have more than one way out of anything, but tiny rooms rated up there. He unrolled the sleeping bag onto the mattress to let it fluff up. He was still wearing his peacoat and watch cap. He pulled the chair over to the open window, leaned on the sill, and allowed himself a goodnight cigar. He turned out the reading lamp behind him to see what he could see outside. The rest of the house was already dark, incognito. The Churchill tasted especially warm and sweet.

Beyond the window was black nothing, but an exceptional amount of it. Even the smell of the cold ocean was vast. From somewhere very far away on the bay, as if defining meaningless distance, came the hollow call of a foghorn. What an unsuccessful mating call that was, Dominick thought. Lonely loons on empty lakes sounded like better company than that. And here on Teapot Island there was no longer a lighthouse to answer. No wonder they were a dying breed, pushed to the edge of extinction.

There he went again, anthropomorphically sexualizing the inanimate world, a bad habit from which he should to try to wean himself, the stuff of mythmakers. What a fun job that would have been—the local mythmaker, supplying the etiological stories to explain and name natural phenomena, human origin stories because this would have been long before science and its alternate, inhuman stories. Yes, your ancestor dragged this island up from the sea as the wedding price for a goddess, which is why it is named after her. Yes, the same trickster god who was blamed when things went wrong was the one whose giant penis slammed into the mountain so that his people could scramble up it escaping attack. Yes, the moon gets eaten every month, which is why women bleed.

He would have a shaman's hovel on the edge of the settlement, to which people would come when they needed an explanation for something. And he would make up something satisfying, something that fit at least loosely into earlier stories. Let acolytes and future believers make sense of it, if they wanted to. As long as they had an answer they were happy. He would be paid in food and cigars and someone to come and take care of the yard and shovel the walk in the winter. The distant foghorn pled again.

His cigar was nearly finished when the door burst open behind him.

"Nickel! Nickel, is this your room? Where are you?"

Dominick switched on the reading lamp. It was Emma, wrapped in her sleeping bag.

"He was in my room. He came in and wouldn't leave. I had to run right through him to escape. You've got to protect me. My god, it's cold in here."

Dominick flipped what was left of the Churchill out into the yard, then closed the window. "Who was that?" He did not appreciate being jerked so suddenly back into the realm of other people's problems.

"The ghost, the old lighthouse keeper. He smelled like he'd been pulled up out of the sea." Emma made a shivering sound and dived onto Dominick's bed, burrowing beneath his sleeping bag, hiding her head.

Dominick went to look out into the hallway lit by the light through the open bathroom door at the end of the hall. Nothing there, but the hallway was a tad warmer than his room, so he left the door open when he came back in. "Nothing there," he said.

"A bad dream."

"It was not a bad dream," Emma said from beneath the sleeping bags. "Get your body in here and warm me up."

Dominick looked at the bed, which with Emma in it looked already full. "Move over," he said. "Make yourself skinny." And he sat down on the side of the bed. He took off his shoes and his peacoat, but left on the rest of his clothes and his watch cap. He turned off the lamp. It took a bit of arranging and shifting around, but he finally got both unzipped sleeping bags on top of them with Emma curled up spoon-style against his back. He left the door open to let in what little heat there was in the rest of the house. There was the smell of Canadian whiskey beneath the sleeping bags.

"I need a big man like you to sleep with to keep me warm," Emma said. She put an arm around him and tucked her knees into the backs of his. She too was still fully clothed except for her coat and shoes. "There aren't enough big men like you left, in my opinion."

"You know, Emma, we almost met once before."

"I know. At The Harp. You were with Starks. I took you for one of his gay sailor liaisons, but you aren't, are you?"

"No, I'm not."

Emma passed a hand gently over Dominick's face and beard. "No, you're not. You are a ladies' man. I can smell it."

"They call you Queen Emma there at The Harp." Dominick was talking into the cold, but his back, where Emma was pressed, was getting warmer. He shifted his weight and stretched. Emma moved easily with him.

"I wouldn't know about that. That's Stark's special world. Faggots like to think that they are special, some sort of royalty. Sweet Jesus, you smell so good, Nickel. And you are so warm." Emma cuddled even closer, pressing her nose into the beard beneath his ear.

This was all very good. Huddled together like this, they both would survive the night fine. But it had been a long time since he had shared a bed with anyone, much less such a narrow bed. He waited for his other brain—the one down beneath his waist—to kick in. This was, after all, a woman holding him, warm and purring as she went off to sleep. Would the shaman be paid with women as well? Once upon a time, *in illo tempore*, such proximity would have canceled all thoughts of sleep; testosterone would have accomplished the brain switch. But now he found himself drifting away himself, his eyelids heavy, his penis already sound asleep. Dominick's final thought as sleep caught up with him was that this was probably a good thing. The old initial genital handshake had gone out of style. All those obligations of performance were bypassed. All those half-truths and false endearments could go unsaid. The lack of urgency itself was welcome. Maybe part of getting older and wiser was no longer being in a hurry. Shamans always took their time. Emma moved slightly behind him, filling in what gaps were left between them. Sleep was sweet.

"Hey, hey, Nickel, wake up. I got to pee." Emma was shaking Dominick's shoulder. There was a dim gray morning light coming in the window. Emma was up against the wall and couldn't get out. Dominick had to sit up and put his feet on the floor for her to climb past. He got right back under the sleeping bag. Yes, that was snow swirling rather wistfully outside the window. Emma returned, and he had to sit up again to let her back into bed. She made herself comfortable. "Was it all the clothes?" she asked.

"All the clothes what?"

"I'm not used to going to bed with a guy and waking up in the morning unmolested."

"You thought I would . . . ?"

"I sort of hoped you would. But you never even started anything. You just started snoring. It's almost an insult."

"Sorry, no insult intended. I guess we both were pretty tired. And all the clothes, yes." Was he apologizing for not molesting someone, a stranger? "You could have said something. You know, asked or given me a clue."

"Nice girls don't have to ask, they just get drunk and let it happen. I may not be as cute or petite as I was twenty years ago, but I still know how to satisfy a man, even big guys like you." Emma's hand that had been resting on Dominick's hip now reached down and grabbed his genitals through his trousers. She kissed his ear and whispered, "How about one of those nice extra hard morning boners for me?"

Dominick rolled over onto his back to look at Emma, who was propped up on an elbow smiling at him. She had let down her long thick black hair. She leaned in and gave him a playful kiss, then another, more serious one. "I like your beard," she said. Her hand kneaded his already thickening member. In the next few minutes Dominick learned that Emma was wearing no underwear beneath her skirt and shirt and sweater, that her skin was smooth and her flesh soft and supple to the touch, that her nipples were large and black and hard as gum drops, that the lips of her vagina were wide and wet and loose and easy to spread and her clitoris could not—would not—be ignored. She squatted above him on her knees, straddling him. She loosened and pulled down his trousers and shorts, and as soon as she got his erection free and firm she gripped it with one hand and jammed herself down on it with a great moan, her head thrown back. She rode him like some rodeo bull. Yes, she needed a big man. He grabbed her flopping breasts, then her hips. With his thumbs he spread her outer lips and watched himself go in and out of her pinkness between the fur as she galloped and ground. Finally, she collapsed onto his chest as spasms spread from her groin throughout her body. "Oh, Nickel," she said, "have you come? Please come and show me how beautiful I am." She reached back and squeezed his testicles, pushing him as far inside her as he could go, and he came, a long and jerking orgasm as her vaginal muscles sucked every last drop of come out of him.

Emma stayed there on top of him, squatting on her knees, her head buried in the crook of his shoulder and neck, his cock still firmly inside her. He managed to pull a sleeping bag up over her back. They were very still, breathing together, with nothing to say.

"So, that's where you are, Emma." Theo was standing in the open doorway. "We don't allow this sort of thing here, Dominick or whatever your name is, taking advantage of this poor girl. This is a good Catholic household. No seducers or fornicators allowed. You will have to leave immediately." And Theo departed, slamming the door behind him.

After a half minute of silence, Dominick asked, "Are you Catholic?"

"Oh, Nickel, I'll be anything you want me to be, just don't come out of me yet. Can you get yourself hard again?"

Chapter 16

There was something eerily peaceful about being out on the bay in the snow. Start with the snow itself—large fluffy flakes drifting straight down with no wind, a uniform whiteness in all directions save down, where the surface of the sea looked like a piece of softly undulating obsidian silk. There was a stillness that swallowed everything—sight lines and sounds. The sharp-prowed speedboat was not speeding, so its passage disturbed little. Dominick and Emma were out on the deck. The cabin seemed all too confining inside this dome of porous whiteness. There being no wind, the air seemed almost warm.

Good to his word, Theo had immediately summoned his boat to come and remove the two fornicators from his Spartan Eden. There had been a breakfast of oatmeal and coffee and silence, Atticus clueless as to what was transpiring. Dominick thought Theo was acting like a jealous schoolboy, but no matter, as long as it got him out of there sooner. Emma treated them all as if they didn't exist. The stairs down to the dock were slippery from the snow. Theo stood at the top like some sort of avenging angel as Emma and Dominick descended. The boat was waiting, purring at the dock. Atticus would not be coming. Theo needed him there for the time being to help in the crisis. Doing what? God knew. Dominick helped Emma onto the boat. Theo had already turned and left.

Dominick and Emma were now pals. It wasn't the sex so much as the getting caught at it. If it hadn't been for Theo's interdiction, they probably would have parted amicably, happy to have had a warm bedmate for the night and a morning lay. But now as sentenced coconspirators caught in the act they were a pair as surely as if they were chained together. Not a pair of lovers, or even of friends, just a pair of pals, almost a Tom and Huck sort of thing.

True, Emma did make a joke about what a fine honeymoon voyage Theo had arranged for them. But they never touched one another, felt no impulse to. Emma left her sexuality in bed, where she let her hair down and lifted her skirt. Out here her hair was pulled back in a bun and she would show you who wore the pants.

"Did you really see the ghost back there?" Dominick asked.

"No, of course not. It was too cold for ghosts. I just wanted to get warm, and you seemed like the sole solution. But I needed a reason to burst in on you. What brand of cigar was that anyway?"

"A Romeo y Julieta Churchill. I have never been in snow like this before. Did you know that scientists think that all the H2O in the world arrived here via meteors?"

"That's hard to imagine."

"I know. That's why they call it a fact, so that you don't have to think it up."

"You don't get to talk to many people, do you, Nickel?"

"No, I guess not. I usually try to avoid it. But you're a chief, right? You must get to talk to a lot of people."

"Well, I'm just a small chief, not the big chief, and there are only several hundred members of our tribe left, and a lot of them don't live in the area anymore. No, my tribal work entails more running errands than talking."

"Are there many other women chiefs?"

"Not so many. In my clan I am the only one."

"What is Theo's trip?"

"Theo likes to control stuff, including people. Take Bay Savers, for instance. No one elected him chief. He just sort of took over, and everyone let him because no one else wanted the job."

"And you?"

"Because I slept with him a couple of times he thinks he's got a claim on me or something. No problem. That was probably my last Bay Savers meeting anyway. Theo will have to find himself another squaw."

"How so?"

"The tribal elders want out. It's the terrorist thing. They want to apply for a casino license, and being tied to a radical group being accused of bombings won't help. That place, Strawberry Point"—and here Emma gave its long native name—"was once our land, a burial ground because it was so well aligned with the stars. It's been desecrated enough, but that plant would be the final insult."

"Tribe looking for compensation?"

"Maybe. I can't say that wasn't part of it, but I was told by the elders to announce at that meeting that the tribe would no longer be part of Bay Savers. But Theo wouldn't give me a chance to speak at the start."

As the snow slowly lessened, visibility increased and with it the speed of the boat. Their passage now caused a stir, a snow wake, but the muffled world was still mute.

"Do you consider yourself a radical, Emma?"

Emma laughed. "What sort of radical? Here, hold this bomb for a sec, would you?"

"I don't know. A Native American radical, a tree hugger radical, a feminist radical, a free love radical."

"No, none of the above. But what a funny question. And if I was any of those, why would I tell you, someone I've just met and don't know? I went to the Bay Savers meetings because I was told to, as a representative of the tribe. None of the elders wanted to do it. If that is what you were wondering about. And if by free love you were referring to this morning's adventure, well, I don't think of having sex as a radical thing to do. Do you?"

"In chemistry a radical is an entity with an unpaired electron looking to mate."

"I never took chemistry, but I do like having sex. And if I was a Native American feminist radical I probably wouldn't be pairing my electrons with white guys like you and Theo, now would I?"

"Never thought of that."

"Ladies in my lineage have been screwing white boys a long time, Nickel. Why not? Sometimes they've got what we need. All the white blood in my veins—and there's a mix, going way back—started out as white sperm. There's not a single instance in my tribe of a white woman and an Indian mate. That would have been called rape in any case. Oh yeah, your hyper-pious forefathers here had red-skinned slaves as well as black-skinned ones, and they spread their seed around. My great-granddaddy's slave family name was Mather. They say he could almost pass for white."

Thanks to the onboard radar and GPS and the crew of two who knew what they were doing, the speedboat purred quietly back into the Quanticut Yacht Club marina under cover of snow. They were smugglers smuggling themselves back home. All was quiet. The boat dropped them off at a deserted outer dock and slipped away as silently as it had come. Dominick's car, now covered with snow, was still parked between the yachts in the adjacent chandler's lot. Emma's car had not been towed, though there was a parking ticket beneath the snow and wiper on her windshield. They parted there, and Dominick walked back to his car. It had been a long time since he had driven in snow. He found it a very disagreeable experience, even though not much had accumulated on the roads.

In New Jerusalem Dominick parked in a restaurant's lot and had lunch before walking to Ms. Arnold's. The snow was the kind that turned into slush on the sidewalks where people stepped so that they left personal trails. Dominick was trying to decide on a story to tell Lydia and Ms. Arnold. Would the truth suffice, or would that be too much information? What they already knew would help determine what else he would tell them. He stopped at a corner convenience store and bought a copy of the morning's *New Jerusalem News*. There was not a mention of the Bay Savers meeting or the raid. Okay, he could go with some innocent story of the meeting running late, Atticus staying to work, and Dominick too tired to drive back alone. All Lydia would want to know was where was Atticus, and Dominick would just say with Theo.

But at Ms. Arnold's house no one was home. There was a small envelope with Atticus's name on it pushpinned to the front door beside the brass knocker. The message inside read, "Lydia and I have gone to Boston Xmas shopping." So Dominick could save his story; he would have no audience. As he waited in line in his car at the ferry dock he flicked through the local radio stations, searching for news. Nothing.

Back on the island the snow had turned to cold rain, a sort of falling slush. Dominick's thoughts turned south again. He had forgotten how miserable winter could be. Really, there was nothing keeping him here, although he had nowhere else to go. Usually he had his moves planned weeks in advance, but he had been remiss the past few months and fallen out of contact with any of the people he might have wintered with or house-sat for. True, he could always just head for his mother's in Virginia. She was never really pleased to see him, but she was polite enough to let him stay there if he was in transit. There were always motel rooms, but he hated them, and there was not a bed and breakfast in the land where you could smoke a cigar. But there was nothing keeping him here. It was not as if he would be missed. Lydia had probably forgotten him already after only one day. Atticus could find another driver to his clandestine meetings. It was time for a change of scene, to something with palm trees.

The black SUV with government plates arrived at Mt. Sinai soon after Dominick did. He was making a fire in the back parlor when they came in. There were three of them this time. They were looking for Atticus. Dominick told them that he was alone in the house, but two of them went to search the house anyway. When the agent who stayed with him asked where Atticus was, Dominick told him he believed the Jamesons were away on vacation, perhaps visiting their children for the holidays. He was just watching the house for them. They left without even asking his name, which Dominick figured meant they already knew who he was and he was deemed unimportant, a mere factotum, a servant maybe. He got the fire going, then went out to bring in more wood. If the weather improved he would leave the next day. When the phone in the hall started ringing he decided to ignore it. But it would not stop ringing, so he went and picked it up.

"Atticus, this is Martha. Are you deaf that you could not hear the telephone ringing?" It was Ms. Arnold. "Atticus, you must come to Boston immediately. Lydia has had a little misunderstanding with the authorities. You have to come and bail us out. Officer, officer, where are we? District D4 station? That doesn't mean anything. Back Bay, yes, Hamilton Avenue? Anyway, Atticus, you'll find it. It's right by that big cathedral or whatever it is. Do you hear me, Atticus?"

"Ms. Arnold, this is Dominick. Atticus isn't here. He is still away on business."

"Well then, Lord Witherspoon, you will have to come and deal with this. Lydia will not allow me to call her daughter, who is right here in Boston. I'll expect you here immediately. Oh, and bring some identification for Lydia." And she hung up.

The grandfather clock in the parlor was chiming a half past something. Dominick went to check. It was three thirty. The last ferry back to New Jerusalem would just be leaving. So much for immediately, Martha my dear.

Dominick missed the first ferry the next day and ended up on the mid-morning boat. He took the main roads to Boston this time, which were cleared of snow but slick and crowded. By one o'clock he was searching for a parking place near the Back Bay police station. In a desk drawer in her room he had found Lydia's wallet, which contained, among other expired cards, a long-expired driver's license. He had stopped at an ATM and taken out the daily maximum of $400. The District D4 Police Station on Harrison Avenue was modern, redbrick, three stories, and could have passed for a high school classroom building. Dominick was pleased to find that Lydia and Ms. Arnold were still there and had not been moved to some other location overnight.

They had, in fact, been given their own private holding cell and a deck of cards, which Lydia returned to the desk clerk in exchange for her purse when Dominick checked them out. They had also been issued blankets and pillows, which were not commonly supplied at the precinct level. When Dominick had told the female officer behind the bulletproof window at reception that he was there to bail them out, he had been greeted happily and buzzed right in. The beefy desk sergeant filled Dominick in as he dealt with the paper work and paid their bail—only $50 each.

The ladies—as Desk Sergeant O'Shea referred to them—had presented a small problem. Normally, suspects brought in on minor charges such as theirs—shoplifting and interfering with an officer's duties—would be charged and booked, post a bond, and be released, all at the precinct. But the ladies had no cash to post their bonds, and one—Miss Lydia—had no identification, so she couldn't even be properly charged. They obviously were not dangerous criminals, and they reminded everyone there of aunties they would not be seeing over the holidays. They should have been sent downtown for overnight lockup, but the loud one, Martha, insisted that someone would be there soon to "spring them," as she put it. So the lieutenant let them stay, and the night shift took care of them. "Hell, it's Christmas," Sergeant O'Shea said. "They were no trouble. They got a lot of tea and Christmas cookies. So, are you this Lord Witherspoon Martha said would be here? She expected you last night."

Dominick did not like friendly authority figures, even overweight Irish cops. They made him suspicious and gave him the creeps. Some basic instinct instructed him to never converse with people in uniform. Always answer their questions with a question. "Is that it for the paperwork then?" Sergeant O'Shea either had not noticed or did not care that Lydia's driver's license was long expired. The sergeant went off to Xerox things. He took Dominick's driver's license as well, his Florida one with the address of an old friend who had since died.

When the sergeant returned he brought Lydia and Ms. Arnold with him. Ms. Arnold looked the worse for wear after a night in the lockup. Her blue-tint hair had lost its coif and her clothes were wrinkled. Lydia, on the other hand, looked fine, refreshed. She was listening to her iPod and smiling, off in her own private Narnia. Formalities completed, Dominick had them wait by the front door of the station while he went to get the car. In the car, Ms. Arnold started to give him a hard time about her having to spend overnight in custody because Dominick had not come immediately. Dominick reminded her that she had called him on the island after the last ferry of the day had departed. No matter, it was still his fault.

"What was the arrest all about?" Dominick asked. Surely she couldn't blame him for that.

"A mere misunderstanding blown up out of all proportion." Ms. Arnold was in the back seat, while Lydia hummed along to her earphone tunes in the front seat beside Dominick. "Lydia just forgot what she was wearing, that's all. But that security man at Anne Klein's had to make a big deal of it so he could feel self-important. Men. I swear, you give them any kind of control and they become monsters."

The disjointed and defensive account of the crime that Dominick slowly extracted from Ms. Arnold, when reconstructed, went something like this: They were just window shopping at the Copley Place

Mall. Neither of them had money to spend on presents. Lydia didn't even have a credit card. In Anne Klein's Lydia had taken some items off to a dressing room to try on while Ms. Arnold sampled different perfumes. When they went to leave, an alarm went off and this perfectly terrible man stopped them. It turned out that Lydia had forgotten which clothes she was wearing and was still dressed in unpaid-for Anne Klein creations. She had just liked the way her new clothes felt.

"But I just paid bail for both of you," Dominick said. They were on fairly open road now. The traffic out of the city was not as heavy as the inbound had been. The late-afternoon sun was trying to break through the clouds. Lydia played with her iPod.

"Well, I couldn't just let them take her off all by herself, could I? The train trip to Boston was my idea after you men didn't return the other night."

"And?"

"I made that man take his hands off her. You know how she hates being touched by strangers. And he just wouldn't, so I hit him with my purse a couple of times. Got him once down there, you know. At Anne Klein's of all places. What the world is coming to."

Dominick couldn't see Ms. Arnold in the rear seat in the rearview mirror, but he could see Lydia beside him. He realized now that one of the reasons she looked so fresh was the new, stylish, and very un-Lydia-like outfit she was wearing beneath her same old coat. "That outfit from Anne Klein would be the one she is wearing now?"

"That's right."

"So, you bought it after all. So what was the problem?"

"We never! I will never buy anything from that place."

"But how . . . ?"

"What were they going to do? Strip her right there? That man was in a hurry. Nobody knew where her other clothes were. I guess the store just wrote it off as they took us away. Which reminds me. I never did ask. Lydia, Lydia dear." Ms. Arnold leaned forward over the seat back to pat Lydia's shoulder, make her take her earphones out. "Lydia, whatever happened to the clothes you were wearing before?"

"Those old things? Why I hung them on hangers and put them back in the closet."

"In the closet?"

"Back where I'd gotten my new clothes, of course."

"You look nice," Dominick said.

"Why, thank you, sir. My name is Lydia," she said, extending her hand.

Dominick shook it. "Nick," he said. "Still Nick."

"I beat you at hearts, didn't I, Martha?" Lydia said without looking back.

"We weren't keeping score."

"But I remember winning," Lydia said, and she pulled out from somewhere in her clothes a playing card, which she held up, the queen of hearts. "You don't suppose they will miss this one little card, will they?"

By the time they got to New Jerusalem it was snowing again, a more serious snow slanting sideways in a steady wind. At Ms. Arnold's house Lydia got out of the car with Ms. Arnold. "Aren't you coming on home?" Dominick asked, but Lydia had her earphones in again and didn't hear him.

"She'll stay with me until Atticus comes to fetch her," Ms. Arnold said before slamming the car door and following Lydia up the front steps. Dominick didn't remember her saying thank you.

He just made the last ferry. The metal grate between the dock and the deck was slick with snow. The van in front of him skidded sideways going up it. Dominick dreaded having to follow him, but he made it, creeping in low gear. His car was the last vehicle they allowed aboard. The ferry crew was in a hurry. Visibility on the bay was shrinking. Dominick was not looking forward to the drive off the ferry and the trip home to Mt. Sinai. He hated that sensation of sliding and slipping and having no traction, that sense of having lost control. He bought a cup of coffee at the concession stand in the top-deck cabin and stood with a handful of other anxious, silent passengers peering out the front windows at the snow blowing at them in the dying light as the boat headed out at quarter speed. It was dark when they disembarked—Dominick last on last off—and he skidded off the ramp onto solid ground.

The streetlamps made cones of white swirling air as Dominick left the village and headed for home. Well, home for at least another day or two until the weather let up and he could leave. He wouldn't be driving in this, given any choice. About halfway home, well out of the village, Dominick's headlights picked up a figure at the side of the road trudging head down into the blowing snow. He or she was going the same way Dominick was headed, so he pulled to a stop along side to offer a ride. Only when he buzzed down the passenger side window did Dominick recognize Atticus. "Give you a lift, sailor?" he asked.

Dominick got the fire going while Atticus fixed a pot of tea. Theo's boat had dropped Atticus off at the village dock. When Dominick hadn't answered the phone at the house, Atticus had had no choice but to hike it. There were no taxis available in the village at that time of year. Atticus was full of Bay Savers news. The fed's case implicating them somehow in the bombings was falling apart. They had had to let Mohammed go—well, they did deport him back to Canada—but that proved they could find no evidence strong enough to hold him or connect Bay Savers with terrorists.

"I don't suppose it's possible for federal agents to do anything illegal, but the raid on our meeting was totally spurious. No judge would give them a warrant to raid a public meeting, and their only probable cause was looking for other members with questionable immigration status. That's why the news blackout. We've got a bunch of lawyers in the group who were there, and they didn't let those agents get to second base with questioning anybody, much less taking anyone in. The Federales really overstepped. We may even sue them for trying. We are well on our way to vindication."

Wasn't that telling? Dominick thought, poking a log back into place to burn like a proper log. The folks who set out to save the bay can count as a victory escaping a charge of blowing it up. How far off the original mark was that?

Atticus was animated. He asked once about Lydia, whom, Dominick informed him, was still safely at Ms. Arnold's. He decided not to give Atticus the rest of the news about Boston and all. Did Napoleon worry about what Josephine had for lunch back in Paris?

They went rummaging for supper in the kitchen, Atticus still going on. "Their case is so busted they are going back to looking for the

fictional Lord Witherspoon. Theo loved this part. At their press conference today when they had to admit to letting Mohammed go, all they
could say was that they had other leads they were pursuing, including
someone passing himself off as one Lord Witherspoon. They never
once mentioned Bay Savers by name. We are off that bogus hook, I tell
you. They won't mess with us again, fucking feds."

Dominick fixed them grilled cheese sandwiches.

Chapter 17

Dominick went through the list—who knew Lord Witherspoon? There was Charlie and Brenda, of course, and Atticus and Lydia and Ms. Arnold; none of whom were going to go running to the feds saying It's Dominick! There were the realtors they played with in the summer, but all they could say was that a Lord Witherspoon had been looking at houses in the area. Then there was Angelica. What would she do when she heard the feds were looking for him? What could she tell them? That Lord Witherspoon had made a bid on her property, that she had met with him once in Boston. But that would only get her more entangled with the feds and her property suspected as being possibly involved in illegal activities. There was no good reason for her to go to them, and she couldn't connect Lord Witherspoon to Dominick. He would probably be getting an e-mail from her, though, canceling any deal on the house. That was it, wasn't it? Starks didn't know. Wait—Theo knew, but he was hardly going to reveal that his fake lordship had helped him escape from the raid. Bay Savers had to have nothing to do with Lord Witherspoon, and the longer he was on the lam the better for them. No, as long as the feds couldn't make the connection between Lord Witherspoon and Dominick, let them search all they wanted. Besides, no crimes had been committed by either Lord Witherspoon or Dominick, and he knew that as long as no charges had been brought against him, avoiding being interviewed was not against the law.

He was half through his grilled cheese sandwich when it hit him. That Boston desk cop, Sergeant O'Shea, had asked him if he was Witherspoon before taking his driver's license off to Xerox. Even though Dominick hadn't answered the question, O'Shea could, probably would, make the connection to the fed's announcement. The Florida address on the license would be useless, but they had Lydia's and Ms. Arnold's addresses on their booking records. Dominick got up and walked to the back porch door and turned on the outside light. The snow was still coming in sideways. It hadn't let up. Pretty soon they would be snowed in.

"I have to leave, Atticus."

"What? In this? Where would you go? If this is about the feds saying they're looking for Lord Witherspoon, forget it. They only said that because they had to say something, just spin. How could they track him here anyway? Don't be silly."

"Then I will just give them a bit longer to prove their disinterest." Dominick went up to his room and packed as quickly as he could. He ended up making several trips out to his car with armfuls of clothes and piling them in the back seat. An emergency exit. He had done it before. There was always stuff you missed. When he had finished he found Atticus back in the parlor with the fire.

"Atticus, I don't want you lying to the feds, so I'm not going to tell you where I am going. Just tell them I left and you don't know where I went."

"They won't come here again," Atticus said. "Why would they?"

Dominick didn't have time to try to explain. "They'll be back. Whatever they ask you, answer them honestly, just don't volunteer anything."

"Why are you doing this?"

"I'm not sure, Atticus. I know it is time to move on is all I can tell you. I wish you luck with your protest and all. Best to Lydia. Now, I've got to get going before I can't get out."

"Wait." Atticus got up from his wing chair beside the fire and came over to where Dominick was standing by the parlor door, his shoes and pants legs melting snow onto the floor. He gave Dominick a hug. "Let me hear from you," he said matter-of-factly. "You want a gun? I've a pistol hidden upstairs."

"No, no guns, thanks. I'll be in touch."

Dominick had to rock the car back and forth a few times to get it loose, but the driveway was downhill to the road, and in reverse he had enough traction. A few more cars had gone down the road since he had come home, and he stayed in their tracks to the intersection, where the going got easier because there had been more traffic. The roads were all but deserted now. He saw only four other sets of headlights between Mt. Sinai and Charlie and Brenda's house, where he shifted to low and plowed right up the driveway to their two-car garage. He retrieved the hidden house key and in the kitchen found the keys to the garage right where they should be. He got the door up and pulled his car into the space Charlie had vacated when he left, beside his summer car, the yellow MGA. He got the garage door closed again and hauled all his stuff into the house. By the time he was done, the blizzard had almost erased his tracks up the driveway. He turned up the heat and turned off all the outside lights. The darkened house inside the storm was like a perfect tomb. Dominick reclaimed his old bedroom. Just to make sure, he checked the phone, and it had been turned off for the season. He retired with a fine sense of relief. He dreamed of Queen Emma. It was all about looking for exits.

The next morning was brilliant and frozen. The snow had stopped, but the sky was almost as white as the landscape. Nothing moved, nothing sparkled. The world was a matte black-and-white photograph, with only the lee side of trees and power poles black. Dominick ventured outside as far as the porch to take photographs while his coffee was brewing. There was nothing alive besides himself. This was his idea of heaven. He spent the day eating, drinking, reading, napping. The cable TV connection had been shut off for the season along with the phone, and if there was a radio in the house Dominick didn't go looking for it. So his removal from the world was doubly blessed.

He returned to reading the collection of Morison's essays, but after a while the know-it-all voice became tiresome. Luckily, he had brought other books from Atticus's, one of which was Carl Sauer's *Land & Life*, a collection of his papers about American geography. Sauer's cold prose suited the situation. In Sauer's world there was the pleasing assumption that man was just another passing natural phenomenon, that the rise and fall of Homo sapiens as a dominant species would occupy in geologic time but a tiny fraction of the time that dinosaurs reigned. There was one chapter entitled "Seashore—Primitive Home of Man?"

Dominick copied out a passage from it in his quotes notebook:

> *Ranging from beach into shoal water, from wading to swimming and diving are steps that Professor Hardy has invoked to explain certain characteristics of the human body, such as the symmetry of his body, the erect and graceful carriage, the loss of body hair and development of hair on the head, the distribution of subcutaneous fat, the streamlined hair tracts.*
>
> *It is a curious fact that no other primates appear to have taken to living on seashores. . . . Most primates seem not to forage in water, and some do not swim at all.*
>
> *May it be that by seaside living our physiologic system established its particular needs of iodine and salt, its apparent benefits from unsaturated fats, and its inclination to high protein intake?*

Dominick satisfied his sudden craving for fish with a can of sardines from Brenda's well-stocked larder. By sundown the sky had cleared.

The next day brought bright sunlight and snow melt from the roof, forming icicles on south-facing eaves. By midday a snowplow had passed down Charlie's street and one or two cars ventured out. Dominick stayed inside and read about nascent culture in the last deglaciation.

The third day after the storm it rained all day, a very mournful insistent rain that melted away most of the snow except for the mound the plow had pushed up along the edge of the street. The morning of the fourth day after the storm was clear and almost balmy, an invitation out. The snow was largely gone. Dominick showered and on an impulse chopped away his beard and moustache and shaved. It took him two disposable razors. The battery in Charlie's MGA was dead, but Dominick found a set of jumper cables in the garage and started it up with a charge from his car and let it run. Instead of dressing like Nick he dressed as Lord Witherspoon in proper slacks, a turtleneck sweater, and the London Fog raincoat he had yet to wear. From the hall closet he borrowed one of Charlie's hats, a tan trilby. He drove into the village in the yellow MGA.

His first stop was the barber shop, where he received an almost military haircut and a better shave. He then checked his post office box—nothing—and stopped by the library to check his e-mail. There was news from his agent and his accountant that the sale of the last of the antique cars had been successfully finalized. The sale, thanks to the sheik, had fetched more than anticipated, and the funds—minus fees—were now safely stashed in interest-bearing accounts. As long as the country stayed solvent and his lifestyle did not change, Dominick could coast to forever now. There was nothing from Angelica at his Lord Witherspoon address, so he was successfully disappearing as well.

He shopped to replace and augment what he had taken from Brenda's larder and Charlie's liquor cabinet. He stopped at the drug-store to buy a pair of dark glasses and some magazines. He resisted picking up a copy of the *New Jerusalem News* as well, though he did check the front page banner to see what day of the week it was. He had lost track again. It was a Thursday. No one seemed to notice him. If he could remain invisible here, perhaps he would stay a bit longer. At least he had a familiar bed to sleep in and he was free of the unwanted domestic entanglements at Mt. Sinai. Having a house all to himself was a plus.

The next day, Dominick drove back to the village in the MGA and parked on a side street near the ferry. Dressed in what he now thought of as his Lord Witherspoon disguise of London Fog, tan trilby, dark glasses, and best clothes, he took the midmorning boat to New Jerusalem. No men talking into their lapels or blondes with bad breath in blue down ski jackets followed him. He needed cigars, and he wanted to retrieve that last batch of photos and negatives that he had left behind at Starks's museum.

Also, he had to admit that he was feeling a flush of excitement and satisfaction, blending in with the crowd of his fellow anonymous passengers as they boarded the ferry and found seats in the heated cabin. He had brought a magazine to read but he could only pretend to read it. He was too absorbed in his fellow passengers and what was and was not going on around him. He was enjoying his camouflage—disguised as what they were looking for, aka Lord Witherspoon, not Dominick or Nick or Nickel. Hell, he had to admit he enjoyed being Lord Witherspoon again, enjoyed the distance that gave him. Distance from what, he was not sure. His clothes felt good on his body. He felt alive, like a total stranger among strangers, passing for one of them. Maybe he should have been a spy, proper employment for a solitary man. Your mission, if you choose to accept it, is to prove that you are a fictional character and therefore uncatchable.

Lord Witherspoon had lunch—oysters—at the Trafalgar, the fanciest eatery on the waterfront. He paid in cash and left a big tip. He strolled up to the central square and stopped in a gallery featuring oil seascapes in fancy frames, paintings suitable solely for hanging in galleries. He stopped in a swank men's haberdashery and purchased a pair of kid gloves and a reversible silk and wool scarf—items his costume lacked. At his tobacconist's he bought a box of Churchills. He was only blocks from Ms. Arnold's place, so he detoured past there. One of the parked cars he walked past on her block had its motor running and a man and a woman sitting in the front seat looking bored. They paid him no attention.

At the New Jerusalem Historical Society Museum Starks did not recognize Dominick when he walked in. Dominick stopped in the hallway to study a display of harpoons. "There is a coat rack by the door, sir," Starks called out from his unseen station in the library room. "We keep it warm in here." Starks enjoyed that invisible voice bit. Dominick hung his outer garments on the antlers then returned to the harpoons, his back to the mirror where Starks could see him, ignoring the invisible voice. Soon enough Starks came out into the hallway. "Welcome to the museum, sir. If there is anything specific I could help you with, just ask."

"Actually, John, I just came to pick up those photographs I left here and to settle up my bill with you," Dominick said, turning around to face him.

Starks took a surprised step backwards and looked Dominick up and down. "My god, you are a bloody spy after all."

"I'm headed south," Dominick said. "That requires a slightly different presentation."

"I'd wondered what had happened to you. Headed south? Good choice. Come on in," and Starks led the way into his library office. "What photographs you left here? I wasn't aware you left any."

"That last batch you developed for me, the seagulls."

"And the black helicopter, yes. I thought I gave them to you. They're not here."

"Oh, I didn't take them. I hid them before I left, in the archival box of photos we were looking at, the ones of Strawberry Point."

Starks made a strange noise in his throat and went off. He came back with an archival box and opened it. There was Dominick's manila envelope. Starks handed it over. "No storage fee," he said. "And forget about owing me anything for developing them, just chemicals and paper, a public service we supply for spies."

"Thank you, John."

"How about you buy me a drink instead?"

"A bribe?"

"Precisely."

"Capital idea. The Harp?"

"I'll close up shop early, meet you there in, say, an hour?"

The phone was ringing. Starks went to answer it. Dominick stuck the envelope of photos into the plastic bag with his box of cigars and let himself out, tinkling the bell above the door. The wind off the bay had picked up, and he raised the tall collar of his coat against it. He was glad for his new scarf and gloves.

Dominick again took the corner booth farthest from the bar. He ordered a pint of Guinness and a shot of Jameson's. He had his magazine to read. It was still early; the place was quiet, just a murmur of conversation from the patrons along the bar where a muted flat-screen TV played a soccer game. It was less than an hour before Queen Emma arrived. She was obviously searching for someone. Dominick just watched over the top of his magazine. She scoped out the bar patrons once, then ordered a drink. As the bartender poured her a glass of red wine she asked him a question, and he shook his head as he answered. Was she looking for Starks, Dominick wondered? Emma sat on a bar stool with her back to the bar, a very unladylike pose except that her ankles were politely crossed beneath her long skirt. She surveyed the room again. There was nothing tentative about her walk across the room, but there was nothing definite either. It was like a stroll through a garden as she made her way to Dominick's booth. She reached out to touch his trilby and coat and silk scarf where they hung on the hook outside his booth. "Nice threads," she said, "but I think I liked you better when you looked less respectable, less groomed. Why didn't you say hello, Nickel? Didn't you know I was looking for you?"

"Hello, Emma. Just trying out my new disguise. Why would I know you were looking for me?"

"Well, isn't everyone? May I?" Emma slid into the booth seat opposite Dominick.

"And why would you look for me here at The Harp?"

"No mystery there. John Starks called me and said you would be here."

"And why would John Starks do that?"

"Because I asked him to contact me if he heard from you."

"And why would you do that?"

"Because I want to help you."

"Help me? Help me do what?"

"Why, hide out, of course. God, you are such a white guy, shaved and with that haircut and those clothes. You look like a Republican."

"Emma, I don't know what you think you know, but—"

"Theo told me all about it," Emma interrupted him. "He called me up, delighted to be able to inform me that my 'new lover' as he put it was now the feds' primary terrorist target. My 'new lover' being 'Lord Witherspoon'—and I said both of those inside quotation marks."

"What is it about Theo?"

"I don't think you two hit it off well. A couple of days later he called me back to let me know that the feds had also put it together that you were Lord Witherspoon. I don't think he told them. Why would he? In fact, he called me the second time to tell me to forget that he had mentioned you being Lord Witherspoon and if the feds questioned me to tell them I knew nothing of Your Lordship or any connection he might have with Bay Savers. He said that's what he told them."

"The feds have questioned Theo?"

"Oh, yes. Theo and Atticus and everyone else identified as 'sitting at the head table'—as they put it—at that meeting they raided."

"Including you?"

"Well, they've had trouble finding me, so not yet."

"Have any charges been brought?"

"Not that I know of. Why?"

"Because if no charges have been brought then you don't have to talk to them."

"Why would the feds want to question me anyway? I don't know anything. They've already gotten me in enough trouble as it is."

"How so?" Dominick motioned to the waitress to bring them another round of drinks.

"No, don't," Emma said, pulling his hand down. "Let's go."

"But I'm supposed to meet Starks here."

"Yes, I know. Starks expects to meet both of us here, the two people left that the feds haven't questioned, the two most likely suspects left. Well, fuck them. I don't trust Starks, and I don't want to talk to the feds."

"Finish up then, and we'll go. Though I think you are being more than a tad paranoid. Starks?"

"Just a feeling. The questions he asked. He seemed to know things he shouldn't have known. Listen, Nickel, the feds went to my family looking for me. That wasn't good. It spooked my dad and the other elders. They are trying to come across squeaky clean to get the okay for their casino, and the feds are investigating one of their chiefs? They threw me out, disowned me. They had to. I have no place to go. I thought I might hide out with you for the time being till this sorts out." Emma still had hold of his hand, the one she had pulled down from motioning the waitress. "There is more, but not here. Let's go before Starks and whoever he is bringing with him arrives."

Dominick got up to collect his things and put on this coat. "What time is it?" he asked. Emma pulled out a cell phone and told him. "We still have plenty of time to catch the late boat. We can eat somewhere."

Emma was helping him on with his London Fog. "No, not the late boat. If they don't find us here, they'll be watching that. Can't we catch the next one?"

"Barely," Dominick said, cinching his coat and putting on his hat, "but we can try."

"Different doors," Emma said and she gave him a peck on the cheek.

Emma went out by the back door onto the alley. Dominick left through the front onto the street. The weather had worsened again. He headed straight down for the ferry dock. No one was following him The legs of his best pants were getting soaked. What a miserable place to live.

Only because the ferry was delayed by the weather did they make it, Emma four or five people ahead of him in the line. On board they ignored each other, and disembarking Dominick lost sight of her entirely. Alone he walked to where he had parked the MGA and started it up, but two minutes behind him Emma arrived and lowered herself into the passenger-side seat. "Lord Witherspoon," she said.

"Queen Emma," he answered.

Chapter 18

It really took less than a day, but Dominick let it go on because he didn't know how to end it. If he had had a chance to turn it down out front, he would have. Oh, the sex was alright the first night, but in a well-heated house he didn't need a bedmate. Some part of Emma's body was always in the way when he wanted to roll over or change positions. She seemed much larger asleep. Also she talked in her sleep—gibberish mainly but disconcerting nonetheless because he would lie awake trying to decipher what she was saying. So, it was not a good night's sleep. Dominick was happy when Emma got out of bed sometime after the sun came up and he could stretch out in his full bed with all the pillows.

But he didn't get to sleep much longer. No sooner had he rejoined his dream than Emma was shaking his shoulder. "Hey, sleepyhead, Nickel, wake up. What's the secret with the TV set? I can't get it to work. I gotta have my morning news."

"Emma, I must warn you. I can be a very cranky person when woken up. The TV set does not work because the cable is turned off for the winter." Dominick rolled away from her.

"What? That too?"

The night before, Emma had gone searching for a computer so that she could check her e-mail while Dominick was fixing something for a late, light supper, and he had told her that there was no computer in the house and that, in fact, the phone line was disconnected for the season. When she pulled out her cell phone instead, Dominick had to ask her to turn it off. "They can trace your calls here, at least to the neighborhood. That's hardly hiding out. No, turn it off. You don't need it."

"I don't believe this. The cable too? How do you know what's going on?"

"I don't. Now go away and let me sleep."

But she wouldn't. She wanted coffee and something for breakfast. She was jumpy and jittery, like someone going through withdrawals. His makeshift breakfast of oatmeal, toast and marmalade didn't suit her either. She wanted eggs, but of course Dominick had no eggs. The day continued apace with its start. All of Dominick's plusses for his hide-away—the seclusion, the silence, the freedom from electronic intrusions—were minuses for Emma. Bored to distraction, she prowled the house. By midmorning she was hitting the vodka, first with orange juice, then straight on the rocks. She spent a while in the garage, listening to the radio in Dominick's car, but that didn't satisfy. A car radio is not interactive. Changing the station is your only control. There was nothing to look at. She came back in to where Dominick was reading at the kitchen table and asked if he wanted to screw. She was looking for something to do. "No, thanks," Dominick said, not just then.

She was beginning to drive him crazy. This was not working out. As a houseguest, Emma was hopeless. And now she was getting drunk, breaking the houseguest's second commandment, thou shall not get drunk on your host's booze. The first commandment about sleeping with your host or hostess she had already broken. He would see how long it took her to get to the third and ask him for a loan.

Dominick disliked tending to drunks, but over the years he had had to do it often enough, starting with his mother. He warmed up two cans of chunky soup for lunch and put out a plate of bread. Emma ate when the food was put in front of her. She was at the entitlement monologue stage, where the drunk seeks through the telling of self-serving anecdotes to establish his or her right to be so self-absorbed. This can be revealing in so far as what incidents of camouflage are chosen. The drunk dresses herself in pieces of her past, laced together with lies of omission. Emma's costume was a typically charming one. The illegitimate daughter of an unemployed chief, she had been farmed out as a child to a Puerto Rican family in the Bronx. Spanish, in fact, was her first language. "I still dream in Spanish," she said. Only after her father's wife died did he admit his paternity and bring her back to the reservation.

There was more. Dominick got up and cleared the table. Emma poured herself another three fingers of vodka on the rocks. He had learned tending drunks to never get between them and their bottle, never even think of trying to get them to stop drinking. Who was he to interfere with someone so lost in the moment? Besides, it never worked and just caused unnecessary scenes. The best you could do was feed them and not let them drive. Emma started talking about people he didn't know as if they were all old mutual friends. She was still making sense, not slurring her words; she was just wandering around in her memory, looking for a place in her past to occupy.

Dominick put some ice cubes in a glass and joined Emma at the table. "May I?" he asked, motioning to the now half-empty fifth of his vodka.

"Let me," Emma said, and she poured him a drink equal to her own. "You're a nice guy, Nickel. How come I didn't meet you years ago when I was a prize worth catching?"

"You are still a prize." They clinked glasses. Emma smiled. She was happy. Now she had a drinking buddy. "Emma, tell me about John Starks, what that gut suspicion of yours was all about."

"Oh, Starks. He's a strange one, isn't he? Little Miss Proper. I've known him for years from the bar. We've done some business now and then. He does like his recreational drugs. How did you get to know him?"

"Doesn't matter. Your suspicion?"

"Well, when I called him to see if he knew how to reach you, he seemed awfully interested in you, had all kinds of questions about you."

"Why would you do that?"

"Do what?"

"Call Starks looking for me."

"Because I'd already called Atticus looking for you, and he just said you were gone. Starks was my only other connection to you. Anyway, I guess I let it slip that Theo thought you were Lord Witherspoon." Emma looked down into her glass and swirled her ice cubes around. "Was that some sort of secret?"

"Doesn't matter."

"So later he called me back, and that's when the strange questions started. About the Bay Savers meeting and where you and I went afterwards and about why I called you Nickel. He wondered if that was some sort of code for something. I got this feeling that he was talking to someone else in addition to me? I couldn't think fast enough to lie, so I pretended my signal was breaking up and asked him to give me a call if he heard from you. Nickel, are you sure you don't want to go up to the bedroom and spend the rest of the afternoon making out?"

"Then he called you yesterday?"

"Yeah, he called to tell me you'd stopped by the museum and that you were going to The Harp. But he wanted to know how soon I thought I might get there to meet you, which I thought a strange question. But then everything sounds the same coming from Starks."

"Sometimes I think irony is his only emotion."

"I'm not going to ask twice, you know." Emma was fading.

"I know. Go take a nap. I'll fix something nice for dinner."

"There is one other thing." Emma drained her glass and pushed it away. "There is a warrant out for me, an old criminal trespass charge, tribal bullshit, that was placed in abeyance if I stayed out of trouble. Well, the feds looking for me was trouble enough to reactivate it." Emma pushed herself up from the table. "I thought you should know that you are harboring a—what-do-you-call-it?—a fugitive."

Dominick talked Emma into turning herself in. His plans did not feature harboring a fugitive. Her story would be that she had been out of town and hadn't learned she was wanted for questioning. As soon as she learned, she came right in. She had done nothing wrong; she had nothing to worry about. Did the tribe have an attorney? No? Bad idea? Then she should ask Theo for one from Bay Savers if the feds tried to detain her for anything. The main thing was not to lie to them or to volunteer any information. Why had she left the Bay Savers meeting? Because the tribal elders had told her to quit and she was worried about being illegally parked. Was he really Lord Witherspoon? No, that was just an old joke as far as she knew. Did she know where he was? No. He would be leaving this place immediately, so she would not be lying.

Dominick had made pasta for dinner—marinara sauce, garlic bread, salad, a bottle of Cabernet. Emma came down from her nap subdued and returned to what was left of the bottle of vodka. Over dinner Dominick persuaded her that going back was the best thing to do. It wasn't that hard to do. Obviously, her idea of a little outlaw idyll with Nickel was not working out. There were no electronic diversions.

Not long after dinner Emma excused herself; rather she came into the kitchen, took the now almost empty bottle of vodka, and said she was going to bed. "Listen, Nickel, is there another bed up there I can sleep in?" She was wavering a little. "If we're through screwing I'd rather sleep alone. You either snore or toss all over the place."

Dominick made up a bed for her in another guest bedroom.

"You're a good host, Nickel, but I worry about your lack of sex drive." Emma crawled under the covers with her clothes on, putting the bottle on the floor beside the bed, and went quickly to sleep.

"I haven't worried about that in a long time," Dominick said to himself, watching her from the doorway as she passed out. Asleep, Emma's relaxed face looked years younger, as if relieved of the need to pretend she was someone she wasn't, some hard-nosed adult, and could for a while be the face of the child she really was.

In the morning, on the drive to the ferry, Emma hit him up for a loan. They were in the MGA. Dominick told her he would drop her off for the midmorning boat so that she could get back, but that he would have to return and close up the house before he could leave. She asked him when she could turn her phone back on, and he told her when she got off the boat back in New Jerusalem. Then she asked if he could spare her a hundred bucks. She would get it back to him later. He had to stop at an ATM to replenish his cash.

At the ferry dock, before getting out of the car, Emma leaned over and gave him a hug and a smooch on the lips. "You're sweet, Nickel, boring but sweet. You'd make some girl a wonderful brother."

Emma could have asked but never did, why, if her turning herself in for questioning was such a good idea, it would not also be a good idea for Dominick to do so too. Well, for one thing there were no outstanding warrants on him, and for another he had never been properly asked. They were looking for him? So, find him. If they were at all interested, they could check his credit cards. He had taken $800 out of the local island ATM in a little more than a week. In any event, if they did catch up with him, his answer would be how was he supposed to know they were looking for him? He had lied to Emma. He wasn't going south. He would hang out at Brenda and Charlie's for the time being.

As Dominick drove away, he mulled over Emma's accusation about his lack of sex drive. It probably wasn't what it once was, but then he had always suspected it wasn't what it was supposed to be. That was another one of those purportedly universal endorphin/dopamine-driven givens. This one was shared with every other sentient species—the essential passion to reproduce. The ejaculative imperative. Well, he had not reproduced. He had never felt the slightest inkling to do so. Oh, he had always enjoyed having sex, but it had never been all that important to him. He liked women well enough and found some more attractive than others, but the attraction was more aesthetic than reproductive. Certain rare women were works of art, a pleasure to behold and be with, but who wanted to screw a work of art?

So, Emma had been miffed by Dominick's declining her offered re-engagement and accused him of being abnormal. Perhaps he was. What was normal? "Normal." Dominick laughed, remembering a flight attendant's pre-takeoff spiel on a flight he had taken years before, a commuter flight filled with harried businessmen. She had started by saying, "Please pretend to pay attention," and he had looked up from his magazine, attracted already. She delivered the requisite set of instructions to her veteran passengers, all of whom had already heard it more times than the average cop-show viewer has heard the Miranda Rights read to captured perps. She did it as fast as possible, like some sort of robotic sorcerer's apprentice, with her own revisions and inclusions. She was a well-practiced comedienne. She was also a classic American woman—tall, trim, well kept, middle-aged, ironic. When she got to the part about the descending oxygen masks and how to put them on and how the balloon would not expand and about breathing normally, she said, "If you can't breathe normally, breathe the way you normally breathe." Dominick wouldn't have minded having a drink and a chat with her after the flight. Not because he wanted her to have his children, but because he liked the way she thought. Normalcy was such an assumption.

Dominick had never thought to ask if Emma was married or not. Probably not—no ring, no mention, no worries about hubby or kids left alone. He couldn't see her as a wife-type or mother. Of course, if her childhood had been as she described it, she had not had much of a model for a typical—or was it a normal?—domestic life. Maybe they would meet up again. Maybe he would get his hundred bucks back. There was certainly one link between them—the fact that they had both grown up as bastards exiled from their fathers' worlds. Who knew what else they shared? Both unwed, no progeny. Was her escape into casual sex the same as his fleeing it? The same reason anyway—the recognition of its meaninglessness? Her lineage's claim to fame was a bastard Mather; his was a bastard Washington. You might say illegitimacy ran in their families. Was there an organization for people like them, like the DAR? The Bastard Offspring of Famous Americans, BOFA. Like all the descendants of Sally Hemings or West Ford.

Sally Hemings, of course, was Thomas Jefferson's slave mistress, his dead wife's half-caste half sister who bore him a half dozen children. West Ford was Washington's purported mulatto son, whose mother was also a family slave with the wonderful name of Venus Ford. Because of Dominick's great-aunt Dorothea's claim to First Father descendancy, Dominick had done the research. Washington had had no legitimate children of his own, a fact that Dominick had found strangely gratifying. Washington had married a widow with two children, and we always think of Martha as a gray-haired old lady, but when they wed she was, at twenty-seven, only a year older than the future general, and her children were still toddlers. Did George, too, see the reproductive thing as more trouble than it was worth—except for his slip up with Venus? The sole progeny of the father of our country had been born a slave. Obviously, Dominick's great-aunt Dorothea must have had some other illegitimate child in mind. There were no Fords in their family tree.

It was several days before Dominick got back to the village on errands—the usual rounds, including the library. He was running out of things to read. He had a list of New England history books he wanted to see, but he had to sign up for a library card first. While he was there he used one of their online computers to check his e-mail. There was something from Angelica: "In light of my father's arrest—see attached—I think we should talk. Please e-mail me back or give me a call. I am confused. Where are you? Is there another Lord Witherspoon or is someone impersonating you? I must clear my father of any charges or we may lose the house as gov't now can seize property involved with federal crimes. Please get back to me. I am desperate."

The attachment was a *Boston Globe* article from a few days before, "Feds ID Old Grofton Bomber":

> *Federal authorities yesterday announced that they had identified a prime suspect in the bombings of the Hercules Corp liquid natural gas terminal site in Old Grofton. Working with British intelligence agencies, the FBI has determined that the suspect is a known international anarchist already wanted in England, Ireland and Italy for terroristic anti-government activities.*
>
> *The suspect, previously known to authorities here as Lord Witherspoon, is a British subject. He was connected to the Old Grofton bombings through surveillance photos and fingerprints found inside an undetonated explosive device found at the scene of the first attack. The suspect is still at large and his whereabouts is unknown.*
>
> *The FBI released a photograph of the suspect supplied by Scotland Yard, which believes his real name is Jake Forrest. In addition to using the name Lord Witherspoon in the U.S., Forrest has in the past used the aliases Sir Reginald Faber and Bishop Fenwick. He is described as armed and dangerous.*
>
> *Forrest is believed to have been associated with the local environmental group Bay Savers, perhaps using them as a cover for his terroristic purposes. A Reggie Fenwick was found on the group's membership list but could not be located. Authorities have questioned members of the group and have detained one of its leaders, Atticus Jameson, for questioning on suspicion of aiding and abetting terrorist activities.*

Accompanying the article was the ICE-released photo of Mr. Forrest, one of those nightclub-photographer shots of a well-dressed man sitting in a padded booth between two handsome young women. Aside from being a big man he looked nothing like Dominick. He looked a great deal like a young Prince Charles, with a long Anglo face and slicked-back dark hair. There was something dated about the photo—the clothes, the setting, maybe just England—but the man in it was a good ten years Dominick's junior. He took an instant dislike to him.

Amazing how the world moved on without you when you paid it no attention. Here he had been deposed from his bogus peerage without even knowing it. Always the last to know. But the news of Atticus's arrest was troublesome. How could he be aiding and abetting terrorists when he didn't even know any? Also, there was no mention of Theo whatever his last name was, the actual leader of Bay Savers. Dominick wondered if Emma had turned herself in or not, and if she had, what sort of questions she had been asked. She wasn't mentioned either.

Dominick wasn't sure what to say in reply to Angelica's e-mail, so he did not respond. He had to sort this out. He checked out the books he had found; others he had to order on interlibrary loan. The librarian had noticed that he had not put down a phone number on his library card application. They had to have a phone number. How else would they notify him when his books came in? Everybody had a phone number. These days everyone had several, she said. Dominick couldn't remember Atticus's number, nor Charlie's disconnected one. He made up a phone number and filled in that space on the application, thanking the librarian for catching his oversight. He had on his Lord Witherspoon outfit. She smiled and thanked him back. "Enjoy your research, professor," she said.

Professor? No, that wasn't right, but he didn't correct her. Professors professed things. He only read things so he could pretend that he lived in another era, could be somebody else. Such as the slave West Ford, son of a president father who had seemingly severed all visits with the boy after becoming president, a father who as Founding Father had established that "'Tis our true policy to steer clear of permanent Alliances,

191

with any portion of the foreign world." Dominick had copied that out in his quote book. "With any portion of the foreign world," both diplomatic and personal? No one knew Washington. That seemed to be part of his pragmatic strength. Martha, in her letters, was certainly nasty to him. You could sense why he spent so much time away from Mount Vernon on campaigns. All the Stoic stuff and his quoting Cato—that was all a loner hiding behind a current pop philosophy. What was it like, being a slave and knowing the most famous man in the land was your father who had abandoned you? Washington's favorite pastime was riding to hounds—he and his cadre of white male cohorts on big steeds chasing small animals through the woods of his vast estates.

It had started to snow again, and on the ride back to Charlie's the MGA had skidded around like a toy on the slick roads. Dominick would have to give up that part of his fake façade. But then if they—the great They, whoever they were—had a new Lord Witherspoon to chase through the snowy metaphoric woods of foreign entanglements, his camouflage was now superfluous. There was still the matter of Atticus in custody, however, and that bothered him.

Chapter 19

On the morning that Benedict Arnold's treasonous duplicity was discovered with the serendipitous capture of Captain Andre, Arnold was supposed to have breakfast with General Washington at West Point. He never made it, escaping instead to a British ship. Washington then offered to exchange Andre for Arnold, but the British refused, and Andre was hanged. How must Arnold have felt, to have another man hanged in his place?

The next morning Dominick caught the midmorning ferry as a walk-on. The weather had changed into what forecasters called a wintery mix, a confused combination of snow, sleet, and freezing rain. He drove his big car to the village, leaving the MGA in the garage. No dawdling this time when he got off the boat in New Jerusalem. With his trilby pulled down and the collar of his London Fog turned up, he headed straight for Ms. Arnold's house. He would learn what Ms. Arnold and Lydia knew about Atticus.

Ms. Arnold answered the door. She didn't recognize him at first in his latest manifestation. "Yes?" she said.

"Ms. Arnold, it's me, Dominick. Sorry to bother you, but is Lydia here?"

"Well, if it isn't the troublemaker himself. Here to cause more trouble?"

"Ms. Arnold, might I remind you who bailed you out of jail in Boston? Now, may I come in? It's wet out here."

"I suppose," she said, stepping back and opening the door. "Just don't drip on the carpet."

While Dominick removed his wet coat and hat and scarf and hung them on the coat tree by the door, Ms. Arnold walked toward the back of the house, where a light was on in the kitchen. The rest of the house was dark and gloomy. There was the flicker and murmur of a TV set from the back parlor. As he followed Ms. Arnold to the kitchen a voice from the back parlor said, "Sistine Chapel." It might have been Lydia's voice; he couldn't be sure.

In the kitchen Ms. Arnold was putting on a cardigan sweater. "You let all the heat out of the house," she said. "What else are you going to do?"

"Lee Harvey Oswald," the voice in the back parlor said.

"Look, Ms. Arnold, I have done nothing to harm you. I do not believe there is any reason for you to be hostile toward me."

"Haley's comet," the voice said. It was a woman's voice, but flat and emotionless like a voice-mail message recording.

"You've done nothing to harm me?" The sweater on, Ms. Arnold now folded her arms across her chest like a disciplinarian. "You caused federal agents to come to my house and subject me and poor Lydia to ridiculous questioning. You got that fool Atticus picked up and taken in. You totally disappeared, making us all look guilty of something."

"The Sun King," the voice said.

"No, wait," Dominick said. "I did not do any of that. I had no control over any of that. So, find someone else to blame. What did the feds question you about?"

"Why, you, of course, or at least you as Lord Witherspoon."

"And what did you tell them?"

"That that was just one of Lydia's pet names for you, some sort of game you two played."

"Jimmy Carter and Thomas Jefferson."

"And what did Lydia tell them?"

"Lydia wouldn't tell them anything, bless her. She just glared at them. She did tell one of them to 'Go fish, Mr. Meriwether.'"

"A short guy?"

"Why, yes, short and unpleasant."

"Did they come back?"

"No. Goodness, do you think they'll come back again? Lydia hasn't been the same since. Why, she didn't even recognize Atticus when he came to get her."

"The fifth commandment."

"So Atticus is out?"

"Oh, yes. They released him after questioning."

"And he's home?"

"I guess so. He's been by twice, but Lydia thinks this is her home now."

"The Emaciation Proclamation."

"And that is Lydia?"

"Yes, talking back to one of her TV quiz shows. She's really quite good when it comes to history and art."

"Can I talk with her?"

"No. She wouldn't recognize you, and I think you have done enough damage already, don't you? So, now that I have been subjected to yet another round of questioning, why don't you just leave? Go find Atticus and get yourselves into even more trouble. Go on, get out. Avaunt."

Dominick left. It was so comforting being around people who could use the archaic imperative. He caught the next ferry back and found Atticus at home. He was not well.

"I thought you'd be way south of the Mason-Dixon Line by now," he said when Dominick came into the kitchen by the back door.

"I thought you were in jail. Are you alright?"

Atticus was hunched over in a kitchen chair in front of the open stove, with a blanket over his shoulders. He looked pale and ancient.

"Just a cold. All this running around has got me wore out."

"Are you eating?"

"There's not much here, and I'm not hungry. I can never remember: Is it starve a fever, feed a cold, or the other way around?"

It was cold in the house. Dominick kept his coat on. "How about some soup?"

"Sure, if you can find some. Lydia's not here."

"I know. I stopped by Ms. Arnold's."

"That witch."

Dominick found a can of chicken noodle soup and put it in a saucepan to warm up. "Atticus, I'm worried about you, your condition and all. Maybe we should get you to a doctor or the ER or something."

"What condition is that? My cold? Anyway, I don't go to doctors."

JOHN ENRIGHT

"No, I mean your other condition, you know, your cancer. Lydia told me about it. Are you in pain or anything? I mean, can I get you something besides a can of soup? Pain pills?"

"What in tarnation are you talking about, Dominick? The only condition I have besides this cold is a wife losing her marbles one at a time."

"You mean you don't have prostate cancer metastasizing and only a couple of moths left to live?"

"No, for Christ's sake, and how would I know if I did, seeing as I haven't seen one of those overcharging quacks in years?" Atticus was stopped by a hacking cough. "Did Lydia tell you that?"

Dominick stirred the soup.

"I thought by now you would have figured out that Lydia sometimes confuses what she hopes for or fears with what is real."

"She had me convinced you were in your final days. I couldn't figure why she would lie about it." Dominick poured the steaming soup into a bowl and put it on the table. "Come eat."

Atticus came to the table and started eating his soup. "Well, you were right. They did come back. Those same two guys that were here before. It was after the storm, a couple of days after you left. They'd made the connection somehow between you and Lord Witherspoon. They were looking for you."

"What did you tell them?"

"That you had left, and I didn't know where to. That Lord Witherspoon was just sort of a joke name for you. That I didn't know anything about you. That you were just an acquaintance, a friend of a friend, passing through. I didn't lie."

"And?"

"And they left. Then a couple of days ago they came back, not the ICE guys this time but two others, FBI. They took me in for questioning this time, a federal office over in New Jerusalem. But this time they weren't interested in you. They wanted to know about someone named Jake Forrest or Reggie Fenwick, whom they claimed was in Bay Savers. All their questions were about Bay Savers." Atticus pushed the bowl of soup away, half finished. "Too salty," he said. "Get me a drink, would you?"

Dominick brought them both glasses with three fingers of scotch. Dusk was gathering. He turned on the light above the stove.

"They had photos of us on the Lucy Anne II, that day you and I went out on surveillance, taken from that helicopter I guess. Only in the photos it was me alright, but it wasn't you. It was your body and clothes, but the face wasn't yours. It was some clean-shaven guy with black hair and a big nose. They kept saying he was this Jake or Reggie guy and asking what we were doing out there. I kept telling them I didn't know who that guy was but that I was out there with you that day. It was crazy. We kept going around in circles."

Atticus looked a little bit better now, a bit less like a corpse. "Then they let me go, told me not to leave the state. Can they do that?"

"I don't know."

"They said I should get a lawyer because the grand jury would probably be charging me with at least lying to a federal agent. Shit, Dominick, I can't afford a lawyer anymore. They just told me I could go. It was a good mile hike back to the ferry dock. Over here I went to my lawyer, but he said he doesn't do federal felony cases. Agnes, his secretary, gave me a ride home." Atticus coughed again.

"Atticus, this house is impossible. You are coming with me. I'm camping out over at Charlie and Brenda's place. They have heat."

"Figured you went there, leaving in the storm like that. How did they do that with the photographs?"

"Digital pictures. There is a computer program called Photoshop that lets them do things like that."

"That's not playing fair. Why would they do something like that?"

"Good question. Listen, let's get the stuff you need and we'll get out of here."

Atticus protested, but Dominick would not take no for answer.

"How will Lydia get in touch with me?"

"We'll come back here tomorrow and call her. Atticus, you know she's not making much sense these days."

"And the feds?"

"You're not leaving the state, you're just disappearing."

Dominick nursed Atticus through the next several days. It was more like the flu than a cold—fevers and chills. Atticus stayed in bed, too weak to move. He probably would have frozen to death at Mt. Sinai. Dominick remembered a story he'd read about a corpse they found in Alaska, some guy in his house trailer in the woods, frozen stiff, sitting at his breakfast nook wrapped in a sleeping bag, looking out the window. Jack London stuff. The weather had taken an arctic snap, minus degrees at night.

It was three days before Dominick got out of the house again, on a multi-errand run to the village. Atticus was resting, breathing normally; the worst seemed to be over. At the library Dominick checked his e-mails—nothing from Angelica—and picked up the books he had ordered on interlibrary loans. One of them—a book about New England ships in the slave trade—had come from the library of the New Jerusalem Historical Society. "That's special," the librarian said as she checked it out. "Usually they don't let their books out on interlibrary loan." When Dominick opened the book an envelope fell out, addressed to him. It was from Starks.

"Dominick: I learned your full name from the FBI when they were here looking for you. Then I saw your name on the library loan request. I cooperated with the FBI at first, after Emma told me you were the Lord Witherspoon they were looking for. I thought it was the right thing to do. But then later, when the feds came out with a totally different Lord W., I realized something fishy was going on and I stopped cooperating. Now I feel badly about being a stool pigeon. Give me a call"—he gave several numbers—"so that I can apologize properly and we can try to figure out what is going on." Signed John Starks.

The next day, Dominick fixed a light breakfast for a now cantankerous-when-awake Atticus and left for New Jerusalem, leaving stuff by Atticus's bedside for him to snack and sip on. Dominick was tired of playing nurse. Atticus had taken to calling him Flo. At least he won't freeze, Dominick thought as he left. He found John Starks at his museum. He was interested to hear what else Starks had found out about him from the FBI. He got there in time for lunch. Starks locked up the museum and they had lunch at a tiny sushi place Starks knew nearby.

"You got the book, I presume. We have duplicates of that volume, so I thought it safe to send it out," Starks said over the too salty miso soup. "You're still over on the island, then?"

"You are still tracking me down?"

"No, no. Wait, bad start. Let me start by apologizing and assuring you that my complicity with the authorities has ended. I should have known better, thought twice. I mean they were already following you around. They knew who you were—not Lord Witherspoon. But when Emma called looking for you and told me that you and the guy the feds were looking to question were one in the same, I . . . I fucked up. Your blonde tail had left her business card. I called her and told her I thought I knew where you would be for the next hour or so. Turned out they were looking for Emma, too, which sort of confirmed things, if you see what I mean." Their main orders arrived.

"So, you called Emma and told her I would be at The Harp so that they could scoop us up together. Two friends with one stone."

"Give me a break, I thought I was being a patriot. You gave them the slip anyway. I gather they missed you by ten minutes."

"You never came?"

"They told me not to go. I think they were afraid I'd give it away or something."

"You did anyway. You asked Emma a few too many questions."

"Glad I did. No, they came back to me after they missed you and quizzed me some more. It was like suddenly I was a suspect, too."

"They have become a bit desperate for suspects."

"I did not appreciate the attention. There are certain aspects of my life style that I must, of necessity, keep off police and public radar."

"I am understandably interested in what the feds told you about me," Dominick said. "If you could flatter me with that information." The maki was too sticky.

"The first time—your blonde in the ski jacket—she led me to understand that you yourself weren't a person of interest, just someone they hoped would lead them to someone. She wanted to know if you'd met anyone at the museum. The second time, they wanted to know everything I knew about you, which is nothing and I told them less. I didn't mention your black helicopters or interest in Darby Point. They wanted to know why I thought you were this Lord guy, and I told them that Emma had told me someone suspected you were, that's all. At about this point I was beginning to feel like a total fool."

"Well, they no longer think I am Lord Witherspoon," Dominick said. "I told you before, it was a case of mistaken identity." The tempura was doughy.

"Yeah, now I guess they have their bead on some other guy, some actual Brit. How could anyone take you for being English? And you don't look anything like that guy."

"I believe they have invented that guy."

"But they said they had photos and fingerprints and a name from British intelligence."

"I said they were desperate for suspects, especially one they can link to the Bay Savers group. You know something about digital photography, John. How hard is it to change a photo, switch faces, say?"

"If you have the right software, not hard to do at all; harder to hide though if someone who knows what to look for examines it—pixel size and stuff. Why?"

"Because our new Lord Witherspoon is showing up at photo ops he wasn't there for. I would not be surprised if his fingerprints on the bomb were post hoc as well." The tea was good though. Dominick poured himself another cup.

"But why? And to think I was cooperating with those people."

"I was hoping they told you something that would help make sense of it."

"All they told me was that they wanted to question Lord Witherspoon. They didn't say he was wanted for anything. But they did ask me if I was a member of Bay Savers, or whatever that group calls themselves."

"But they didn't say anything about me—Dominick?"

"No. Why? You got something to hide?"

"Nothing," Dominick said, sipping his tea. "Nothing that means anything."

Starks insisted on paying for lunch.

Lydia's dementia was like the weather. It could be overcast and gray for days, then come up dawn bright and sparkling off the snow so that it hurt your eyes. Lydia answered the door at Ms. Arnold's house when

Dominick knocked. She was dressed in clashing blue sweatpants and sweatshirt, wearing mismatched earrings. She looked ready to go for a jog. "Dominick, thank god you have come. I am ready to go. Where is Atticus? Is he okay? He hasn't answered the phone for days."

Ms. Arnold appeared behind her. "Do come in, Dominick."

"No, don't come in, Dominick," Lydia said. "Wait here. I'll get my purse and coat." Lydia brushed past Ms. Arnold. "You leave him alone," she said.

Dominick flashed a fake smile at Ms. Arnold, who shut the door in his face. There were voices behind the door before it opened again and Lydia appeared in her full length mink, carrying a small pink backpack. "Oh, Martha, just go find someone else to boss around," Lydia said, as she took Dominick's arm. "Let's go."

"Mark my words, Lydia, you'll regret this, you . . . you turncoat," and Ms. Arnold shut the door behind them.

"Is Atticus in the car? Where is the car? Did you know what the local Indian word for this time of year was?" And she said something unintelligible—"Which translates, I think, as something like 'we're not dead yet.'"

"No, Atticus is not in the car. He's home. I didn't bring the car. We're walking to the ferry. 'We are not dead yet'? I like that."

"Can we stop for a candy bar? There is no chocolate in that house. What's a house without chocolate? You know, shaved and with that haircut you look a lot like that movie star, Ray Milland. Remember him? I think a lot of Indian words were like that. I'm sure there was a chief whose name meant something like windchill factor." They stopped at a corner store to buy candy bars. "You know, without chocolate I just get all bound up. Irregular hardly describes it."

Lydia continued to chat all the way to the ferry dock as she polished off a KitKat and an Almond Joy. There were more candy bars and a bag of barbeque chips in her plastic sack. When she wasn't eating she hooked her arm inside Dominick's and walked close beside him. "Just out for a stroll with my movie star. Remember him in *Dial M for Murder*? I guess that would make me Grace Kelly. Did she go crazy?"

"I don't think so. One of the few who didn't."

"That's right. I marry a prince and kill myself in an automobile accident."

"In Monaco."

"I just won't go to Monaco. Doesn't that sound like a show tune? 'Just Don't Go to Monaco.'" She did a little dance step down the sidewalk, her mink-covered arm looped in his.

At the dock they had to wait for the next ferry, and Lydia couldn't sit still. She toured the small waiting room and adjacent shop, humming her show tune. When it came time to board, it had started raining. Lydia emptied the remaining contents of her plastic sack into the pockets of her mink coat and slipped the white sack over her hair like a rain hat, the white loop handles below her ears. As they walked through the rain to the gangway she presented a look different than the other passengers, in her dirty white running shoes, turquoise sweatpants, full-length mink with pink backpack and her makeshift white plastic rain hat. Dominick thought the other passengers envied her, or should have.

Chapter 20

Dominick had learned the word for it once—soteriophobia, the fear of dependence on others—the professional opinion of his old friend Dr. Sarah Baum, after years of his passing in and out of her life and house in Savannah. Sarah had always been a good sport about his need to move on until she finally gave his disease a name and married a jealous pharmacist. Dominick wondered if she hadn't gotten it backward, but he didn't know the term for the opposite phobia—the fear of others depending on him. Now he had both Atticus and Lydia staying with him at Charlie's house. This was not good. He was not a host.

Lydia did not like it there. She wandered away. It was well over a mile from Charlie's to Mt. Sinai, but the second day back she snuck out and walked over there. They found her in her studio, trying to thaw her paints on a tray atop her electric space heater. This did give Dominick an idea, however; and the next day, after a series of yellow-page phone calls from Atticus's phone, he located a business in New Jerusalem that would deliver two electric space heaters to Mt. Sinai. They were almost a hundred dollars apiece, plus delivery; but he happily charged it, a gift of warmth. Anything to get them out of his house. He figured they could put one in the kitchen and one in their bedroom. If they needed a third, he would buy them a third.

Atticus, of course, was dead set against the idea. "Do you have any idea what that will do to my electric bill?"

"Well, you can't stay here and you can't go back to a freezing house. I wouldn't be surprised if your water pipes haven't already frozen."

"I drained the upstairs pipes and left the kitchen and downstairs bathroom taps running," he said. "This cold snap will end."

Lydia was all for going home. "We'll make Angie pay the electric bill. She claims it's her house anyway."

So, the next day all three of them were at Mt. Sinai, awaiting the delivery of the space heaters, when Angelica arrived. Lydia was out in her studio. Atticus, still weak, was up in bed, huddled under a layer of quilts. Dominick was in the parlor, feeding the fireplace. He was dressed again in his peacoat and watch cap. He was wondering if the house would ever heat up, when the front door swung open and Angelica called out, "Father, mother. Is anybody here?"

The hall door to the parlor was closed to hold in the heat. Dominick heard her walk past to the kitchen, where the stove was on and open. "Daddy?"

Dominick opened the parlor door to the hall and called out, "In here," then he stepped back into the room and went back to the fire. Very little gray daylight came through the draped windows, and aside from the flickering light of the fire, the sole other source of illumination was the little lit-up Christmas tree. Angelica came to the door but didn't come into the parlor.

"Your father is upstairs in bed. He is recovering from the flu," Dominick said, his back to Angelica as he bent over to stoke the fire.

"That's your car with Virginia plates out there?"

"That's right."

"And who are you?"

"Just a neighbor, a friend of the family."

Lydia walked to the hall table that held the telephone. Dominick heard her pick up the phone and then put it back in its cradle. She came back to the doorway. "The phone is working. Why doesn't anyone answer it?"

"No one's been home," Dominick said. He listened as Angelica went up the front stairs. She hadn't a clue, he decided. Perhaps he could just leave. But the heaters had yet to be delivered, and he had to sign and pay for them. What was the point of continuing to hide from Angelica, anyway? Besides, the fire was now happy and leaping, and he hated to let a good fire like that go out.

Angelica came back downstairs to the parlor just as the delivery truck pulled up in the driveway. "He's asleep," she said, walking up to the fire, "or dead. I can't tell. Frozen to death."

"Excuse me," Dominick said, leaving the room and the fire to her as he went to the front door. The space heaters came in boxes, which the driver brought up to the front hall one at a time on a dolly. Dominick had the man unbox them and take their packaging back to his truck. Angelica came out to the hallway to watch Dominick sign and pay for them. Then he carried one up to Atticus and Lydia's room and plugged it in, turning the thermostat up to high. Then he set the other one up in the kitchen and turned it on high. Angelica had gone back to the fire. When Dominick finally rejoined her he brought two mugs of steaming tea.

"It is you, isn't it?" she said, taking her cup of tea. "I didn't see it at first. You look so different. But you came back to take care of them and the house. You truly care about this old place, don't you? It's like you're already moving in or something. Why didn't you answer my e-mail? Tell me you were coming?"

"You never asked about your mother. She is out in her studio trying to paint with frozen paints."

"I had no idea you knew them so well."

"There's a lot you don't know, Angelica."

"I suppose you came back to defend your good name against this terrorist imposter?"

"Something like that," Dominick said, as he positioned another log on top of the fire. "And to help Atticus out of a jam."

"I've been trying to reach him for a week. I learned he was out of custody, but I didn't know where he was."

"He was with me, recuperating."

"You have a place . . . ?"

"Just visiting, friends on island."

"You know, Lord Witherspoon, clean shaven and groomed like that you could be a movie star."

"Don't tell me, Ray Milland."

"No, more Raymond Burr maybe, without the wheelchair. You know, if Daddy is charged with some terrorist thing, we may lose this house."

"He's done nothing wrong."

"How can you be so sure?"

"Like I said, Angelica, there is a lot that you do not know."

"And why is that? Why would you know more about my father's affairs than I?"

"Because you know nothing about your father's affairs."

"Does he know anything of ours?"

"Was that an affair?"

"It could be. If we can keep the house. A summer affair anyway."

"Angelica, I think the only way you are going to get your parents out of this house is in a hearse. Why don't you just accept that?"

"Your puny space heaters are hardly going to solve the problem of their staying here."

"Then put a proper heating system in here and some insulation."

"And you don't know anything about the state of my affairs. The house has to be sold, and I am not putting any more money into it."

"Well, you can hardly sell it to Lord Witherspoon now, seeing as the feds are claiming he's the bomber."

"Then you have to clear your name. That man they are claiming is passing himself off as Lord Witherspoon looks nothing like you."

"You don't understand, Angelica. I am not Lord Witherspoon either. There is no Lord Witherspoon. It's just a name I have used in the past."

"You've lied to me?"

"Absolutely. Why not? To keep you from selling this place out from under your parents."

"Why, I never . . ."

"Get over it. No harm done. Right now your problem is getting your father and this house out from under suspicion."

"I guess I knew all along you weren't really a lord. That's why I wanted to meet you. But your e-mail address, the way you checked into the hotel, the realtor calling you that . . . I really didn't care if you were a fake or not. I just wanted to sell the house, and you were the only bidder. So, do I just call you Dominick now?"

"Please." They were seated on the settee in front of the fire, both leaning forward to be closer to the heat.

"Are you married, Dominick?"

"No, and I have no children." Dominick put two more logs on the fire, and they sat in silence, just watching the flames.

After a while Angelica asked, "So, how do we get my father and the house out from under suspicion?"

"I really do not know," Dominick said. "It's like proving a negative. Or is it disproving a negative? You see, the feds are lying, too. How do we prove that someone they say exists and is associated with Atticus and Bay Savers really does not exist?"

"Oh."

"Where are you staying?" Dominick poked at the fire. He was tiring of company.

"At a bed and breakfast in the village, the Oswalds on Washington."

"Why don't you stay around a few days and look after your dad. He'd like that."

They heard the outside kitchen door slam shut and then Lydia's voice calling out, "Dominick, what is this machine doing in my kitchen?"

Dominick was still wearing his coat and cap. He walked to the kitchen door. "That's the space heater, Lydia, just let it be. I'm off now. I've been spelled as nurse and sitter." Angelica came up behind him in the hallway.

"Oh god, what is she doing here?" Lydia said.

Dominick turned and headed for the front door, brushing past Angelica. "Ta-ta."

"Mother," Angelica said.

At the foot of the front stairs Dominick could hear Atticus calling out from his bed, "Dominick!"

Dominick kept on going, out the front door. Ah, the happy family reunited at home. On the ride back to Charlie's, Dominick pondered what, if any, were the differences in real life between being dependent on others and having others dependent on you. They were equally uncomfortable states.

Dominick could pack more leisurely leaving Charlie and Brenda's than he had fleeing Atticus and Lydia's—no agents looking for him, no blizzard setting in. He even had time to do all his laundry and return the house to the state in which he had found it. He considered leaving a check to cover the costs of the excess electricity and heating oil he must have consumed, but then decided against it—an admission of his long stay. They could afford it and probably wouldn't even notice. Who knew if he would ever see them again? The weather was fine and the roads were clear. He had been meaning to leave for weeks. Now was the time, the time to sever the entanglements of dependence.

He didn't return to Mt. Sinai. He spent a day in the village, shopping and running errands. He had the oil in his car changed and the tires checked and rotated. He got another haircut and returned his borrowed books to the library—all save the one from Starks's collection. Dominick had been reading Joshua Slocum's *Sailing Alone around the World* and he felt the same sort of pre-departure flush of anticipatory excitement that Slocum described when he was preparing to take leave of these same shores on his epic voyage in the *Spray* a hundred-plus years before. Everything was pointed outward. Dominick could not believe he had lingered so long in this freezing backwater. The village and the villagers seemed laughable in their predictable, practiced, prideful simplicity. Leaving here would be like waking from a somber dream.

The night before Dominick left the island he had a solitary celebratory meal in the one fancy restaurant still open, overlooking the bay and the distant lights of New Jerusalem. He drank a fine bottle of Merlot and took his brandy on the porch with a cigar. It didn't matter where the road took him, only out of here. The Gulf Coast, maybe all the way to California. He drove onto the midmorning ferry the next day, feeling that he was sailing away a la Slocum into sweet anonymity again.

His last stop was at the New Jerusalem Historical Society Museum. He wanted to return the book on slave ships in person and say good-bye to John Starks. He parked in the museum lot besides Starks's aged Jaguar. The bell above the museum front door jingled as he went in. He hung his jacket on the antler coat rack near the door.

"Dominick," Starks called out from his hidden vista.

"John, I have brought your book back before leaving town," Dominick said, holding up the volume.

"Come in, come in and meet my new assistant." Starks was standing in his usual spot at the high work counter in the middle of the library, papers and photographs spread out in front of him. Beside him was an attractive middle-aged woman, as tall as Starks and dressed in a turtleneck and business jacket with padded shoulders wider than Starks's. "Constance, Dominick. Dominick, Constance. Constance is my savior, my emancipator."

"Mr. Starks," the woman said, rebuffing him as she leaned across the counter to shake Dominick's hand. "Hello." She was every bit as masculine as Starks. Her dark hair was cut short and she wore no jewelry. Her grip was firm and very male.

"Well, you are my great emancipator, dear, because your being here allows me to take a luncheon meeting with Dominick without having to close up shop or worry about leaving it in incompetent hands. You can see what I want to do here? Combine these files and send all duplicates to the archives? I'm afraid there's a lot of such tidying up to do." Starks went to his desk to turn off his computer and get his coat. Coming back he told Constance, "Any calls just take a message. There shouldn't be anything pressing. It's only history after all. It's all already happened. I'm going to spend some time with my famous author here."

So now Dominick's new imposed pretense was to be a famous author? He put the slave ship book on the counter and led Starks out the door.

"Let's walk," Starks said. "I know you don't like sushi, so let's go to The Harp."

"A new assistant?" Dominick asked as they set out. "Since when did you rate an assistant?"

"Isn't she dreadful?" Sparks asked. "I've been asking for help for years, even wrote a grant for one, but it was never forthcoming. Then Constance just shows up, hired by someone, not me. I'd never met her before, never interviewed her. I don't trust her. I'm not even sure she is a she."

"You don't think . . . ?"

"No, not your paranoia, something much less serious and more mundane. Someone to spy on me."

"So, you can't just step out to lunch? You have to step out with a famous author?"

"Oh, not currently famous perhaps, but once at least infamous."

"Are you talking about me?"

"I am talking about the author of *Coca Exotica*."

It took several steps for Dominick to do the mental math. It had been almost thirty years since his only book's publication, issued by a small university press in England. It had gone almost immediately out of print. He had almost succeeded in forgetting it. How would Starks even know of it?

"You're not an Internet sort of guy, are you Dominick? There are some pretty amazing search engines out there."

"Search engines that search the past? Digital backhoes for digging up graves? Is nothing sacred anymore?"

"Somehow the past is sacred? How does that work? You were a pretty thorough historian. You got the history of cocaine down pretty well."

"You've seen the book? How is that possible?"

"Well, when I learned your name from the FBI lady, I did a search for you and came up with your book. I found a used copy for sale on the Internet and ordered it. It cost me almost a hundred bucks, by the way. There were only two copies for sale out there. I got it a couple of days ago. A good read."

"Is it? I don't remember writing it, just the research."

"Oxford degree. I was impressed."

"Different chap altogether."

"Nothing after that though."

They had reached the back alley door to The Harp. Dominick stopped. "I think I'll smoke a cigar out here before going in," he said. This was not the anonymity he had been savoring.

"I'll bring you a pint then. Guinness?"

"If you must."

There were still Christmas lights up around the door to the pub and its small brick courtyard. How those things always lingered, avoiding dismantlement, the small inanimate objects too unimportant to disappear. What was found in graves was what refused to rot, everything once alive having vanished, dust to dust, muck to muck. Only meaningless objects survived. A copy of *Coca Exotica: The Illustrated Story of Cocaine* unearthed from beneath almost thirty years of temporal compost. "Nothing after that though?" No, that's right. Nothing after that. Screw you, John Starks. The book's publication and hysterical reviews were a career ender. The suddenly unemployable young historian, suspected dope fiend, addict apologist, misplaced American, slanderer of both Freud and Coca Cola. How quickly members of a tribe could coalesce against the outcast. It was reason enough for his wife to decide to leave him.

"Nothing after that?" No, nothing after that but this, where he was, smoking a cigar in the cold outside the back alley door of a midday pub. Starks brought him a pint of Guinness and a shot of Irish whiskey then went back inside. Starks was clever enough not to hang around. But the cigar and the drinks and the cold calmed Dominick down. He could stuff all that eclipsed history back into its folder and send it back to the non-digital and not even analog memory archives. He found the end of the extension cord for the Christmas lights and plugged it in. Most of the bulbs still worked. He took his empty glasses back to the bar and ordered refills, then joined Starks in their far corner booth.

Halfway through their lunch Emma arrived. Starks had forewarned Dominick that he had called her. She wanted to say goodbye as well. Emma was looking her best. Her hair was down and she was wearing makeup and jewelry, a long denim skirt with tall boots and a stylish leather jacket. She gave them both a kiss when she came to their booth. Emma had Bay Savers news. Theo had called her several times in the past week, trying to get back together. She had even had drinks with him one evening. Theo wanted to be sure that Emma's version of events was the same as his if and when she next spoke to the feds.

"Version of what events?" Dominick asked.

"About the new Lord Witherspoon. You are better looking than he is, by the way, Nickel. He looked like some pimp in that newspaper photo. Theo told me that he had just guessed the wrong friend of Atticus's was the wanted man, that's all, but that it didn't matter because the feds had the right suspect now and he was still one of Atticus's additions to the group."

"He's admitting the suspected bomber is connected to Bay Savers?' Dominick asked.

"No, he is admitting that their suspected bomber is connected to Atticus, not the group, some sort of sleeper cell within Bay Savers, not the group itself. He said the group was cooperating fully with the feds."

"Sounds like this Theo guy is throwing this Atticus guy overboard," Starks said, finishing his lunch and pushing his plate aside. "You two lead such interesting lives."

"Don't we, though?" Emma said. "Theo said it wouldn't hurt if I told the feds I had suspicions about Atticus all along, how gung ho he was."

"Theo wasn't gung ho?" Dominick asked. "Didn't you tell me he pretty much made himself the leader?"

"Yeah, but all along he wasn't so much opposed to the LNG plant per se, just the LNG plant at Darby Point. It was a real local issue with him, which is why he got the tribe's support."

"Wait, is this Theo Neisner you are talking about?" Starks asked.

"I don't know. Is that right, Emma?"

"Yes, Neisner, Theo Neisner. Why?"

"There aren't that many Theos around. New comer, big bucks. I only know the name because several years ago he made some enemies hereabouts by buying up a lot of land across the bay, around Dogshead Bay, including some historic properties the State Historic Land Trust wanted."

"Including a lighthouse?" Dominick asked.

"Yes, the one on Teapot Island, which was already on the National Register of Historic Places."

"Dogshead Bay," Emma said. "I know that name. That's right. It was the Hercules Corp's alternative location for their LNG terminal. They rejected it because the land-based costs for infrastructure development like roads and stuff were too high."

They all three sat in silence for a minute.

"Oh," Emma said.

"Your Bay Savers must succeed in stopping the plant at Darby Point," Starks said.

"So that the plant will be moved to Dogshead Bay, where there is no local opposition," Emma said.

"Even if that means tossing Atticus to the feds to save Bay Savers," Dominick completed the paragraph. "That sort of sucks, doesn't it?"

Chapter 21

Dear Editor:

I am writing this letter to set the record straight. Federal authorities are once again engaged in a campaign of misinformation. The FBI would have the public believe that the recent actions on behalf of energy sanity and freedom in Old Grofton are somehow the responsibility of the local group Bay Savers. Nothing could be further from the truth.

Those warning shots across the bows of the Hercules Corp at Darby Point were fired by us, the International Gaia Brigade, on behalf of all Earth's living creatures and future generations in their fight for freedom from fossil fuels.

The IGB is dedicated to confronting and stopping the proliferation of liquid natural gas and all other new fossil fuel facilities worldwide, not just here in your precious estuary. Bay Savers is only a small nonviolent collection of not-in-my-backyard patriots incapable of effective action against new-world-order monster conglomerates such as Hercules Corp.

But the FBI and their fellow federal gestapos choose to ignore the global movement for energy sanity and instead cast aspersion and blame on local innocents. Bullies always pick the easiest targets.

Inform yourself about the evils of fossil fuels and the ecological catastrophe of natural gas fracturing extraction. Go to our website at gaiabrigade.uk or antilng.org to learn the truth about liquid natural gas. Hercules promises LNG to be the future. The only promise they can make is that the future will be worse than the past and much, much shorter.

Lord Witherspoon
IGB

Dominick thought the letter could have been better, but things written by committee are never perfect. He objected to "precious estuary," for instance; but John Starks liked it, so it stayed in. The IGB was Emma's invention. By the final draft they were all three tired of it. The idea got started over the third round of drinks at The Harp. If the feds were going to throw out a straw-man suspect to make it look like they were on the job, then they would set fire to it. They would commandeer the simulacrum. No crime there. But how? A new Lord Witherspoon would have to be born, one with the face and fingerprints and history of the fed creation but beyond the control of his inventors.

Starks especially was excited by the prospect. He wanted to get back at the feds for having sucked him into their schemes, and, he said, he was bored. He called Constance at the museum to tell her he wouldn't be back that afternoon, that he would be making some long overdue visits to potential donors. "Donate something," he said when he hung up, and Emma ordered another round of drinks. They repaired to Starks's house. Emma rode with Dominick as he followed Starks's Jag out of town. First, they all got stoned on Starks's hashish and fixed themselves fresh drinks. Then Starks got out a pad and pen, and they brainstormed a campaign. The opening act would be a letter to the *New Jerusalem News*. Starks went online to make sure there was no organization named the International Gaia Brigade. There wasn't, but there was an antilng.org website with all the negative facts about natural gas and its extraction.

"I had no idea," Emma said. "There's very little natural about it. They pump millions of gallons of water and chemicals and diesel fuel back into the earth to force the gas out? It causes earthquakes? It's like a mega earth enema."

Starks made a phone call and had a large pizza delivered just as night was falling. That was appropriate food, as they were acting like college kids conspiring on a prank. Starks recalled dressing a statue of Jesus in a ball gown and feather hat once in the chapel of the Catholic college he had gone to. "You know, he had his hand raised like a blessing, and we stuck a cigarette between his fingers, gave him some lipstick." Emma confessed to an early career as a midnight urban graffitist. "I'd spray paint other girls' names to get them in trouble."

Starks typed out and printed the final version of the letter to the editor. He put on some cotton archivist's gloves before pulling the page out of the printer and made Emma wear gloves as well when she addressed, stamped, and stuffed the envelope. "It should be mailed from somewhere else," Starks said. Dominick volunteered to mail it from somewhere on his trip south, if Starks would give him a pair of those gloves. Pretty soon they were all wearing archival gloves and things got just silly. They smoked some more hashish.

At some point Starks walked off down the hallway, saying, "You know where your bedroom is, Dominick." There was some cable show Emma wanted to watch, so she curled up on the couch in Starks's study in front of his flat-screen TV to watch it. Dominick went out to his car to get his overnight bag. It was very cold, too cold to stop and light a cigar. A half moon. The coyote was silhouetted against the white snow field. It had seen Dominick first and was frozen there watching him, its head turned toward him in predator vision. Dominick froze in response. It was only ten yards away. Flight or fight, Dominick thought, and the memory file he thought he had closed hours earlier fluttered open, of Linda leaving him, mute, putting her bags in the trunk of a taxi and taking off. As he stepped toward the trunk of his car, the coyote retreated an equal distance, its intensity never wavering. What if it attacked? What if he had tried to stop her? Volitional acts.

The coyote turned and took a step toward Dominick. This was one of those "bad" coyotes, and this was its test. Dominick rushed at the critter—"Scatter, bitch"—and it left, trotting halfway across the snowy moon-streaked field before stopping and looking back. They stood for a while staring at each other, as if trying to implant a long-term memory. In its shaggy, Rasta-matted winter coat and defiant upright stance, the coyote was an encapsulation of the wild. It had no fear. Death was its business. Dominick gave it the finger, got his bag from the car, and went back up the stairs to the house. Once there had been wolves here.

Emma was stretched out asleep on the study couch in front of the TV, softly snoring. Dominick fetched an afghan from the living room sofa and covered her. Wolves roamed in packs, they were not lone hunters like his coyote. He turned down the sound on the TV set. A pack could bring down bigger game. Again Emma looked years younger asleep, her face in just the flickering light of the TV screen, turquoise earrings. Hunting in silence in the dead of night. For the first time in years Dominick wondered what had ever happened to Linda? Where was she tonight? For sanity's sake had she erased all memories of him?

It was a good laugh—rolling, inviting, infectious. Dominick could hear it coming all the way from the kitchen. He was still in bed. The morning was bright out the window. Starks had Emma in stitches over something. Dominick liked this house. He felt comfortable here. He would be sorry to leave it, coyotes and all. When he got to the kitchen, Emma was still chuckling, but they would not tell him over what, which probably meant it had something to do with him. They were both wearing the archival gloves again. That was part of the joke. Starks made breakfast—an omelet and leftover pizza, with lots of coffee. Starks would take Emma to town on his way to work. She had to be someplace. Dominick could take his time. Starks made it clear that Dominick was welcome to stay. Their little game with the feds was just beginning. Didn't he want to stay and play?

"You know, this morning, out of curiosity I did a search for their famous terrorist—Jake Forrest—and his supposed aliases—Sir Reginald Faber, Bishop Fenwick, Reggie Fenwick, and Lord Witherspoon—and came up empty on every one. Their famous international terrorist is totally unknown, a blank canvas to paint on."

"Well, I will leave the fun and finger painting to you guys," Dominick said. "I need some warmer weather."

Starks left the kitchen to get ready for work after putting their dirty dishes in the dishwasher. Dominick poured himself another cup of coffee.

"You will be coming back, won't you, Nickel?" Emma asked. "I've grown accustomed to your company. You covered me up last night, didn't you? That was sweet. You know, I got up later to come and join you in bed. I really wanted to be with you, but you were spread out like a hibernating walrus or something across the bed, making walruslike sounds, so I went back to the couch."

"You snore, too, you know," Dominick said.

"I do? Nobody ever told me that."

"It's a pleasant enough sound, something between a cat and a flower."

"You do like me then?"

"You do grow on one."

"I wish you would come back. Starks, for all his weirdness, can be fun, can't he?"

"I can't say if I'll be back or not. I never know where I might end up. I've had a bellyful of this place." There was silence for a while as they both moved their coffee mugs around. "You are pretty when you sleep, by the way. I guess that's what I meant about a flower snoring."

"You're prettier when you're awake."

"That would never work out."

Emma got up and came around the table. She pushed Dominick in his chair back so that she could sit in his lap and put her arms around his neck. "Nickel, what if I told you I wanted to come with you?"

"That would not work out either," Dominick said. He was talking into her bosom. "I need some downtime from people."

"Then I'm going to have to make you promise to come back." Emma pulled Dominick's head back and leaned down to kiss his mouth. They lingered in the kiss. Emma shifted her weight. Hands moved on backs and hair. Tongues touched. "Come back or I'll put a curse on you and that thick dick of yours," she said.

"'Tis you, 'tis you must go and I must bide." Starks's fake Irish tenor from the kitchen doorway was quite professional. "But come ye back when summer's in the meadow, or when the valley's hushed and white with snow, for I'll be here in sunshine or in shadow. Oh Dommy boy, oh Dommy boy . . ."

"Oh, shut up, Starks." Emma was laughing. "Better put your gloves on."

"Is it examination time again?" Starks asked. "Is his equipment really that thick?"

Dominick hit the road an hour or so after Starks and Emma left, after a shower and a good-bye toke on the hash pipe. They both had left wearing their archival gloves, holding their hands up like surgeons entering an operating room. "The world awaits its examination," Starks said as he exited. It was nice and quiet after they left, and the morning sun flooded Starks's rooms with their walls of windows. It was hard to leave, but he did.

The initial leg of the trip south, past New York City, was all on interstates and dreadful, but once out of New Jersey he cut off onto state roads and could relax. Dominick had decided to mail their letter from Valley Forge, which was about as far as he wanted to go his first day on the road. That seemed appropriate somehow, he was not sure how. From Pennsylvania he meandered south through western Maryland into Virginia, giving Washington and his mother's house in Alexandria a wide pass. Snow piles shrank and then vanished from the side of the road. He stopped just south of Shenandoah, at an inn he remembered, and stayed there for three days before continuing on the five hundred miles to Charleston.

In Charleston he discovered that the old friend he was about to surprise with a visit was in the hospital and, from the sound of the report he received, was not expected to come out alive. Stroke. The past few years that sort of thing was happening with increasing frequency among his list of hosts. He called ahead to Tallahassee to his next planned visitation and was told that a recent fall and broken hip had made that stay impossible as well. Another call to Boca Raton raised just an answering machine.

Charleston was nice enough, and the temperature was almost springlike; but now he knew no one there. Dominick's taste in hotels and restaurant meals was expensive, and he disliked feeling like just another spendthrift tourist. But his options were dwindling. Was his tenure of permanent guesthood coming to an end? He could always head back to his mother's and regroup there. She might not even be there this time of year. She hated the cold. For all he knew she, too, had broken a hip or had a stroke. It had been a year since their last contact.

Dominick called John Starks first. He still had Starks's apology note with his phone numbers. He wondered whether their Lord Witherspoon letter had appeared in the *New Jerusalem News*.

Dominick called him at his work number, and Starks couldn't talk. Dominick could tell someone was there with him, probably what was her name the new assistant, Constance. Starks took down Dominick's hotel phone number and said he would get back to him after he saw whether the museum had any information about that.

When Dominick got back from dinner the red message light on his room phone was blinking. Starks had called back; call him at home.

"We may have kicked a bit of a hornets' nest," Starks said. The *New Jerusalem News* had published their Lord Witherspoon letter, which had then been picked up as a news story by the *Boston Globe* and then by the *New York Times*, which led to an editorial in the *Wall Street Journal*. A new terrorist outfit was good for newspaper sales. Before all that broke, Starks and Emma had already moved on to phase two of their campaign, which Dominick had assumed was just a joke when they wrote it down. They had mailed out envelopes containing harmless white powder—Sweet'N Low—to the Hercules Corp headquarters in Houston and Dubai with courtesy notes—a sufficiently vague Bible quote, "He shall suck the poison of asps; the viper's tongue shall slay him"—signed IGB.

"I had a meeting in Boston," Starks said, "so I mailed them from there, from Concord, actually. Somehow that seemed appropriate."

"Yes, I can understand that part," Dominick said, "but not the rest."

"Well, Emma is fond of her Gaia Brigade. She wanted to give it a little muscle."

"What did you mean about the hornets' nest?"

"You haven't been watching the news?"

"No."

"The FBI put their Lord Witherspoon aka Jake Forrest on their most-wanted list, splashed his picture all over the networks—new photo, same guy. Then they had squads of feds and local cops with cable news crews embedded conducting raids all over eastern Pennsylvania and around Boston. I can't believe you have missed all this. Where were you? On another planet?"

"That would be nice."

"They picked up a bunch of illegals and some other people whom they had to release after questioning. Big show of force."

"That stuff isn't good for you, is it?"

"What stuff?"

"That sweetener you mentioned that people put in their coffee."

"Listen, Dominick, this is serious. They picked up Emma. Some old warrant, but they made a big deal of it."

"Emma?"

"They need suspects that badly, I guess."

"Any details?" Dominick asked. There was a balcony to Dominick's Charleston hotel room out some French doors, with white wire chairs and a table. The phone on the desk had a long cord that stretched out there. He opened the doors and went out and lit a cigar, cradling the phone against his shoulder. "Have you talked with her?"

"No, no I haven't. They picked her up at The Harp. I got the story from people there. They must have had the place staked out, looking for her, because as soon as she got there two agents came and took her."

"FBI?"

"No, ICE guys, I was told, wearing their black-and-white uniform jackets, which people there thought strange. I mean, you can't get more Native American than Emma."

"A tall guy and a short guy?"

"Yeah. How did you know? Liam, the bartender, called them Mutt and Jeff. Where are you now? I didn't recognize the area code."

"South Carolina."

"How's the weather?"

"No snow on the ground, but it's not spring yet. The feds haven't gotten back to you?"

"No. Why would they? I'm not part of Bay Savers, and the only information I ever gave them was wrong. Where to next? Farther south, I'd guess, in pursuit of spring?"

"Probably. Sure. Do you know if Emma has a lawyer yet?"

"Don't know. Probably not. He would have to be court-appointed. Bay Savers wants nothing to do with her, I gather. They denied she was any longer part of the group. I'd bet your Mr. Neisner is claiming she was part of his fictitious sleeper cell. Her warrant, I gather, had nothing to do with any of this."

"How did The Harp feel about having its queen abducted?"

"Oh, this was her absolute coronation. She's queen for life now. A raid by federal agents? They'll probably name a drink after her."

After he rang off from Starks, Dominick stayed out on the balcony to finish his cigar. The view was of the backs and roofs of houses in an old neighborhood. There were five church steeples in his panorama. The few taller new buildings of Charleston were all behind him. The future was all behind him. In front of him were buildings that predated the Civil War. Down there somewhere was the Old Slave Mart, where slaves had been auctioned off. Around him were strangers. The only downside to solitude was this occasional feeling of pointlessness. But then maybe everyone felt that, not just aspiring anchorites. Without others is there any meaning, any need for it? Alone, don't we all find someone to talk to inside our head? Doesn't everyone sometimes crave the solace of feeling watched over, observed? Or was that all just another layer, the undergarments as it were, of hubris and learned vanity that had to be finally shed in order to learn the naked truth? Which was, yes, pointlessness. Only the observed exist; unobserved you vanish.

Check out was at twelve. Dominick loaded his car and left. He had nowhere to go. He headed back north, but on a different and much more desultory route along the coast, avoiding the interstate, through Myrtle Beach and other coastal towns. It was if he was looking for something, but he didn't know what. As dusk descended he crossed a bridge into a town called Washington, North Carolina. That sounded right, so he stopped at a roadside motel and checked in. The bed had known many tortures. From Washington it was only a half day's drive to Yorktown, Virginia, on back roads through peaceful farm country and along the edge of the Great Dismal Swamp. Driving was a form of meditation.

Dominick had never been to Yorktown before, and really there was nothing there, which somehow seemed appropriate. Like every other battlefield he had ever visited it was empty and mute and forlorn, its moment of significance passed. He knew by now that he was headed back to his mother's house in Alexandria, only a few hours' drive farther north. To compensate for his poor sleep the night before, he checked into the best hotel he could find. He called his mother's house, hoping she would not be home. He still had a key, if she hadn't changed the locks. But she was there, alive and complaining. Someone had died. Or was it her dog? She didn't forget to remind him how his conception had ruined her live. He didn't tell her where he was. She didn't ask.

The next day Dominick drove past his mother's house. It was raining. He didn't stop but he slowed down. Nothing had changed. That piece of the past was frozen. As he left her gated community a local cop tailed him then pulled him over. The tag on his Virginia plate had expired. Dominick apologized, said he had been out of state on a business trip and had just returned and would renew his registration. He got a ticket anyway. Home is where when you return you get a ticket for having been away. He thanked the cop for reminding him. Beyond Bethesda he headed west, back toward Shenandoah and the inn where he had started this loop through the Confederacy. His route took him past the battlegrounds of Manassas and Bull Run, where he stopped, and through the tiny Blue Ridge Mountains hamlet of Washington, Virginia. So many Washingtons. Did he deserve so many? Was there a little town named Venus anywhere?

Chapter 22

The sound came from a neighboring room at the inn where the TV set was never turned off. After the first night Dominick asked for a different room, but there were none available. The place was full. There was some sort of Civil War reenactment or reunion or something going on up the valley at the Cedar Creek Battlefield. The inn was awash with men dressed as Confederate officers. The clanking of swords in scabbards was a curious sound Dominick had never heard before. The men's Southern accents seemed exaggerated, but he noticed the license plates on the SUVs in the parking lot were primarily from the deeper Southern states. He wondered if the officers had any troops, and if so, where were they staying? Not in this expensive inn. In campgrounds somewhere else in the valley? And if it was a battle reenactment, where were the Union officers? And if he could not get another room, could the manager at least request a curfew for the TV set?

This was the problem with staying in public accommodations—there were always other guests. Back in his room, he could still hear the TV, so he decided to address the problem directly and knocked on the door of the offending room. No answer. He knocked again, harder. No answer. He tried the door. It was locked. There would seem to be no one home, just the TV set on. Back in his room he tried to read. He had picked up a brochure at the desk about the Battle of Cedar Creek, about which he knew nothing. It was General Philip Sheridan's ultimate victory in driving the Confederate Army out of the valley. The Confederate general was Jubal Early. Dominick loved that name. So joyous a name for a general, though in this case the opposite of jubilant. Now all he could hear from the other room was a laugh track.

He went for a drive. This whole valley had been a battlefield once. He wondered how many men had died in pain here. At Cedar Creek alone there had been more than 8,500 casualties. He had brought his camera but found nothing to photograph.

That evening after supper Dominick called Starks again to see if there was any new word about Emma. Surely some sort of bail had been set. Had she triumphantly returned to The Harp? Starks had heard nothing new from or about Emma, but he did have other news.

"That man you and she mentioned, Atticus, Atticus Jameson? I don't know how close you were to him, but he's dead. It was on the news. He'd been taken in again for questioning, and he died while in custody. A heart attack, they said. They said the grand jury was about to indict him, but they didn't say for what."

"John, is that offer of a place to stay for a few days still open?"

"Yes, of course, you're always welcome."

"I may take you up on it. I'll let you know."

Starks never asked where he was calling from, and Dominick didn't mention it. He went down to the pub attached to the inn, which was by now full of liquored-up rebels, many still in their gray uniforms. He found a stool at the end of the bar and ordered a Guinness and a Jameson's. He wondered how many Atticuses were now left in the world. For the original Atticus that wasn't even his real name, just a pen name meaning he was from Attica. Dominick couldn't recall his actual name, just a friend of Cicero's.

The trip back north took four days as Dominick studiously ignored the interstate and cities. Again he was trying to avoid the present and people. Back roads that were headed in his general direction were fine. Driving was still meditation, but being out on the road had become contrary. Other drivers irritated him, so he sought out roads where there were none. He stayed at 1950s-style cabin motels where cars came and went all night long as locals checked in and out by the hour. One night near Wilkes-Barre there were gunshots off in the woods but no sirens. At some point in western Connecticut it started to snow again. He ignored it and it went away.

Dominick reached Starks's house late in the afternoon while Starks was still at work, and he drove past the carriage house up to the big empty house at the top of the drive. Broadmoor, Starks had called it, another of those century-old monuments to show-off elegance. Each mansion—called cottages in typical Yankee false humility—was designed as if in a contest of wasted space and money. They reminded Dominick of the distinctive pampered breeds in a Westminster Dog Show, each hoping to win best of show. Broadmoor's distinction was its femininity, its long vertical lines, tall narrow windows, two asymmetrically placed turrets—a wistfulness and delicacy that the macho Gilded Age profiteers who commissioned most of these places did not go in for. A woman's touch on the architect's drafting table, the set for some Victorian romance. It stood on a lonely windswept moor, not a bush or a tree within hundreds of yards of it. Why was the past always so cold, Dominick wondered? He sat there in his car and smoked a cigar and watched a non-sunset until at dusk he saw the headlights of Starks's Jag pull in through the gates and disappear behind the carriage house.

Dominick still didn't move. He didn't know why he had returned. He had no reason, no story to tell Starks. He was just back. What did they call it in physics? Brownian motion? The random directionlessness of a wandering iota. Did direction need to have a meaning?

He parked beside Starks's Jag and went up the stairs. There was music playing, something classical with lots of violins. It was loud. He knocked to no answer, then opened the door and stepped in. "John?"

Starks answered from somewhere, "Dominick, come on in. I'm fixing martinis for us."

Dominick walked into the main room, taking off his coat. Starks appeared in the doorway to the kitchen with a remote control in his hand, which he pointed into the room and clicked a few times to turn down the music. "Why? you ask, as well you may. Because I was expecting you—I saw your car up at the big house—and I haven't had an excuse to make martinis in a while, and it's been one of those days." Starks went back into the kitchen, then came out with a tray bearing a large silver shaker and two tall martini glasses. "Lots of olives, of course. How was your trip?" It was a strange feeling, almost like coming home.

"John, how is it you have no mate? You would make some guy a wonderful catch."

"Please, Dominick. The same person day after day? The routines you have to put up with? It's like having a pet, and then they get sick and die. No fun. But again you have answered my question with one of your own. Last you told me you were in South Carolina."

"You know, Americans are basically very friendly people. They love to talk, about themselves."

"Take any photographs?"

"Tried once or twice. Too many people. I visited battlefields."

"Dreadful places."

"Aren't they, though?"

"My condolences for the loss of your acquaintance, Mr. Jameson."

"Funny, the last thing Atticus told me was that he was in good health and not about to die."

"One shouldn't make assumptions like that, at least not out loud."

"Nothing suspicious about his death?"

"Seemingly no, just an old man collapsing. They tried to revive him. He died in hospital. That piece of news sort of got buried under the rest."

"I suppose I must hear it," Dominick said, holding his martini glass out for a refill.

"More olives?"

"Please."

Starks came back from the kitchen with four olives skewered on a fresh swizzle stick. "Well, there was our Sweet'N Low campaign."

"How did that go?"

"Oh, swimmingly. They discovered almost immediately what it was, of course, but not before the Houston police had emptied the entire Hercules Corp headquarters building and shut down the downtown Post Office. And then there were the dragnet raids in Concord and Pennsylvania. Is that where you mailed your letter from?"

"Yes, Valley Forge."

"You masochist, you. But the bigger news, strangely enough, was our envelope to Dubai, which was just an afterthought on Emma's part when she learned online that Hercules Corp's real daddy was some Arab outfit there. That girl is a natural troublemaker."

"Anything new from her?"

"Nope.

"Well, the *Globe* picked up the Dubai story and made the connection and followed it up, and bingo, big news—coordinated attacks in Texas and Dubai by the Gaia Brigade. The story was now several news cycles thick, so all the talking heads got onto it. I can't believe you missed all this. Did you go someplace where there's no TV?"

"That's right, just old sitcoms and laugh tracks."

Starks shook the last liquid out of the shaker into his glass. Dominick had eaten only two of his olives. Starks reached over and took the remaining two. "But there's not much of a story there because it's just Sweet'N Low and no one dies, so they end up talking instead about the Arab connection, about how natural gas was supposed to be the patriotic solution to depending on foreign cartels and all, and about how no one knew Hercules was just a front for some Arabs. I guess they wanted that kept a secret, and nobody had paid it much attention before."

"Tangled webs." Dominick's stomach growled. He had not eaten since breakfast.

"Right," Starks said. "I'll warm something up. Leftover lamb stew sound alright?" Starks headed off to the kitchen. "There's more news, but it will keep. Somehow I get the impression you don't want to hear it."

Dominick picked up the tray with the empty glasses and shaker and followed Starks into the kitchen. "It's not that I don't want to hear it. It's just that I thought I had escaped it all."

"All what?"

"All the craziness. I don't know."

"You'll never escape that. By the way, I've cleared off a shelf in the fridge for you, and there are towels in your room. You can find the washer and dryer. There are no secrets there. You'll probably need them. We do recycle. Figure it out. There's a bottle of Pinot Grigio in the fridge door. Open it for us, will you? The corkscrew is in the second drawer there. Have you ever noticed how most American kitchens are so predictable? I mean where people put things. Tomorrow we'll see what has happened to Emma. See? You knew just where the wine glasses would be, and somewhere in the fridge is a jar of mint jelly."

Dominick didn't mention that he probably knew strangers' kitchens better than anyone, and that only the surprises held any meaning. In Starks's kitchen, for instance, all the sharp knives were hidden somewhere. Over supper Starks quizzed him about his trip, and they enjoyed some laughs at the expense of their fellow Americans. Dominick skipped over his visit to Alexandria and his drive past his mother's house. Nothing entertaining there. Starks's final words before retiring were a warning—that he and only he could load and run the dishwasher.

Emma was out, on her own recognizance. The district court judge had not liked the feds picking her up on the strength of what was, after all, an old local warrant. "Overreaching," the judge called it. A hearing date was set, and he ordered her released, telling the feds to get their own warrant from their own court if they chose to charge her with something. "Don't try your dragnets in my district," he told them. Starks found this out through a couple of phone calls to friends at the courthouse. They were at his museum office. Starks had sent Constance off on an all-day errand to the state archives.

"This is in line with the other news I've been hearing," Starks said. "A local judge telling the feds to go stuff it. There's some sort of local uprising going on, especially in Old Grofton. I guess the national news coverage forced folks to pay more attention. There have been letters to the editor and callers to talk radio shows criticizing the Old Grofton mayor and their congressman for backing the Hercules project. I get the feeling that few people up there ever really liked the project, but no one was saying so out of politeness or resignation or something. It was always presented as a done deal until Bay Savers started asking questions.

"Some ultraright group calling themselves Christians for American Values or Americans for Christian Values or something like that has started a drive for signatures on a petition opposing the LNG plant as part of an Islamic plot to take over the government and subvert the culture, and according to the news anti-LNG and anti-Hercules graffiti has been springing up all over the city."

"Graffiti?"

"Some Reverend down in that neighborhood is planning a protest march."

"Too bad Atticus isn't around to see it taking off," Dominick said.

"I don't think it has much to do with the environment or saving the bay. It's just a new enemy."

"Do we care?"

While at Starks's office Dominick borrowed some time on Starks's computer to check his e-mail. It had been a month. There was nothing much there, a few queries from his accountant to answer about taxes and expenditures. Before signing off he remembered to check his Lord Witherspoon address. There was just one message there, from Angelica, the only person who knew that address:

Dear Dominick, I don't know where you are right now. Except for the times when I've been in the same room with you that's been true as long as I've known you. The last I saw of you was your back walking out of my parents' house. Like the Lone Ranger or something, after nursing Dad through the flu and buying them those space heaters.

Daddy died four days ago. I thought I'd let you know. A heart attack, the doctors said. I wasn't there. I had to come back to work in Boston. I had him cremated. We had no ceremony.

You know I do not care if you are not lord somebody. What matters now is that you were Daddy's friend. He liked you. And I miss you. Miss someone to talk to about Daddy and what was going on before he died. You were right I do not know anything about what was going on with him.

Please get back to me. I would love to meet and talk. I need someone to hold me.

XO, Angelica.

Dominick replied: "My condolences on your father. Where is your mother?" Then he paused. There wasn't much he wanted to say. Then for some reason he broke one of the houseguest rules and gave her John Starks's home number—which he remembered because it had three zeros, his favorite digit, in it—and told her he could get a message there if he got back on island. He sent his reply and immediately regretted it.

"John, I have just made a mistake," Dominick said, signing off.

Starks was at his usual workstation at the library counter. "What's that?"

"I just gave out your home phone number to get personal messages. I don't know what came over me."

"To whom?"

"Atticus's daughter. She seemed lonely."

"Gotten laid recently, Dominick? Don't worry, we'll deal with it. You'll just have to tell me all about her if she does call. Price to pay."

The next day Starks was off to a conference in Albany, and Dominick had the carriage house apartment all to himself for five days. He had plenty to read, and the days were getting longer and warmer. The snow was gone from everywhere the sun could reach, but the country was still stark, dead and monochromatic. Dominick explored the neighborhood and the grounds of Broadmoor. He took his camera with him. In a kitchen drawer he found some keys and he tried them on the locks of the big house. One of them worked in the bolt lock on a side door. He explored the house as well, taking photographs of shadows. There was still some furniture in the rooms—pieces too large to move or that would have been out of place in any other house. In one of the turrets there was a wide window seat that caught the full afternoon sun, the only warm spot in the otherwise glacial rooms. He took to reading there.

The phone never rang. Starks had told him that the landline was only still there because he was too lazy to have it disconnected. It was all cell phones now. There was an answering machine, as vestigial as the instrument it was attached to. On the third day, when Dominick returned to Starks's apartment around sunset, a red light on the answering machine was flashing. It was a message from Angelica: "This is a message for Dominick. I'll be arriving this Saturday, the twelfth, staying at the Oswald's on Washington. He knows who this is."

Starks was scheduled to return on Saturday. Maybe he would like his home to himself for a day. So, Saturday morning Dominick parked his car in a lot near the docks and caught the midday ferry out to the island. It was like an old commute he thought he would never repeat.

He stopped at the deli for a roast beef sandwich and to watch the young waitresses. The one who had reminded him of Linda wasn'twas not there. He was in his Lord Witherspoon wardrobe today. He left an overlarge tip. Washington Street was just a few blocks away and only two blocks long. The sign was small and tasteful, carved in wood above the porch steps, Oswald's Bed & Breakfast. At the curb was a silver Camry with Massachusetts plates that Dominick had seen before in Atticus's driveway.

They had drinks at the fancy restaurant overlooking the bay. Midafternoon, off season; they were the only patrons. Dominick sipped a Pinot Grigio and listened. In a way it was refreshing, in that Angelica wanted to know nothing about him. There were no questions about where he had been, where he was staying, how he was doing. It was all about her. She was hurting. She had let her dad slip away, as if he were going to live forever. The last time they had talked they fought. Her mother hated her. The feds were threatening to take the house. The people she was working for were very image conscious; they were not thrilled about her father dying in custody, about to be indicted by a federal grand jury. His life insurance was all in Lydia's name. Her husband was no help or support at all.

"What's his name?" Dominick asked.

"Whose?"

"Your husband. You've never mentioned him before,"

"Dexter. His name is Dexter. That's not important."

"Is he gay? Your father thought he was gay."

"Dex's sexual orientation is not an issue here. Daddy never liked him."

"Just curious. Why would you marry someone gay?"

"This is not about my husband or my marriage. Oh, Dominick, don't be mean to me. Please. I came all this way on the hope you would be here for me, and here you are, like the Lone Ranger again. Help me, please. Help me keep the house."

"How?"

"By proving Daddy wasn't part of any terrorist plot, that the house wasn't where the terrorists met and planned and kept their weapons."

"Who says it was?"

"Those agents, the ones that kept hounding him."

"The FBI?"

"No, not them so much, the other ones, that pair from Homeland Security."

"I don't know what I could do, Angelica. They have no reason to believe anything I could tell them."

"But you know Daddy wasn't one of those people, whoever they are."

"What I know doesn't mean anything, dear. Drink up." Dominick ordered another bottle of wine and a dozen oysters on the half shell. "I think what you need is a good lawyer. I hate to say it, but Atticus's dying may have been the best gift he could have given you. They can't indict a dead man, so they may not be able to seize his property either. But it's a new law and all on the government's side. You need a pro, not an amateur like me."

They shared a second dozen oysters and finished the second bottle of wine. Angelica mellowed. She shed some real tears for her father, and they toasted him.

"You remind me of him, you know," she said. "So sure of yourself, so masculine that way."

"You flatter me," Dominick said. "All I am sure about is that I don't know the answers."

On the way to her car in the parking lot Angelica took Dominick's arm. "I believe you have gotten me a little bit tipsy, Dom. Would you mind driving?"

Back at the bed and breakfast on Washington Street, Dominick went with Angelica up to her room. There was a dance she had started that they would see through to the end. They weren't exactly strangers. It was a slow dance. Neither of them was in a hurry. There was no need for words. They lingered over kisses. Caresses lasted until they became familiar. Clothes were leisurely shed. It was like they had been lovers a long time. Not until he entered her, on top of her, her thighs pressed back against her breasts, her hands guiding him into her, did she call out. "Oh yes. Oh lord, lord, yes. All of it, give me all of it. Oh lord, yes, fuck me."

Chapter 23

I t was not pleasant. It was not pleasant at all. It was the sort of scene that Dominick had customized his life to avoid. There were the three of them. Two of them basically out of control as far he could judge, and the third now with her earphones in listening to her iPod. If it had been three men perhaps it could be worse. It would have gotten physical. Punches would have been thrown, furniture broken, maybe even concealed weapons put to their intended use. It was just Angelica and Lydia and Ms. Arnold, but all three of them were between him and the front door exit.

Dominick knew when he came that it was a mistake. He had missed the last ferry off the island the night before and had spent the night in Angelica's room at the bed and breakfast on Washington. Over another bottle of wine she had told him her life story according to Angelica—tomboy, drugs, abortion, a stint in New Zealand with a Kiwi boyfriend. Her sister Rey was the favorite, Daddy's little girl and her mother's perfect little baby doll. Then Angelica went to bed and slept soundly, leaving half the queen size bed for Dominick. At some point in the night she curled up spoon style against him and purred.

In the morning they had the breakfast part of the bed and breakfast. Angelica was headed back to Boston. She had wanted to check on the house—she refused to call it Mt. Sinai—but discovered she hadn't the stomach for it. Dominick went back with her on the midday boat. On deck she insisted on holding his hand—not the way old couples do, but the way teenagers do when they are dating. She chatted about his coming to Boston, the things they could do, like the amphibious Duck ride around the harbor. She had never done that. They could go to museums, and she knew this great little restaurant in Little Italy. It was not necessary for Dominick to say anything.

It wasn't until they were driving off the ferry that Angelica mentioned Lydia. "I have to go see her," she said. "She's staying at that Ms. Arnold's place. Do you know where that is? I can never find it."

"I will show you where it is, but you can never find a parking place in that neighborhood, and I'm not going in. The last time I was there Ms. Arnold threw me out, and I think she was right."

"Oh, Dominick, help me out here. You know that mother and I don't communicate that well. With you there things would go better, I just know they would. She likes you. Maybe with you there she won't act up. You know, she was asking for you, as Lord Witherspoon. She was sure that the feds had killed you, too. She kept saying, 'I saw it coming. I saw it coming.'"

"She thinks the feds killed Atticus? Turn left here, up the hill."

"Sometimes she thinks they're just hiding him away in solitary confinement somewhere."

"Another left. Keep your eye out for a place to park. What's going to happen to Lydia?"

"I'm trying to get her to go to London and stay with her favorite daughter, but mother doesn't have a current passport. Mother doesn't even have a current driver's license."

"Go around the block. You can only take left turns in here. That reminds me, did she and Ms. Arnold make their court date in Boston?"

"Court date? What court date! For what?"

"They didn't tell you? I had to go bail them out for shoplifting. Wait. That person is pulling out. You're only a block away, take it."

"At least stop in and let mother know that you are still alive."

"But I'm not Lord Witherspoon anymore. That's someone else now."

Angelica parked her car, and they were walking back to the cross street. She grabbed his arm. "Dominick, sweetheart, just do this one little thing for me and I'll let you go again. I can't stand that woman Ms. Arnold. It's like making me go to the dentist all by myself. Don't be mean to me." She would not let go. She dragged him up to the steps of Ms. Arnold's house. He would have had to hit her to make her let go. There was no avoiding it. Angelica was still attached to him when she raised and lowered the front door knocker.

Ms. Arnold answered the door. She was carrying a large, seemingly comatose gray cat.

"Hello, Martha. I'm here to see mother," Angelica said.

"Why didn't you call first? You know you are supposed to call first."

"I did call yesterday when I got in. I talked with mother."

"You have to talk with me, not her. I see you have brought trouble."

"You know Dominick. He came along to say hello to mother. Is she here?"

"Where else would she be? This gentleman is not welcome here."

"Fine. Then I'll just be going," Dominick said, pulling his arm away from Angelica's grip. "Good day, Ms. Arnold, Angelica."

"Nick? Is that you Nick?" It was Lydia's voice coming from somewhere behind Ms. Arnold. "You've escaped! Is Atticus with you?" Lydia came up from behind Ms. Arnold and, with a firm hand on her shoulder, pushed her aside.

"Hello, Lydia," Dominick said. "Yes, it's me, Nick and, no, Atticus isn't with me. Atticus is dead. And I have to go now."

"But you just got here," Lydia said. "What are you doing with her? Wait here. I'll get my coat and we can go." Lydia turned and went back into the house. "We'll buy some chocolates and take the ferry ride again." Her voice trailed off down the hall.

"Lydia, no. You are not going with him," Ms. Arnold said as she turned to follow her.

"Mother!" Angelica said, following them.

Dominick retreated back down the steps, shaking his head. Time to avaunt. He was on the sidewalk and headed away when Lydia came rushing out the door. She was wearing her mink coat and carrying the gray cat by the scruff of its neck. Ms. Arnold was not far behind her.

"Here, kitty, you're free, too," Lydia said and she flung the cat up into the air. It did not land well. It didn't have the air time to right itself. It bounced off the railing and off the porch like a hairy bag of random objects. Ms. Arnold let out a sound like the scream equivalent of a stifled yawn. Lydia bounded up to Dominick and took his arm. "You'd like a drink, wouldn't you, Nick. Let's go find you a drink. I'll pay. Oh, darn. I've forgotten my purse. Wait just a sec." And Lydia bounded back up the steps into the house, brushing past her daughter standing in the doorway. "Out of my way," she said.

Ms. Arnold was already off the steps, down out of sight beside the porch. Purely out of morbid curiosity, Dominick found himself standing beside her, looking down at the twitching pile of gray fur.

"Oh, do something, do something," Ms. Arnold said. "This is all your fault after all."

Dominick couldn't see any blood. Maybe the cat was just stunned. He bent over and reached down, but the cat still had enough life in it to try and bite him. There was a snow shovel leaning against a corner of the porch. Dominick managed to get the cat onto the shovel and he carried it on that, at a safe distance, up the steps and into the house. Ms. Arnold was right behind him. "To the kitchen," she said.

In the back parlor the TV set was still on, and as Dominick passed by the door he got a brief glimpse of Lydia and Angelica tussling over Lydia's purse. They each had a grip on the handle and were pulling in opposite directions. Their voices were raised and mixed in with the sounds of gunshots and screams from the TV show. Something snapped, someone fell with a crash, and there was the sound of the purse's contents spewing out onto the floor.

Dominick slid the cat off the shovel onto the kitchen counter beside the sink. He could see now there was blood congealing around the cat's nostrils and eyes. That was probably not a positive sign. Otherwise it looked the same as when Ms. Arnold was carrying it around.

"What should we do? Should I call 911?" Ms. Arnold asked.

"Let it rest for a minute. See what happens," Dominick said. "You know, nine lives and all."

"How can you say that? How can you say that?" Angelica was yelling at her mother as they came into the kitchen. Lydia was still wearing her mink, but now she was also wearing blood, running down her cheek from a cut on the side of her forehead.

"Don't try to tell me different," Lydia said. "You are nothing but a liar." She didn't seem to notice the blood.

"I never did anything of the kind!"

"Liar, liar, pants on fire," Lydia said. "You took them all."

"Lydia, you've cut yourself," Ms. Arnold said, going toward her with her hand extended.

"Don't touch me, you witch. My ancestors used to burn the likes of yours at the stake."

"You're the murderer. You've killed my precious. You're just a crazy, dangerous old lady!"

The blood was now dripping off Lydia's cheekbone onto her mink.

"Don't you talk to my mother like that," Angelica said, coming all the way into the kitchen.

"You shut up, you cheap harlot," Ms. Arnold said. Voices were now raised to a level that drowned out the car chase and sirens on the TV. "You fobbing your poor addled mother off on me to take care of, never contributing a penny. You . . . you geriatric abuser."

They were off to the venom races then, all three of them. Dominick ran some tap water onto the end of a dish towel and went over to Lydia. She let him dab at her face. He showed her the blood on the end of the towel, and she scowled. Then she saw the blood on her coat and she took the towel away from him to wipe at her fur. Angelica and Ms. Arnold were still going at it. Dominick drew Lydia aside to try to stop her bleeding, feeling like he was pulling an injured bird out of a cockfight.

"How dare you! How dare you!" Angelica was yelling. "It's not as if anyone ever trusted you or any of your family. My father was right about you."

"Your father? Your father was one the most useless . . ."

Dominick sat Lydia down in a kitchen chair and gave her the towel to clean her coat. He went to get a fresh tea towel. He knew what drawer they would be in. When he came back Lydia had slipped her iPod out of her mink coat's pocket and was putting in her ear pods. The fight no longer interested her. She took the fresh towel from Dominick and pressed it against her cut brow without a word. She looked more distant than dazed.

"No, no. She is leaving today, right now, with me. I wouldn't think of leaving her here with the likes of you for another minute," Angelica was saying as Dominick slipped behind her and out of the kitchen, down the hall, and out the front door.

It was Sunday and sunny, almost the Ides of March. The first pale tourists of the season were venturing out in New Jerusalem. As

Dominick walked back to the dockside lot where he had left his car he walked past them. He remembered a bumper sticker from the summer before: "If there is a tourist season, why can't we shoot them?" When he got to Starks's house, Starks's Jag was there but he wasn't. Dominick showered and changed, ridding himself of the smell of Angelica. When he came back out of his room he could hear the sound of a blender in the kitchen.

"Margarita?" Starks asked as Dominick came into the kitchen. "Sunshine, hope, tequila."

"Welcome back," Dominick said. "How was the trip?"

"Always answering questions with questions." Starks was running a slice of lime around the lip of a tumbler. He then twirled the upside-down glass once in a plate of salt. "Two can play that game. How was your tryst with the grieving daughter?"

"Lucky guess?"

"Who doesn't erase messages from the answering machine?'

"Who knows how?"

"Can you imagine a language that only used the interrogative?" Starks poured a thick slurry mixture into two tumblers.

"What would that be like?"

"Wouldn't that be interesting?" Starks put one of the tumblers down in front of Dominick.

"Did you know there is a language that only uses the passive voice?"

"Really?"

"Basque. It's an ergative language."

"That wasn't a question, you know? You lose." They clinked glasses.

"Thanks, I will have a margarita, though it's hardly the season yet. Where were you just now? Your car was here, but you weren't."

"Down in my darkroom off the garage, developing film I shot on my trip, which went fine, by the way. Was your visit worth the trouble?"

"Oh, no trouble. What did you take photographs of?"

"Houses primarily, old houses. Oh, come on, Dominick. What's her name? What's she like in bed?"

"Angelica. Appreciative."

"Well, one word answers are better than none, I guess." Starks went to the stove and lifted the lid off a pot to give it a stir. There was a wonderful waft of fish chowder. "Emma is coming out for dinner," he said. "She heard you were back, and wanted to fill us in on developments."

"She heard I was back? Was it on the radio or something? That smells good."

"Oh, was your return a secret? She called me on my cell phone while I was away to ask if I had heard from you, and I told her you were back and staying here. There's a second messge for you on the machine, from yesterday, from Emma. I guess you didn't get that one. Pretty soon you're going to need a secretary to keep your social calendar straight."

"Developments?"

"The LNG thing, I'm sure. That is her new pastime and passion. Unless, of course, it's just to see her dear Nickel again."

Emma arrived in a taxicab and asked Dominick to pay the man. But first she gave him a big hug and smooch and said, "I knew you'd come back." *Coconspirator* had always struck Dominick as a cozy term, hinting at a bond unknown in everyday lives. It carried an aura of covert closeness, of secret sharing. It was certainly never a term he would have expected applied to himself, but at dinner that night, over chowder and French bread, Emma ordained him and Starks as her coconspirators. She acted as if it were a gift she was giving them.

Emma's enthusiasm—a convert's eagerness—was inviting. Starks had been right; there did seem to be some sort of sudden weird groundswell of public opinion against the LNG terminal in Old Grofton, some sort of Yankee closing of the ranks against an intruder. Emma seemed to know all the players and all the details. Even schoolkids were making posters opposed to the Hercules Corp's project. The TV news especially liked covering the right-wing anti-Arab group's antics.

"Graffiti?" Dominick asked.

"Some pretty good stuff," Emma smiled. "Even if I do say so myself."

Emma's "kidnapping"—as she put it—by the ICE agents at The Harp had been her confirmation to the cause, that and a documentary she had seen on the dangers and evils of natural gas and its extraction.

"You've got to see it." Her release from custody had been for her the validation and proof of the righteousness of her cause. She was disconcertingly full of self-confidence and had all sorts of ideas about what their International Gaia Brigade could do next. "And to think," she said, "that it all started right here at this table with your guys' idea to reinvent Lord Witherspoon."

"The hashish revolution," Starks said.

"And all to save poor Atticus's ass," Dominick said.

"Well, Atticus is becoming a bit of a martyr to the cause now, you know. There are people who think he didn't just innocently drop dead while being questioned."

"Oh, come on," Starks scoffed.

"The whole world knows that the feds don't mind using extreme methods of interrogation when they think they are dealing with terrorists."

"That's the CIA and those types and not on US citizens." Starks seemed offended.

"CIA, FBI, ICE—it's all the same to most people. And they have used torture on American citizens. They had already questioned Atticus more than once. He had nothing to tell them. Why pull him in yet another time? I'm just telling what people are saying. It didn't help that there was no autopsy and that they had him immediately cremated."

"Wait," Dominick said. "His daughter told me that she had him cremated."

"Did she? Or did she just agree to it? In any case, it looks like a cover-up. The hospital they took him to was a veteran's hospital, Army doctors."

"Don't you think this all sounds, well, a bit paranoid?" Starks said. "Like some conspiracy theory?"

"The fact remains he died in custody and would probably still be alive today if they had just left him alone."

"Okay, so he qualifies as a martyr," Starks said. "Does that make your Gaia Brigade some sort of church?"

"Oh, please, John. People can believe in something without making a religion out of it. Our little campaign, or more properly the feds' overreaction to it, sparked something. Suddenly it was a federal crime to question something being pushed down our throats?

Atticus's death put a human face on the protest, a local face. Not some guy named Muhammad. You couldn't get more New England than Atticus Jameson."

"Spoken like a true zealot," Dominick said. "Emma d'Arc."

"You two are such cynics. I think that's why I like you."

"No, you're cute when you've got a cause," Starks said. "That warpath look suits you."

"I don't think Atticus would like the idea of his being a martyr," Dominick said, "but no matter, as he isn't around to like or dislike anything now. What's next?"

"I don't know. It's all gotten pretty out of control. No coordination, different groups doing their own thing. Bay Savers has pretty much fallen out of the picture with Atticus gone and Theo cooperating with the feds. There was an interesting development in court in Boston today, though—a deadline that the Hercules lawyers missed, which is unlike them. They were supposed to respond to a show-cause motion that had been filed requesting a delay and an expanded environmental assessment, and they didn't respond."

"Which means what?"

"No one knows for sure. Just a dropped ball or what? But I was told that their not filing a response means the judge—a federal judge— pretty much has to grant the request for a delay. But they wouldn't give up that easy. They've won every court decision thus far. They may have something up their sleeves."

"Lawyers wear a lot of sleeves." Starks opened another bottle of wine.

"I think, right now, your best course would be to just sit back and see what happens," Dominick said. "Don't get any more involved. I mean, do you want to find out personally if the feds are using torture or not?"

"The problem is I can't think of a single funny thing to say about torture," Starks said, refilling their wine glasses.

"It comes from the Latin for twisted," Dominick volunteered.

"Emma, you do not want to become a twisted sister. It is not a wait-loss program."

"Are you implying that I should lose some weight?"

"No, just that you should lean toward waiting. Patience, princess."

After dinner Emma went to watch her cable news shows and Dominick went out to the porch to smoke a cigar. He wondered where his bad coyote was hanging out tonight. When he came back in, the house was quiet. Starks had retired and Emma was not in the study watching TV. He looked into his room, where an end-table lamp was lit and Emma was curled up under the covers on one side of the queen-size bed. Her back was to him.

"I want to sleep here tonight, Nickel. That couch is uncomfortable. I won't bother you, if you don't bother me. I've got my period anyhow."

"Okay, go to sleep before I come in and start snoring." Dominick went to the kitchen and poured himself a nightcap. This sharing of beds would have to stop. It disturbed his sleep.

Chapter 24

"John, I want to make it clear that I will be out of your hair as soon as possible. I know I have already overstayed the few days I asked for." Dominick and Starks were seated at the dining room table the following evening, eating the braised lamb chops and risotto Dominick had cooked for supper. Dominick felt that some sort of apology was in order. That morning when Emma had left for town with Starks there had been no witty routines. Starks had seemed mildly irked by their presence and by Emma's assumption that he would give her a ride. She hadn't noticed, of course, just full of her cause and her plans, but Dominick noted it, a houseguest's red flag—irritated host. So he had gone shopping and cooked dinner, entering into houseboy mode, and now he was broaching the delicate topic of EDD—estimated date of departure.

"Was I that unpleasant this morning?" Starks said. "I hate Mondays, always have, the end of make-believe and the start of their world. It was nothing personal, more universal."

"But Emma staying over again . . ."

"Please, Dominick, do you flatter yourself by thinking I'm jealous?"

"It is your house."

"And she was my guest as well. Although I fear Queen E is becoming a tad unhinged."

"It's not a game with her anymore."

"Anyway, Dominick, stow your apologies. I enjoy your being here, and you can cook supper every night, if they're all as good as this."

"Then let me do that. It would be my pleasure. You can call in your menu requests."

"You're not worried about Emma?"

"Not my worry. She is a big girl, if you haven't noticed."

"You said you took some photos on your trip. Black-and-white, I presume. Shall I develop them for you?"

"That would be good, thanks. I've been shooting that film you gave me. And as long as we are exchanging favors, may I use the computer in your study to check my e-mail? I'll be searching for the next place to go."

"No problem, no hurry. No porn sites, please. Too many viruses."

As a matter of fact, Dominick had already begun using Starks's landline in search of his next destination, leaving messages with his e-mail address to respond to. Coming back had been a mistake.

It was several days later when Starks's phone, which never rang, rang around midday. It was Starks. "You've been killed. Or at least Lord Witherspoon has been. Turn on the news, channel four." Of course, by the time Dominick turned on the TV and found channel four there was an erectile dysfunction drug ad on and it took another half hour for them to circle back to their "top breaking story."

The Coast Guard and federal authorities had released some details about an explosion and fire in the channel off Darby Point the night before. According to the Coast Guard, the vessel destroyed was a Chris-Craft powerboat that had been stolen the day before from a local marina. According to the federal authorities, the boat had been engaged in another terrorist attack on the Hercules Corp's LNG compound in Old Grofton when it was intercepted by the authorities. A warning shot across the boat's bow was answered by a burst of automatic weapons fire. When the fire was returned there was a violent explosion, destroying the vessel and all aboard.

Special Agent Kaczynski of Homeland Security affirmed that the stolen craft and its crew of three had become the object of an intense search since earlier in the day when through anonymous sources and surveillance it had been determined that one of its crew was the fugitive terrorist Jake Forrest, known locally as Lord Witherspoon. "Mr. Forrest was observed through night-vision goggles on the deck of the vessel firing an automatic weapon moments before the explosion." Pieces of at least two bodies had been recovered, but positive identification was doubtful. Agent Kaczynski was briefly interviewed on camera. He was their abbreviated ICE man. He looked suitably grim and victorious. In a World War II movie—Audie Murphy—he would have been smoking a Lucky Strike. Another erectile dysfunction drug ad followed, as if men who watched the news had a chronic problem, one that could not be cured purely by buying a bigger pickup truck. Dominick clicked the set off.

Well, Agent K would be quite the hero now, having tracked down and eliminated a number one terrorist enemy of the state. At least he hadn't thanked the lord for the professional courtesy of his assistance. Maybe that was in the part of the interview edited out. After all, was it not a godlike act to create someone and then destroy him? There was something almost biblical about it.

This called for a cigar. It was a sunny day, not spring yet but headed there. Dominick put on his jacket and walked up toward the big house. There was a south-facing terrace there with a stone bench from which he could see the bay. He would take a broad view of things. This, after all, no longer had anything to do with him. This was now entering the realm of history. An historic event had transpired. A transnational villain of mythic proportions—Jake Forrest, aka Lord Witherspoon, aka Nobody—had been vaporized right there on their bay. A terrorist attack on the homeland had been repulsed. A red letter day for America. And for Hercules Corp, which could proceed unimpeded by bombs. Agent K's feat could now be entered into the register of patriotic exploits, and Dominick could brag that he had actually met the man himself, had the honor of being frisked by him.

Now, there was a perfect example of revisionist history. It had been the tall agent, not short Agent K, who had frisked them at Charlie's, but that unnecessary detail would only dilute the impact of the story. Dominick was now smoking his cigar on the stone bench, looking down the rolling brown meadow toward the bay. The historic record had been diddled with like that long before digital photographs. Sometimes actual events made lousy narratives, and *story* was the important part of history. Soon the story of the battle of Darby Point would begin its petrifaction into historic fact and Agent

K would need a publicist. It would not make any difference that it was all invention. But body parts? Those were more difficult to produce than faked photographs.

Dominick fixed Cajun short ribs for supper that night. Starks told him that their local news was now national, with the old photos of Jake Forrest and even the faked one of Forrest and Atticus on the boat playing on cable news. "The International Gaia Brigade is now infamous," Starks said.

"Excuse me for being so vain," Dominick said as he brought the food to the table, "but am I to understand that a photograph of my body—albeit with a different face—is on national TV?"

"International, and it's your hands holding the camera, too."

"Fame, so fleeting."

"Aren't you lucky? They identify your friend Atticus by name, as a probable accomplice."

"Tying it all up. I hope it's not too spicy for you."

"Well, there is still the question of who the other two men on the blown-up boat were, and the Coast Guard is conducting a pro forma inquiry, but, yeah, it is a bit over the mark with the cayenne."

"It's what the recipe called for. Of course, I do sometimes confuse teaspoons and tablespoons. Has anyone asked what all those explosives onboard the Chris-Craft were for? I mean, there's nothing really at Darby Point yet to blow up."

"Question unasked, along with why the ICE guys were out there alone without FBI, Coast Guard, or local assistance when a so-called intense search was in progress."

"I guess it doesn't really matter," Dominick said. "Here, more bread. Want another beer?"

"Thanks. It was a pretty bold move on their part anyway. Do they think this will end it?"

"And who exactly are they? I made a flan for desert. That should ease your palate."

After supper Starks loaded the dishwasher and went off to his darkroom downstairs. Dominick went to the study to watch the cable news.

He did want to see his body on TV, but he had to wait through the other news. Starks came to the study door. "Dominick, we have to talk," he said, and he turned and walked off toward the front room. Dominick followed him. Starks dropped a pile of photographs and contact sheets on the dining room table. "I developed your film," he said. "A few good shots."

"Thanks. What's wrong?"

"Dominick, when I invited you here I opened my house to you. I did not grant you entry into my past."

"What are you talking about?"

"This," Starks said, sorting out some black-and-white prints from the pile and laying them out for Dominick, shots of the shadows inside Broadmoor. "This is my past, not yours. My parents' home, not yours. My dreams and nightmares, not yours."

"John, I . . ."

"You had no right to go there. You trespassed. You broke into and entered my private world."

"No, I found the keys to an old and deserted house and I wandered around in empty rooms, a space that had been empty a long, long time. If that is your past, John, god help you."

"Look at your photographs, Dominick. You wanted to own that space."

"I was photographing shadows, for Christ's sake, dust motes not memories, contrasts not crime scenes."

"Why did you say that? Why?" John Starks was suddenly as Dominick had never seen him before. He was angry, furious. He stepped back and flexed as if punched. "What do you know? Why, really, are you here?"

"John, I . . . really, come on. If I was trying to hide something I would not have given you the film to develop. I'm sorry if I crossed some line by going up there, but . . ."

"This and this," Starks flopped two more prints in front of Dominick. One shot was of a corner of the Broadmoor kitchen where the slanting barred light from an unseen window did a disappearing trick above a counter. The other was of sunlight coming down the staircase from one of the turrets into an otherwise darkened hall.

"Do you know why all my sharp kitchen knives are locked up and I had to show you how to unlock the drawer to get one to use? Because my mother stabbed my father to death in that kitchen, against that counter, in a jealous rage. You knew that, didn't you? Somebody told you. And this, this." Starks jabbed his finger into the other photo, into the shadows at the end of the hall. "You even caught her face watching you; just as she watches me whenever I go there."

Dominick picked up the print to study it, and, yes, there in the shadows of the dark hallway were the faint symmetrical highlights of what might be construed as the cheekbones and brow and nose of a face.

"I've destroyed your negatives and I will destroy these prints, stolen property, and you will have to leave, Dominick. Not tonight. I won't throw you out into the cold, but as soon as you can. Our continuative present has ended. Good night."

When Dominick got up in the morning Starks was already gone. Once again Dominick could leisurely pack and load his car. He was in no hurry. He had no idea where he was going. As he left he slipped the spare house key under the tread on the bottom step where Starks kept it. He was feeling rather numb, not at all philosophical.

Not a hundred yards down the road, Emma was drudging along, talking on her cell phone. She either didn't notice or didn't recognize him driving by. She had her head down as she walked and talked. Dominick turned around in the next driveway and headed back. There was no other traffic on Starks's road. He pulled up beside her and buzzed down the passenger-side window. "Emma, if you are headed to John's house, no one is at home."

"Oh, oh it's you," she said. Then into her phone, "Gotta go. Do you think you can find it? It's a house with two turrets up on a bluff. There's a cove with a dock. I'll have a light. Bye." Emma clicked her phone shut. She was wearing a small backpack that she slipped off and tossed on the seat between them before getting in. "O Lover, am I glad to see you."

"What's up?" Dominick asked. He pulled back onto the road and drove back the way he had just come, but past Starks's driveway.

"Where?" Emma asked, expecting them to turn in.

"I'm not there anymore. John has gone solo, guest-free again."

"I was hoping you guys could put me up again, just until dusk. It's sort of urgent."

"How so?" The roads here circled around the big estates. Dominick took a left onto a smaller back lane.

"I've got to escape. Someone will pick me up in a boat."

"I gathered that. Escape from what?"

"The feds are after me. I'm headed for Canada."

"Emma, what in the world? What have you done now?"

"There were bomb threats today, e-mailed to the local ICE and FBI offices."

"And?"

"They were signed by the IGB, supposedly in retaliation for the murder of Forrest and Atticus."

"And?"

"The feds think I did it."

Dominick took another left. "And did you?"

"No. Honest Injun, Nickel, I wasn't responsible, but they have their plants in the movement. They know who to blame. Someone fingered me, and I can't prove I didn't do it. I'm no good to the cause in the slammer. Been there, done that. Not this time, sweetheart." A variety of delightful youthful energy emanated from Emma as she leaned forward in her seat. "Not this time, baby."

"But your cell phone, can't they trace that?"

"Oh shit, I never thought. What should I do?"

"Make another call, to anyone. No, wait." Dominick took another left, back onto a main road that led to a shoreline stretch with plenty of new houses at least two miles up the coast from Broadmoor. "Now. Then after they answer give it a minute, hang up, and turn it off."

"You're so clever, Nickel."

"I'm just guessing."

She did as he said. Dominick turned the car around and headed back to Starks's. At the carriage house Dominick had Emma wait in the car while he retrieved the apartment key from the bottom stair tread and went up and let himself in. The ring of keys with the key to the big house was still there in the same kitchen drawer. He drove up there and unlocked the house. Emma followed him in. He led her through the empty rooms and up the main staircase to the second floor, then up the circular stairs to the turret. "You'll hide here," he told her. "I'll come and get you when the coast is clear."

"I have to be down at the dock by dusk."

"How did you know there was a cove and a dock?"

"John and I used to run dope in there from visiting yachties now and then in the old days. Before they'd hit customs. It's secluded. Nickel, I don't know what to say."

"Just don't say anything over your phone."

Dominick locked the house behind him as he left. He drove back to Starks's and went up into the apartment. He needed to take a piss and he wanted a drink. He wasn't sure what to do. Was he aiding and abetting a fugitive? Could he believe Emma that she hadn't placed the bomb threats? Should he stay or go? He decided to leave—best not to deal with cops if you could avoid it. But as he walked out the front door, a drink in hand, the road at the end of the driveway filled up with police vehicles and two pulled in the driveway. Dominick turned and went back inside, finishing his drink.

He watched from the windows as two officers—they were State Police—went around to the back of the carriage house. The doorbell rang. Two more officers were at the door. One said they were in pursuit of a dangerous fugitive and would like to search the premises. It wasn't exactly phrased as a request. Dominick could imagine what Atticus would have told them, but he stepped aside and gestured them in. Their search was quick and perfunctory, but every room and closet was visited. The garages downstairs? one of them asked. Dominick knew they were locked, but guessed that one of the keys on the key ring would open them. The key ring was still in his pocket, but he went to the kitchen to pretend to fetch it. It took several tries, but he found the right key, and they searched the garages and darkroom as well.

The house up there? One of the officers said, gesturing toward Broadmoor. The two other officers were already headed up there in their cruiser. Empty, Dominick told them. No one had lived there for years. Did he have a key? Otherwise they would have to break in. Dominick wanted to ask them if they were familiar with the Fourth Amendment, but instead he said, yes, he had a key. He got into the back seat of the cruiser and drove up there with them. It had been a while since he had graced the back seat of a police car, but at least this time his hands were not cuffed behind him.

"What is it your fugitive has done?" Dominick asked them. "I didn't hear anything on the news."

"Federal case, terrorist."

"Oh, an Arab?" Dominick said.

"No, this one is homegrown, I gather, an Indian." The officer held up a poor-quality faxed photo of Emma with her hair pulled back, a mug shot. She had never looked more like Geronimo. "Seen her in the neighborhood? Maybe she works as a domestic for someone?"

"Do Native Americans work as domestics?" Dominick asked.

"Just a guess. They traced a call from her cell phone to someplace near here. I don't know what else she'd be doing in a neighborhood like this."

Dominick unlocked the house and the same two officers went in while the others circled outside. Dominick followed them in.

"This place is like a tomb," the officer said. "You're sure no one's been in here?"

"I come up now and then to check on the place. Only ghosts."

The other officer went upstairs. Dominick could hear him opening and closing doors. Then there was the sound of the radio in both of the cruisers squawking, and a voice called from outside. "Todd, Todd, they've got a new location on her up the road. She's still on the move."

"Yo, Luke," the officer with Dominick yelled up the stairs. "Let's go. We're out of here. Thank you, sir. We'll give you a ride back down."

Dominick locked the door behind them and rode back to the carriage house with them. "Well, good luck," he said, getting out of the car. "Be careful, those Indians can be dangerous." He liked the idea of their having to search all those houses down by the beach. Maybe somebody there would have the guts to ask if they had a warrant. The cop cars were all gone from the road, though now and then one raced by in one direction or the other. A black helicopter passed overhead in a hurry.

Dominick poured himself another drink. He would wait till all was calm, both outside and within his gut, before going up to release Emma. She had until dusk and she was safe where she was. His car was packed. This would all soon be history. He went into the study and turned on the TV—it was still tuned to the news channel—and there was Emma's mug shot. The announcer identified her as a leader of the IGB—even they were using just the initials now—successor to the slain Lord Witherspoon and wanted by the authorities. She was armed and dangerous, they said. The FBI had released the text of the bomb threat, which read in part, "You have killed innocent people. If this is now war, then you are war criminals." It was signed Commander Em, IGB.

This time Dominick walked up to the big house. He let himself in and walked up the stairs to the second floor. "Emma, all clear. It's just me, Nickel," he called out as he walked down the hall toward the door to the turret stairs. But as he went to open the door it was locked. "Emma, the cops are gone. Come unlock the door." He tried the knob again, but it would not open. "Emma!"

Emma's voice came from behind the door. "That is you, isn't it, Nickel?"

"Me and just me, Commander Em. Come on, it's time to go. Unlock the door."

"I didn't lock it. Someone else did, from the outside."

"What? When?"

"After you and the troopers left. The trooper opened the door, you know. I heard him. I guess he didn't feel like walking up more stairs." Emma was now shaking the doorknob from the other side. "It was after that. I saw them leave and was going to come down, but you had told me to stay, so I did. Then I heard someone lock the door."

"Step back, go back up the stairs," Dominick said. He backed up and kicked at the door above the latch, trying to spring it. Nothing. A few more tries had the same result. Then a kick missed and hit a central door panel, which splintered around his foot. A few more kicks removed the rest of the rotted-out panels. "Can you make it through there?" he asked. Emma managed to squeeze her way through, ripping her poncho.

"I thought you had sneaked up here and locked me in for some reason. To keep me from escaping or something, to wait for them to post a reward. I had bad thoughts about you, Nickel. It wasn't you?"

"No, it wasn't me, and nobody else came up here either. Old houses do strange things. Let's go."

Emma reached back through the busted door and pulled out her backpack. "What do you mean, they do strange things?"

"Old houses have memories. Sometimes they repeat themselves out of habit."

"Well, did this place used to give people the creeps? Because that's what it is giving me."

The path down to the dock on the cove was obvious enough once they found the entrance to it in the scrub. Dominick left Emma there. He wanted to get back and leave before Starks returned from work. "You did send those bomb threats, didn't you, Emma?" he asked as they stood at the top of the path, looking out at the empty cove.

"Actually, yes, I did have a hand in it, Nickel. I lied to you because I was afraid you wouldn't help me if you thought I was guilty of what they were chasing me for. Forgive me? This is just the beginning, Nickel. Extreme times demand extreme measures. We won't stop until they are stopped."

"They is a huge number."

"Gotta try."

"Good luck. Watch your back. Don't trust anyone who makes being trusted a big deal."

They hugged and Emma headed off down the trail to the dock. Dominick walked back to the carriage house, put the ring of keys back in the kitchen drawer and the apartment key under the bottom stair tread, got in his car, and drove away. Twilight was just coming on. He had nowhere to go. He drove away from the direction Starks would be coming home, which took him down the road past the new beach houses. There were police cars everywhere. He was stopped at a roadblock. They checked his backseat and had him open his trunk.

"Moving?" An officer asked him.

"Just on vacation," Dominick said. "What's going on?"

"Nothing to do with you, bud. Just move on along."

Chapter 25

Names on the land should have meanings, a reason for being there. After all, every place name had an origin, a footprint in history. Someone or some group of people at some point in time had decided to call their place either Pleasantville or Tombstone. Some place name origins were dictated by what was there—Fall River, Grand Canyon, Cedar Creek. Others were acts of religious devotion—Providence, Trinidad, Virginia, all of the Saints—or politics—Pittsburgh, Louisville, Georgetown—or patriotism—Jacksonville, Lincoln, all the Washingtons. Then there were, especially here in New England, all the News, homage to places left behind—New Bedford, New Brunswick, New Wherever.

Place names as exits in white letters on green signs showed up in his headlights as Dominick drove away from New Jerusalem. People should know where their place's name came from. Why Tiverton? Why Wareham? Even the original names that somehow remained. Who knew the meaning of Acushnet or Weweantic, Mattapoisett or Popponesett? What had those words once meant? Why had time's renaming passed them over?

Destinationless, Dominick wandered back roads for a while, then found himself headed not south but east, out the cape. It was late when he pulled into the Radisson Hyannis, but it was off-season and there were rooms. He took one with a balcony and smoked a cigar out there before retiring. Hyannis, he decided, had probably been the name of some big man, the chief who had taken a gift to let the white guys stay. Who knew what Massachusetts meant? It sounded descriptive. He wondered if Emma had gotten away.

Dominick bought a *Boston Globe* on the way to breakfast. The news was that Commander Em, the homegrown terrorist, had not yet been apprehended. The local judge who had released her from custody was catching a lot of flak. Bay Savers was mentioned, and Atticus. No bombs had been discovered. The FBI let it be known in no uncertain terms that it did not like being threatened. ICE had no comment. Emma was now wanted on charges of terroristic threatening.

A sidebar article was entitled "Coast Guard Continues Investigation." The Chris-Craft destroyed in the Old Grofton attack had been identified as one stolen from a marina in East Haven, where, ironically, it had been mothballed after being seized a year previously in a drug raid by ICE agents. Divers were searching for additional wreckage. None of the detonated suspects had yet been identified. Forensics on the recovered body parts was continuing.

Dominick disliked Hyannis. He headed on to Provincetown, only an hour further out at the end of the Cape, which was deserted and encased in a frozen fog. He found a nice enough inn and decided to stay. He was reading Philbrick's book on the Mayflower people. What presumptuous bastards they were. He avoided the news and newspapers, but he still checked his e-mail each morning on the inn's guest computer to see if he had any leads on where to head next. On the third day there was a message from Angelica:

Once again, dear Dominick, where are you? Mother has escaped. Would you have any idea where she might be? The police checked Mt. Sinai, but she wasn't there. I have no idea how she could get there anyway. I had to put her in a home here in Boston. She was just impossible to live with, and Dex wouldn't put up with her. It was supposedly a secure facility, but she managed to get out, after stealing cash from other residents and the office. I'm afraid she's gone too far this time. If she does contact you, please let me know. By the way, I did not appreciate you sneaking out on me at that witch's house. Angie.

That evening he finished Philbrick's book, and the next morning he headed back down the Cape, out of Pilgrim territory. He stuck to the coast roads to New Jerusalem and caught the late-afternoon ferry back to the island. At Mt. Sinai he parked out front and walked around the house and back through the brown and winter-blasted garden to Lydia's potting shed studio. He called out, "Lydia, it's me, Nick. Okay if I come in?"

There was no answer, so he went on in.

"Hold it right there, mister, or I will shoot you." Lydia's voice came from behind him, from behind the door.

"Lydia, now you're supposed to tell me to put my hands up where you can see them."

"I know that part. Put your hands up, and they better be empty. Now turn around, slowly."

Dominick did as she told him.

"What are you doing here?"

"Looking for you. Your daughter e-mailed me that you were missing, so I came to see if I could help you hide."

"You came alone?"

"You know me, Lydia. I'm always alone."

"Have you been sleeping with her?"

"Lydia, what kind of question is that to ask?"

"An easy one to answer. Yes or no?"

"But there is honor and privacy involved."

"So you did get on her privates. I hope you had a doctor check you out."

Dominick laughed.

"What's so funny?" She raised the handgun she was holding toward his face.

"You are, my dear. Look at you."

Lydia was dressed in Atticus's clothes—baggy brown corduroy pants, a plaid woolen shirt, and a bulky green cardigan sweater. She was wearing Atticus's battered old fisherman's hat. She looked like a girl dressed up in her daddy's clothes.

"No mirrors out here and no laughter either. I don't like laughter."

"Lydia, could you put down the gun or at least point it in some other direction? Those things are made to go off."

Lydia looked at the gun in her hand as if wondering what it was doing there. "Oh," she said. "No funny stuff?"

"No funny stuff, cross my heart."

Lydia went to put the gun down on the potting shed counter and it went off, sending a slug through a windowpane. "Mercy, that's loud," she said, putting her hands to her ears as if the gun might go off again by itself.

"Is that Atticus's old gun?" Dominick asked.

"Yes, the one he took to hiding beneath his pillow. Lot of good it did him." Lydia wandered off toward the studio end of the shed, leaving the gun where it was. Dominick went over and found the gun's safety and switched it on before following her.

"Are your ears still ringing?" Lydia asked. "I can't hear my crickets anymore."

"Lydia, how did you get here?"

"What do you mean, how did I get here? Why, I walked all the way from the ferry dock."

"How did you get to the ferry?" The daybed in the studio's far corner was now piled with pillows, quilt, and a comforter. There were a teakettle and a saucepan on top of the space heater and a large oblong canvas up on her easel. "From Boston, I mean."

"Why, the way I always have, the train and a taxi. I know my way home, you know. I'm not totally addled."

"You stole money from folks at the nursing home?"

"They weren't using it, bunch of zombies. And it wasn't a nursing home. It was an asylum, a loony bin with bars on the windows."

"How did you get out?" Dominick noticed that the canvas was up on the easel backwards, with its frame side out. She had already gessoed it.

"Kitchen door. They never locked it after taking out the garbage. Was she any good in bed? Angie, I mean."

"Does it matter?"

"Not really. I'm not sure what that means anymore anyway. You know, people used to sleep around in my day, too. Especially here on the island. Summertime, parties, drinks. A lot of times husbands weren't around, either still back in the city working or out sailing or fishing. But we didn't have all these diseases you've got now back then."

"People look at old folks and can't imagine them doing it, so they think they never did."

"She married a homosexual, you know. They catch even more diseases."

"Didn't they give you pills in there?"

"I never swallowed them. Held them under my tongue."

Dominick looked in the saucepan—the remains of a can of chicken noodle soup. "Have the police been by?"

"I guess so. Maybe. They never came out here. You're the first. You are right, you know. It's hard to imagine George Washington in bed with someone."

"What's the painting going to be?"

"I am waiting to find out. I'm still trying to find the picture behind the painting, so I thought I would start from the back looking out. But so far all I can see is white, all the colors together, like looking at the sun."

"Weren't we told as kids never to do that?"

"Who remembers what we were told as kids? Most of it was lies anyway."

"And shall I continue in that tradition and lie to your daughter?"

"Oh, please do. About what?"

"About your whereabouts—a lie of omission—and not tell her I found you here?"

Lydia was staring intently at her reversed canvas. She answered almost absentmindedly, "Oh, she really doesn't care where I am, as long is it's not around her. That geriatric prison they had me in must have been costing them a small fortune. They're glad I'm not there. What was it that was supposed to happen to us if we looked at the sun?"

"I think it was supposed to burn a hole in our retina, a blind spot for life."

"That's right," Lydia said, still staring at the canvas as her right hand rummaged among brushes in a jar, "a blind spot for life." When she stepped up to the easel she was holding a rusty Exacto knife and she reached out and with a flip of her wrist opened a teardrop-shaped hole in the canvas. "That's a start," she said.

Lydia stood there, her head bent to one side, silhouetted against the pale canvas. Most of the daylight had left the room. Atticus's fishing hat now looked jaunty on her. She shifted her weight and the tilt of her head, put down the knife and picked up a brush. "Turn on the lights when you leave, please, Nick. And if you return, bring me some chocolate doughnuts, the kind that never go stale."

Dominick checked himself back into Charlie and Brenda's that night, his old room with the clean sheets. The next day he brought Lydia her chocolate-covered doughnuts, along with candy bars, cheese and French bread, canned peaches and cider, a rotisseried chicken and a bottle of Chardonnay. He only stayed a few minutes. She was busy with her painting on the back of the canvas, which had grown more holes, blocks of bright colors, and stippled outlines of trees. She called him Lord Witherspoon. He told her to make a list of whatever she might need from the village. At the library he checked his e-mail but did not respond to Angelica.

It was officially spring now, and the forsythia bushes and maple trees were showing buds, but otherwise the world was monotone drab and dreary. A high point in Dominick's day was stopping by Mt. Sinai to look in on Lydia. She had begun drinking prodigious amounts of cocoa, and he would have a cup with her and chat. One day she would be fine and the next disconnected. One day she called him Atticus the whole time he was there. She finished the canvas she had started and nailed it to a tree in the garden where she could see it from her studio window. "It needs to be weathered now," she told him. "It's just a baby."

She had started a new work that was actually several—three smaller canvases, all different sizes and shapes and pastel shades. She was doing them simultaneously, "treating them equally," as she put it, torturing them. The canvases were backward again, built up with layers of paint and glued-on fabric, then stabbed with pieces of broken glass, pierced with wires, and spattered with blood. At first Dominick thought it was just red paint, but as it dried it darkened like blood, and he asked.

"It doesn't take much," Lydia said, holding up a bandaged hand. "It was an accident, but then they each deserved their due, and I got to like the effect." She was flicking drops of black paint from a brush among the blood spatters. She called them her seascapes, and as they grew they did take on an abstract sense of rolling waves, stormy skies, and rugged coastline.

It was on the fourth or fifth day of this routine that Dominick got an e-mail message at the library from Rob and Laurie in Key Largo. Rob and Laurie were part of Dominick's old cycle of hosts that he had contacted. It had been several years since he last stayed with them. They were one of those couples who had had so much money for so long that they were bored with it all, and houseguests constituted a form of distraction. It was a come-on-down. They were going for a Caribbean sail and he was welcome along. This was his ticket out. It was a four-day drive south on the interstate, but with a known destination he could zone out and do it. He e-mailed them back that he was on his way. It felt good to be back in play. Perhaps his old life was not over yet.

Dominick packed his car one more time and put Charlie and Brenda's place back to rights again. He took pleasure in totally covering his tracks, in erasing all evidence of his stay. As he went one last time through the house, he carried a dishcloth and wiped all the surfaces he might have touched as if removing even fingerprints. He remembered to turn the thermostat down to where Charlie had set it.

In the village he picked up one last load of groceries for Lydia. After this she would be on her own. Whatever happened next would happen. He had no solution. She was wily enough that she would not starve, and now that spring was here she would not absentmindedly freeze to death. Maybe she would go feral like his coyote. Maybe her favorite daughter Desiré would arrive from London and rescue her. Surely, Angelica had put out the word that their mother had gone AWOL. He stopped at the liquor store to buy another bottle of wine, then changed his mind and bought a bottle of Dom Perignon instead. They would properly toast their fare-thee-well.

Encased in a leaden light, the village seemed deserted, as if the winter had taken a mortal toll. The shops were empty. The clerks were pale zombies. No one spoke. It was a silent, somber, historical diorama of a New England village. Dominick felt invisible, the quick among the unseeing dead. He thought that if he walked out of the store without paying, no one would notice or care to stop him. Even the bay was lifeless and empty, a flat and hammered sheet of pewter blending seamlessly into a horizonless fog that hid distant New Jerusalem. It was as if all this was already part of the past, a halftone memory on a just-turned album page.

When Dominick drove up to Mt. Sinai there was a black SUV with federal plates parked in the driveway out front. With its tinted windows up he couldn't tell if there was anyone inside. He drove on by. The next house down the road, the Benson place, was winter-empty and shuttered. He pulled in there. You couldn't see one house from the other, but Dominick knew there was a path through the brush that connected their backyards. He would just walk over and see if Lydia needed a way to escape, although the feds would not be looking for her. They had more important tasks than tracking down rest-home escapees. He carried over her bags of groceries and the bottle of champagne. Why let uninvited visitors interfere with their goodbyes?

When he got to her studio Lydia was not there. He put down the groceries and considered the possibilities. Most likely she was out in the garden spying on whomever was spying on the house. He went back outside to look for her. He didn't want to go up to the house if the feds were there, but he could scout around and see what Lydia was up to. Maybe she didn't know that the feds were parked out front and was just out starting her spring gardening chores.

The sound of the gunshot came from inside the house—flat, loud, declarative, final. Dominick froze. There was no mistaking it. Half a minute later there was another identical shot. He waited for a third shot, for a scream, for any other noise. There was none. He was halfway to the house, behind an arbor that partially hid him. He stayed there, frozen from flight like some garden statue, and listened. Off in the distance a crow cawed, then closer to hand some other birds chirped and tried a song, trying to make it sound like just a normal early spring day. After a minute or two he began to feel silly, just standing there. He peeked out and looked around. Nothing was moving. There were no crouching agents with guns leveled in two-handed grips like on TV, no sound of footsteps or of doors opening and closing.

Slowly, hesitantly, he walked up the path toward the kitchen door. He couldn't recall if the porch steps creaked or not. They didn't. He looked in the door window. Nothing strange, nothing moving. He opened the door and went in as silently as he could manage. The line of pegs along the hall, now empty of coats. In front of him the wall where Lydia had nailed the toast, the nail holes still showing. There was the smell of gunpowder or cordite or whatever it was called in the chill air of the house.

Lydia was seated at the kitchen table, her back to him. She was still wearing Atticus's plaid shirt and cardigan, but she had lost his fisherman's hat. Her gray hair was loose and long over her shoulders. On the table beside her was Atticus's revolver. "That you, Nick?" she said.

"That's me." Dominick came up beside her at the table.

"Well, we settled that score," she said.

"Um, what score is that, Lydia?"

Lydia gestured with her head toward the closed door to the front hall. "Meriwether," she said. "The one who killed Atticus."

Dominick carefully slipped the revolver away from Lydia down to the other end of the table. "Are you okay?" he asked.

"Never been better."

Dominick opened the hall door. There, halfway to the front door in a pool of blood on the hall carpet was the twisted short body of Agent K. The back of his head was missing and fluid still seeped out of a hole in the front of his shirt. His right hand was on his gun in its holster. He had managed to unsnap the clasp. Now all Dominick could smell was Agent K, a most unpleasant smell. He returned to the kitchen, shutting the door behind him.

"Was he alone?" Dominick asked.

"Yes, just him."

"That's strange. I didn't think they let them out alone."

"He said he was just here to put locks on the house. He said I would have to leave. Nick, would you fix me some tea?"

"Lydia, you shot him twice."

"He wouldn't stop moving." She played with the bandage on her hand. "None of those Meriwethers were ever any good except for Bobbie."

"No tea, not right now. What are you going to do?"

"I had no idea there would be so much blood. That carpet is ruined."

"You can always claim you thought he was a burglar."

"No, I thought this all out a long time ago, when Atticus was still alive and I realized I was going to be one of those crazy old ladies who lived forever and would be just a burden. I'd commit a felony—I always wanted to—and they would put me away for life. For free. I wouldn't be a burden to anyone. The state would take care of me, three squares and a cot, and I wouldn't notice because I'd be gaga. I thought it might be like a convent, just me and the other ladies, only more interesting because they wouldn't be nuns."

"I don't think you know what you're talking about, Lydia. Prison's not like that. You can take my word for it. And the idea of you in a convent is laughable. They won't let you do your artwork in there. No gardening."

"That carpet is totally ruined. Why don't you roll Mr. Meriwether up in it and take it somewhere then, if you don't like my plan? Get Lord Witherspoon to help you. He's a devious sort. He'll think of something. He has that big car."

"No, Lydia, neither I nor Lord Witherspoon will be doing your corpse disposal dirty work for you."

"Well, be that way," Lydia said, and she got up to put a kettle on. "If Atticus was here, he'd know what to do."

Oh, Dominick knew well enough what to do, which was to get out of there, and he would not be taking Lydia with him. Key Largo beckoned. This time he would make his escape. He took a tea towel from the drawer beside the sink and wiped off Atticus's gun where he had touched it. Lydia put two teacups on the table. "No, Lydia, I won't be staying for tea, I'm afraid. I have to catch the last ferry to New Jerusalem." The smell of Agent K's corpse was still in his nostrils. "But I did bring us champagne for a goodbye toast."

"I have always despised champagne," Lydia said, "ever since my honeymoon. But go on, get out, skedaddle, and don't worry. I won't tell a soul that you've been here."

Dominick gave Lydia a kiss on the top of her head where she stood at the stove and went out the back door. He stopped at her studio to wipe his fingerprints off the bottle of champagne as well, and then, remembering what Lydia had said, took it with him.

Dominick pushed it hard that first day out. It was going on midnight when he finally pulled off the interstate in the middle of New Jersey.

It wasn't like he was fleeing anything. It was just a relief to be finally on the move again, with a destination, an invitation, a whole new situation to look forward to. He checked into a Motel 6. He didn't need anything fancy. He was just another trucker, trucking himself south. He didn't even turn on the TV; he just hit the bed.

Of course, there was a radio in Dominick's car, but he never turned it on. What was there to listen to? Music, ads, and news—three sets of things he did not need—and the noise would only distract him from the hypnotic meditation of the road. The second day, he drove another five hundred miles, pulling off after crossing into North Carolina. A Days Inn this time. The TV set was on in the small lobby as he waited his turn to check in. It was tuned to a news channel, the volume turned down low.

Dominick was still in his road trance, and the image on the screen didn't register at first—a female reporter with a microphone standing in front of a yellow crime-scene tape between her and the house behind her. Nothing unusual about it except that the house was, yes, the house was Mt. Sinai. Dominick walked over and turned up the volume, catching the reporter midsentence, "by local and federal authorities, who tell us the property is believed to have been used as a safe house by the terrorist group IGB. We've been told that there is evidence that the house and another building on the property have been recently occupied and that the terrorists are the focus of the investigation, but thus far no suspects have been identified in this gruesome execution-style slaying. Back to you, George." End of story. Dominick turned the sound back down.

"Those crazy Yankees, heh? Killing federal agents who aren't even revenuers." It was the desk clerk. It was Dominick's turn to check in. "I don't know how people live up there, with all that crime and killings and terrorists."

Dominick was filling in the registration form. "Ever been up there?" he asked.

"Up north? Nope. No reason to go there. Don't like Yankees much. You?"

"I have been in and out a couple of times. Different country. Smoking room?"

"Sorry, all full up. But if you open a window you'll be alright unless you're smoking a stogie. Can't get that smell out. Two thirty-seven, that's around the back."

In the morning Dominick picked up a USA Today to read over breakfast. The story was there, already relegated to page three. It went into some detail about the IGB and the LNG protest, but did not mention any names. In passing it was mentioned that Hercules Corp had scrapped its plans to build a LNG terminal in Old Grofton, moving it instead to a more secluded and less controversial location at a place called Dogshead Bay, and in a curious development the coroner had determined that body parts recovered after the recent firefight and explosion at Darby Point had belonged to bodies that had been quite dead for some time before the event.

Dominick carefully refolded the paper and left it for the next diner. That would be it for news for a while, especially Yankee news. In Rob and Laurie's gated world all outside news was unnecessary, and paying any attention to it was déclassé to the point of being impolite. The very rich did not live in the mundane present. No news was the only news. Maybe that was why Dominick liked history so much—it was by definition the opposite of news. The past was a safe place.